Jet

BY JAY CROWNOVER

Jet
Rule
Rome

Jet

A Marked Men Novel

JAY CROWNOVER

wm

WILLIAM MORROW

An Imprint of HarperCollins*Publishers*

HarperCollins books may be purchased for educational, business, or sales promotional use. For information please e-mail the Special Markets Department at SPsales@harpercollins.com.

FIRST EDITION

Library of Congress Cataloging-in-Publication Data has been applied for.

ISBN 978-0-06-230241-0

13 14 15 16 17   OV/RRD   10 9 8 7 6 5 4 3 2

I am always asked who inspires me, and instead of writing a dedication page, I thought I would just answer that question instead.

My mom. I love my mom—she is all the things a mom should be. She's loving, she's strong, she's kind, she's fun, she's my biggest fan, and whenever I need her to, she puts me back together and reminds me that I am great and deserve great things. She's my best friend and anything great I have ever done was because she never doubted me or questioned me. Even when I made bad choices or she hated what I was doing to my hair she never, ever let me down.

My dad. My dad is the guy we all read about in these books. He is a living, breathing hero who would die for my mom and has always—I mean ALWAYS—done whatever I needed him to do, be it fix my car or race over to my house because I'm freaking out about this or that, and only he can handle it. He is flat out my hero and you will never meet a dude who is more badass in real life.

My gram. My gram is amazing. She is the matriarch in a family of strong, willful women and she is the basis for all of us knowing our own minds and appreciating how important family is. She has never turned me away when I asked for help, and even with various health issues, she is still one of the sassiest and sauciest ladies I have ever met.

My aunt Linda. My aunt is the smartest person I know, and when I emailed her in a panic because *Rule* was starting to sell and I had no clue what I was doing, she didn't hesitate to tell me she would help me and straighten me out. I run any business decision I make past her and frequently send her rambling, stressed-out emails, to which she simply replies, "You're fine. Calm down and enjoy your success." When I was younger, I wanted to be her when I grew up. Sometimes I still do.

My bestie. My best friend is 100 percent the voice of reason in my life. I tend to be melodramatic and hot tempered; my bestie is the only one in the world who can make me see the forest for the trees. She is the best time ever, and is actually from Kentucky, so has all the Southern sass anyone could want. She's an amazing mom, supergenerous, and never, ever gets fed up with me and the million and one questions I have about everything, all day long. I love her to bits and pieces and when my life went haywire, hers did simultaneously, and I don't think either of us would have come out on the other side without the other.

Finally, he who shall not be named. If my life hadn't ended up dismantled and upside down, I never would have been forced to figure out a new game plan. I never would have forced myself to do something just for me, to challenge myself to prove I could. I win.

I do want to thank all of you bloggers, tweeters, Facebook followers, and anyone who took a second to email or share my work with a friend. I learned fast how important you all are to this process, and how your embracing what a writer puts out there can impact the success of a story. Thank you for sharing the love, and please keep reading on. It means the world to me and each of you has played a significant part in my figuring out the next phase of my life! Thank you from the bottom of my tattooed heart.

Ayden

Jet Keller was all kinds of temptation wrapped up in too-tight pants and with too many personal demons hidden in those dark, golden-rimmed eyes. He was every girl's rock-and-roll fantasy, with an edge that made him just sharp enough to be hard to handle. And boy, oh boy, did I want to handle him in every way possible.

The trouble was that I was supposed to be making better decisions and walking a clean and much narrower path now. There could be no stops for the kind of things Jet inspired along the way, and no detours for the spontaneous combustion he brought with him. Unfortunately—or fortunately, depending on who was looking at the situation—it was a two-against-one battle, with my brain coming up short and my body and heart repeatedly overruling my better judgment.

Jet

Ayden Cross was a puzzle that, every time I thought I was close to solving, proved to have five extra pieces and no corners. For a long time, I thought she was a Southern belle, complete with mile-long legs in cowboy boots, but then she would turn around and do something that knocked me on my ass.

I had the feeling I didn't know the real Ayden at all. I would gladly spend the time it took to unravel it all, to undo her in every way I could. But I knew firsthand what happened when two people who had opposite ideas of what a relationship should be tried to force it to work. I wasn't up for that, even if she made all the parts of me that scorched and blazed manageable in a way no one else ever had.

Ayden

IT WAS TOTALLY AGAINST everything I was supposed to be doing in my new life—to ask a really cute boy in a band to take me home. There were rules. There were standards. There were simply things I did now to avoid ever going back to being the way I was—and sticking around to wait for Jet Keller was right at the top of the no-no list. There was just something about him, watching him wail and engage the crowd while he was onstage that turned my normally sensible brain to mush.

I knew better than to ask my bestie what was wrong with me.

She was all about boys covered head-to-toe in ink and littered with jewelry in places the Lord never intended boys to be pierced. She would just say it was the allure of someone so different, someone so obviously not my type, but I knew that wasn't it.

He was entrancing. Every single person in the packed bar had their eyes on him and couldn't look away. He was making the crowd feel—I mean really feel—whatever it was he was screeching, and that was amazing.

I hated heavy metal. To me, all it sounded like was yelling and screaming over even louder instruments. But the show, the intensity, and the undeniable vibe of power he was unleashing with just his voice—there was just something about it that drove me to drag Shaw to the front of the stage. I couldn't look away.

Sure, he was good-looking. All the guys who Shaw's boyfriend ran around with were. I wasn't immune to a pretty face and a nice body; in fact, at one point those things had proven to be weaknesses that had gotten me in more trouble than I cared to think about. Now I tended toward guys who I was attracted to on a more intellectual level.

However, one too many shots of Patrón and whatever crazy pheromone this guy was emitting right now had me forgetting all about my new and improved standards in men.

His hair looked like he had just shaken off whatever girl had messed it up. At some point during the set he had peeled off his wife-beater to reveal a lean and tightly muscled torso that was covered from the base of his throat to somewhere below his belt buckle in a giant black and gray tattoo of an angel of death. He had on the tightest black jeans I had ever seen a guy wear, decorated with a variety of chains hanging from his belt to his back pocket, and they left little to the imagination.

That might have been why Shaw and I were nowhere near the only female fans at the front of the stage.

I had seen Jet before, of course. He came into the bar

where I worked on a pretty regular basis. I knew that the eyes, now squeezed shut as he bellowed a note that was enough to have the girl to my left spontaneously orgasm, were a dark, deep brown that gleamed with easygoing humor. I knew of his penchant for outrageous flirtation. Jet was the charmer of the group and had no qualms about using that, combined with his heartbreaking grin, to get what he wanted.

I felt a warm hand land on my shoulder and turned to look up at Shaw's boyfriend, Rule. He towered over the rest of the crowd and I could tell by the twist of his mouth that he was ready to go. Shaw didn't even wait for him to ask, before turning to me with guileless green eyes.

"I'm going with him. Are you ready?"

Shaw and I had a "leave no man behind" policy, but I was far from ready to call it a night. We had to scream over the blaring guitars and the ear-splitting vocals bombarding us from our prime location, so I bent down to holler in her ear.

"I'm gonna hang out for a bit. I think I'll see if Rule's friend can give me a ride."

I saw her speculative look, but Shaw had her own boy drama to handle, so I knew she wasn't about to try to tell me any differently. She hooked her hand through Rule's arm and gave me a rueful grin.

"Call me if you need me."

"You know it."

I wasn't the kind of girl who needed a wingman or wing-woman. I was used to flying solo and I had been taking care of myself for so long it was really second nature. I knew Shaw would swoop in to grab me if I couldn't get a ride home or if calling a cab took too long, and knowing she was there was enough.

I watched the rest of the show in rapt fascination, and I was pretty sure that when Jet threw the microphone down after his final song, he winked at me before slamming back a shot of Jameson. Even with all of the things I knew I should be doing pounding in my head, that wink sealed the deal.

I hadn't been on the wild side in too long and Jet was the perfect tour guide for a quick refresher course.

He disappeared off the stage with the rest of the guys in the band, and I wandered back over toward the bar where everyone had been posted before the band had started playing. Rule's roommate, Nash, had apparently been dragged home by the lovebirds. There was no way he was making it out of the bar under his own steam. Rowdy, Jet's BFF, was busy sucking face with some random girl who had been giving Shaw and me the evil eye all night. I gave him a *you could do better* look when he came up for air, and then found an empty stool by the bar.

The thing about heavy-metal bars is that there are heavy-metal guys in every corner.

I spent the next hour fending off come-ons and free drink offers from guys who looked like they hadn't seen a shower or a razor in years. I was starting to get annoyed and, in turn, nasty when a familiar hand with a plethora of heavy silver rings landed on my knee. I turned to look up at laughing dark eyes as Jet ordered me another Patrón, but got water for himself.

"Got ditched, did ya? The way those two were looking

at each other, I'm surprised they made it halfway through the set."

I clicked the tiny shot glass against the rim of his glass, and gave him the smile that I had always used in the past to get whatever I wanted. "I think Nash had a fight with the tequila and the tequila won."

He laughed and turned to talk to a couple guys who wanted to congratulate him on the show. When he turned back to me, he looked a little embarrassed.

"I always think that's so weird."

I lifted a dark eyebrow and leaned a little closer to him, as I caught sight of a redhead in too-tight clothes circling. "Why? You guys are great and obviously people like it."

He tossed back his head and laughed and I noticed for the first time he had a barbell through the center of his tongue.

"People, but not you?"

I made a face and shrugged. "I'm from Kentucky." I figured that would explain it all.

"Rule sent me a text saying you needed a lift home. I have to go pull Rowdy off that chick and help the guys load the van, but if you can chill for, like, thirty, I'll totally give you a ride."

I didn't want to seem too eager. I didn't want to let him know how much I wanted him to give me a ride of an entirely different kind, so I shrugged again.

"Sure. That would be nice."

He squeezed my knee and I had to suppress the shudder that moved through me from head to toe. There was most definitely something up if just a little touch like that could make me quiver.

I turned back to the bar, ordered myself a glass of water, and tried to close my tab. I was surprised when the bartender told me it was already taken care of and a little annoyed that I didn't know who to thank. I swiveled around on the stool and watched closely as people fought their way through a bar full of overly enthusiastic guys and overly obvious girls. I wasn't a saint by any stretch of the imagination, but I really had no respect for any girl who was willing to degrade herself, to offer herself up for a single night of pleasure, just because Jet looked hot in tight pants.

Whatever was happening to me went deeper than that; I just couldn't name it. And tonight I was drunk enough—and missing some of my old self enough—to ignore it for now.

By the time Jet came back, I was faking interest in a conversation that some guy who looked like he had raided Glenn Danzig's closet was forcing on me. He was telling me all about the different genres of metal and why the people who listened to each different kind either sucked or ruled. It was all I could do not to shove a stick of gum in his mouth to stop him from breathing heavy, boozy fumes all over me.

Jet gave the guy a fist bump and hooked a thumb over his shoulder.

"Let's roll, Legs."

I made a face at the generic nickname because I had heard variations on it my whole life. I was tall, not as tall as his six-two, but I towered over Shaw's five-three and I did indeed have very long, very nice legs. At the moment they were a little wobbly and a little unsteady, but I pulled it together and followed Jet to the parking lot.

The rest of the band and Rowdy were piling into a huge Econoline van, and shouting all kinds of interesting things out the window at us while they peeled out of the parking lot. Jet just shook his head and used the control on his keys to pop the locks on a sleek black Dodge Challenger that looked mean and fast. I was surprised when he opened the door for me, which made him grin, so I folded into the seat and tried to plan my attack. After all, he was a guy who was used to groupies and band sluts throwing themselves at him on a daily basis, and the last thing I wanted was to be just one more.

He turned down the music blasting from the obviously expensive sound system and wheeled out of the parking lot without saying a word to me. He had found the time to put his shirt back on and it was now covered by an obviously well-loved leather jacket, complete with metal studs and a patch of some band I had never heard of. The combination of cute rocker boy, too much tequila, and the heady scent of leather and sweat was starting to make my head spin. I rolled down the window a little and watched as the lights of downtown bled by.

"You okay?"

I tilted my head in his direction and noticed the real concern in his dark gaze. In the dim light of the dash, the gleaming gold circle that rimmed the outer ridge of his eyes looked just like a divine halo.

"Fine. I shouldn't have tried to keep up with Nash for the first hour."

"Yeah, that's not a good idea. Those boys can put it away."

I didn't answer because generally I could hold my own with anyone when it came to matching shot for shot, but that wasn't something I liked to talk about. I changed the subject by running a finger over the obviously new and pristine interior of the car.

"This is a supernice ride. I had no idea screaming into a microphone paid so well."

He snorted a laugh and gave me a sideways look. "You need to branch out from cookie-cutter country, Ayd. There are all kinds of great indie country bands and even some amazing Americana bands I bet you would totally dig."

I just shrugged. "I like what I like. Seriously, is your band famous enough that you can afford a car like this? Rule said you guys were popular in town, which was clear after tonight, but even with that crowd it doesn't seem like you would make enough to live on just playing music."

I was prying, but it had suddenly occurred to me I didn't really know anything about this guy other than he was making my heart race. He was also making my head create all kinds of interesting scenarios that involved both of us and a whole lot less clothing.

He was tapping out a rhythm on the steering wheel with his black-tipped fingers and I couldn't look away.

"I run a recording studio here in town. I've been around a long time so I know a bunch of bands and guys in the scene. I write a lot of music that other people end up recording and Enmity is big enough that I don't ever have to worry about starving. Lots of people make a living just playing music.

It's just hard and you have to be dedicated to it, but I would rather be broke and do something I love, than be wealthy working a nine-to-five job any day."

That was something that just didn't make any sense to me.

I craved security and a future with a foundation rooted in safety. I wanted to know that I was going to be able to support myself; that I would never have to rely on anyone else for life's basic needs. Happiness had nothing to do with it at all.

I was going to ask more questions but the apartment I shared with Shaw was quickly coming into view, and I hadn't even tried to let him know that I was interested in more than a lift home.

I turned my entire body in the seat so I was fully facing him, and plastered my best *do me* smile on my face. He lifted an eyebrow in my direction but didn't say anything, even when I leaned over the center console and put my hand on his hard thigh. I saw the pulse in his throat jump, which made me grin. It had been a long time since I had been so overtly interested in anyone and it was nice to know that he wasn't immune to me, either.

"Want to come up and have a drink with me? Shaw is staying with Rule, so I'm sure she'll be out of commission for at least a couple days."

His dark eyes grew even darker with something I didn't recognize, because we really were strangers, but he put his hand over mine and gave it a gentle squeeze.

I wanted to inhale him; I wanted to get inside him and never come back out. There just something there, something special about him that pulled on all the strings I thought I had neatly trimmed away when I had left my old life behind.

"That sounds like a bad plan, Ayd." His voice was low and had undercurrents floating through that I couldn't identify.

I sat up straighter in the seat and with my other hand turned his face to look at me. "Why? I'm single, you're single, and we're consenting adults. I think it sounds like a fabulous plan."

He sighed and took both of my hands and placed them back in my lap. I was watching him carefully now because, while I might have undergone a dramatic life change over the last few years, I was still smart enough to know I was way better looking than most of the bar trash who had been circling him all night. That—and *no* guy ever turned down no-strings sex.

"We have friends who are dating. You drank half a bottle of tequila tonight, and let's be real—you're not the type of girl who takes a guy she barely knows home for the night. You're smart and ambitious, and you have no fucking idea what that Southern drawl does to me or how fast it would cause us to end up naked and tangled up. You're just a good girl all around.

"Don't get me wrong. You're beautiful, and in the morning when I replay this conversation over and over in my head, I'm going to absolutely want to kick my own ass, but you don't want to do this. Maybe if I knew for a fact we would never have to see each other again, never have to spend time around each other, I could do it with a clean conscience, but

I actually like you, Ayden, so I choose not to mess that up."

He was so very wrong.

I totally wanted to do this; to do him, but something about him thinking he knew what kind of girl I was shocked my libido like a bucket of cold water. I jerked my head back so hard that it hit the passenger window and the car suddenly felt like a coffin. I scrambled to open the latch and bolted out. I heard Jet call my name, heard him ask if I was all right, but all I needed to do was get away from him. I jabbed the security code into the door and ran into the apartment.

It wasn't until I had the doors locked and had a hot shower pouring over me that I realized how close I had come to letting everything I had worked for unravel around me. Whatever it was that Jet made me feel tonight, it was far too dangerous to try to act on. Not only had it ended in humiliation and panic, but I had also risked all the things that mattered to me now, and I just couldn't allow that.

I was going to have to keep Jet Keller locked in the box where I kept pre-Colorado Ayden. Only now, I was going to make sure that the lid was on so tight, there wouldn't ever be a chance of it coming off. The risk just wasn't worth it.

CHAPTER 1

Ayden, One Year Later

I HAD MY COMPUTER open and was working on something for my biochem class. My roommate Cora was sitting on the couch in the living room painting her nails a startling neon green before she left for work, when the door to the bedroom at the back of the house opened. I pushed the glasses I was wearing up on my nose and gave Cora *the look*. She swiveled around on the couch, so that her arms were dangling over the cushions.

We waited and we watched.

This had become our ritual over the last three months, since Jet had come to live with us. At least two to three times a week, we subjected whichever random chick he had brought home with him the night before to a (humiliating for them, hilarious for us) walk of shame.

Cora and I had taken to ranking them on a scale of one to ten depending on how thoroughly worked over they looked the next day. So far, Jet was coming in with solid sevens or eights, but a couple of the girls had left so pissed-off at his lack of interest in a repeat performance, that we had to give them fours and fives. The one who had locked herself in the bathroom and refused to leave until Cora threatened to mace her got a one.

This one today was pretty good.

She was a blonde and was all big boobs and long legs. Yesterday's makeup didn't look so hot running down her face now, but she had a nice whisker-burn going on under her chin and she had that dreamy, lovesick look that most of them wore when they came wandering out of that room.

I automatically upped her score because, instead of wearing her bra, she was clutching it in one hand like a lifeline. I was pretty sure her silky top was on inside-out. Her gaze shot from Cora to me and back again, and an embarrassed blush heated her face.

I couldn't figure out why Jet never told these girls he had female roommates. I assumed it was because he was a sick bastard and liked the fact they had to run this gauntlet when he was done with them, but he never confirmed or denied it when I asked him about it.

"Uh, hey." The poor thing stammered out an awkward greeting, which had Cora grinning like a lunatic. Cora was mouthy and loud on a good day; give her ammunition or show her a weakness, and she was like a piranha that smelled blood in the water.

My roommate looked like a pint-size fairy princess; well, a princess gone punk rock for the day. Cora's diminutive size often left the poor things that trekked through the living room unprepared for the attack she was just waiting to launch. This one was all blissed out on a postorgasmic high, and I knew it was only a matter of time before Cora unleashed all of her East Coast sass and brass.

"Did you have a good night?"

It was an innocent enough question, but coming from the feisty blonde with the two different-colored eyes, I knew it was anything but.

"Sure. I'll just, uh, be going now. Tell Jet I left my number on the dresser."

Cora waved a hand around in front of her. "Sure, because he is so totally calling you again. Right, Ayd? He won't want to lose that number."

I didn't like it when she tried to draw me into her verbal games, so I just shrugged and lifted my coffee mug up to my face to hide a reluctant grin. It was like watching a car accident happen in front of my eyes.

Cora waved her arms around in a dramatic sweeping gesture and told the bewildered blonde, "I'm sure he called the redhead that left yesterday morning. I'm sure he called the brunette that stayed the entire weekend, and I'm absolutely sure he's probably going to call you. Right, Ayd?"

She rolled her eyes and flopped back on the couch, as if she hadn't just demolished this poor girl's romantic hopes and dreams.

The girl looked at me and then back to Cora. I saw her mouth tighten before she uttered "bitch" and stomped out our front door. I upped her points even more when I saw she had her panties from the night before sticking out of her back pocket.

Without looking up, Cora held her hands up over her head and extended seven fingers in the air. "She didn't even have any fight in her. I would've given her at least an eight if she had told me to fuck off or get bent. Anything."

I shook my head. "You were kind of a bitch."

She snickered. "Gotta find my fun somewhere. What do you give her?"

I was about to answer when another figure came out of the room. You'd think that after three months of running into him coming in and out of the bathroom we shared, or catching him running around without a shirt on while he was getting ready to go out, or even watching him dance around half naked onstage I would have built up an immunity to seeing Jet Keller's bare chest.

But as he made his way down the hall, pulling on a plain black T-shirt, I forgot every single thought as my mind blanked, just like it always did.

After the disastrous incident outside my apartment last winter, we had developed an odd sort of friendship. I knew what boundaries I had to keep Jet within, and he treated me like I was some kind of virginal goddess he wasn't allowed to mess up. That was working for us, sort of.

When Shaw had ultimately decided to go live with Rule and Nash, Cora and I had worried about who was going to take up her share of the rent. Luckily, the girl Jet had been living with went bat-shit crazy, and dumped all of his stuff on the lawn while he was on his last tour, not to mention she found someone else to take his place when she got lonely. He ended up homeless and in need of a place to crash, so here he was. I saw him every day and spent plenty of time just hanging out with him.

But still, the sight of those abs, the ink that covered them and the twin hoops through his nipples turned all my good intentions and strictly marshaled thoughts to all things sexy and naughty, where they clearly didn't need to be. When I looked at him I had a hard time remembering the rejection and what I should be doing and instead let his wicked grin ruin all my self-control.

I averted my gaze and ordered myself not to inhale when he leaned over me to snag the other half of my untouched bagel. I wasn't allowed to go around sniffing him, even if he smelled like temptation and rock and roll.

He lifted a dark eyebrow in my direction and motioned toward Cora with the bagel.

"What kind of havoc are you two wreaking in here? I heard the front door slam all the way from the back of the house." He stretched his long legs, clad in supertight black jeans, out in front of me and I wondered again how he got into them. I had never seen a guy wear such tight pants, but they worked for him. I spent an obscene amount of time wondering how to get them off of him.

"Cora was just wishing your latest conquest a safe trip home."

He paused before biting into the bagel and focused his eyes at the back of Cora's head. "What did you really say to her?"

We could see Cora's shoulders shaking with silent laughter, but she didn't turn her head around. "Nothing. Well, nothing that wasn't true."

He took a big bite out of the breakfast treat and narrowed his eyes. They were so dark it was hard to tell where the iris and the pupil met.

"I think you're just pissed Miley Cyrus copied your haircut and you're taking it out on innocent girls across the land."

Surprised laughter shot out of me as Cora jumped to her feet and hurled the nail polish bottle she had been using at Jet's head. Luckily, he had good reflexes and caught it in the air before it smacked him in the face or broke all over the wood floors.

"I've had this hair forever! It's not my fault she decided to be rock and roll all of a sudden." She huffed out of the room and I shared a grin with Jet.

"She's sensitive about that. Be nice."

"It's not nice that you two have a sliding scale for every girl I bring home, either, but you don't hear me complaining, do you?"

I didn't have an answer for that so I turned back to my computer screen.

"One of these days there's going to be a ten and you're not going to know what to do with yourselves."

I was surprised he was aware of what we were doing. That didn't speak too highly of his respect for the girls he brought home with him on a regular basis.

I tucked the ends of my hair, which was now styled in a short, sleek bob, behind one ear and looked at him over the top of my glasses. I wasn't sure how I felt about it now that I knew he was in on the game.

"Why didn't you say something, if you knew what we were doing?"

He lifted a shoulder in a shrug and I watched as his mouth turned down in a frown on one side. Jet had an expressive face. I think it came from trying to project his every feeling, his every passion, to a crowd of people while he was onstage. I knew the half frown well—it meant he was thinking about something he didn't particularly want to talk about. I always wondered what put it there.

"They get what they come for and then they go home satisfied. If they have to tangle with you two knuckleheads on the way out, I just figure that is part of the price of admission." He cut his look back up to me and frowned for real. "Where were you last night? Everyone came to Cerberus and hung out for a few hours. Shaw said you were supposed to meet us there, but you never showed."

I cleared my throat and fiddled with the handle on my coffee mug. "I was on a date with Adam. He didn't want to go, so I just had him drop me off here and I did some homework I've been putting off."

I saw his eyes widen and the gold rings flashed bright and clear. Jet wasn't a fan of Adam, and Adam hated that I lived with Jet with every fiber of his being. I tried to keep the two of them apart, a task that was getting harder and harder now that Adam was pushing for us to be more than casual dating partners. We had been seeing each other for about four months, and logically I knew it was time to move one way or the other, but something always stopped me.

"Of course Adam didn't want to go. When does that dude ever do anything you want to do? Geez, Ayd, how many freaking operas, ballets, and boring-ass art exhibits are you going to let that moron drag you to? Why can't he just come and meet your friends and chill at the bar for a minute?"

We'd had this conversation more than once, so I just sighed.

"My friends intimidate him. Rule and Nash don't exactly scream 'welcoming committee' and you and Rowdy take way too much pleasure in making fun of anyone and everyone that you don't like. It would be awkward for all of us, so I would rather avoid it altogether. Adam is a nice guy."

I told myself that at least ten times a day. Adam was a nice guy and he was far more suited to a secure future than a guy who planned to play heavy metal for a living. Not to mention Adam didn't make we want to lose control and throw caution to the wind at every turn, not the way Jet did.

"We're your friends, Ayden, and Shaw is your girl. If this guy plans on sticking around, don't you think he needs to suck it up and get used to all of us? Or are you planning on just ditching us for the upper crust as soon as you can?"

There was something in his tone that spoke to a deeper conversation than the one we were currently having. But as usual, before I could probe further, he decided to change the subject to something he obviously deemed safer.

"Besides, if he didn't want Rowdy and me to clown on him, he wouldn't wear a damn sweater vest everywhere he goes. Who even owns a sweater vest anymore?"

I kicked him lightly under the table. "Be nice. Sweater vests aren't that bad."

He made a face and climbed to his feet. I tried not to drool when he stretched his arms above his messy hair and the hem of his T-shirt rode up over the edge of his pants. It would take torture to get me to admit it, but my main goal in life was to see how far down that damn angel tattoo went, and to trace the entire thing with my tongue.

I cleared my throat to try to get my head out of the gutter, and noticed he was watching me closely.

"That's the whole point; you don't see anything wrong with dating a dude who thinks a sweater vest is badass, and I don't see anything wrong with picking up a chick who gets ranked by my shithead roommates the morning after. Two different worlds, Ayd, two totally different worlds."

He ruffled my hair, getting several of the longer strands stuck in his rings as he walked away. I watched him solemnly until he disappeared in his room, before releasing the breath I had been holding. It took a minute for me to unclench my fingers from the coffee mug.

Jet had no idea what I was really like under all the polish and primer I had slapped on before moving to Colorado with nothing but the clothes on my back. No one really did. I had talked to Shaw about it briefly and vaguely, but even my bestie had no clue about the kind of life I had lived before starting college three years ago.

I was only twenty-two, but felt like I had lived a hundred lifetimes in this short amount of time. The good girl, the girl who Jet saw as so untouchable and so different from him, was all an illusion I fought on a daily basis to maintain. Having him so close and so present put my desire to leave the old Ayden buried in the rolling hills of Kentucky to the test, every minute of every day.

JET   23

"Hey!" I sputtered indignantly as a dish towel suddenly slapped across my face. Cora plopped down in the chair Jet had just vacated and gave me a knowing look.

"I thought you might want that for the slobber on your chin."

I narrowed my eyes at her. "Knock it off."

"Whatever. Every time, Ayd—it's like you're in heat or something. I don't know how you guys ignore all the snap, crackle, and pop that happens whenever you get within breathing distance of each other, but I'm telling you it's exhausting to watch."

I opened my mouth to tell her, in no uncertain terms, that we were not attracted to each other, but she held up a hand and lasered a pointed glare at me before I got one word out.

"And don't give me that bull about just being friends. I have guy friends. In fact, I have more guy friends than I do girlfriends and I do not look at a single one of them like I want to have hair-pulling, bite mark–leaving, bed-breaking sex with them. When you look at him when he's not paying attention, Ayd"—she made a big production of fanning herself down with the towel she reclaimed—"I feel like I need a cold shower."

I didn't know what to say to that so, I stuck with what I knew.

"We're friends. We aren't each other's type and I told you what happened the one single time I let alcohol try to convince me otherwise."

She leaned back in the chair and regarded me with her

crazy eyes. The dark brown one was all censure and knowing regard, and the turquoise one was all good-humored
mirth and friendly compassion. It was hard to pull anything
over on Cora, but that didn't mean I ever stopped trying.
In order to build the life I wanted, the life I so desperately
craved, I had to convince everyone that it was what I had
deserved all along. Who I was before wasn't allowed to be a
factor in who I was now, and no matter how hot Jet was or
how much he made me want to wander off the path of good
intentions, I just couldn't allow it.

"Besides, we fundamentally want different things out of
life. Once I graduate I'm going right into a master's program.
Jet has been playing at being a rock star since he was a teenager. I can't understand not having the ambition to want
something more than that, to want a secure future. We want
different things all the way around." Not to mention the way
he made me want to forget everything I already knew about
the dangers of the wild side totally freaked me out.

She shook her head looking like a judgmental version of
Tinker Bell. It was hard to fathom so much attitude packed
in such a little frame.

"I'm going to be honest with you, babe. From the outside looking in, you and that boy want exactly the same
things, only you're both too scared of something to admit
it. And FYI, nobody, and I mean nobody, looks good in a
sweater vest, so you should just stop trying to sell that poor
Adam guy as boyfriend material." She climbed to her feet
and gripped the back of the chair, and in typical Cora fashion
switched gears while I was trying to process the last bit of

insight she had dropped on me. "So you never gave me your ranking for the groupie of the day, what do you think?"

It bugged me every time a girl came stumbling out of that room, but I refused to acknowledge it, so I held up nine fingers and played along just like I was supposed to.

"She had a seven thanks to the missing bra and inside-out shirt, but after calling you a bitch and stuffing her underwear in her back pocket, she moved up."

Cora burst into boisterous laughter and grabbed her sides. She was cackling so loud I was worried all the noise was going to bring Jet back out of his room.

"Crap, I totally missed the panties. You know he's right; one day he's going to have a ten, a girl so thoroughly worked over that it won't even be fun anymore, because we're going to know she got the best stuff."

I bit the inside of my cheek to keep from scowling at her. "I can't wait."

I didn't fool Cora for a minute. "Sure you can't."

Frustrated with the conversation and the morning in general, I shut the laptop down and got to my feet.

"I'm gonna go run before I have to leave for class." I announced this to no one in particular, because Cora was messing around on her phone and Jet had not reappeared. I changed into clothes that were warm enough for a February in Denver and put on my well-worn running shoes.

I loved to run. It helped me clear my head, and since I lived in one of the most health-conscious states in the union, I was always just one of a hundred other people out for a little exercise when I took to the pavement. I put in earbuds and listened to what Jet called "that god-awful pop-country," as loud as it would go. I liked music that I didn't have to think about, and most country songs spelled it right out for the listener. The girl was mad because the guy cheated, the guy was mad his pickup got trashed, everyone was sad the dog died, and Taylor Swift had about as much luck with men as I did.

I knew Jet preferred stuff that was loud and heavy, but in reality the guy was a music snob, and after knowing him for more than a year, fighting about what was good and what wasn't ceased to faze me.

The cold air burned against my face as I found a steady rhythm and headed toward Washington Park on my usual route. When I ran I liked to block everything out, to shut the constant buzz of all the things hounding me, and just feel the ground under my feet and the brisk air on my face. But it wasn't working so great for me today.

I couldn't ignore the fact that I was pretty much living a lie. There was Ayden Cross, nobody, from Woodward, Kentucky, and Ayden Cross, chemistry major, from Denver, Colorado. They were two parts of the whole and at times I thought one was going to smother the other and there would be nothing left but ash and bad memories.

Woodward wasn't a bad town, but it was small, really small, and everyone knew everyone. When your family was the family in town that everyone the same age as you gossiped about, that everyone older than you talked about, that everyone coming and going told stories about, life wasn't exactly easy.

My mom wasn't a bad lady, just nowhere near equipped

to handle being a mother at sixteen, and way less ready to be a mom to a hard-to-handle daughter and to a son who was born looking for trouble. My older brother, Asa, had never met a crime he didn't want to commit or a law he didn't want to break. Since neither one of our dads had stuck around, Mom was left alone with us running wild and trying to keep the damage down to a minimum. I learned the hard way that if you heard you were one thing enough times, eventually you had no option but to start believing it.

Even though I knew better, I fell in with the kind of crowd that could destroy a perfectly good future, led there by the hand of a big brother looking out for only himself and his current scam. We were trash; we were never going to amount to anything, and with all the trouble and drama Asa created, it was a wonder any of us was still breathing.

If it hadn't been for a well-meaning and overly perceptive science teacher in my high school, I would have more than likely ended up just like Mom, knocked up and forever living under the judgmental eye of everyone else in Woodward.

But I applied myself at school, got scholarships, and worked my ass off day in and day out to make sure I never ended up back there. I was never going to give anyone a reason to think I was easy, stupid, and worth nothing ever again. I was going to take care of myself, build a future that was rock solid, and, Lord willing, pull my mother out of that tiny town. I was going to show her there was more to life than a case of Miller High Life, a pack of smokes, and whatever truck driver she had hooked up with for the month. As far as I was concerned, Asa was a lost cause, and the last I had heard was doing time—but I was the first to admit that I drifted in and out of the Woodward gossip mill, so I didn't really know for sure, and I was way past the point of always wanting to save my brother from himself.

I had made plenty of mistakes and done plenty of things wrong, but I was on the right track now. I figured my reward for living my life the right way, finally, was getting good grades in school, keeping friendships with good people who loved me no matter what, and never having to worry about waking up with nothing ever again.

If that meant I had to bury the attraction and choking lust I felt for Jet, then that was just the way it was going to have to be. If he wanted to treat me like a Catholic schoolgirl who was never allowed past the gates, then all the better for making me act properly. There was no reason for me to let him know that not only was he misguided, but that I could probably give any of those girls he brought home for one night a decent run for their money when it came to being the type of girl that knew all about the price of admission.

I rounded the corner of the park, and started to slow down as I got into a heavier flow of people out walking their dogs and playing with their kids.

When Cora had initially asked about letting Jet rent out Shaw's old room, I had wanted to say no. After the incident in the car last winter, I'd had a really hard time being around him at all without reliving every mortifying detail in slow motion. I thanked God every day I hadn't actually made a move. I doubted there was any way I would ever be able to face myself after that, but when I considered the horrific experience Shaw had gone through with her ex, the idea of letting a stranger stay with us was too scary, so I reluctantly relented.

I thought brutal, in-my-face exposure might do something to kill the persistent crush I had on him. After all, he was sarcastic and pushy at times. Only the opposite had happened: I liked him. I mean, I still wanted to do really naughty things to him on a regular basis, but I liked him as a person now, too.

He was surprisingly funny and smarter than a guy with that many tattoos and such horrible taste in music should be. He took all of Cora's attitude with a grain of salt, and never bothered me when I retreated into myself. We usually had breakfast with each other, and at least once a week all of us got together and had a drink at some bar or another. Even though I hated—and I mean hated—the music he played, I went to hear his band at least twice a month.

He was by far my favorite drinking partner. He didn't have all the raw edges that Rule had, he wasn't prone to broody moodiness like Nash, and he wasn't into making a scene like Rowdy. He was just laid-back and liked to have a good time. It wasn't until someone started to talk to him about his band or tried to treat him like he was a big deal that he got closed off and distant. For a guy who was born to be a rock star, he sure had a lot of issues being semi-famous and admired. It was odd, but it was also endearing and just another reason I enjoyed being around him.

I stumbled a little as a German shepherd pulled free of his owner's grip and dashed past me. I took a minute to catch my breath and bent over to put my hands on my knees. Now that I wasn't moving, the air wicked across my sweat-soaked skin, making me shiver. I should have put on a hat and maybe some gloves, but it was too late now, and I had to get back if I didn't want to be late for class.

I was plowing through my undergrad classes with my sights set firmly on a master's program, all before I was twenty-five. I had always been good with numbers, and science came naturally to me, so when I had applied to schools I made sure to look for ones that were as far from Woodward as I could get, but also had top departments in my field. I wasn't sure what I wanted to do when I graduated, but I knew I wanted no less than a six-figure income, continuous growth potential, and a generous retirement plan. I knew those were lofty goals for someone my age, and from someone with my lackluster background, but I didn't set low standards anymore.

I fell into a light jog and pulled my earbuds out as I got closer to the house. I pulled up short when I rounded the corner, because I could have sworn I recognized the guy walking on the other side of the street from somewhere.

Granted, I was still jumpy after Shaw's attack and looked at most strangers like they were a danger, but there was something about the way this guy carried himself that had me stuck to the sidewalk, trying to figure it out. He walked right past me on the other side of the road without once glancing my way, so I shook off the heebie-jeebies and dashed up the stairs to the front door. I was about to pull it open when Jet came out the other side, causing me to almost topple over backward on the front steps. I let out a squeal and tried to grab the railing, but it was no use. I had too much momentum and went flying back toward the concrete.

Jet grabbed for me, but I was moving too fast. When he caught my hand, all that did was drag him forward, so that we were both suspended in air for a split second. Our eyes locked before we went tumbling to the ground, hard.

He landed half-on, half-off me. I swore softly as my head made contact with the solid slab of sidewalk hard enough to make me see stars. His chest pressed into mine, and between my thin running pants and his painted-on jeans, there wasn't an inch of us not pressed intimately together. I forgot to breathe, forgot I was injured, and mostly forgot why I knew that he was such a bad idea.

I wanted to rub up against him. I wanted to put my hands in his messy hair. I wanted to kiss and lick the spot on his neck where his pulse was hammering hard and fast, but none of that was going to happen. He levered himself up in a stiff push-up and looked down at me with wide eyes. The gold had swirled in from the outer circle, making him look like some kind of wild animal as he gripped my head in his hand and whispered, "Are you okay? I'm so sorry. I didn't know you were there."

His rings were freezing cold on the side of my face and the sidewalk at my back was making me go numb.

"I'm fine. I was distracted. It wasn't your fault." My accent was a little stronger when I was upset and I could see that Jet had noticed.

"Are you sure? I can take you to get checked out. We can't risk having that giant brain of yours rattling around."

I wanted to be having any other conversation than this one while he was practically lying on top of me. I wrapped my hands around his wrists and tugged at him to get him to let me go. "Seriously, I'm fine. Wanna let me up?"

Something moved across those dark eyes that I hadn't seen before. It was like he was considering the question and answering "no," but it passed, and he shoved to his feet, pulling me up with him. He didn't let me go and where he still held on to my hands, I burned. I needed to get away from him, fast. I had to bite back a groan as he turned me around and started to brush off the back of me with the palm of his hand.

"Are you sure you're all right? I'm not exactly a lightweight."

He wasn't. He was tall and solid, but not muscle-bound or ridiculously pumped up. He was in good shape from running around the stage and from hauling equipment back and forth, but I knew he didn't have a steady gym ritual he followed—not that it mattered. I shook him off because I had to, in order to catch my breath, and shoved my hair away from my face.

"Yep. Nothing's broken and we both know I have a pretty hard head. I was lost in thought. I just need to pay closer attention when I run or I'm going to end up falling on my face again."

He gave me a funny look and shoved his hands in the front pockets of his leather jacket. I always wondered how he could wear it when it was wintertime. I figured the zippers and studs had to be icy cold, but it was such a part of his look that he just wouldn't be Jet without it.

"Okay, if you're sure you're fine. I gotta get going. I have a session with a band from New Mexico this afternoon, and then practice later. One of the bands we played with at Metalfest last year is going on tour this summer, and they need some new stuff."

I shivered because I was getting cold and because I hated the idea of him going on tour again. It actually made me sick to my stomach. I had heard the stories, listened to the tales the guys told about what happened when a guy in a popular band went on tour, and it wasn't pretty. I forced a smile and took a couple steps back toward the stairs. "Well, that sounds like a busy day. I have class, and then I close tonight, so I won't be home until really late."

He was watching me and I was watching him, and I realized that Cora was right. I was a genius when it came to chemistry, and what was going on between us was bound to explode eventually. I had been keeping it under pressure and on a slow and steady boil and nothing reactive could handle that kind of heat for long.

He scratched his chin with a finger and lifted an eyebrow at me. "Maybe if the guys and I get done early we can swing by for a beer."

I gulped down a surge of panic and forced a smile that I'm sure he didn't buy for one second.

"Sounds great."

I didn't wait to see what his response was as I darted for the door. This time I made it into the house without incident, but I was running late, so I had to scramble into the shower, throw on some jeans and a long-sleeved top before getting into my Jeep and racing toward the campus.

The University of Denver wasn't too far from home, but parking tended to be a pain in the neck and I was already stressed out, so when my phone rang I didn't bother to dig it out of my bag. I was the last person into the classroom and had to suffer through questioning looks and irritated glowers as I interrupted the professor while I made my way to my seat. I tried to pay attention, but my mind was a million miles away, and after sleepwalking through my lab and my second class, I realized I had better get my head out of the clouds or work tonight was going to be a nightmare.

I worked at a popular sports bar in LoDo, or lower downtown Denver, where we had to wear ridiculous outfits that showed more skin than they covered. We were right down by Coors Field, so even with football season over, we were still packed with hockey and basketball fans. I made enough money to easily make rent and whatever my scholarships didn't cover for school. I didn't mind shaking my ass a little, as long as it got the bills paid.

I had to be on alert, though, because there was no shortage of drunken, grabby hands and overly affectionate regulars who wanted to touch things that were not allowed. I also had to keep my head in the game when it came to dealing with my catty coworkers. Those girls lived for gossip and any kind of dirt they could find. Shaw and I had a longstanding feud with Loren Decker, the reigning queen bee, and if I showed up for my shift like I was now, she would find an opening and make the night hell for me.

It wasn't until I was in the changing room at the back of the bar, getting into my silly cheerleader outfit, that I remembered my phone ringing earlier, and I blinked in surprise when I saw I now had five missed calls from a 502 area code. I didn't know why anyone in Kentucky would be trying to get ahold of me, let alone how they had gotten my number. There were no voice mails or text messages, so I just tucked the phone into my bra, where it lived for my shift, and made a note to try to call the number tomorrow.

I was slicking my black hair down and shoving a sparkly bobby pin in the front, when Loren's sickly sweet voice came from somewhere over my shoulder. I so wasn't in a mood to deal with her, so I just gritted my teeth and turned to look at her.

She was the perfect fit for a bar like the Goal Line. She was every guy's cheerleader fantasy all grown up, complete with fake double Ds. She had about as much sense as a bobblehead doll, and I couldn't figure out why she tried to go toe-to-toe with me, because she never won. Besides, she was, like, three inches shorter than me, even more than that when I wore the spiked heels I used to up my tips, and I always ended up looking down on her. Both figuratively and literally.

"How's it going, Ayden?"

"I'm having a crap day, Loren, what do you want?"

She played with the ends of her hair in a way that made me want to strip them out of her head, one perfect blond strand at a time.

"I was wondering if you could do me a teeny-tiny favor?"

I rolled my eyes and slammed the locker shut behind me. "I already work all weekend, so I can't cover you."

She blinked her big cornflower blue eyes at me, and I swear in that second it solidified my hatred of her until the end of time. I had to take a deep breath, because I knew I was being irrational and irritable for no reason.

"No, I was wondering if you could talk to Jet and see if he could get me and a couple of my girls in to see Bryan Walker at the Ogden. He has a bunch of connections, doesn't he?"

Bryan Walker was a pop singer, along the lines of Justin Bieber, but way less famous. There was no way on this green earth I was ever going to ask Jet if he could get this nimrod into that show. I moved past her with a frown.

"Why don't you ask him? He said he was probably going to come in tonight for a beer."

She looked at me like I had just landed from another planet. "I can't talk to him."

That brought me up short and I turned to look at her in confusion.

"Why the hell not? He's in here all the time. I know you've waited on him before."

She shook her head like I was an idiot and shared a smile with one of her girlfriends. "Oh, Ayden, you are just so sweet. I just think it's so cute how you hang out with all those superhot, superyummy boys and yet you don't know the first thing about wrapping one around your finger. If I ask Jet for a favor it means *he* knows that *I* know who he is and what a big deal he is in this town. If I want him to notice me, I have to ignore him and treat him like he's no one special. Otherwise I'll be like you, forever stuck in the friend zone, and dating a guy who has a sweater vest in every color of the rainbow."

I was so stunned, I just stared at her. I was pretty sure all the blood went from my head straight to my face because, for one, I couldn't believe she was interested in Jet after her interest in Rule had been shut down so mercilessly by Shaw. I also couldn't believe she was criticizing Adam or my taste in men.

Loren was custom-made to be a trophy wife who would be cheated on after she lost her shine. She had no idea what a real future looked like or what a steady guy like Adam had to offer.

I was about to unleash a torrent of shit at her. I was ready to pull her apart verbally, and maybe even physically, with the mood I was in. But the urge passed when Lou, the bar's door guy, stuck his head in and told us to haul ass. He said that a busload of after-work guys had just piled in, and paying my bills was way more important than putting Loren in her place. The straighter path didn't have stops for taking down bimbos on it, either.

I gave her a tight-lipped smile and tossed over my shoulder, "And I just think it's so cute how you drool all over those superhot, superyummy boys I hang out with, like you have a chance in hell of ever even getting into the friend zone. Those guys can spot a fake a mile away, Loren, and that's why, even with all your attributes"—I sent a scornful gaze over her very fake boobs—"they don't give you the time of day."

I flounced to my section, hoping all the talk of asking Jet for favors was put to bed. The guys *could* spot a fake; in fact, I had seen them do it on more than one occasion. As far as I was concerned, it was a miracle they all still thought I was such a good girl, still worthy of their friendship and protection, and if it took learning to love sweater vests to keep the act up, then by God, I would do it, and I would do it with a smile.

CHAPTER 2

Jet

THIS STUPID DANCE I was doing around Ayden was getting old and tired pretty damn fast. When I first moved into their place, I thought having Cora and her big mouth there would make it easier. When that didn't happen, I thought having a revolving door in my bedroom might do the trick, but nothing seemed to be working.

She was on my mind all the time—in my head when I was trying to work, under my skin when I was with another girl—and I swear that soft, Southern drawl was designed to turn me inside-out every time she spoke to me. I hated that I didn't know what to do with it. Girls always came easy to me, but that girl was anything but.

A year ago, I had a shot to do everything to her I dreamed about at night. In fact, I think I had fallen a little bit in love with her the first time I saw her at the Goal Line in her sexy uniform, wearing heels up to the sky. She had a "take no shit" attitude wrapped up in superlong legs and whiskey-colored eyes that did way more than Jameson when it came to going to my head fast and hard. I wanted her, wanted her like an addict wanted a fix, but she was so far out of my league, and played on such a different field than me, it was a wonder we even managed to maintain a loose form of friendship.

Rule had warned me in no uncertain terms that if I upset Ayden, and if that, in turn, upset Shaw, there would a reckoning like Denver hadn't seen in years.

I could hold my own in most cases and spent a fair amount of time trying not to get my ass kicked in mosh pits across the country, but Rule was someone I knew firsthand not to mess with. He was even scarier now that he was all caveman-protective over Shaw.

So I had done the right thing, the decent thing, and told her no when all I wanted to do was tell her yes. Now I was stuck in this awful place where we were friends, but not, and where I had endless dreams about that voice and those legs while she slept soundly across the hall. It sucked to epic proportions, and I didn't know what to do about it besides either moving out or quit talking to her altogether—options which were neither practical nor enjoyable. I liked living with the girls. Cora was a riot and Ayden was hardly there as it was, but when we all got together it was fun and easy. I didn't have to worry about all my shit ending up on the curb with the garbage because I pissed one of them off while I was on tour.

My studio was in an old warehouse off California downtown. The acoustics were great and after the band's last tour, I had enough money to really trick it out.

I knew everyone, and I mean *everyone*, in this town who had anything to do with music. Granted, Denver isn't

L.A. or New York, but it is right in the center of the country. It has such a huge and diverse population that it really is a destination for bands, some more famous than others, to come and record.

My band was really popular locally, and after going on tour with Artifice for Metalfest last year, we were getting better known nationally. What paid the bills was the studio and putting together tracks for other people. I didn't care—as long as I got to make music and got to write songs, I was a happy guy. Music was what made me get up in the morning and what followed me to bed at night. Sure, I sang in a heavy-metal band, but when I was younger it had been all about punk rock and the indie scene. The reality was I just liked good music. I didn't care what color or creed it came in, even if I gave Ayden endless shit about her addiction to Top 40 Country. The truth was, I liked to get her riled up just to see those amber eyes of hers shoot sparks.

Today I was planning on losing myself in work. The band that was booked was good and we had already put together a solid track layout for their new album. What I hadn't planned on was pulling into my spot by the door to find my old man waiting for me. I couldn't help the frown that automatically pulled across my face, and it took a conscious effort to uncurl each and every finger from around the steering wheel in order to get out of the car to confront him.

He had on aviator shades and jeans that were too baggy for a guy his age, but that was my pops, refusing to let go of his youth and all the good times, no matter who it hurt along the way.

I sighed and pushed open the door, watching him warily as he came around the hood of the car. "What are you doing here, Pops? I have work to do. I can't stand around and shoot the shit."

Sometimes it was better to just cut him off before he got started, but today apparently that wasn't going to work.

"You got back from tour three months ago and didn't think to give your old man a call? I've been dying to hear about Metalfest. Did you boys get signed by a big label yet?"

It would have seemed like a typical question for a parent to ask his child, if it was any other parent than mine. Dave Keller had lived his life as a professional roadie and had gone on tour with everyone from Metallica to Neurosis and whatever band he could find in between. And now, all he wanted was for his one-and-only son to hit it big. Not so I could take care of him or buy him a mansion in the Malibu hills, but so he could go back on tour and live the wild days of illicit sex and drugs, as if he were still in his twenties. It drove him crazy that I was happy staying local, that I made plenty of money recording and doing an occasional tour, and that the idea of fame and worldwide recognition scared the living piss out of me.

Not to mention he had bailed on me and Mom over and over again and was less than an ideal candidate for husband or father of the year. I never understood why my mom, my sweet, loving, kindhearted, generous mom, stayed married to such a scumbag. But no matter how hard I pushed or how much I pleaded with her, she refused to leave him, which, in turn, made it really hard for me not to hate his lazy, cheating, lying ass.

"I don't talk to major labels, Pop. I've told you that a million times."

He scoffed. "Do those other guys in the band know that you're holding their future hostage? What do they have to say about you making decisions like that?"

This wasn't a conversation I cared to have with him. I didn't really care to have any kind of conversation with him, but he wasn't going to go away unless I made him. The band I was recording was going to be here any minute, and the last thing I wanted was for him to act like a middle-aged groupie.

"The guys know where I stand and they know where the door is if they don't like it. I've played with Boone and Von since we were fourteen years old, so I doubt much I do surprises them. Catcher came from a band that already hit the mainstream and hated it, so the last thing he wants is to be in another one that's blowing up. Stay out of my business, Pop. It doesn't concern you, unless you're asking to borrow money—in which case, have Mom call me. I'll transfer it to her, not to you."

He pushed his sunglasses to the top of his head so that I could no longer just watch myself glower in the reflection. I got my dark eyes and my dark hair from him, but that was where the resemblance stopped. He was lived-in. A life of too many drugs and too many hard nights had taken its toll, and all I could think about when I looked at him was to wonder how someone so awful was able to convince someone as wonderful as my mom to marry his sorry ass. He made me furious in a way I couldn't express with normal words.

The only way I ever got it all out was to purge it on stage, in bleeding vocals and ear-shattering melodies.

"You better watch what you're saying to me, son. I'm still your father and I go home to her, unlike you."

There were a million things that I wanted to say to that, but I didn't; I never did. As much as I loved my mom, there was no way I could stay in that house and watch him tear her down time and time again. It upset her so much when the old man and I got into it over his blatant disregard of her and her feelings that I had moved out when I was barely fifteen. It was either that or put my dad in the ground. Luckily, Nash's uncle Phil was practically running a halfway house for unhappy teenage boys and hadn't had any issue adding me to the fold.

I knew it bothered her that I didn't come home often, considering they lived just a few miles down the road. But I couldn't abide him stepping out on her and constantly hurting her. I knew he did a number on her emotional state, and I wouldn't put it past him to have taken it further, to take it to a level none of us would be able to ignore anymore, but I was at a loss as to what to do about any of it. My mom was a great lady and she deserved someone who treated her like she was a queen, not a consolation prize.

"What do you want?" My patience was running thin.

We stared at each other in silence for a long minute before he pulled his shades back down and crooked the corners of his mouth up in a grin that made me want to punch him in the face.

"That band you helped get signed—Artifice—they're

pretty huge right now. You wrote most of their album didn't you?"

"So?"

"So I'm thinking they owe you pretty big, and it wouldn't kill you to put in a call to them to see if they want any help on the European leg of their tour that's coming up."

I was two seconds away from grabbing him by the collar of his stupid bowling shirt and shoving him against the side of the building, when he held up a hand and smirked at me.

"I know you love your momma, son. What about her? You really want to leave me to my own devices for an unknown amount of time where she's concerned? Who knows what that will look like this time? Neither one of us is getting any younger."

The challenge in his voice was clear—as was the threat to my mom. I glared at him and consciously talked myself out of ripping his head off his neck and kicking it across the parking lot like a soccer ball.

"You're out of your damn mind, old man. I already hate your guts. You really want to go this route with me?"

"She ain't ever going to leave me, son, and you know it. There ain't a damn thing you can do to me while you're worried about her at home with me, and we both know it. Set up something with Artifice. I'm not asking to be their tour manager, or even the sound tech, but I want in on the show. I need a little adventure and a whole lot of good times."

I was going to skin him alive and then use his bloody carcass as a stage prop. I pushed past him with a growl.

"I'll see what I can do, but if she calls me and it so much

as sounds like you upset her or were even thinking of upsetting her, I swear I will run you over in the street like the dog that you are. If you think blackmail is the way this relationship is going to play out, you don't know me at all."

"You're damn straight I don't know you. No son of mine should be wasting his God-given talent in this town, when he could be all over the map making millions and dropping panties in every city."

I looked at him over my shoulder as I unlocked the door. "It is my undying wish that I was no son of yours, but neither of us is that lucky. Go away, Pop, before you make me do something that one of us will be sure to regret."

I went into the darkened space, turning on lights as I went. It took a real honest effort to lock back down all the aggravation and resentment that always boiled to the surface when I had to deal with the old man.

It bothered me on an inexplicable level that he insisted we were so similar. I had been born with the talent he so desperately wanted. I had the life he longed to live practically banging down my door, and it infuriated him that all I wanted was for my poor mother to recognize that she deserved better and get away from him. I would never claim that I was an angel when I went on tour, and I would never deny that being in a band was a surefire way to get laid by the ready and willing. But I never left someone behind with a promise that I would behave, and I never had anyone in particular waiting for me to come home. I didn't make promises I couldn't keep. I learned that firsthand from him.

I set up the recording area and leafed through the list of

songs the guys in Black Market Alphas dropped off. It was a stupid ass name, but the kids were talented and had a lot of potential to make it big. They were more poppy than I liked, falling more along the lines of Avenged Sevenfold. They were hard enough that teenage boys would dig them, but with enough harmony and melody that teenage girls would rock out to them as well. Plus they were young—the lead singer was only like eighteen or nineteen, so they had a lifetime to get better or flame out and die, which was probably more likely. I agreed to work with them because the drummer who wrote all the songs had a ton of talent and reminded me a lot of myself when I was younger.

Being in a band was hard work and being in a good band was often more work than the reward was worth. I was lucky that the guys I played with understood that I was happy being a big fish in a small pond here, rather than a speck in the ocean that ate new bands alive elsewhere.

I might be conceited in other ways, but I knew that wasn't the case when it came to my ability to play good music. I knew I could sing and I could rock any guitar you put in my hands. I had enough fury at my old man and anger and angst built up over a lifetime to fuel me to write songs that were both powerful and relevant.

I also knew that I had enough swagger and attitude to own any stage I walked on, and that if I wanted my audience to feel what I was feeling, I could pull them in and refuse to let them go until I was ready. I was a good front man. What I didn't have was the patience to play the game, or the desire to let others think that they had a right to what I had created.

I didn't have the necessary tolerance for bullshit and ass kissing that it took to be a major player in the industry.

I was also terrified by the idea of what would happen to my mom if my dad ever found out I signed with a major label. That would just spin the old guy right off his axis, and he would take her right along with him. She just deserved better than that. He would up and leave her in the blink of an eye. He would hitch himself to my coattails, the all the pomp and circumstance that went along with being a big name band on a big name label, and I always wondered if she would ever be able to forgive me if I was the cause of the old man ultimately walking away for what he deemed his just rewards.

I looked up when the outside door opened and the group started filtering in with their instruments. The lead singer was a kid named Ryan, who was a decent kid but full enough of himself that he could easily rub you the wrong way. He had a lot of attitude and the requisite presence to lead a band, but he was immature and way more interested in the money and the girls than in putting out a quality product. I noticed he had his upper arm wrapped in cellophane and medical tape when he reached across the mixing board to pound fists in greeting. I nodded at the obviously new ink and asked, "You go to one of my boys?" When we had been on tour, all the guys in BMA had been enamored of the artwork the Enmity band members sported courtesy of the Marked, the tattoo shop where all my boys worked.

The angel that stretched from one side of my collar bone to the other and went way below my navel was probably my most recognized piece. I also had a Japanese dragon that covered one whole arm that Nash had done when he was just starting out, and my other forearm was covered from elbow to wrist in a complicated mélange of Salvador Dalí paintings that Rowdy had recently finished. It looked more like a painting on flesh than a tattoo.

All of the guys had their strengths. Rule was all about heavy lines and gothic pieces that covered huge amounts of skin, and he tended toward the traditional style. Nash loved big color and bold design. It was easy to see his street style and new-school aesthetic in everything he did. Rowdy, though the most irreverent of all of us, really treated his work like art. He believed in creating custom-designed pieces that no one else would have, and honed his talent like a true craftsman. Tattooing was just another art form to him, and I think he took what he did more seriously than the other guys. In fact, I had enlisted him to design all of our album covers and T-shirt designs for the band.

Cora's hands and needles had been in places that I didn't care to think about, but all the staff at the Marked did a great job. I had zero complaints and didn't hesitate to refer anyone who asked about them.

"Yeah, dude, it was badass. I totally name-dropped, and the guy with the flames tattooed on his head worked me in on the spot." He rolled his eyes dramatically and looked at me like I should have disclosed pertinent information before suggesting they hit the shop. "You didn't tell me the place was packed with talent. The blonde that ran the desk, holy shit, man, she was like my dream girl."

I bit back a laugh because Cora was every rock and roller's dream girl until she opened her mouth. With her mismatched eyes and undeniably general cuteness, her looks were deceiving. Guys like Ryan were attracted to her crazy hair and the fact that she had a full-sleeve tattooed on her left arm and tiny, solid black gauges in each ear. The fact that she was mouthy, bossy, and treated us all like we were wayward kindergartners never came up until the poor, unsuspecting guy was already head over heels in love.

I shook my head at him and warned, "She's too old for you and way more trouble than she's worth. Trust me. What did you get done?"

He peeled the protective covering off and proudly displayed a snarling gargoyle. It was cool, well done, but honestly kind of generic. I could tell Nash had done his best to put some flare into it to make it unique, but it was really just a tattoo that some kid got because he thought a big ol' piece of ink would make him look cool while onstage and in photos. Because they were paying me more than a grand an hour for my time, I just nodded and told him to get into the studio with the rest of the guys in the band. I could tell he wanted more props, but I was almost out of patience for dealing with people's shit today, so I just kept my mouth shut before I said something that would get me in trouble.

For the next three hours I tweaked vocals and mixed instruments to get the first five songs done. The rest of the guys in the band were pretty committed to putting together a solid debut album, but Ryan was difficult, and I could tell he was getting irritated that I kept deferring to Jorge, the band's drummer, because he was the main songwriter.

I needed to understand what was behind a song before I could do it justice, but Ryan clearly wanted all the attention on him and it was making getting anything laid down hard. The kid had decent pipes and a butt load of charisma, but if he didn't pull his head out of his ass all they were ever going to be was a really good opening act for far better bands.

The recording session ran so long that when the guys in my own band started showing up for our practice, I was still working on getting the bridge for the chorus in song number two right. My bandmates were used to having to kick it while I paid the bills, and when the kids saw that they had an actual audience to impress, they pulled it together, and I managed to get everything hammered out up to track five.

Von was my lead guitar player and songwriting partner, Catcher played bass, and Boone managed the drum kit. We were a pretty tight group; had to be since we spent so much time together. So I didn't have to say anything to them, just offer up a grunt and a narrow-eyed stare when they jokingly asked how it was going.

The kids came bounding out of the studio to say hey to everyone, and I wanted to smack Ryan when he asked if they could hang around and watch our practice. I was over teenage metal heads and had just wanted to knock out a quick practice so we could go grab a beer and some wings and bug Ayden. I knew I should stay away from her, but I couldn't seem to do it for too long. Our band had a big show planned for Valentine's Day the following weekend and I figured it would just be easier to agree to let them stay than to argue about it.

I led everyone to the back room that we used for our practice and the guys and I took our places like we have at least twice a week for the past five years. We were a well-oiled machine; we knew what we were doing and that no band worked when someone's ego was the driving force. I thought that maybe watching what an actual band looked like might help Ryan get off his pedestal. Boone tapped out a lead-in beat and looked at me over the top of his kit. "We gonna play the set for the show or you need to do some harder stuff?" They knew when I was in a mood, really we were friends first and a band second, they just understood where I was at.

I shoved hands through my dark and usually messy hair and rolled my shoulders around. The microphone felt like an extension of my arm when I pulled it out of the stand. I met curious looks all around and nodded at him.

"Yeah, let's go black and then do the normal set."

Before I even finished the sentence, deep rhythms were coming off the drums and low bass tones were shaking the ground under my unlaced combat boots. Von made the air ring with guitar chords that were sharp enough to peel the paint off the walls and I started singing. I let all the anger at my dad stream out. I let the frustration of trying to wrangle young talent explode into vocals that ebbed and flowed with every emotion that was trying to strangle me. By the time we had moved to the second song, the guys in BMA had all taken seats on empty instrument cases and were watching us with wide eyes and slack jaws. When we moved on to the mellower stuff, what we played for the bar crowd, I could see that Jorge was really listening to the power behind the lyrics that meant something. I could also see that Ryan was probably going to try to emulate everything I did to a T at their next performance.

After I had yelled, dripped, and purged every bad thing that happened today out of me, I dropped the mic on the floor and pulled the edge of my T-shirt up to wipe my face. I felt empty, but better.

I turned to the guys and told them I was hooking up with Rowdy for a beer if they wanted to come. Usually, we tried to hang out once a week and just touch base, but Catcher was doing some demo work for another band, Von and his girlfriend had just had a baby, and Boone was struggling with a pretty short bout of sobriety. Lately I had been kicking it more and more with Rowdy and the guys from the shop.

I had known Rule and Nash since high school, but those two were a pretty tight unit, and when Rule's older brother, Rome, was in town, it was worse. I often ended up on the outskirts of whatever they had cooking up. I was stoked when Rowdy had started coming around because he was quirky, unpredictable, and always a hell of a good time. They were all good friends to have, and I liked to think they felt the same about me, but Rowdy and I just clicked and had an understanding so he typically ended up being my go-to bro.

The rest of the guys in both bands filed out the door but Jorge stayed behind as I chugged a bottle of water and moved to put all our stuff away. "What's up?"

He rubbed the back of his neck and looked at the tips of

his tennis shoes instead of at me. "You guys are so much better than us, so much better than half the bands we were on tour with at Metalfest. Why are you helping us out, and not in the studio making albums of your own? I'm just wondering how that happens?"

"You guys are pretty solid, but if you don't get Ryan to tone it down, you're going to end up breaking up before you get anywhere. You got a lot of attention from Metalfest, so you should capitalize on it. You're paying me to help you, Jorge, but that doesn't mean I don't recognize talent when I see it. You write really good songs but anyone can sing them. You don't need a front man who doesn't appreciate that."

He looked up at me and grinned. "Thanks."

"No problem."

"That song you closed with, 'Whiskey in the Morning,' it's about a girl, isn't it?"

I sighed and clapped him on the back of the neck as I guided him out of the warehouse.

"Aren't all the best songs about a girl? It doesn't matter if it's metal, if it's country, if it's blues or rock and roll; all the songs that make us remember and make us want to sing along are about the best kind of girl, the kind you can't live without but can't ever get ahold of."

"You have one of those?"

I barked out a bitter laugh and stopped by the Challenger. "Oh yeah."

I texted Rowdy to let him know I was on my way, and he shot back that I had better hurry because the place was packed. The girls were all smoking-hot and dressed in sexy little sports-themed uniforms that made Hooters girls look like they were dressed for church. The bar was typically packed so that wasn't anything new. We went there enough that Lou, the door guy, usually hooked us up with a seat, even if there wasn't room or if the bar had a long wait.

When I walked in, I noticed the blonde with the giant fake boobs giving me the eye, but I never even blinked in her direction. I knew Ayden hated her and that it was my duty as her friend—god, I hated that word when it came to her—to keep all common enemies at bay, even if said enemy looked like she wanted to give me a bath with her tongue the first chance she got.

Lou gave me a head nod and pointed a meaty finger toward the section of the bar that was off to one side. It was the closest to the patio that was open in the summer, and I had no trouble spotting both Ayden's dark head and Rowdy's much blonder and far more prominent one. I don't know when he decided that a pompadour, long with perfectly groomed chops, was a style he could rock in the real world, but for the last year or so he had been wearing his hair like James Dean and dressing like a cat from the fifties. Rowdy was eccentric and liked flash and attention, so I just rolled with it because it was just part of who he was and not much made me chuckle like he did.

I caught Ayden's eye and gave her a grin. She looked at me for a second, then looked away without so much as a twitch of her lips. It made me frown as I settled onto the stool across from Rowdy. Even if there was some serious sexual tension between us she was always usually happy to see me.

"What's her problem tonight?"

I still felt bad about knocking her off the landing, but she had insisted that she was fine, so I didn't know what I had done to piss her off between then and now. Unless she had felt the instant hard-on that lying on top of her had caused. I couldn't be held accountable for that uncontrollable response. She was beautiful, and if she had any idea how badly I wanted to be on top of her all the time, it would make her do a lot more than frown at me.

Rowdy pushed a shot of amber liquid the same color as Ayden's eyes in my direction and used a finger that was tattooed with a picture of a miniature skull and cross bones to point at the bar. "He showed up about twenty minutes ago, and she's been acting like she has a metal pole crammed up her backside ever since."

I swiveled my head around and swore under my breath when I saw him through the crowd gathered at the bar. I didn't know what she saw in the guy. Sure, he was enrolled in the same school as her. Sure, he was interning with the government, doing some kind of groundbreaking research for biochemical fuels or some shit. Sure, he was all-right looking—in that dry-toast, plain-yogurt, white-rice kinda way. Sure, he was, by all accounts, a perfectly nice guy and a gentleman to boot, but everything about him screamed *boring!*

All of that aside, he wore a fucking sweater vest and didn't look like he had any idea what to do with all that was Ayden Cross. She was something special, something that grown men in another era would have battled to death to win with shiny pistols or clashing swords. But this guy, this nerdy, sweater vest–wearing idiot wouldn't even tell me to shove it where the sun didn't shine, even though I knew *he* knew that I had dirty, sexy, X-rated dreams about the girl he was dating. Try as I might to tone it down, I'm sure as hell it was all spelled out in my eyes when I looked at her.

"Awesome."

I tossed back the shot and took the one Rowdy hadn't touched yet and downed that one too. He gave me a look and leaned back to cross his arms over his broad chest. We were about the same height, an inch or so over six foot, but he looked like he could wrestle a bull to the ground due to his past life as an all-star football player. We never really talked about why he had quit playing ball, but I figured since he had found his niche in the tattoo world it didn't really matter, and if he wanted to tell me, he knew I would listen.

"He brought her a huge bouquet of flowers and some stupid box of chocolate or some shit shaped like a heart. I think he's trying to pin her down for Valentine's Day."

A cold chill raced down my spine, and I felt my eyes harden involuntarily. "She's supposed to come to the show at the Fillmore with Rule and Shaw." It was big deal for the band. It was a big deal for me, and I wanted her to be there. I had just assumed she would be.

Rowdy shrugged a broad shoulder. "They've been hanging out for a while now. I bet it's the night he's planning on going all out. You know what I mean, fancy dinner, expensive gift, and the night closing with a trip to a high-end hotel room. He looks like the type and he's been giving her the hard press for the past few months if I understand correctly all that girly jabber Cora annoys us with at the shop."

I gritted my teeth and repressed the urge to get out of my seat and strangle the guy with his own argyle outerwear. Another tumbler was set down in front of me, along with a plateful of wings. A pitcher of beer landed in front of Rowdy, and I narrowed my eyes to match Ayden's careful look when I noticed she was scowling back at me.

"Stop it."

I tried to look innocent, but had to admit that even on a good day, it wasn't a look I pulled off. "What?"

"Stop making faces at Adam. He just stopped by to say hi. I told him to come over and have a drink with you guys, but then he saw Jet looking like he was plotting someone's murder, and decided against it."

I wasn't going to deny it, so I picked up the shot and let my gaze travel over her outfit. Today was the cheerleader, my personal favorite. Her tiny pleated skirt was orange and blue, Bronco colors, and it was topped off with a supertight white sweater that left little to the imagination. She was already taller than average and when she put on those do-me heels, she was almost eye to eye with me, which made her legs—which deserved their own ode-to-greatness— look even better. I was lost somewhere in my own world, where those legs were wrapped around my head or my waist—I wasn't picky—when she jolted me back to reality.

Ayden smacked me on the side of my head. "Knock it off. I don't know what's wrong with you tonight, but get your mind out of the gutter. Are you sure you aren't the one who got banged up when we fell earlier?"

I rubbed the ear that had the little spike pointing out the top of it, where she had made it sting. I tossed back the shot she brought and pushed the plate of wings in Rowdy's direction. Maybe I needed to get drunk, so I could blame my sudden need to act a whole lot of wrong on something.

"Are you bailing on the show on Valentine's?" I heard the intensity in my tone and I hated it. It wasn't supposed to matter what she did or who she chose to spend her time with, but it did. I wanted her to pick me, even though I knew I wasn't allowed to pick her. She shifted on her shoes and fiddled with the edge of her skirt.

"I don't know. Shaw will be all wrapped up in Rule, and Cora usually takes off and does her own thing. You"—she pointed a finger at Rowdy—"always ditch me for some bar skank, and Nash offered to be DD, so he won't be drinking and will be grumpy and nasty all night." Those eyes that flashed with every color of gold and bronze landed on me and she bit her lip. "You'll be onstage, so that leaves me to fend for myself. Adam asked me to dinner and has a whole night planned, so I just don't know."

We stared at each other silently for a while, so long that it ultimately became awkward and strained. I wanted to ask her to ditch Adam and come, and I think she wanted me to ask her to ditch Adam and come, because she would do it. But if she wanted a boring, predictable Valentine's date with a douche bag in a sweater vest, who was I to stop her? I was never going to be a guy who had an advanced degree and a

five-year fiscal plan. I was never going to be a guy who valued safety and security above passion and creativity. I sure as
fuck was never going to be a guy who wore argyle in public.

"Well, you should have a nice time. Let Adam take you
out and give you a nice romantic night. You deserve it." I
almost choked on the words, but I got them out.

Something moved across her pretty face that I couldn't
read. Ayden was really good at that, hiding her emotions
behind a flirty smile and a sarcastic comeback. Whatever it
was disappeared as she picked up my empty glass and asked
if I wanted a refill. I nodded silently and turned back to
Rowdy. He was watching me dispassionately and pushed his
full pint of beer in my direction.

"We getting shit-faced?"

I tried to exhale around the band that had tightened in
my chest, and nodded sharply.

"Yep, sounds about right."

CHAPTER 3

Ayden

ICALLED THE KENTUCKY number back every day for the rest of the week and never got an answer. I called my mom and she had no clue who it might be. She insisted that she hadn't heard from Asa in months and got mad when I asked her if he was in jail. My brother was an easy guy to take up for—charming, unassuming, and effortlessly attractive and suave. He was the kind of guy who could steal the shirt off your back while you were still wearing it and then convince you it was your idea to give it to him all along. He made you want to take care of him at all costs even though he would never, ever return the favor.

I couldn't fathom why he would suddenly have a pressing need to get ahold of me, but it still gave me a sense of apprehension that I couldn't shake. On top of that, I swore I had seen the same guy I thought I recognized earlier, walking in the neighborhood near the house the last two times I had headed out for a run. I was tempted to stop and ask him if we knew each other, but I still kept my distance from strangers after the attack on Shaw at our old apartment. Granted, she had been cornered by a lunatic ex-boyfriend bent on making her his by any means necessary, but I figured better safe than sorry.

I would have mentioned it to Jet, as the de facto man of the house, but over the last few days I got the impression he was upset with me and was purposely avoiding me, so I hadn't had much of a chance to say anything to him. Something had happened when I told him I didn't know if I was going to the show on Saturday, some subtle shift that changed things between us, and I didn't know what it was or what to do about it.

In all honesty, I didn't want to spend Valentine's Day with Adam. He was such a sweet guy and he was exactly what I was convinced I should be looking for in a long-term partner. But when he had come strolling into the bar with those ridiculous flowers and that box of chocolates, just like a scene out of *Pretty Woman,* all I wanted to do was find a place to hide.

I knew he wanted Valentine's Day to be a big night. He had been pressing for our relationship to get more serious the last couple times we went out, but even though I tried, and gave myself pep talk after pep talk, I just couldn't drum up an inkling of the desire for him that I felt for Jet.

In fact, the last time I had sex with a guy was with a fellow chem major named Kyle. I had used him to try to rid myself of the memory and humiliation of Jet's rejection the previous winter. The only purpose it had served was to make me feel worse than I had before and to remind me that good-girl sex was entirely boring and unsatisfying. That was why such a huge part of me was so drawn to Jet. Sure, his future plans, or lack thereof, concerned me, but the real reason I needed to stay as far away as possible had to do with more than that. The way he simply made me want to let it all go and just *be* with him made my blood freeze up and my better judgment scream and holler.

I might hate that girls wandered in and out of his room across the hall on a fairly regular basis, but I was honest enough with myself to admit that not a single one of them looked like they left wanting more or like they were in any way unsatisfied. It made me want to tie him down and have at it myself, but that wasn't in the cards. So in the meantime I had to decide what I was going to do about Adam.

I knew it wasn't fair to keep stringing him along if I wasn't willing to commit to something more serious. I knew it wasn't fair for me to try to keep fitting these perfect guys into a role I needed them to fill for my perfect vision of the future, only to ultimately deem them not right. Unfortunately, I didn't know what the alternative was. Deep down, I knew what I really wanted, what I ultimately desired, but we didn't fit. Jet didn't fit into my flawless vision, and I had a feeling that trying to make him fill any other role than the one he was already occupying would destroy more than just our friendship. Jet wasn't the kind of guy that respected boundaries.

I was sitting at a table outside the library at the college mulling all of this over and not paying any attention to what was going on around me, when a heavy anatomy book slammed down in front of me on the table. I jumped a little and glared at my best friend as she lowered herself into the chair across from me.

Shaw Landon was the opposite of me in every way one could imagine. She was short, with almost white-blond hair, leafy green eyes, and came from a background flooded with wealth and privilege. She was also shy, sweet and, as of late, so ridiculously happy and in love, it took a concentrated effort not to gag all over her.

Don't get me wrong. I was very happy she had finally come clean about her feelings for Rule and that after some serious damage and some serious making up, they had figured out how to make things work between them. I had to admit I was a little jealous that even though they seemed to be so different, it was incidental when it came to just simply being together. I didn't know how to do that. If I did, I wouldn't be sexually frustrated and contemplating hurting a very nice guy for no other reason than he just didn't do it for me or have me daydreaming about skintight pants and what was inside them.

"I called your name like four times. You looked like you were trying to figure out something pretty serious over here."

We both went to DU and were both in our junior year. Shaw wanted to be a doctor so she was looking at a longer haul than I was, but it was nice that a couple of our upper-level undergrad classes now overlapped. I rarely saw her unless we went out or were at work together, and even then, chances were she left early to go home to Rule or to study. I missed her, and while Cora was fun and I enjoyed spending time with her, talking to her was different from talking to Shaw.

I traced the image on the front of the book with a fingernail and refused to look up at her. "I'm thinking it's time to cut Adam loose."

"Hmm . . . This wouldn't have anything to do with Valentine's Day would it?"

I made a face and sat back in the chair with a sigh. "Maybe."

Looking into those green eyes of hers was like looking into a raw piece of emerald. She watched me for a second before sitting back and copying my pose with her arms crossed over her chest.

"What do you want to *do* tomorrow night?"

I think the more accurate question was *who* did I want to *do* tomorrow night and the answer was clearly not Adam. I huffed out a breath that sent my dark hair sliding across my forehead.

"I wanted to go to the show with everyone, but then Adam showed up at the bar with flowers and chocolate and made a big production about making plans. Rowdy was there and saw the whole thing. Jet came in and told me I should go have a romantic night, that I deserved it—so now I don't have any idea what I want to do, but I know I'm irritated at both of them for different reasons."

Shaw lifted a pale eyebrow and tapped the edge of her fingers, tipped in a crazy leopard-print polish, on the cover of her book. "So tell me the reasons."

"It's stupid."

"If it has you sulking outside the library when it's barely forty degrees out, then it isn't stupid. Something is bothering you and we should talk it out."

I sighed again and ran aggravated hands through my hair. I normally wore it much shorter, but between school and work, I was unsuccessful in finding time for anything that might be labeled trivial or a waste of time, which included my current state of boy confusion.

"I like Adam. He's nice and we have a pretty good time together, but it bothers me that he never wants to hang out with my friends. He's almost *too* cookie-cutter, you know what I mean?" I waited until she nodded. "He has a great future all planned out, he has an awesome family all from here and I know that he really likes me. He's cute enough and we have a million and one things in common, but . . ." There shouldn't be a "but," yet there it was.

"But what, Ayd?" She wasn't going to let me sugarcoat it.

"But when he kisses me or tries to touch me, I might as well be filing my nails or watching CNN. There is no spark— Hell, there isn't even a stiff wind. It's boring and dull, and I hate it."

"Well, that's not good."

I scoffed at her, "You think? I'm not attracted to the guy I'm supposed to be dating, but if, God forbid, the guy who lives across the hall comes out of his room without a shirt on, instantly I'm ready to spontaneously combust. Watching Jet onstage, being close enough to accidentally touch him and smell him, does more to get me off and turn me on than anything Kyle or Adam has done in the past year, and that's why I'm irritated and frustrated with him.

"I don't want to be attracted to Jet, Shaw. I want to be attracted to a guy like Adam, who I can potentially build a future with, and it bugs me to no end that no matter how hard I try, I can't seem to make that happen."

She gazed at me knowingly for a long minute. Shaw knew all about my disastrous attempt at seduction with Jet and she always told me that something seemed off about it. Sure, he thought I was all virginal white-gloves and untouched purity, but she was convinced there was more at work than Jet just trying to be chivalrous. She was always encouraging me to let a little bit more of the old me out, so he could see that I wasn't above whatever lofty pedestal he had decided to place me on.

The last time I did that, he hurt me and made me run away, so I wasn't too keen on letting the old Ayden out again for him to reject all over again. Frankly, I was terrified of the way he made we want to throw all caution to the wind.

"Well, we both know you can't maintain a relationship of any kind with a guy you aren't physically attracted to, and as for Jet, maybe you just need to get him out of your system. Maybe once he's not the one that got away, you won't want him so bad. That thing that happened last year between the two of you has always lingered. Maybe you just need to take a full dose of whatever he's packing, and it will go away. Then you can focus on finding a guy more like Adam to work on building a serious relationship with."

"I tried that already. He said it was a bad idea, remember?" I couldn't help the bitterness that colored my tone.

Shaw laced her fingers together and leaned across the table, so that I couldn't look away from her super-green eyes.

"So make him think it's a great idea. You really think if you set out to seduce him, he's going to say no? I heard what you told me happened last time, Ayd. He put up a little tiny protest and you ran away as fast as you could because it reminded you too much of something you might have done in another life. We don't talk about Kentucky much, but I get the distinct impression that the girl from Woodward wouldn't have let Jet go that night, the way the girl from Denver did."

I groaned and dropped my head into my hands to cover my face. "The girl from Woodward wouldn't have ever given him the impression that she was some good little girl, just trying to play with fire. Who I was before wasn't pretty, Shaw. I tell you that, but I don't think you really get the enormity of it."

She waved a dismissive hand and got to her feet, hefting her heavy book as she went. The thing looked like it weighed more than she did.

"None of that matters. It's *this* Ayden that I'm worried about. This Ayden deserves to be happy, regardless of what the future holds, and *this* Ayden is the one who has to decide why she is settling for milk and cookies when what she really wants is edible body paint and furry handcuffs."

That startled a laugh out of me and I got to my feet to follow her. "What do you know about edible body paints?" She flicked her long hair over her shoulder, and the black underneath shimmered under the pale blond.

"Tattoo artist boyfriend, remember? He likes to draw."

We shared a knowing look and parted to go our separate ways to class. I hated that she was right. I could drag things out with Adam forever and still end up nowhere. He was too nice for that, and I was too good of a person now to make him suffer and wait around needlessly for things that I just wasn't willing to give him. I knew that being with someone like Adam helped me keep all the bad traits from my past at bay. Dating a guy like him didn't allow for the spontaneity or the reckless decision-making that so often ended up making me suffer harsh consequences. Adam was steady and didn't offer up much in the way of excitement or passion, and my logical side knew that was what I should want. However, the bigger part of me that operated on instinct and emotion knew he just wasn't ever going to cut it on the more basic, physical fronts.

I spent my entire next class worrying about it and getting nowhere. Unfortunately, Adam was the teacher's aide for the I-chem class that was directly across the hall from mine so when I exited the classroom he was waiting for me. I had to try not to flinch when he leaned down to press a light kiss to my unyielding mouth. It shouldn't be this hard. He was nice enough looking, with brown hair and clear blue eyes. Regrettably, he dressed like he was about to burst into a lecture about cell division or the effects of global warming at any minute. There was just nothing there; no spark, no tingle, no nothing.

He offered to take my books from me but I shook my head no.

I was getting ready to tell him that we needed to cancel

Valentine's Day and that I didn't think it was a good idea
to see each other anymore, when he grabbed my hand and
placed a kiss on the back of it.

"I know you were on the fence about spending Valentine's Day together tomorrow, so I went ahead and made us
a reservation for dinner at that Brazilian restaurant you like
so much. I really want us to spend the evening together, Ayd.
This relationship is very special to me. You are very special
to me."

I gulped down a mixture of bile and guilt, and tried to
give him a smile that I knew ended up more like a grimace.

"That's really sweet, Adam, but like I said, I just don't
know about dinner and the night together. I don't think I'm
in the same place with this relationship that you are."

I could see that my words hurt him and it made me feel
awful, but I knew it was the truth. I couldn't use him to
keep myself from acting in a certain way. Maybe I had really
changed or I was just pretending, but either way, he didn't
need to be jerked around while I figured it out. He didn't need
to be mentally rejected while I was busy getting Jet's pants
off in my mind every five minutes.

"I'm sorry, I know that's not what you wanted to hear."

He squeezed the hand he was holding and gave me a
grin that was sad and sweet. "Well, how about this, we go
to dinner and you let me try to charm you? After, you can
decide what you want to do. We have to eat, and the reservation was tricky to get on such short notice. I think you'll be
missing out on something really great if you don't give this
thing between us a shot."

I wanted to groan, but just tugged my hand free and used it to twist the straps on my book bag around. I knew the right thing to do was to walk away, but he looked so bummed out. He had given it his all for the last four months and I was having a hard time just pulling the Band-Aid off clean.

"Look, I have plans to go see a friend's band tomorrow night. I'll go to dinner with you but you have to understand that all it's going to be is dinner. I don't think my mind is going to be changed. You're a really nice guy, Adam, but there's just something missing here, and after four months I know when to pull the plug."

He laughed and I heard a chord of bitterness. "I know what it means when a girl says I'm a nice guy, Ayd. You don't have to try to spare my feelings. You're bored with me. I've seen the guys you hang out with when you aren't working or at school. No one in their right mind would ever call any of them nice guys, especially that one you live with, the guy with the band."

We had reached the parking lot and my car, so I popped the lock and tossed my stuff inside. I shifted on my feet and tried not to look guilty.

"It doesn't have anything to do with that. I just know that something isn't working and I'm not going to draw it out for either one of us. Trust me, Adam, there was a time when I would have just kept dating you until I had wrung you dry, and then walked away without an apology or bothering to look back. I know we both deserve better than that now, so if you want to cancel dinner I totally understand."

I was secretly hopeful that he would do just that. I didn't

want to sit through an awkward dinner with a guy whom I had just told, in no uncertain terms, that I didn't find him attractive. But Adam was a gentleman and his good manners just wouldn't allow it.

"No. I already made the reservation and I would still like to take you. I don't want to be alone on Valentine's Day, especially not when I thought things were moving in a much more favorable direction with you."

Man, he was even being nice about being dumped. I sighed and climbed up into the high vehicle. "All right. I really am sorry, Adam."

He gave his head a rueful shake and slid his hands into the pockets of his slacks. "To be honest, Ayd, sometimes when we were together I felt like one minute you were there with me, and present, and then the next second it was like a stranger was staring back at me. You're very difficult to get a handle on, but I really thought it was worth the effort to try."

That made my eye twitch and I needed to get away from him. "I'll see you tomorrow."

"I'll pick you up at eight." It was on the tip of my tongue to just tell him I would meet him at the restaurant, so I could go to the show right after without him having to drop me off, but I figured I had done enough damage for one day. His comment about me being two different people was still spinning in my head, so I just left.

I was surprised when I got to the house to see that Cora's little Mini Cooper was parked in the driveway. She normally closed down the tattoo shop where she worked and did the bank deposit for the night. She was usually just getting home when I was leaving for my shift at the bar. I was also irritated and relieved to see that the Challenger was gone. Jet had been scarce lately, which in turn made me curious as to what he was up to and grateful I didn't have to deal with his unpredictable moods as of late.

When I walked into the living room I was brought up short by the tiny figure curled up on the couch. Cora wasn't the type to wrap up in a fluffy blanket and watch sad movies on Lifetime, so the fact that both those things were happening right now made me drop my bag on the floor and rush to her side. I was startled to see that both the brown and the blue-green eyes were glassy with tears, and that her normally cheerful smile was hidden under a quivering lip and flushed cheeks. Cora was a couple years older than me, but right then she looked all of five years old.

"What's wrong?" I didn't know what to do, so I patted her on her knee under the blanket.

She blew her nose into a Kleenex and swiped at her damp face with the back of her hand. She looked like a sad pixie.

"I just had a really bad day."

I frowned and settled even more fully onto the couch. "I've known you awhile now and you've never even called in sick, not even when we all got food poisoning from that bad Thai food. What happened?"

She sighed and flopped over on her back. She tossed an arm over her swollen eyes and gritted out through clenched teeth, "My ex-fiancé is getting remarried at the end of the year. The asshole sent me a wedding announcement in the mail."

I blinked in surprise because I didn't even know she had

ever been engaged and because I never would have figured her for the type to carry a torch for someone. "I'm sorry. That has to be rough."

She let out a string of swear words that would have made Rule and the boys proud and shoved up into a sitting position so that she was hugging her knees. "It shouldn't matter. He was a bastard and cheated on me the entire time we were together. He owned the shop I worked at in Brooklyn. I came back late one day because I forgot something, and walked in on him putting it to one of his clients in the back room. That wasn't even the worst part. I thought we were family, that the shop was home, but everyone knew and no one ever said a thing. I looked like a fool."

She ran her hands through her short hair and growled like an angry puppy. "He was the first guy I ever really loved, ya know? I was so sure that I was over it, but then I saw that stupid announcement and I felt like I was reliving it all over again. If Phil hadn't pulled me out of the city when he did, I don't know what I would have done. It just sucks that he's moved on to some other unsuspecting girl, and I go day after day alone."

I went to the kitchen to grab her a bottle of water and hand her a paper towel to wipe off her face.

"It's not like you don't have every opportunity to date and have a boyfriend. I've been out with you. You get hit on all the time."

She rubbed her multitoned eyes and sighed. "I get hit on by the same kind of guy over and over again; tatted up, restless, and only looking for a good time. I work with guys like them, and some of my best friends are guys like that, Ayd. I know how they operate. I've had my heart stomped on, so even though I could probably hang out with one of them for a minute, in the long run I would still end up heartbroken and alone."

"So date someone different."

She looked at me from under spiky eyelashes and a hint of her old attitude started to surface.

"Says the girl who is dating a guy who looks like he should be smoking a pipe and reading Chaucer."

Now it was my turn to sigh and flop on the couch. I crossed my arms over my stomach and looked at her out of the corner of my eye.

"I broke it off with him today."

She lifted a pale eyebrow, the one with the pink stud in it at me. "Really? I thought you were planning a perfectly boring future of going to the cinema and breeding supergeniuses with tedious bouts of vanilla sex."

"Yeah, well, I would actually have to want to have sex with him in order to breed anything and it just isn't happening—vanilla or otherwise. I just couldn't string him along anymore."

She popped me on the shoulder with her tiny fist and gave me a huge grin. "Good. Now you can stop pretending that you don't want to get all kinds of naked and horizontal with Jet."

I snapped my head around and stared at her with my mouth hanging open. "You're the second person today who has told me I should just go ahead and sleep with him."

She shrugged and tossed the blanket to the floor. "Shaw and I talk about it all the time. Jet is sexy, like it-hurts-to-look-at-him sexy, so we totally get it. What we don't get is why you so obviously struggle to keep him at arm's length. I see you stare at him day in and day out, and when he's onstage, Ayd, you should see the way you look at him."

I fidgeted nervously, again unaware that I was being so transparent about what he did to me and the struggle I had with myself to keep my hands off.

"Everyone watches him like that when he's onstage. He's amazing and talented."

She got to her feet and stretched her arms above her head. She patted me on top of my head with the hand of the tattooed arm on her way out of the room, calling over her shoulder, "Yeah, that's true, but you're the only one he ever looks into the crowd for. You're the only one he makes sure is watching if he knows you're there."

That made my breath catch in my throat and my pulse slip and slide. I wasn't oblivious to the fact that Jet and I shared a pretty potent amount of attraction, but I was also smart enough to know that after turning me down last winter, he hadn't had an empty bed or a serious relationship since.

A relationship needed more than fire and flames to make it work. Plus, he didn't know the real me, and the me he did know, he had deemed too clean to mess up. Having someone else tell me that he might be looking at me, realizing all the forbidden things I wanted to do to him and seeing through the perfect image I tried to project, really made me nervous. I struggled around him now, and if he had an inkling as to what I really wanted, I didn't know that I would be able to keep my hands to myself and out of his pants any longer .

Grumbling to myself I picked my stuff up off the floor and wandered back to my room. I scowled at his closed door and settled in to do some homework and brood. I didn't want to go to dinner with Adam, and now with Cora's startling revelation, I didn't really want to go to the show afterward, either. Maybe when I packed up and left Kentucky, I should have looked into becoming a nun. Right now, that seemed like it would be a whole lot easier to handle.

WITH MY DARK HAIR and odd-colored eyes I looked good in red and since it was Valentine's Day, I thought that my dress with its flared skirt and off-the-shoulder boatneck in lipstick-red was a perfect choice. My hair was too short to do much with so I curled it around the front of my face, and pinned the long bangs back with a bobby pin that had a big rhinestone heart on it. I had been to enough of Jet's shows to know that heels weren't exactly the best choice in footwear, but I didn't have anything else that would fit with the dress, so I settled on a pair of black patent leather Mary Janes.

When I looked in the mirror I had to acknowledge that I looked way too good to simply be having dinner with my ex-sorta-boyfriend, and that I was dressing for someone else entirely. And that wasn't smart, but I didn't care or change my outfit.

Adam arrived right on time in his very sensible Subaru, and drove us downtown. The conversation in the car was stiff and strained, even though he told me I looked lovely and was being perfectly polite. We devolved into talking about school and chemistry. By the time we got seated at the restaurant, it was all I could do not to check my phone every five minutes to see the time. I was antsy and still a little concerned about his comment that he felt like I was two different people. That was something I battled with on a regular basis and had thought I'd figured out how to keep the old me totally locked down tight.

I would be the first to admit that I was probably the worst Valentine's date in the history of the holiday. When he ordered a bottle of wine to have with dinner, I wanted to groan because that just seemed too datelike, but I owed it to him to at least try to be pleasant. I let him pour me a glass and forced a smile.

"Thanks, Adam."

"I'm glad you came. I really wish you would reconsider and think about trying to work this out between us. I really do like you, Ayden. You're smart, funny, and beautiful. Plus, we have so much in common."

What was wrong with me? This guy was nice, cute, and clearly thought I was awesome. He was like the dream guy most girls wanted, but for some reason, the more he extolled all my virtues, the more turned off I got. I pushed the glass of wine away and picked up a glass of water.

"Adam, I don't think you really know me. For instance, I hate wine. I usually drink tequila, a lot of it, and then hate myself in the morning. We have our chemistry majors and school in common, but beyond that, not much. I really don't like the ballet or the opera, and I'm more of a line dancing, rodeo kind of girl. I thought that it would do me some good to try to date a guy like you, because you're just so thoughtful and nice, but all it did was show me that trying to force something to happen just won't work."

He cleared his throat and set his wine down as well. "You could have told me all of that months ago, Ayd. You never even gave me a chance to get to know you. You already decided, before we even began, which version of you that I was going to date, without considering that I might like both of them enough to stick around. Maybe I like to line dance as well."

He was absolutely right and that just made me feel even worse.

I spent the rest of the dinner sulking, and to his credit Adam still offered to pay for the entire bill. I couldn't let him do that, so I paid for my half and for the tip, to make up for being such a jerk. He drove me to the Fillmore and I had every intention of jumping out of the car and dashing inside, but for some reason when he caught sight of the crowd waiting out front decked out in a whole lot of denim and spikes, he decided that he had to park and walk me in.

I wanted to tell him that it was unnecessary. I had been to plenty of these shows over the past year, and while my fancy dress might garner a few weird looks, most of these guys could care less about me. They were here for the music. But I had already rained on his parade enough for one day, so I let Adam guide me up to the front doors. I didn't miss the scowl on his face when I told the girl taking tickets I was on the list.

She double-checked my name and wrapped a bracelet

around my wrist that said I was over twenty-one. She looked questioningly at Adam, who just shrugged and paid for a ticket. He stood out like a sore thumb amid all the other miscreants milling around, and I didn't have the heart to tell him it was going to be even worse when we got inside. We had to wait in a little bit of a line to get to the front doors, and I tried to tell him I was fine, but he kept insisting on at least getting me to my waiting friends. Since Enmity was the headlining band, I knew that Jet would have arranged for them to have one of the VIP tiers up in the balcony by the bar. It took a little work, and a lot of waiting for Adam to stop gaping at barely clothed girls and guys who looked like they ate glass and metal for breakfast, to get to the rest of the group.

Shaw was pressed up against Rule and looked cute in a black dress with pink polka-dot hearts scattered all across it. Rule's nod to the holiday was to have dyed the front of his dark hair a shocking hot pink. Only a guy like Rule could rock pink hair and not have to give a second thought to getting his ass kicked.

Nash was in a deep conversation with Cora, who looked much better today. Rowdy was saying something to Jet, trying to get his attention. It was to no avail, because as soon as Jet's gaze locked on Adam and me making our way over, those dark eyes went pitch-black and the gold on the outside started burning like embers. I had to swallow a lump in my throat, because for the life of me I couldn't figure out why he was so mad. Before I could say anything, he pushed away from the table and stalked away without saying anything to me or anyone else.

I stiffened automatically when Shaw slipped away from Rule to wrap me in a hug. "Hey, girl, you look great."

I cleared my throat and waved a hand around the table. "Adam, this is everyone, everyone, this is Adam."

I didn't wait to see if anyone talked to him. I focused my gaze on Rowdy and moved toward him with purpose. He was staring past me at Adam, and sucking on a Coors Light tall boy. I put myself right in his line of sight and crossed my arms over my chest.

"What's Jet's problem?" I was one second from tapping my toe like a disgruntled kid and I think he could tell, because he just smiled at me and tipped the beer up.

"You should probably ask him."

Annoyed, I poked him in the center of his solid chest. "I'm asking you. He's been acting pissed off all week. What's going on with him?"

He moved the beer and narrowed his eyes at me. Rowdy was your typical blond-haired, blue-eyed, perfectly sculpted God's gift to women, but there was always something lurking just below the surface of that ocean-colored gaze that let people know there was more to him than just an easy smile and a good time. There were depths beyond all that tattooed skin and perfectly coiffed hair. I didn't know him as well as some of the others, but in him I felt a kindred spirit I didn't bother to try to define.

"It's Valentine's Day, Ayd, and you showed up looking like a goddamn pinup model, on the arm of a guy that dresses like someone's dad. Like I said, maybe you should go ask him what's wrong. I think it's long past time that the two of you have an honest conversation, before one of you—or both of you—end up doing some kind of irreparable damage to the other."

I sucked in a hard breath between my teeth and put a hand on my racing heart. The opening band was starting their set, so I knew Jet would have gone backstage to make sure the band was getting ready to go. I looked over my shoulder and noticed that Adam was alternately looking at Rule like he was an alien from another planet, and at Shaw like she was crazy for cuddling up to him like he was a giant teddy bear. He just didn't get it, and even if I had tried to make a relationship with him work, he never would have gotten it.

"Will they let me backstage to talk to him?"

"Sugar, looking the way you look right now, nobody in their right mind would try to stop you."

I had to give him a smile for that. "Will you keep an eye on Adam? Make sure Rule doesn't murder him or that Cora doesn't convince him to do something stupid, like move to Antarctica."

He nodded briefly and went back to his beer. "I got you covered, Ayd."

I spun on my heel and dashed down the steps and across the wide general admission floor to the stairs at the side of the stage. The first band was playing and it was getting more crowded, so I had to wiggle and shimmy a little more than I planned. At the top of the stairs, the security guard tried to stop me from going by, but I told him I was with the band. I said that I was with Jet, and like Rowdy had said, the guy did a quick sweep of my outfit (and lingered on my legs) before letting me by. It took me a minute to find the right room, and when I did, I found only Von and Catcher sitting in big leather chairs messing around with their instruments. They looked up at me in surprise and I felt my heart trip when I didn't see Jet anywhere.

"Uh, hey."

"Hey," they chorused in unison.

"I'm, uh, looking for Jet. Have you seen him?" They shared a look that I didn't understand, and Catcher cleared his throat. He inclined his head toward the door at the back of the room.

"He came in and smashed a bottle of Jameson against the wall. He went in there a few minutes ago."

I looked at the door and back at them. If the door was locked and he didn't let me in, I wasn't sure what I was going to do. I stepped gingerly around the piles of cords and switches littering the floor. I was about to try to pull the door open when Von called out, "We sorta need him to get his shit together ASAP, so try not to get him even more riled up than he already is."

I nodded absently and knocked lightly on the door. "Jet?"

There was no answer, but the knob turned easily under my hand, so I slipped in and silently prayed he wasn't doing something that would embarrass us both. He had his back to me and was leaning over the sink staring at himself in the dingy mirror. His gaze snapped up to mine in the dirty glass and there was no misreading the hostility stamped on his handsome face or the wildness in those dark eyes. The gold rims were melting and hot, and he looked like he was on the very edge of losing control. His biceps flexed and tensed like he was going to pull the sink off the wall and hurl it.

"What do you want, Ayden?"

That was a loaded question if there ever was one.

"I just wanted to see what was wrong with you. You've been acting like you're mad at me all week and I don't understand why."

I saw his hands tighten and his fingers flex. I also noticed that instead of his usual black nail polish, he had painted the middle fingernail on each hand the same bloodred as my dress. That shouldn't be hot, but on him it just totally was.

"Why did you bring that guy to my show?" The bathroom felt stifling and small. I could sense the intensity of whatever he was feeling, vibrating across my skin. I had never seen him this raw unless he was on stage performing, and I wasn't sure how to handle it in such close quarters.

"I didn't bring him. We went to dinner and I was planning on getting dropped off, but he kind of freaked out when he saw everyone running around outside and insisted on coming in with me. What does that have to do with why you're acting like such a prick toward me? You can't be mad I'm hanging out with a guy I've been seeing for months, when you had a girl leave your room with her panties in her back pocket less than a week ago." I paused.

"Come on, Jet, what gives?"

I thought maybe he was going to lay into me. I thought maybe he was going to tell me that I had no right to judge him. I thought maybe he was going to yell that I shouldn't be bringing someone I knew he didn't like around, when he was getting ready to play a big, important show.

What I wasn't prepared for was for him to let go of his death grip on the sink and stalk toward me with fire and something else burning in his dark eyes. Or for rough hands heavy with rings pushing me back up against the bathroom door, and then traveling up higher, through my hair. Jet slammed his mouth down hard enough on mine that it made me whimper, and for a second I was so shocked all I could do was stand there and let him devour me with those hands I'd stared at for months and with a tongue that had the glide of metal in it.

By the time my brain reengaged, he was starting to pull away, but now that the seal had been broken there was no stopping the flood. Desire blazed first and foremost, and I wrapped my arms around his neck. keeping him right where he was. He tasted like whiskey and the sweetest kind of temptation there was. Lust had me pressing as close to him as I could and I felt his knee slide up under the skirt of my dress. The shock from the contrast of cold and hot as the barbell he had through his tongue moved back and forth across my own, made me gasp. That only gave him better access to everything he was trying to invade. On my tiptoes now, all of the best parts of him were pressing hard and insistent against all the wanting parts of me, and I couldn't ever remember a simple kiss being something as powerful as this.

I didn't want to let him go.

CHAPTER 4

Jet

I WAS LIVING IN a state of perpetual fury. I was still furious that my narcissistic and overbearing father thought he could blackmail me, using my mom. I was livid that my mom would let him use her like that. I was incensed that I couldn't get Ayden out of my head, and I was just flat-out angry that it mattered to me whether she wanted to spend Valentine's Day with me or with Mr. Perfect. As a result I was acting like an asshole to anyone and everyone that dared cross my path the past few days. The guys in the band were sick of my shit and if Rowdy told me to just take her to bed and get it over with one more time, I was pretty sure I was going to knock all his front teeth out.

All I wanted to do was get through the show, figure out what I was going to do about my folks, and maybe set up a short tour so I could get out of town and put some distance between me and a certain brunette who was buried under my skin.

But then she had to show up in a bloodred dress, looking like she just stepped off the pages of a hot rod magazine, with that sweater vest–wearing douche trailing behind, her like a lost dog. She was just too much for me to handle at the moment. Those endless legs and bright red lips had my head going to all kinds of places it shouldn't. She was there with a date, so I walked away in the middle of whatever Rowdy was trying to tell me, and headed to the band room backstage. The rest of the guys were warming up and getting ready, but the idea of going onstage while I felt so volatile made something inside me snap. I grabbed the closest thing to me—a bottle of whiskey I had been drinking from earlier—and chucked it against the wall.

The guys all stopped what they were doing and watched me with curious and careful eyes. I felt like I was about to fly apart into a million pieces, so I just barked, "Not right now!" and decided to barricade myself in the bathroom until I managed to pull it together.

I was breathing hard and I could see how wild my dark eyes looked in the mirror. I was just about to splash cold water on my face to try to get some level of control back, when I heard my name, spoken in a soft Southern drawl, from the other side of the door. I was going to growl at her to leave me alone, but I didn't get a chance, because she pulled the door open and met my gaze in the mirror. All I could do was stare at her while everything swirling under the surface suddenly broke through. I heard her ask me what was wrong, and was aware that I demanded to know what she was thinking by bringing that guy here.

But all of it was white noise against the roar of something far louder and far more powerful thrumming in my heated blood.

I wasn't aware of moving toward her. I wasn't aware of pushing her up against the door with the entire length of my body. I wasn't aware of tangling her silky dark hair around my fingers and getting it caught up in my rings. I heard her gasp when my tongue ring hit the warm center of her mouth. I was going to pull away, going to apologize over and over again and tell her it had just been a shitty week, but before I could, she wrapped her arms around my neck and I felt any resistance she had, any control I retained, melt away under a soft little murmur of pleasure.

We were exactly at the right height for me to get my knee between her amazing legs and press even more fully against her, as she collapsed against the door behind her. She tasted like wine and invitation and I was pretty sure both things were going to my head. When she whispered my name, any rational thought that I shouldn't be touching this girl in this way, especially not in a backstage bathroom, went out the window.

The fingers of one of her hands moved from my neck and crawled down the back of my T-shirt. Even though it felt better than anything I could remember in a long time, to be pressed head to toe against her wasn't enough, so I let go of her hair and moved my hands under the hem of her poufy skirt. Gripping her toned thigh, I expected more resistance when I wrapped it around my waist and trailed my eager fingers up to the part of her I had no business at all being anywhere near. It was a short trip met with zero resistance and little gasps of surprise.

I saw her amber eyes get wide, but instead of asking me

to stop or telling me to go to hell, she whispered my name. I felt the edge of her fingers dig into the base of my spine, right above my ass.

We were eye to eye, foreheads almost touching, and I could see every single reaction she had to my touch shimmering in those liquid depths. When I got my fingers under the edge of her lace panties, I saw something flare there that made my already hard dick get even harder. I knew it sure as hell wasn't very comfortable. She shivered, and I didn't know if it was from the press of the metal on my fingers against her bare skin or because I had her pinned and exposed and was about to touch her in ways I had only dreamed of. Either way, her other hand tightened almost painfully in my tousled hair and her bright eyes fell to half-mast. She tugged my head closer, so our mouths were lined up and she kissed me. I got inside all her wet heat, her mouth and more, and swore because she was hot and slippery and felt like molten fire against both my tongue and my questing fingers.

I leaned down so that my forearm was braced on the door above her head, and settled even more fully into her. My tongue ring clicked against her teeth and I pulled away to suck on the pulse that was rapidly fluttering right below her ear. Her hands were tense in my hair and on my skin. I moved my fingers in and out of her, and slicked over the part of her that was throbbing and burning for my touch. Every whimper, every gasp made me move faster, made me touch her in a way that was guaranteed to send her over the edge. I felt her flutter against my fingers and moved back to kiss her hard and fast, just before she went limp and her eyes burst into a fireworks display of desire and satisfaction. Her chest was moving rapidly up and down, and clarity was slowly starting to filter back in, when a fist pounded on the door behind her lax head and made her jump.

"Jet, man, we go on in, like, ten minutes. Can you stop acting like a spaz and get out here so we can do this shit?" Von's voice was irritated and I couldn't blame him. I was acting erratic, and we did have a huge crowd out there that had paid good money to see us perform.

I pulled her from against the door and let my hands fall away from her. She leaned back and we watched each other warily, without saying a word. I ran my hands over my face, which was a mistake because I smelled like her, and it was doing nothing to tame the more than uncomfortable situation I had going on in my pants. They were already tight; she'd made them unbearable.

"I have to go."

She sucked her plush bottom lip between her teeth, and all I wanted to do was find the closest flat surface and demand she put that pretty mouth to better use.

"Jet?" I didn't have the time or the wherewithal to get into any of the consequences of this little dalliance with her, so I just shook my head and reached around her for the door-knob.

"Look, we both know that's what a guy like me has to offer, a quick fuck in a bathroom backstage, and we both know you deserve a night in a king-sized bed with silk sheets. I'm not going to apologize, but I can tell you it won't happen again. All right?"

I thought she was going to look remorseful or ashamed; I wasn't prepared for her to be mad. Those whiskey eyes lit with a fire I had never seen in her and before I could react, she slapped me across the face hard enough to make my back teeth rattle and my face flame.

"What the fuck, Ayd!"

She brushed down her dark cap of hair, and turned to pull the door open herself. I hated that I loved how wrinkled and well-loved she looked, and that I was the one who had gotten her all messy and rumpled.

"In case you forgot, I offered *you* a night in a king-sized bed with silk sheets, asshole. You turned me down. You told me I wasn't the type. If you took a freaking second to stop trying to tell me what I do and don't deserve, maybe you could see that the location doesn't matter, but the person does."

She had stunned me into silence, but she was good and pissed and clearly not done.

"And just so you know, I broke it off with Adam yesterday because every time he tried to touch me, every time he tried to kiss me I had to pretend it was you to even fake getting through it. But you're right, Jet, it won't happen again, because you don't know half of what you think you know about me. Every time I think you're figuring it out or at least trying to, you just end up making me feel like an idiot."

She threw the door open in a swirl of red and righteous indignation. The guys in the band were all staring at me with knowing looks, as she swept out of the room like a regal goddess. I saw Von open his mouth, but I just squinted my eyes and pointed a finger in his direction. "Don't even start."

I picked up my electric Les Paul and fit the strap over my shoulder. I shook my head to try to get my brains and my libido to settle back down, and shoved a guitar pick between my teeth.

"I wanna start with something a little different. You guys think you can just follow me in?"

We had played together for years, and there hadn't ever been a time when I had spontaneously changed up a set that they hadn't been able to just fall in line or pick up the rhythm and follow my lead. Boone narrowed his eyes at me and picked up his bass.

"It's going to be one of those shows?"

I blew out a breath and tried not to think about how good Ayden felt, how perfect she had tasted and moved against me. Granted, I had had a thing for her for a hell of a long time, but I hadn't been prepared for the reality to profoundly beat the crap out of the fantasy. She was a girl who wanted things in life I was never going to be able to give her. It shouldn't make me go sideways every time we were close, when I knew that nothing was ever going to come of it. While I wasn't opposed to being any pretty girl's good time, something told me that when she walked away after having her fun, she would be taking with her more of me than I wanted to give.

The sound tech running the board at the venue called us onto the stage, and as soon as we walked out, the crowd erupted. I lifted a hand and saw Von give a little salute. Here, we were kings and what happened elsewhere didn't matter, couldn't matter. I loved to play live. Loved to give the crowd

a show that made them move and sing. It was my way of
getting all the poison that filtered around in my blood out,
so that it didn't kill me. The house lights went down and the
red spotlight hit me squarely in the face. I looked around
the crowd, refusing to admit I always searched for a certain
dark head in the masses. I forced a wicked grin and shoved
my hands through my hair, and heard a few ladies offer up
loud whistles.

"It's Valentine's Day, motherfuckers!!!" Everyone
screamed and Von struck a long chord on the guitar. I
grabbed the mic with both hands and squinted into the
light. "Unfortunately, for all you lovebirds out there, you
came to see a rock show. We don't sing songs about love."
There were more cheers and someone screamed "I love you,
Jet!" at the top of her lungs. I laughed and felt the intensity
ratchet up and up. I cocked a hip to the side and gave my
best sneer, feeling all the things that had just happened with
Ayden blazing under my skin.

"We don't normally do cover songs, but tonight, oh
tonight, I think we'll introduce a little metal to one of my
ol' faves."

I felt the anticipation blow across my skin, saw Von and
Catcher share a slightly worried look, but before they could
stop me, I strummed the opening bars to Crosby, Stills,
Nash and Young's "Love the One You're With." I loved old
rock and roll, when songs were written for a reason, and
this one seemed to be a perfect fit for my night. I took the
bluesy notes, the folksy undertone, and bellowed it out over
suddenly screaming guitar riffs. Stephen Stills would be

appalled, as I sang with every bit of dissonance I was feeling.

I was singing it directly to her, even if she didn't know it. The crowd ate it up. The older group was singing along, and the younger kids were embracing it as an anti–love song. By the time I was done, the entire place was electric and the guys in the band were done worrying about me going eruptive and messing everything up.

We blazed through the rest of the planned set and I knew it was a good show. When I threw my guitar pick in the audience after our last song, I saw three girls wrestle each other to the ground to try to collect it, and that was a sure sign of success. We went backstage and I was instantly bummed that I had trashed a perfectly good bottle of whiskey in my rage earlier. I had to settle for doing a shot of tequila with Von and Catcher, while Boone stayed steady and chugged a Red Bull.

Von clapped me hard on the shoulder and looked me straight in the eye. "Want to tell us what the oldies were all about?"

I couldn't meet his gaze so I picked up my guitar case and shrugged. "You know that I like to mix it up every now and then."

"True, but why do I get the feeling that was directed at someone specifically? It's not like you to throw a dedication out there like that."

He wasn't wrong. I never dedicated a song to anyone, ever, but tonight I was feeling turned inside out and I couldn't get a handle on it so I shrugged.

"There's a first time for everything."

Normally, we had a huge after-party when we played a weekend show, but with Rule and Shaw being all coupled up and Nash and Rowdy surely hooked into whatever girls it was for them tonight, I knew no one was going to be lingering around. The idea of trying to pick up some girl, or more than likely letting some girl pick me up after what had happened with Ayden, made me kind of queasy. I didn't really want to go to the house, but after killing as much time as I could backstage, I finally had to go. There was no one left to hang out with or tell us how wonderful we had been, so I left and made my way across town to Wash Park, dreading a confrontation with my sexy roommate the entire way.

It was dark when I walked in the front door, but there was a light coming from under Cora's door. I tried to be quiet as I made my way down the hall to my room, but my combat boots sounded like a herd of buffalo on the old wooden floors. Ayden didn't stick her head out of her room, which I was both grateful for and seriously annoyed at. After stripping down and showering off all the sex and sweat that clung to me, I went to my room and sat on my bed, rubbing a towel over my head and staring at my closed bedroom door until I couldn't take it anymore. I pulled on a pair of black sweats and walked barefoot across the hall to tap on her closed door.

"Ayd? We need to talk." I waited for a second and frowned when I got no response. Granted we had crossed a major line tonight, but we lived together and were just going to have to figure it out so things weren't weird or weirder than they already were.

"Ayden, come on. Don't be like this, open the door so we can talk." I pounded the door with the side my fist and was seriously contemplating taking the damn thing off the hinges to get at her if I had to, when I heard Cora's door open and saw her blond head poke out. She was glaring at me, but the effect was kind of lost, considering she had on hot-pink fuzzy pajamas.

"She isn't here." She sounded surly and I didn't like the nasty gleam in her eyes.

"Where is she?" The idea that she might have gone home with that jackass and his idiotic sweater vest made my blood start to explode in my head. I felt my hands curl into fists at my sides and had to concentrate to keep from putting a fist all the way through the door. Cora crossed her arms over her chest and lifted a pale eyebrow at me.

"Do you care?"

I gritted my teeth and counted to ten to avoid shaking her tiny frame like a rag doll. "Of course I care. I wouldn't have asked if I didn't care."

"Well, that's interesting, because she came back from talking to you looking a little . . . manhandled . . . and a whole lot pissed off. Shaw offered to take her home, but she said she wanted to stay and watch the show, that is, until you started with that song. What in the hell were you thinking, Jet? Ayden isn't a moron. She isn't one of your groupies who think you're just perfect because you have a pretty voice and a nice ass. She knew exactly what you were trying to say and it made her flip out."

I felt my heart lurch in my chest and my throat go tight.

I closed my eyes and let my head fall back so that it banged against the bedroom door. "Where did she go?"

"That guy she's been seeing offered to take her to his place." I bit out a swear word so loud I saw her start. "Chill out. She told him no and said she would figure it out, but lucky you, Rowdy is an awesome friend and he swooped in to play knight in shining armor. She went home with him, and hopefully you'll take this time to get your head removed from your ass, because if you don't, I'm going to take that ring I put through the tip of your junk and do things to it that will make you cry every time you even think about having sex. I don't know what's going on with either one of you, but knock it off."

She turned in a huff of spiky blond hair and fluffy pink, slamming the door behind her with enough force to make me grimace. I was just pissing off every important lady in my life lately and it was wearing me out. I shuffled back into my room and went to dig my phone out of my pants, which were in a pile on the floor. I tapped on Rowdy's name and waited for three rings until he picked up.

"What's going on?"

He was silent for a minute and when he spoke, I was surprised to hear the censure in his tone. "I don't know. Why don't you tell me?"

I sank down to sit on the edge of the bed and rubbed my forehead. "I fucked up."

He snorted. "Big-time. I've got the girl you've been pining for sleeping on my couch because you're pissed off at your old man and acting like an idiot. You need to figure your crap out before you blow whatever shot you might've had with her. She had one foot out the door with that guy who dresses like a high school teacher, and I don't think he even cared that she came back looking like someone had put it to her, twice."

I swore softly under my breath and let his words ring in my head. I flopped back on the bed and stared at the dark ceiling.

"I don't have any idea what I'm doing with her."

"Messing shit up."

"Besides that."

"No one is perfect, Jet. We all have things that have happened, that are going to happen that make us who we are, and maybe you need to look past all the superficial stuff you see when you look at this girl and see what's underneath." I was starting to think that she had been right, that I didn't know half of what I thought I did, but he went on.

"Yes, your dad turned your mom into a shadow of who she once was, and that sucks, but get over it. That doesn't mean you can't be in a relationship or that history has to repeat itself."

"Dude, I don't even think it's like that between us. It's just a lot of mutual attraction that finally reached a boiling point. My future and her future don't really click."

He muttered something I didn't hear and then called me another name that made me grin, despite how awful I was feeling. "I seriously doubt she was thinking about your futures clicking when she was busy letting you sex her up in a backstage bathroom. She told me she has to work tomorrow at ten, so get your ass over here to pick her up and make this right. I thought you would have managed to figure it out on your own by now, but after that stunt tonight, I'm starting to wonder why we're even friends."

I snickered a little laugh and rubbed a knuckle between my eyes. "Because we're idiots and no one else really wants to hang out with either of us."

"Good point. Jet . . ." I could hear the seriousness of his tone so I shut up. "I'm not letting you screw this girl over. I like her, she's smart and sassy, plus she's Shaw's girl and I don't want to deal with Rule if you make an even bigger mess of this. Get your head on right, or just let it go, but knock off the middle-of-the-road bullshit because honestly, dude, it's pissing off more than just me."

I didn't have anything to say to that, so I told him "later" and tossed the phone on the stand next to my bed. I lay across the mattress sideways and crossed my hands on my chest and continued to watch the shadows on the ceiling.

Rowdy had a very valid point: I wasn't my dad. I hated everything about the man, so I tried day in and day out to purposely make decisions that would lead me in the opposite direction from the road he walked. Part of that meant I didn't allow room in my life for any one girl to get close. I dated, I slept around, and I crashed with girls who were easy to leave, easy to walk away from. I tried to pick ones who knew the rules so that when I left on tour or moved on, it was no big deal. I was twenty-five, successful, had an awesome group of friends, and more opportunities at my fingertips than I could count, and yet I had all of that alone.

There was no one to share it with, no one to enjoy it all with, because I was always deathly afraid of what would happen if I let someone matter that much.

That night with Ayden, all those months ago, I think I knew.

I think even then, when we were still basically strangers, I knew that if I had gone into that apartment with her I wouldn't have been able to just walk away, to just shake her loose and let her not matter. I think even then I recognized how important she could be to me and was absolute terrified by it. I could suddenly see myself starting to worry about my nonexistent financial portfolio or what tax bracket I was going to fall into, and that just wasn't cool with me. She set me off balance and I didn't like it at all.

I didn't know if hooking up with Ayden for anything long-term was even something worth contemplating, but I did know that the idea of morphing into a stockbroker to make her happy wasn't an option, not when I knew I was never going to sacrifice music and what I loved for any girl. I just didn't know what to do with any of that from here, because after that kiss things clearly had to change.

CHAPTER 5

Ayden

I HARDLY SLEPT AT all, even though Rowdy went out of his way to be a good host. He bundled me up in a pair of track pants that were way too long and way too big, and gave me a T-shirt with a logo on it from the tattoo shop where he worked. He gave me a soft blanket and a pillow for the couch, and even more helpfully, he gave me a shot of Jäger from the freezer and let me bitch about how pissed off at Jet I was for more than an hour without trying to defend him or justify his actions.

He was like a gigantic, blond teddy bear, only covered in ink and rocking badass chops and sporting a wicked tattoo of an anchor on the side of his neck. He did a whole lot of nodding and grunting in response, but never interjected or told me to calm down. The sun was coming up by the time my eyes were finally too heavy to keep open, and even as I drifted off to sleep, all I could see was Jet sneering and telling the crowd that he didn't play any kind of love song.

I woke up *done*. Done feeling caught between the past and the present. Done trying to think twenty steps ahead, because no matter what I did, good or bad, I ended up getting hurt and feeling awful. I was hurting good people and acting impulsively, and all I had to show for it was some seriously twisted feelings for a guy who I couldn't even get to see the real me.

The resolve was great, and I felt ten feet tall until the front door to the apartment opened while I was folding up the blanket and putting away my makeshift bed. I turned to see the current cause of all my strife come waltzing in with a couple of coffees, as if he hadn't turned my everything upside down last night with a simple touch and a kiss to end all kisses. Those dark eyes were even more shadowed than normal, and his mouth was pulled tight, like he had to stop himself from saying something that would set everything off once again. It pissed me off even more when I remembered that he looked really, really good with a little overnight scruff on his face in the morning.

I glared at him and crossed my arms over my chest. "What are you doing here?"

He offered me one of the coffees, but I shook my head and moved to put the couch between us. I didn't know if he had gone home alone last night, didn't know if he had gone home at all, and that was one of the major reasons I had taken Rowdy up on his offer to crash on his couch. If Jet had been alone, I would have been tempted to smother him in his sleep. If he had come home with another girl, not only would I have had to move out the next morning, but I also would have had to hire a lawyer because a double homicide would have been certain.

"Cora told me you were here, and I was hoping we could talk before I took you home to get ready for work."

He sounded kind of lost, like he wasn't really sure what he was doing here himself. I couldn't forget that he thought I was just some innocent little flower who shouldn't be touched by dirty hands. I was so sick of him thinking he knew anything about me or how I really felt about him.

"I heard everything you had to say loud and clear last night, Jet. No need to repeat it—in fact, please don't. I've had enough of you telling me how things are between us to last a lifetime."

He sighed and I felt how deep down it came from. He set both the coffees on the table in front of the couch and shoved his hands into his jeans. I wondered how he had room.

"That was a shitty thing I did last night. I'm sorry."

I bristled automatically, because even though I was madder than hell at him, I didn't want him to be sorry for touching me and for making me feel more than I had felt in years. I wanted him to be as affected by it as I was, and to not be able to stop himself from doing it again.

"I thought you weren't going to apologize for it, that you were just going to make sure it didn't happen again." There was bitterness there I couldn't disguise.

His velvety eyes flared suddenly and the golden rims blazed with a passion that burned across the distance separating us. "I'm not apologizing for that, Ayd. God, I was up all night thinking about it, thinking about you. I'm sorry about the song, sorry for making you feel bad, sorry for being an asshole. You keep telling me I don't know you, and that I don't have a clue, but the truth is, we don't know each other, and I don't know that either of us is really ready to handle the other. What I do know is I want you more than I want to keep breathing."

He sounded so sincere, and looked so earnest, that I felt something start to break loose in the center of my chest. And then it cracked wide open when he continued in a gruff voice. "My dad is a nutcase and an emotional wrecking ball. He knocked my mom up when she was just a kid and has spent all of his time since then beating her down emotionally. He has made her into this version of herself who has no will, no desire, and no drive to do anything but please him. He cheats on her, and he takes off for months on end and doesn't call or say when he's coming back. He's never had a steady job, and to this day she works herself to death to support both of them, while telling me over and over again it's not as bad as it really is."

I saw his dark eyebrows pull low over his eyes and his hands turn into fists.

"I know I don't ever want anything like that—I don't ever want to be like that. I also know that no one in a long time has gotten to me the way you do. Girls come and go. I like to think we always have a good time, but none of them has ever stayed with me the way you do. Maybe you aren't this paragon of virtue I try to make you into. In fact, after getting my hands on you and in you, I'm pretty sure you're not even close. Why don't you give me a shot to get to know the other side of you?"

"What exactly are you saying, Jet? You want to be friends with benefits? You want to wander across the hall and hook up occasionally? You need to clarify what we're talking about because last night I could have happily strangled you." My voice cracked a little, betraying just how badly the sting of his words and his dismissal of it all had hurt.

He moved a few steps closer to me and I struggled not to suck in a nervous breath. Given the chance, I was afraid all the things I kept locked down where this guy was concerned would break free and the decision as to what we would be to each other would simply be taken out of my hands. He always seemed so much bigger and more powerful than all the other things I was constantly battling with.

One side of his mouth kicked up in a grin and I felt the effect of it in the pit of my stomach. He didn't have to flirt or try to be charming, not with a grin wicked enough to promise so much more than a fantastic time.

"I wanna have sex, Ayd. Lots and lots of sex . . . with you and only you. Does it have to be more than that right now? After last night how can you deny that you want it, too?"

I shook my head a little and let out a slow exhale. I was going to ask him what had changed, since all the complications he seemed stuck on when we first met still existed, but he went on and rendered me silent.

"I'm not saying it couldn't eventually lead to more, but right now I feel pretty broken and I'm not really sure there are enough pieces lying around to put me back together."

That was heartbreaking and I couldn't fault him for his honesty; in fact I think I appreciated that more than the back-and-forth tug and pull that had been eating at me over the last year. We just stared at each other in silence until my phone rang from somewhere over by where he was standing. He picked it up and threw it at me without looking at the display. I frowned when I saw it was the same Kentucky number that had been calling me the other day. I swiped the screen to answer it and was greeted with dead air. I called "hello" into the phone several times and got no response. I tossed the phone on the couch; that particular problem could wait for now, and turned back to Jet.

"Let me be absolutely clear, Jet. We live right across the hall from each other, we have all our friends in common, and we have very different views on the fundamentals of what is important to our futures. None of those things has changed since the first time you told me we couldn't start anything up, so how exactly does this play out for you?"

I knew what I wanted: him. I felt like I had wanted him forever. I wasn't going to be all crazy and say that I was in love with him, that I couldn't live without him, but he did something to me, got to me in a way no one else ever had. He might think he was broken, but I knew the truth—that he was funny, sweet, and undeniably talented and there were more than enough pieces of him at my disposal if I wanted to try to put him back together. He had so much to offer even if they weren't the things I had spent years telling myself I wanted, and I wondered if I could share all my secrets with him and finally be done lugging them around all by myself.

He rocked back on the heels of his boots, and the spikes in his ears made him look extra devilish. A half grin twisted his mouth and it was easy to see why girls all across town were so in lust with him. "It plays out day by day and moment by moment. I get the feeling that anything more than that would send you sprinting in the opposite direction."

I felt my eyes widen in surprise and my mouth fall open. I guess there was something to be said for in-your-face forthrightness, but I hadn't been expecting that. I didn't realize he knew me well enough to know that's more than likely exactly what I would have done. I didn't get a chance to respond because apparently he was done talking. He moved toward me and scooped me up in hard arms.

This time when he kissed me there was none of the anger, none of the desperation and hurt that had filled the space between us last night. This was a kiss that was filled with promise, filled with all the things that had been hot and heavy between us for so long. I forgot I was standing in Rowdy's apartment, and that I was furious at him moments ago. I forgot everything except how he felt and how he made me feel, and I lost myself in the glide of his tongue across mine and in the grip of his fingers on my hips. I had waited forever for this boy, and had wanted him, coveted him for so long it felt like the longing was a living, breathing thing inside me.

Jet just reached right into the heart of where all that desire lived, where all that lust had percolated and boiled, and he pulled it to the surface with nothing more than a soft brush of fingertips and an artfully twisted tongue. He kissed me like we had all the time in the world to do it over and

over again. He kissed me like he was trying to memorize
every action, every sound, and every taste, so that he could
write songs about it. He kissed me like I was the only girl he
was ever going to kiss again, and it made my head spin and
my breathing choppy. I wanted to suck on that bar in the
center of his tongue like it was a lollipop.

I had my hands wrapped up in that choppy black hair
and was working my way up to climbing him like a tree,
even though we were out in the open in his best friend's living room, when we heard a throat being cleared and saw
Rowdy come meandering out of the kitchen. He was holding a banana and watching us with humor dancing in his
bright blue eyes.

"I wasn't going to interrupt but I like my couch and don't
need Jet getting it all sexed up. Besides, I doubt either one of
you is paying attention to the time. Ayd's gotta get going if
she's going to make it to work."

I swore and dashed to where I had tossed my phone earlier. He was right; I barely had time to get back to the house
and grab my uniform. I looked at Jet with wide eyes. "I need
to go."

He nodded, looked at Rowdy and pointed to the abandoned coffee on the table. "Even though you're a cock-
blocker, you can have that."

Rowdy chuckled and lifted an eyebrow. "I saved your
sorry ass and you know it."

I didn't know what they were talking about and I didn't
have the time to get into it, so I gave Rowdy a quick kiss
good-bye with a mumbled "thank you," grabbed Jet by

the elbow, and towed him out of the apartment. We were both pretty quiet in the car on the way back to the house. I wanted to ask if he had gone home alone last night, but figured if he hadn't, there was no way Cora would have told him where I was. I barely let him pull into the driveway before dashing inside to scoop up all my stuff. He hovered uneasily at my bedroom doorway, watching me run around like a madwoman. I looked at him over my shoulder as I shoved my uniform in my bag and frantically ran a brush through my hair.

"What's wrong?"

He shrugged a shoulder and propped himself up in the doorway. "I just don't know what we do now."

I wasn't entirely certain how to answer that, either, so I stopped in front of him and kissed him long and hard on a surprised mouth. "Me, either, but we have time to figure it out later. How about right at this minute we just work on the lots and lots of sex part, and go from there? I think we both agree that that part is going to be a no-brainer for us, and like you said, moment to moment works just fine for me."

When I brushed past him, I didn't miss the anticipation gleaming in his midnight gaze. He didn't say anything else, which I was grateful for because I was feeling like I had jumped off a very high cliff without any knowledge of what was waiting for me below, and that was terrifying. There were no guarantees that he was going to stick around once he had the entire picture laid out in front of him, but I wanted to give him the benefit of the doubt. In reality, I wanted to give him a whole lot more than that, which was enough to make me break out in nervous hives. I held on tenuously to my control, to the protection it offered my life here, and I had a sinking feeling he could make me give it all up.

When I got to work, a familiar truck was parked at the curb and I could see one very blond head and one darker one with hot pink spikes, turned toward each other. The windows were up, so I couldn't hear what they were saying, but Shaw looked mad and Rule was frowning, hard. When she caught sight of me walking by, she waved and started to scoot across the seat to the passenger door. I laughed to myself when Rule promptly pulled her back and planted a steamy kiss on her open mouth before letting her go. She was flushed and breathing hard when she walked around the front of the vehicle to stand by me. I gave her a look and she rolled her eyes at me. The driver's window rolled down and Rule stuck his head out. No boy should be that good-looking, especially when half his face had holes and jewelry in it, but there was just something about him that commanded attention and refused to be ignored.

I had to grin at him when he asked, "Do you need me to go stomp on Jet's head for you? That was a total dick move he pulled last night and I will gladly do it."

I shook my head and let Shaw lace her arm through mine. "Naw, we kind of made up."

He lifted the eyebrow with the rings in it and gave me a lascivious grin. "Does that mean you finally got naked together?"

Shaw gasped and snapped, "Rule!" but I just laughed

until tears came out of the corners of my eyes. "No, not yet, but I'm working on it."

He smacked the side of the truck with the flat of his hand. "Atta girl." He pointed a finger at Shaw. "You think about what I said this morning, Casper."

Shaw made a face next to me, but hollered, "I love you, jackass!" at him when he started to roll up the window. He blew her a kiss, which made her flip him off, and started to tug me toward the bar. I tried to get her to slow her frantic pace but she was clearly worked up and in no mood to be soothed.

"What's going on with you two?"

She cut me a sideways glance and pulled open the heavy back door. "Shouldn't I be asking you that? You tore out of there like the place was on fire last night, and I never heard a word. I know you had to have been pissed at Jet, so what happened?"

I threw my bag on the bench and started digging around. "You go first. You talk and I'll get dressed, and I'll tell you what happened with us after." I was feeling like I needed a little oomph today after yesterday's debacle, so I went with the football uniform. I liked the white-hot pants with the blue piping and laces, and in all actuality they covered more than either the referee uniform or the cheerleader uniform did. Plus, I could wear tennis shoes with it and still look hot enough to get good tips. I heard Shaw sigh and watched as she twisted her long, two-toned hair into a braid.

"Rome is coming home in a few months. Like home, home. He'll be out of the army for good." Rome was Rule's older brother and they were super close, but due to a recent, startling family secret being brought to light, he was furious with his parents. I guess he was not even getting along all that well with Rule at the moment, but he supposedly had forgiven Shaw for her part in keeping the secret for years and years.

I slimed some junk in my hands and ran it through my hair to get it to lie flat, and then tugged the front up into a little poof. I shoved a blue-and-orange silk flower behind my ear and worked on doing some basic maintenance to my face.

"Well, that's good, right?"

She groaned and let her head fall against the closed locker she was leaning against. "Rule has it in his head that when Rome gets back, he won't go to his parents' home at all, and is going to need a place to stay. He wants to buy a house for us and let Rome take over the lease on the apartment with Nash."

I stopped smacking my lips and doing my lipstick to look at her incredulously. "Why aren't you excited? That sounds amazing. Most girls get flowers and chocolates for Valentine's Day, and you get your dream guy offering to buy you a house."

She turned to look at me and I saw her chew on her bottom lip like she did when she was nervous or worried about something. "I don't know. I guess because I always thought I would do things in order, you know? Fall in love, get married, buy a house, have kids. All of that stuff goes hand in hand and I'm not even close to being done with school yet.

It just seems like a huge step and if he changes his mind or whatever, then what do I do?"

"Shaw, that guy loves you like you're his reason for being. He isn't going to change his mind, and unless you think this isn't a forever thing, then what should the order it happens in matter?"

She sighed again and played with the ends of her braid. "I know for me it's a forever thing, and I believe that he feels the same way, but Rule gets dangerous when he feels trapped. It scares me what he might do when he has to pay a mortgage and come home to the same person every night."

I poked her in the shoulder. "He comes home to you every night now. Stop making it into something it isn't. You guys love each other and it doesn't matter if it's in an apartment or a mansion or a freaking tent in the wilderness. You're still going to love each other, and Rule will be fine. Besides, did you ever stop to think maybe he wants to do something to make Rome's life easier? Rome has always protected both of you. Maybe this is Rule's way of trying to return the favor."

I saw something in her green eyes flare and a little bit of the tension in her face release. "Thanks, Ayd, I needed to hear that."

I shrugged and situated my phone in my bra. "No problem."

"Sooooo, what about you and Jet? I saw how you looked when you came back to the table. I thought we were either going to have to make up an alibi for you and help you move the body or hose you down."

"Rowdy took me home and let me rage at him for an hour. I was pissed, but then Jet showed up this morning and we talked. We're good now."

"What does 'good' mean?"

"I'm not really sure. I guess we agreed that for now we're attracted to each other on a pretty serious level and we should see where that goes."

She lifted a pale eyebrow as we went to find Lou and get our stations for the day. "So you agreed to have sex?"

I rolled my eyes at her. "We agreed to see how things play out while remaining friends. Jet isn't the kind of guy you marry and have kids with. He's the guy who makes you forget your name and rocks your world. We like each other and it's getting old trying to pretend something isn't there, but we have very different ideas about some things, so it's unlikely that it'll ever be more than some intense chemistry and hopefully really good times for as long as it lasts." I was proud at how calmly I said this, because my heart was hammering under Shaw's intense scrutiny.

At first she was silent, and I wanted to say more, but Lou wrapped us up in a giant bear hug. The front doors were opened and we had to hit the ground running. She looked at me over her shoulder and tossed out, "Be careful, Ayd," which I chose not to read too much into.

I knew Shaw was the kind of girl who believed in a great love. She had fought long and hard to get Rule. She had battled her family and his family, and her biggest hurdle had been Rule himself. I don't think I would have ever put that much effort into it. The only thing I focused on, the only thing I ever labored over and sweated about, was building myself a life that couldn't topple over, and establishing a future that was rock solid and indestructible. I wanted old Ayden buried so far under new Ayden there could be no way for her to claw her way back to the surface.

Security would always win in any game where love or any other emotion was a consideration, and that was just the way it had to be. I was willing to see what Jet and I could do with all the heat that burned between us, as long as the fire was controlled. As soon as it got out of hand, burned too hot, I would have to put it out and walk away, no matter how bad it might hurt me or him.

CHAPTER 6

Jet

I WAS AT LOOSE ends, with time on my hands and restless because I still didn't know exactly what I was going to do with this thing happening between me and Ayden.

She was at work, Cora was in a mood, and the guys were all scattered across town doing this or that. I found myself heading to Federal Heights, and to a familiar brick house that I normally avoided like the plague. I called first to make sure the old man was nowhere around and parked on the crowded street. I made enough money that I could move my mom somewhere nice, somewhere closer to downtown, somewhere safer and more upscale, but I wouldn't do it until she left that asshole. She just refused to see the light. I jogged up the cracked cement steps and rang the doorbell, gritting my teeth when, instead of dinging, it gave off a little shock. If he couldn't be bothered to fix something as simple as the doorbell, it made my head go crazy with all the other stuff he was bound to have neglected.

I pounded on the door with the edge of my fist and

scowled at my mom when she pulled open the door. She was a slight woman, several inches smaller than me. Even under the premature lines on her face and beneath the crown of dull brown hair, it was easy to see that at one time she had been a beautiful woman. Now she just looked tired and worn. The smile she gave me was fragile and so fleeting I might have imagined it had she not embraced me with birdlike arms in a hug that felt like it was equal parts desperation and sorrow.

"Hey, Ma, it's been a while." I patted her awkwardly on the back and felt a shudder go through her. Everything about her made me want to take my dad out and use him for target practice. He had done this to her, stolen her vibrancy, made her into this walking shadow of a woman. The hatred I had for him was coiled inside me so tightly I knew it was going to be dangerous for everyone when it finally snapped. The flames of my anger were already starting to lick and curl up my spine.

"I thought you were on tour still."

She ushered me into the drab house, and I tried not to shake my head at the scattered beer cans and ashtrays filled with cigarette butts littering every available surface. Not much had changed since I had left when I was just a kid, only now it looked worse. It was clear my dad was escalating on the worthless-piece-of-shit scale. I followed her into the kitchen and sat at the old dinner table. The wood groaned in protest as I stretched out my legs and took the beer she offered me from the fridge. I popped the top and took a long slug.

"I've been back awhile. Dad didn't tell you?"

She shook her head, and I saw something that went beyond sadness shadow her searching gaze. "Why didn't you call me yourself? I could have made dinner or something."

I never told her when I was coming or going, because inevitably she would want to spend some kind of family time together, and that never went well. I barely tolerated my dad on a good day, and watching him demean her and order her around in the house she paid for was just too much.

"I've been busy working with some new bands, and I met a girl." It was fudging the truth a little, considering I had known Ayden for more than a year, but after this morning I felt like I was finally getting let in, being introduced to the real her. I saw my mom's eyes brighten at the mention of a girl and she reached out to pat my hand. I could see the blue veins running so close to the surface of her skin and again I wondered how she had allowed herself to become this delicate creature that a stiff wind could blow away forever.

"That's wonderful! You need a nice girl to settle down with. You are too special and have too much to offer to be spreading it around all over town, like I know you and your friends like to do."

I lifted an eyebrow and rolled the Pabst Blue Ribbon can between my palms. "How do you know what me and the guys like to do, Ma?"

"I was young once, Jet. I know the allure of a handsome young man in a band. All you boys were a handful when you were younger, and I can only imagine the kind of trouble you find yourselves in now that you are all grown and independent. Tell me about this girl. She must be something, if you couldn't remember to mention to me that you've been back in town for a while."

I could hear the accusation in her tone. She knew why I didn't come around much, didn't stay in touch. Yet she couldn't stop herself from trying to hold me close. I took another swig of the beer and looked at her with a lopsided grin.

"She's different—smart, ambitious, and driven. She's different from what I'm used to. I like her, a lot actually."

I saw my mom's eyes get big, and for the first time in a long time, there was an emotion in them other than abject despair.

"Well, that's good. You need someone who is as ambitious and as talented as you are."

I wasn't sure what *it* was going to end up being so I just stayed silent and finished the beer and got up to toss it in the trash. I crossed my arms over my chest and gave her a level, serious look as I decided to change the subject from my sex life.

"Ma, did you know the old man hit me up to send him back out on the road with some of my friends in a band?"

Instantly, the light that had filtered in her hazy gaze at my earlier good news died. It was replaced with the flat look of loneliness and the acknowledgment that she only existed to him as a doormat and place filler, while he went out and lived his life without her. She twisted her hands together and looked down at the table.

"You father is an old man now. Why would he want to go back out on the road with a bunch of young kids? What purpose would that serve?"

I raked my hands through my hair, and bit my tongue to keep from snapping at her that there was no purpose other than his indulgent, self-centered way of living. But that kind of attack never got me anywhere. I blew out a breath through my nose and clicked my tongue ring against the back of my front teeth.

"Mom, when has he ever done anything that served a purpose? He straight up told me that if I didn't make it happen, he was going to come home and take it out on you. How can you just sit back and let him do that to you? How can you let him manipulate either of us like that?"

My rings rapped out a fast beat on the counter while I waited for her to answer me. For years, I had waited for her to see that I could take care of her and that she didn't need to subject herself to his whims and his thoughtless behavior. I couldn't stand that she just told me over and over that she loved him and that she wouldn't let her family fall apart, even though I hadn't willingly been in the same room with my father since I was a teenager.

She wouldn't look at me and her voice was barely a whisper when she replied, "You just don't understand how it is with us, Jet. You never did."

I pushed off the counter and walked to where she was actually folding in on herself in front of me. I put a hand on her shoulder and squatted down so that she had no choice but to meet my searching gaze. "Ma, don't you think the problem is that I understand it too well? You know you can do better than him, better than this. You always could."

I saw her bottom lip tremble and that pulled at something under all the anger that lived in my chest. I hated that every time I tried to pull her out of this nightmare, I ended up hurting her. She should be thanking me, running as fast as she could away from this place, and yet she stayed rooted so firmly that no matter how hard I dug, I couldn't get her out. The roots were planted too deep.

"If you can make him happy by sending him back out on the road, maybe you should. It's not like he really asks that much from you."

I abruptly stood from where I was kneeling beside her and felt a white hot blaze shoot down my neck. I wanted to shake her. I wanted to shove my fist through the closest wall. I wanted to storm out of that shabby kitchen in this awful house on the wrong side of the interstate and never look back. What I did instead was close my eyes, bend, and kiss her on the top of her head.

"We'll see, Ma. I have to work with these guys. I don't know that I want to ask them for that big of a favor. It was good to see you. Take care of yourself."

I was going to go before I did something stupid, like scream at her, but she grabbed my forearm, her fingers digging into the melting clocks all over my skin. Her eyes were so sad when she looked up at me, that I literally felt a part of my heart die. "Bring your girl by. I would love to meet her."

This was the last place on earth I wanted to bring Ayden, but I forced out something that had to resemble a grin. "Sure, Ma, maybe someday I can swing that."

Ayden was the opposite of this woman I loved, in so many ways it almost hurt to think about it. She was so strong and so independent that she would never let another person dictate the direction her life or actions would take, or devalue her worth. I hated the idea that Ayden would see my broken-down mother and wonder why I hadn't done more to help her or been able to stop this from happening to her in the first place. Those very questions picked me apart from the inside out every day. Looking at my mother now, I remembered every time she had chosen this life and that asshole over me, and it burned away some of the safeguards I had put into place to protect my heart from the inferno of the rage that lived inside me.

My phone picked that minute to ring, and Memphis May Fire came blasting out of my pocket. I told my mom I had to go and wasted no time in running down the front steps. I felt like I was not only running away from her, but also from every bad thing that had ever happened in that house. Nash's tattooed head was staring back at me from the face of my phone, so when I poked at it to answer the call I didn't bother to fake a cheery greeting.

" 'Sup, dude?"

"Where are you?"

I slid into the car and rested my head on the back of the driver's seat. "I went to visit my mom. The old man has been on my case about setting him up with Artifice and I thought maybe for once I could just shut it down, but no. As usual, I just don't understand, and she's just going to let him run around on her and run her over. It fucking sucks."

Nash knew my history with my folks better than the other guys. When I left as a teenager, he had been having his own issues at home with his mom and her richer-than-God new husband. Luckily, for both of us, Nash's uncle Phil had been bound and determined to keep us out of jail and in school. He scooped us both up and, with a mixture of tough love and simple badassness, made us act right. No one went against Uncle Phil, and to this day he was our go-to grown-up when we couldn't get our act together on our own.

"One of these days you're just going to have to give up the ghost, Jet. It doesn't make any sense to keep trying to pull her away from him if she's dug in that deep."

"I know, but she's my mom and I can't seem to stop."

He muttered a swear word and I heard him talking to someone else. "We're all going bowling. You should meet us at Lucky Strike on Sixteenth."

"Why bowling?"

"Because football is over and Rule is pacing the apartment like a caged tiger. It's driving me nuts. Rowdy will be there in twenty, plus they have beer. What else are we going to do on a Sunday?"

I really wasn't in the mood, but hanging out by myself was sure to be a recipe for disaster in my current mood. "Did you call Cora and see if she wants to go? She's been acting a little off the last couple days."

"No answer. I left her a couple messages though."

I frowned because she had been home when I left, moping around the kitchen about something. The shop was closed on Sundays, so I knew she didn't have to work, and it wasn't like her to blow off a call from any of the guys.

"Let me swing by the house and see what's going on with her, and then I'll hit you back."

"Sure thing. By the way, that was a real shit thing to pull last night at the show. Ayden is a down chick; you're lucky she didn't hang you up by your balls afterward."

"I know. I apologized. We're working on trying to figure something out."

"Good, because if Rule doesn't break you in half for messing with her, I will."

I didn't need him to warn me twice. She wasn't a groupie, a stranger who no one cared if I blew off and forgot about from one heartbeat to the next. She was a girl that was woven into the fabric of our lives, into the pattern of our unit, and if I hurt her on purpose they wouldn't let it go lightly. The ironic thing was that she was more than capable of taking care of herself and that the threats from the guys were completely unnecessary.

I shoved the phone in the console and cranked Morbid Angel on the radio as I ran back across town to check on Cora. The screaming lyrics and insane bass made some of the anger still floating around under the surface burn out. I could hate my dad all I wanted, I could beg my mom to leave until I was blue in the face, but things were never going to change and it just couldn't be my cross to bear forever. I had built my life trying to live beyond the legacy my dad had left me. Now I was starting to see it was well past time to start living it based on the legacy I was making for myself.

I parked on the street with every intention of just running in real quickly to see what the little blond fireball was up to. As I was climbing out of the car, the front door to the house slammed open and a guy I didn't recognize came flying down the front steps, with Cora hot on his heels. I felt my jaw drop open when I noticed she was waving a Taser around and screaming obscenities at the top of her lungs. I went to move, to run after the guy, but before either of us could get to him, he threw a leg over a motorcycle that was parked at the curb and took off like a bat out of hell. I tried to look at the license plate, but Cora threw her tiny frame at my chest so hard that I fell back a step and almost toppled over.

"What the hell?"

She was shaking a little and I took the Taser out of her hand just in case she accidentally stunned me.

"I don't know. Someone knocked on the door and I just thought it was a neighbor or a solicitor. I mean, come on, this is Denver, not Brooklyn; that crap isn't supposed to happen here. As soon as the door was open, he shoved me back and started coming into the house. I ran to the kitchen, because I still have all the stuff I bought for protection when Shaw lived here and was worried about her ex. He came after me and kept asking where it was."

I shook my head in confusion because she was talking a mile a minute. "Where what was?"

"I don't know. Just *it*. He freaked when he saw the Taser and I think he heard your car pull up. He took off."

"We should call the cops." I patted her back because I could feel her quivering. Cora was a tough chick, and not very much rattled her, but having a stranger force his way into her home had to have been terrifying. She puffed out a little breath against my chest where she was tucked and she thunked a fist on my ribs.

"No."

"What? Why the hell not?"

"Because they can't do anything. He didn't take anything and never got a chance to put his hands on me. They'll come poke around and tell us tough shit. I'm an idiot for opening the door anyway. I know better than that."

I set her away from me with a sharp frown. "You could have been seriously hurt."

She waved a hand in front of me. "No, I couldn't have been. He was after something, not after me. It just spooked me, is all. What are you doing here, anyway? I thought you went to play nice with Ayd."

I didn't like it one bit. Everything inside me said call the police, that one girl I cared about had already been put through the ringer by a loose cannon. I wasn't about to let it happen again. I picked her up in a full body hug that had her squealing and laughing at the same time. "You need to be careful, Cora. We wouldn't know what to do without you."

She scoffed. "You really think I'm about to let you guys roam around this city unsupervised? The female population of Denver would never survive it. We have to be sure to tell Ayd to be careful. I don't know what would have happened if she had been home and not me."

I liked that thought even less. I don't know how all the fury and fire that I barely kept banked would stay contained if something happened to Ayden. If I let it go, not only would

I go up in flames but there was a chance I would end up burning anyone close to me to dust as well.

"I don't like this, Cora. I want both of you to be safe." She hooked her arm through mine.

"It'll be fine, Jet. Seriously, he probably just had the wrong house, or was looking for money for drugs or something. No place is perfect and we can take care of ourselves. You never answered me"—her crazy eyes narrowed at me—"did you fix things with Ayden?"

I sighed and let her drag me into the house. "Sort of. I apologized for being an asshat last night and told her I couldn't fight this thing between us anymore. I don't know what that looks like to her but I can take it day by day for now."

"She was okay with that?"

"I guess, Honestly, I think that's the only way she's okay with it. She's a hard chick to pin down."

"Don't be stupid, Jet. You have a lot to offer anyone. The cool thing is Ayden isn't the type to take it all. She can provide for herself, and be happy just taking what she wants from you. It's up to you to make her see just how much you're willing to give and how much better she is off with the entire package. Make her want to be pinned down and not just in the sexy, fun way."

I just looked at her in silence. This little pixie ran us all ragged and at times I think she had our lives figured out far better than we did.

"I'll keep that in mind." She tapped me on the chin with her finger.

"Good."

"The guys all went bowling. Do you want to go? Nash was worried you weren't answering your phone, so I decided to come and check on you."

She scrunched up her nose and ran a hand over her spiky blond hair. "No. I think I've had enough excitement for one day. Plus, I had a pretty good sulk going before the breaking-and-entering portion of the day. I think I'd like to finish it."

I felt my eyebrows dip sharply down. Cora wasn't a sulky person. She was cheerful and honest to a fault. "Why are you sulking around? That isn't like you."

She sighed and flopped down heavily on the couch. "Watching Rule take such good care of Shaw is kind of hard for me. I never thought he was going to fall in love, never thought anyone would be able to get him to see past himself, but she did, and they are just so perfect together. I thought guys like him—guys like you—were hopeless. Now I'm wondering if I'm the one who is hopeless. I mean, you're amazing, Ayden is amazing. So, whatever you guys work up is bound to be amazing and I just feel like I'm missing something."

We were friends and I cared a lot about her. There were plenty of mirrors in the house, so I knew that she knew she was hot enough to make men stupid. I didn't really understand it, but all I could figure out was that she was alone because she wanted to be alone.

"Cora, come on now. You can find a guy in, like, a second flat. Half the guys in the band have you on their laminated list."

She rolled her expressive eyes at me. "I want something

real, Jet. Something that is life changing and dramatic, something that makes me forget anyone else ever existed. I just can't see that happening and it makes me sad."

"I think you're maybe reaching for something that doesn't exist."

"You see Rule and Shaw. It exists."

I couldn't really argue that point with her, but I didn't know what else to say. I believed in love. I just didn't trust it and what the end result could be if two people weren't ultimately right for each other. Every great song was sung from a place of love. I knew love was strong enough to change people. My mom held on to her love for my dad, like it was a raft in the center of the ocean of horror that was her life. It was just my experience that love never changed anyone for the better, with Rule being the exception to the norm. He always did his own thing anyway, so it wasn't like he was going to even love someone within the conventions of how it normally worked.

"Well, if some guy does come along, that's an awful lot of pressure to be putting on him."

"I know, so I'm destined to be alone and grumpy for the rest of my life. Not to mention sexually frustrated."

"Stop being ridiculous and shake this crap off. Go put on some shoes and come bowling with us. It'll be fun."

She grumbled until I eventually got tired of it, and just picked her up and hauled her to her room. She argued the entire way, but after I pointed out that I was wearing pants that were bound to make it impossible to throw a heavy ball down the lane without ripping in half, she begrudgingly put

on some Chucks and followed me out the door. I refused to
ride in her little circus car, so we hopped in the Challenger
and roared down to the sprawling blocks of the Sixteenth
Street mall where every tourist and degenerate in town hung
out. I normally avoided this part of the city. It brought back
too many memories of skipping school and sneaking booze
from Phil with Rule and Nash. However, after a spectacu-
larly nasty day, I didn't mind the noise and hustle as much.

The bowling alley was lit in blue and had velour couches
scattered all over the place. Personally, I thought it looked
more like a strip club than a bowling alley. The guys had
beer and it looked like they were having a great time giving each other shit as they rotated turns. The pink bowling
ball looked like a tiny toy in Rowdy's beefy hands, and when
he tossed it down the alley it bounced hard enough that it
went right into the gutter. Cora laughed and gave him a high
five, while Rule and Nash offered up a round of ridiculous-
looking golf claps.

There was a group of teenage girls a few lanes down
openly gawking, and I thought they were going to need the
paramedics called when Nash winked at them when he got
up to take his turn. I sat next to Cora on one of the benches
and ducked just in time to avoid getting knocked upside the
head by the flat of Rule's palm. I scowled at him, but his gla-
cial gaze made it clear he wasn't playing around.

"You ever pull a stunt like you did last night again and I
will use your intestines to string your Les Paul."

I swallowed, because from most people that was an idle
threat, but not coming from him. I nodded.

"I know, dude, I know. I tried to make it right. We're good, she doesn't hate me."

Those cold eyes regarded me seriously and he must have decided whatever he saw was sincere, because some of the tension left his body.

"Good, because if she hates you, then Shaw has to hate you, and by default that means I have to kick your ass all over town and I would hate to have to do that."

I snorted and took a pint of beer that Rowdy handed me. "You wouldn't hate that at all."

He shrugged and nodded at Cora who was having some kind of argument with Nash over exchanging her Chucks for bowling shoes.

"What's up with her?"

I felt my mouth pull down at the corners and my eyes sharpen just a fraction. Rowdy sat down on the low lounge table and all three of us bent our heads together so that they could hear me when I lowered my voice.

"Bad stuff going down at the homestead, guys. When I got there, she was chasing some guy out the door. She said he shoved his way in and was demanding to know where 'it' was. She has no clue what he was looking for, but she was pretty shaken up. He took off on some souped-up bike way too fast for me to do anything about it. After everything that went down with Shaw, I don't like it one bit."

Rowdy whistled and Rule growled like a wild animal. "Did you call the cops?"

I sat back and laced my fingers behind my head. "Cora wouldn't let me. You know her, she thinks this is the Wild

West still and things like that just don't happen here like they do in Brooklyn. She seems to think it's a onetime event and that the guy was just a meth head or something looking for money. That bike was cherry and there was no way he just picked out our house at random. We're way too far away from downtown for a junkie just looking to score some cash."

"This isn't cool." Rule sounded a little unhinged and I couldn't blame him. He had gone a little off the rails when Shaw had been attacked and we were all now just starting to settle down from it all.

"I know, but I don't want to get all worked up over something if it turns out to be nothing. I'll tell Ayden to keep an eye out and remind Cora that things here can be just as bad as the East Coast, but I'm hoping this was an isolated incident."

Rule shoved hard hands through his spiky hair and squinted eyes that were glittering like ice on a frozen lake. "It better be because I'm not going to make it through something like what happened to Shaw again."

I lifted a dark eyebrow. "I'll keep an eye on them. I do live there, you know, and I'm trying to figure shit out with Ayden."

He shook his head. "It's not that. You have no idea what it's like to have someone you care about, someone you love, facing a danger like that. It changes you, it turns you into a different person. I barely made it when Shaw got hurt. If someone hurts Ayden or Cora, there is no telling what's going to happen."

Rowdy reached out and gave him a shove with one of his hands. Rule glowered at him but there was just something about Rowdy that made you want to listen to what he had to say.

"We all care about those girls, Archer. Nobody wants to see anything happen to either one of them. Let Jet handle the home front. You tell Shaw to keep her eyes open and remind Ayden to be careful and on the lookout. We're a god-damn team and no one better forget it."

It took a minute before Rule relented, but when he did his shoulders relaxed and his tattooed hands unclenched. I nodded in agreement, but the conversation was cut short because Cora flopped herself on the couch between me and Rowdy and pouted about Nash forcing her into regulation bowling shoes.

The topic was essentially dropped, but I couldn't stop thinking about what he said, that when you cared about someone so deeply it changed you, made you into a different person. In his case, deciding that he could love Shaw, and more important, that she could love him, had turned him into a totally different guy. He was still a pain in the ass, but now he was a pain in the ass that could see beyond himself, and he was a shining example of love changing someone for the better.

I didn't know how going from friends to something more was going to play out for me and Ayden, or that I nec-essarily needed to be better or worse. All I knew for sure was that she was inside me like cold drops of water next to all the burning things that had lived there for years. I was in no hurry to get her out, because something about her was cool and soothing to all the parts of me that had been on fire for far too long.

CHAPTER 7

Ayden

I WAS TIRED WHEN I got home. Work had been busy, which was nice because I was tired of dodging Shaw's questions and speculative looks about my relationship, or nonrelationship, with Jet. I wasn't ready to get into it with her—hell I wasn't even ready to get into it with him. When Rule had shown up to get her, he had almost strong-armed me into letting him take me home. When he got distracted by Lou, I had literally ducked out the back door to take my own car home. Something weird was going on, because while Rule was normally bossy and overbearing, he usually toned it down with me because I didn't acquiesce to him in the least.

When I was pulling out of the parking lot, I got a text from Cora telling me that I needed to park in the driveway and that they had left all the lights on for me. It was all clandestine and overly cautious, and was making the hair on the back of my neck stand on end.

The house was quiet when I got in the front door. Cora's light was off. I still wasn't sure about this new territory I was treading on with Jet, so even though his light was on under his door, I decided I needed a shower and a minute to collect my thoughts before trying to talk to him. I collected a pair of yoga pants and a stretchy tank before padding to the bathroom on silent feet.

I shared the second bathroom with Jet, and before I had started sticking my tongue down his throat I never really thought about how intimate that was. For instance, all the junk he used in his hair was scattered all over the counter, right next to all the stuff I used to smell good and look pretty. He had a collection of thick silver rings on one side of the sink and a bunch of random guitar picks in the soap dish, next to the fancy bottles of perfume I left out because I was too lazy to put them away. One of his belts with the metal studs was curled up on the back of the toilet and the skirt of my cheerleader uniform was in a discarded pile on the floor. Somehow, without even noticing it, my life had intersected his so thoroughly that it was just seamless and so easy. I liked having all my stuff mixed up with all his. It made for a more interesting mess, kind of like us.

When I was walking back to my room, I had to stop outside the door because there was music drifting from across the hall. It wasn't the screaming, ear-bleeding, headache-inducing noise that he usually had blaring, but soft guitar and the most beautiful voice I had ever heard. I couldn't make out the song because it didn't sound familiar, but it was alluring enough that I threw everything on my bed and went back across the hall without any hesitation. I knocked and the guitar stopped long enough for him to tell me to come in. When I did, my breath stopped somewhere in the middle of my chest, and my heart did a slow slide all the way down to the bottom of my feet and back up to my throat.

Jet was sitting in the center of his bed, his long legs crossed at the ankles. He didn't have a shirt on, which was already hot and distracting, and the huge black and gray tattoo that covered his entire torso looked menacing behind the acoustic guitar he was holding. It was a sight that made my breath catch and made me remember why he put every good intention I had to the test. His dark head was bent down and he was scribbling something on a notebook he had open next to him. He looked rumpled and sexy, the rock star at rest, but the things he was doing with that guitar and the way he sounded when he sang the next verse made my knees go weak. I walked across the room in a daze, unaware that he was pulling me in with his voice alone. I sank to the edge of the bed and watched him with wide eyes.

He didn't acknowledge me until he was done, and by that time I had a film of tears in my eyes and felt that something in my soul had been touched by what this boy could do. He leaned across me and put the guitar down on the floor and shoved the notebook into a drawer of his nightstand. His dark eyes regarded me quietly and I couldn't help but reach out and touch him. I grabbed his thigh and leaned over so that we were eye to eye.

"If you can sing like that why in the world do you get onstage and scream and yell so that no one can understand you? You're amazing. That was so beautiful, it made my heart hurt."

He cleared his throat and his shoulders moved up and then down. There was a lot of tattooed skin on display and even though I was used to seeing it onstage or in passing in the hall, it was pretty impressive and very distracting up close and personal, and I wanted to touch all of it. I wasn't sure where to let my gaze land, so I decided that his midnight gaze with the gold halo was my best bet.

"It's just music, Ayd. It all speaks to something inside us."

"But you have a beautiful voice. You could be famous, like famous on a ridiculous level."

He shoved his hands behind his head and leaned back, making his abs contract and flex under the ink that covered them in a drool-worthy way. My fingers itched to run along the faint trail of dark hair that poked out the top of those too tight pants and across abs that were defined and taunt under a cover of black and gray ink.

"I could be famous on a ridiculous level singing metal or singing nursery rhymes. That's not what I want."

I bit my lip because he was way more complicated than I had ever given him credit for. I thought the band was just a way he killed time, a way he got validation. I had no idea he was as skilled as he was, or that he was actively avoiding being a big freaking deal.

"What do you want in the long run, Jet? Where are you going with all this? Wasting a talent like that should be criminal."

The corner of his mouth kicked up in a grin that made my skin tingle. "As long as I can continue to write songs that are good enough to bring beautiful, dark-haired girls knocking at my door in the middle of the night, I can be happy. I'll sing you anything you want, Ayd, if it means you keep looking at me the way you're looking at me right now. The long run can take care of itself much later."

I knew if I let him, he would own me. If he sang to me with that beautiful voice and played the guitar for just me, with those hands covered in heavy rings and tipped in black fingernail polish, he would just simply own me. He was already close and I was doing my best to keep him at a distance. I knew none of those things, his beautiful voice or his rumpled hair or ink-covered skin, belonged in my future, but letting that take care of itself was sounding better and better by the second. I slid my hand a little farther up his thigh and watched as little sparks shot off the golden rim of those midnight irises. He was my temptation, and had been for a long time now. Good Ayden or Bad Ayden, we both wanted him, only him.

I leaned even farther over him so that both my hands were flat on either side of his hips. We were eye to eye, and only our breath separated our mouths. No part of either of us was touching, but I could practically feel the electricity jump from his colorful skin to mine.

"Why do I feel like I'm always the one coming after you, Jet?" My voice was barely a whisper, and I saw when it hit his lips, it made them twitch. He pulled his hands out from behind his head and I felt the chill of his rings brush across my cheeks as he tunneled his fingers into the hair at my temples.

"I don't know, Ayd."

I probably would have had a smart remark to throw back

at him, but he was pulling me across his legs and turning us so that I was on my back and he was hovering over me in all his toned and tattooed glory. I'd had his mouth on mine before so it shouldn't be shocking, shouldn't be startling, but there was something about being horizontal and having nothing but thin cotton pants between me and a very impressive erection that made our previous kisses seem like practice for the main event.

Before Jet, I had never been interested in guys who were decorated from head to toe, but now I wanted all the things that just made him *him*. That included the artwork that was imprinted everywhere and the metal hoops he had in each nipple that I could feel pressing against my own chest. I was also lucky that all that decoration came with a pair of corded pecks, tightly defined biceps, and an ass that looked better in this bed than it ever had on stage.

I couldn't decide what to put my hands on first. It was like getting all the presents I ever wanted at one time. Jet seemed to run naturally hot and I felt like if I didn't get to all of him at one time, he was going to melt both of us into the comforter on the bed.

I felt like I had been starving for this my entire life and now the seven-course meal that was Jet Keller was mine for the tasting and I was about to turn into a gluttonous beast. He was doing a pretty good job of making me lose track of every thought by assaulting my mouth with kisses that had more bite and more sting than I was used to. He was holding my head still, and playing a game of attack and retreat with his tongue that was making me moan. My only recourse was to slide my hands around his narrow waist and dig my fingers into the tight muscle above his ass. The pressure was enough to get him to lift his head, and when he did, I couldn't help the dart of satisfaction that flared in me at the obsidian glimmer in his dark eyes, the gold completely obliterated by a hazy, passionate gleam. His mouth was damp and when his tongue brushed over it, my knees instinctively bent so that he was cradled right at the heart of where he needed to be.

I slid a couple of fingers under the tight edge of his pants and lifted a dark eyebrow. "How do these come off?"

He had lowered his head and was doing something amazing with his tongue on the tendon of my neck, so his reply was muttered against skin that was quivering at his lightest touch. I hooked a long leg around one of his and pressed up against the part of him that I wanted and was being denied access to. "Seriously, those pants are ridiculous. How am I supposed to get them off?"

Everything I had on was stretchy and designed for comfort and cuddling in bed. I made a face at him and he pushed up off me, and had zero trouble taking my tank top with him as he went. The look that crossed his face when he stared back at me had heat surging up my chest and into my face. I took pretty good care of myself, and I wasn't an idiot, so I knew I was better than all right to look at. But when he looked at me, I had never felt more appreciated, more valued, more adored than I did in that minute. Something serious was going on in those dark eyes, and if I stopped to think about it, I was going to freak out and bolt for my own room.

Luckily, he must have felt it brewing, because he clambered over me to climb to his feet and started working on the buckle to his belt.

"They aren't that tight."

I propped myself up on my elbows to watch the show and implore him to hurry with my greedy eyes.

"Yes they are, and right now they are in the way."

He stopped messing with his zipper for a second to stare at me, but I was shimmying out of my yoga pants and that was enough to spurn him back into action. The denim and leather hit the floor with a clatter and I blinked in surprise when I was face-to-face with not only an impressive erection and ripped abs, but another hoop that I hadn't been expecting. Since Shaw and I talked about everything, I knew that this group of guys was into this kind of thing, but I had never seen it before, let alone had one anywhere near me. I licked my bottom lip and twirled a finger in the air in front of him.

"What am I supposed to do with that?"

He laughed a little and pushed his hair back from his face. "Enjoy it?"

I shook my head a little as he grabbed my ankle and pulled me to the edge of the bed so that I was way closer to it and to him than I was ready for. Anticipation was building and steaming under the surface, but the fear of the unknown was still lurking, and the metal in the unexpected place was a welcome distraction. "Doesn't it hurt?"

He laughed again and I wanted to touch it. I was reaching out tentatively, worried that it would hurt him, worried that I was going to do something wrong. He grabbed my hand

and wrapped the whole thing around the shaft and gave it a squeeze. "I've had it forever. I don't even think about it. You can touch it, you can lick it—in fact why don't you do both of those things on a regular basis?"

I slid my hand back and forth and felt him shudder a little under my light touch. I let go and used my index finger to gently brush the metal. It was hot from being pressed against his skin and the little ball in the center of the ring was smooth. I could only imagine what it felt like when he did his thing. It was as hot as it was intimidating.

"This should be interesting."

He winked at me and leaned over to grab a condom out of the nightstand next to his bed. I was sure the anticipation was going to kill me. He handed me the little foil package and shoved me back on the bed. I wrapped my arms around his broad shoulders and looked up into eyes that held everything I ever wanted in them.

"We have to get you to step outside the box, Ayd. None of the best stuff is found in the mainstream."

He was right. But the mainstream was safe, and no one ever got hurt or judged or ostracized in the mainstream. Now wasn't the time for that argument, because he was kissing me again and doing things to my puckered nipples that only a guy who played the guitar like he did could do. There was something in the way he touched me, the way his fingers pressed into my skin, the way his teeth left marks, and the way the metal scattered here and there sent goose bumps chasing after it, that erased any and all others who had ever tried to get to me. He was hard and he was soft; his mouth was all velvet and steel, and I wondered if there was no going back from this point with him.

Only Jet made that happen. Only Jet had me forgetting that I wasn't a girl who simply gave herself over to passion and mindless oblivion, and only Jet made me scream his name when he pushed my legs apart and touched me, stroked me, did all the things he did to me in that bathroom the other night. Only this time, it ended with me seeing stars and pushing him over onto his back so that I could climb on top of him. This boy could play a woman as well as he could play a guitar; there was no doubt about it.

I looked down at him lying beneath me and something inside me shifted. I had wanted him for so long. He was impressive, talented in a way that hurt, and undeniably gorgeous in a way that spoke to something primitive and instinctual inside me. I didn't care about the future when I looked at him, didn't care that his plans did not go beyond a guitar and a pretty song. All I cared about was that he never stopped looking at me the way he was right now, and that when he said my name in that beautiful voice, he said it like it was the lyric to his favorite song.

I used both hands to cover him in the latex, because I still wasn't a hundred percent sure what to do with that ring at the tip, and frankly I was nervous. Sex was just a thing I had done before. Sometimes it was good, sometimes it wasn't, but whatever was happening here was on another level. I knew that once the bridge was crossed, that whoever came after him was never going to stand a chance. I could feel it as I breathed him in and watched him watch me. This had been a long time coming and now the actuality of it was as potent as the act itself.

There was something in the way he touched me just a little harder, the way he kissed me a little longer, the way he pushed me a little farther than I normally wanted to go that made this different. It was like every place he touched, every place his lips landed, became extra sensitized and overstimulated. I felt like I was going to come right out of my skin.

No part of me escaped his thorough and attentive ministrations; no one had ever been as attentive to my body. I think he even managed to discover new spots, parts of me that I didn't even know turned me on, like the back of my neck and the inside of my wrist. Everywhere his hands landed— the curve of the underside of my breast, my rib cage—his mouth followed, and it felt like he was trying to leave his mark on every inch of my skin so that no one else could ever be there. There was just something about the startling contrast between the soft caress of the tip of his tongue and the hard metal ball in the center that was more erotic than anything I had ever experienced before. There wasn't a place on any part of me that didn't get a nip of teeth, and by the time I couldn't take anymore, by the time I was past wet and wanting, it was all I could do to keep it together when he pulled me up and over him.

I placed my hand over his heart. I felt the steady thump under my fingers and looked at the skeletal mask of the angel of death peeking out at me from between my fingers. Jet put his hands around my waist and lifted me up like I weighed nothing. Before he could pull me back down, before he could impale me with all the burning flesh that was stretched out taut between us, I hissed out a breath between my teeth and dropped my forehead down so that it was resting against his.

"This is going to change everything."

Those words were strangled out as just the tip, and that damn little ball, pressed into places that were greedy for it all. I could feel his stomach contract under me and feel my own reaction. It burned in the best way possible. He was hot, he was hard, and he touched places inside me that I swore had never been touched before. That little ring at the tip of his cock dragged and pulled across tender flesh that couldn't resist the sensation, which made my breath come faster and my heart race. I wasn't going to last long at this rate. Between the wait for this to happen, and just the fact that this was Jet, I was going to be over the edge between one stroke and the next. Flutters ran along the length of his cock that I felt all the way to my toes as he pulled me all the way back down, and we both gasped at the intensity of the contact. His dark eyes drifted shut as I began to move, to find a rhythm that made me pant and had him growling at me low in his throat. Nothing was ever going to be this good, feel this right. I put my hands on the planes of soft and inked skin, stretched taut over straining muscles and let the way he moved, the way he touched me, like I was something precious, take over.

When I was getting close, he put his hands under my ass and flipped us over in one neat move. He kissed me long and hard, put his hands in my hair, and I discovered in short order that really, all I had to do was sit back and enjoy when it came to that ring at the end of his dick. The metal ball brushed against my clit one time, one single time, and it was over. I caught my breath and let him manhandle me however he wanted, and when he was done and we were both lying spent and limp, he turned and looked at me out of eyes that were as dazed as I felt.

"Sometimes, things need to change, because there just isn't any way for them to stay the same."

I didn't know what to say to that. We were supposed to do this, should have been doing this for the last year—that was all too clear now. Sex was incidental and forgettable. This was not.

After he came back to bed from cleaning up, he wrapped an arm around my middle and hauled me to his side. As he reached over my head to flick off the light, I thought this was a change that I liked too much for my own peace of mind. I fell asleep with him winding his fingers through mine across my stomach and humming the chorus to "Tennessee Whiskey" by George Jones. Jet was going to undo me in every way he could, and I just didn't know if I was going to be able to stop him.

THE NEXT MORNING, THE alarm on my phone went off and I had a moment of panic when I woke up surrounded by a lot of naked skin. I hurt in really good ways, and had to fight not to cuddle back into him instead of slipping silently away. It took me a minute to find my discarded clothes and get back to my own room. When I caught sight of myself in the mirror above my dresser, I cringed; I looked well and thoroughly debauched. My hair was sticking up everywhere and my eyes looked heavy lidded and dreamy. I had a very distinct bite mark on the side of my neck and there was no denying that I looked like I had been truly worked over.

There was no ho-hum with Jet. He knew what he was doing, and it was stamped all over me from head to toe. The fact that I had absolutely and completely lost control with him and gotten caught up in the moment was not lost on me or in my reflection, either, and that had me fighting back a heavy flood of panic.

I changed into running clothes and pulled my snarled hair up into a stubby ponytail. I was going to grab my iPod, but for some reason, listening to cookie-cutter songs about love and loss just didn't sound appealing, so I dashed down the hall hoping Jet would stay asleep and that Cora would still be holed up in her room. I was filling my bottle of water in the sink when Cora's singsongy voice came from the living room, "Someone looks well rested."

I closed my eyes for a second and swore under my breath. I looked over my shoulder at her. She was still in her fuzzy pink jammies and her dual-colored eyes were gleaming with mischief.

"Yep."

She wagged a finger at me and suddenly looked more serious. "You need to be careful, Ayd."

I frowned because it was too early, both literally and figuratively, for this conversation. "Careful is my middle name, Cora."

"But Jet's is passion, and he can get really wrapped up in things that are important to him. If you don't want to be wrapped up, you better be honest with him about it."

I couldn't talk about this with her, not when I didn't know what I was doing myself, so I grabbed my lightweight fleece and zipped it up.

"Noted. I'll be back in a few."

"Hey, keep an eye out. Weird stuff has been going on."

I lifted an eyebrow. "You noticed the guy lurking around, too?"

"What? No! But some creep tried to break in yesterday."

A shiver of alarm worked from the base of my neck down my spine. Between the calls from Kentucky and the repeated sightings of the same guy over and over again, I couldn't chalk an attempted break-in to coincidence.

"Did you call the cops?"

She shook her head. "I threatened to taze his ass and he took off. I'm sure he was just a crazy meth head or something, but you need to be aware of your surroundings if you're going running alone."

I nodded, but in reality I was thinking I had to be aware of my surroundings for a lot more reasons than that. I was walking to the front door, contemplating what could possibly have someone threatening my new life, my new home, when Cora called my name. I should have known by the glee in her tone that I was going to regret turning back around. She was standing on the couch with both her hands in the air, waving all ten fingers back and forth, and chanting, "You're a ten!" over and over again. If I'd had something lighter than my water bottle on hand I would have thrown it at her. Instead I rolled my eyes and bounded out the door.

She was right. I was totally a ten and that sucked, because I just couldn't get it in line with how after last night I was supposed to juggle just being friends with a whole lot more and not eventually cross the line into wanting more. I couldn't deal with that. Jet made old Ayden want to get in on all of the good-time action and that was just dangerous to my peace of mind and carefully constructed façade.

I hit the ground hard and tried to let the physical exertion do its thing to get my head to stop spinning. I was almost to the park and breathing hard already, when a nondescript sedan rolled up next to me on the road. I looked at it out of the corner of my eye and would have never even noticed it if I had had music playing. I slowed down and did a double-take when it came to a complete stop next to me on the road and the window rolled down. Normally, I would have kept running. In fact, if I had been smart, I would have kept running, but when the driver leaned out the window and that familiar devil-may-care grin lit his face, I had to step off the sidewalk into the street.

I leaned against the hood of the car with one hand and met amber-colored eyes the same shade as mine. It was really the only trait we shared, since we had different dads. Asa had blond hair and was about the same height as me, but he was beautiful and he knew it. He also had to know that I was less than thrilled to see him here.

"How did you find me?"

He smiled up at me and I felt my heart squeeze. When he

looked at you like that, it was nearly impossible to deny him anything, even though I knew from cold, hard experience that the only person Asa cared about was Asa. Loving my big brother was the hardest thing I had ever done in my life.

"What kind of big brother would I be if I didn't keep tabs on what my lil sis was up to?"

"The kind you've always been. What are you doing here?" I couldn't give him an inch or he would take the thousands of miles I had worked so hard to put between us.

"I need to talk to you about something. I got some trouble brewing back home and I might need a little help."

There was always trouble with Asa and if he said it was brewing, the truth was that it had probably already boiled over and both of us were looking into the eye of a full-on shit storm. That was just his way. Stir up the mess and leave it for someone else, usually me, to figure out how to clean up. He never even stopped to ask how I managed to do it time and time again, just took for granted that I would, and always did, find a way.

I shook my head and pushed off the car. "No."

He lifted a blond brow at me. "What do you mean, no?"

I rubbed my hands up and down my arms, because I was suddenly freezing even though it wasn't that cold out. "Just no. No, I won't help you. No, I won't give you money. No, you can't stay with me. Whatever it is, the answer is just, hell no. I have a good thing going on here Asa. I'm kickass at school, I have awesome friends and a cool job. You aren't going to show up and mess with any of it."

He just smiled at me in a way that used to make me

shake my head and follow him into whatever crazy scheme he was in the middle of at the time. Now it made the tiny hairs on the back of my neck stand up.

"You forgot your fancy boyfriend in that list, sis."

I frowned because no one in their right mind would call Jet fancy, but I wasn't going to give him any ammo to work with. "I have to go, Asa. Stop calling me and hanging up, and if you have friends lurking around tell them to back off. Those guys I hang out with aren't afraid to get physical."

Something moved across the shimmery amber depths of his eyes. I knew the look well. I saw it enough in the mirror. It was fear.

"I haven't called you, Ayd, and I just got to town today. Alone."

I narrowed my eyes at him because he might be telling the truth, but there was just as much of a chance that he was running a game on me. "Seriously."

I had to steel the reserves up. I couldn't get dragged back into whatever Asa was running from. I had spent way too much time doing things I'd struggled to forget, in order to keep him alive and out of jail, when I should have been having sleepovers and trying out for cheerleading.

"I wish I could say it was nice to see you, Asa, but I don't lie like that anymore. I hope you figure out whatever it is you're running from, but it isn't my job to fix it all for you anymore. Mom should have warned you of that before you tracked me down."

I turned to go back to the sidewalk and I could feel his eyes burning into my back as I walked away.

"It looks like you're still running, Ayd. Haven't you figured out the horizon just gets farther and farther away, and the past stays exactly where you left it?"

That was part of what made Asa so dangerous. He could read a stranger from a hundred miles away. But me, me he already knew inside and out, and he didn't even have to try to guess my weaknesses and fears. I didn't answer him, and started running as fast as I could toward the park. I didn't delude myself into thinking that this would be the last run-in I had with Asa. If he was in trouble, he wasn't going anywhere. I needed to make sure that whatever he had brought with him from Woodward didn't have the chance to bleed drama and chaos all over everything wonderful I had built here in Denver.

CHAPTER 8

Jet

I WOKE UP ALONE, which wasn't entirely surprising. What caught me a little off guard was the fact that it kind of pissed me off.

Friends with benefits was all fine and dandy, but after the night before, it felt like there was something else at work that neither of us should be able to ignore. We just fit. We just worked. If two people were ever supposed to be having sex on a regular basis, it was us, and the fact that she had such an easy time walking out after, irked me to no end. I wasn't arrogant enough to think I was the end all and be all of lovers, but like I had promised her, it was a good time and it bugged me she was gone so soon. I wasn't sure if it was my ego or something else and I didn't like it.

I rolled out of bed and hopped in the shower. By the time I was out, my phone was blowing up where I had tossed it on the nightstand the night before. I pulled on a pair of bright red jeans and a black T-shirt and was shoving my feet into my boots and ignoring another call from my dad, when I saw that the first round of missed calls had come from Dario Hill, the lead singer of Artifice. I had worked with him a ton on the last album and they were the main reason we got signed on to tour with Metalfest last year. They were in the big time now and Dario found less and less time to just call and chitchat, so I started to freak out a little, wondering if the old man had circumvented me and tried to get in touch with them about the European tour without my help.

I pushed my mop of wet hair out of my face and twirled the ring that circled my thumb around and around while I called him back. I was prepared to leave a message, but Dario picked up on the second ring.

"Dude, I've been trying to call you all morning."

I picked my guitar up off the floor where I had laid it down last night and ran my fingers over the stings.

"Yeah, I had a late night so I was slow getting to it this morning."

He laughed. "Sounds fun."

I don't know that *fun* was the right word, more like life-changing, but Dario was an old-school metal head and he wouldn't understand the significance of any of that, so I didn't bother to try to explain it. "You could say that. So what's up? I thought you guys were getting ready to head to Europe on tour for the new album."

Going to Europe was a big deal. The global exposure was huge and it was just fun and exciting to play new venues and reach audiences that expected so much more. Metal overseas kicked the shit out of American metal any day of the week.

"That's actually why I'm calling."

I was mentally preparing myself for him to tell me that having my dad badger him crossed both our friendship and professional boundaries, and I missed a chord on the song I was absently strumming. I swore and set the guitar to the side.

"The band that the record label had planned on going with us fell through. I dunno what happened. They're out though and we need a replacement act stat. They tossed around a few names, but I'm not stoked on being on the road with any of them for three months. I dropped your name, on the off chance they would be down for it, and I thought the head of the label was going to shit his pants. Why didn't you ever say anything about them being after you to sign for, like, ever?"

I sighed. "Because I don't want to sign with anyone, let alone someone that big."

"Goddamn, Jet, you are one complicated, messed-up dude."

"Be grateful. That's how I write you such badass songs."

He laughed again, but got serious again real quickly. "Come on tour with us. I shouldn't ask, because Enmity is way better than we are, but it'll be fun and the exposure can't be matched. It's only three months and you know you guys are perfect for it."

Three months was three months, and being that far away from my mom while my dad was in town to do his worst, made my skin crawl. Plus, I had to figure out what was going on with Ayden. If I left for three months, I felt like I would come back and she would be cuddled up to the first guy she could find who was rocking a tweed jacket with those leather patches on the elbows. I knew what she wanted, but what she actually needed was entirely different. If I was in Europe, I had no trouble seeing her talk herself into going back to boring and predictable.

"I don't know, man. One of the guys just had a kid and I have all kinds of jacked-up stuff going on here. That's a pretty big commitment to make."

I heard him sigh. "Jet, you are by far the most talented musician I have ever met and I don't just mean because you can rock a metal song, but all across the board. No one is better onstage than you, no one can write a song like you. I get that you're happy being a big shot in the local scene, but come on now, is that really all this is ever going to be for you? When are you going to see the big picture? How can you realistically pass up the chance to tour Europe on the record label's dime?"

Logically, I knew what he was saying was true, but the part of me that lived and breathed in anger, in fear of what my dad could ultimately do to destroy my mom, just couldn't relent right away.

"Let me talk to the guys and get back to you."

Another sigh, and this one I could practically feel across the phone line. "You only have a couple of days, dude. We need to have the opening act hammered down before the end of the week and then we leave the first of March."

I didn't feel like that was enough time to turn it around in my head, but I had to at least see what the other guys in the band thought about it, before abjectly refusing it. I was going to tell him "later" and hang up, but he stopped me with what I had dreaded hearing when I first saw that I had missed a call from him.

"Hey, before I let you go, the label got a call from some guy saying he knew you and that he wanted to get hitched into the tour. Do you know anything about that? I told the guys I would ask about it before we agreed to anything, but honestly he sounded like kind of a nutjob."

Now it was my turn to sigh. I rubbed my thumb hard between my eyes and felt my back teeth click together. It was a struggle on a daily basis not to choke the old bastard out, and the older I got, the harder and harder it got to keep from pummeling him.

"Tell him no. In fact, tell him hell no. If he calls again, tell him you're going to have security put eyes out for him. He doesn't need to be anywhere near your tour or near your band."

Which meant I was going to have to find some other way for him to spend his time, other than making my mom's life miserable. Maybe the best thing to do would be to just send him off to Europe with Dario and hope that he didn't come back. Disgustingly though, he was my problem, always had been, and I wasn't about to pawn his sorry ass off on a friend.

"All right, but seriously Jet, think long and hard about the tour. This is perfect for you and it couldn't happen to a better guy or a better band. You deserve to get the recognition."

I grunted a good-bye and shoved the phone in my pocket. I made a quick trip to the bathroom to get my hair under control, ending with the black strands hanging shaggily over my forehead. I brushed my teeth and laced my belt through my pants. It looked like Ayden had already come and gone, because all her girly crap was put away and her normal collection of abandoned clothes was nowhere in sight. I went back to being irritated that she could just bolt on me after last night, and muttered obscenities under my breath all the way to the kitchen.

Cora was puttering around, already ready for work, and looked up at me with knowing eyes when I flopped into one of the chairs at the kitchen table.

"Did Ayd already leave for the day?"

She came toward me with a mug of coffee and a grin. "She did. She was up early and went running, then left for class. Everything okay with you two? She seemed a little abrupt when she got back from her run."

I let my head fall back on my neck so that I was staring up at the ceiling. "I have no idea."

She sat down across from me and I lowered my head so that we were staring at each other. There was something about those multicolored eyes that made a person just know that she saw more and understood more than she ever let on. Cora could read people better than almost anyone I had ever met, and if she had any insight into what was going on with Ayden, I was all ears.

"I think Ayd has more going on under the surface than she lets on. I mean, I've lived with her for a while now and she never mentions home or her family, and she never talks about what her life before college was like. Even Shaw has only the basics. It's like she didn't exist before moving here for school. Sometimes it's what people choose not to say that tells the more important story."

I just gawked at her, because I had no idea how she saw the whole picture so clearly like that. Sometimes it was easy to miss all she had going on because her punk-rock, fairy-princess persona was so distracting.

"Like you." She pointed a neon-tipped finger at the end of my nose and flicked it. "You didn't mention that you went to see your mom yesterday. Why is that?"

I groaned and shoved both my hands through my hair getting gunk all over them. "Because I don't like to talk about it. Nash has a big mouth."

"No, Nash is a good friend who knows how hard you are on yourself when it comes to taking responsibility for your parents' shitty marriage. One day, you're going to have to recognize that your mom is a grown-ass woman, responsible for all the choices she's made and continues to make where your dad is concerned. You did your best to help her, to get her out of there, and she clearly doesn't want to go. That can't be your burden to bear for the rest of your life, Jet."

It was pretty much the same thing Nash had told me yesterday, but understanding that they were right, and being able to just put it down and walk away, were two different things entirely. So I told her the same thing I told Nash, "She's my mom."

Only Cora wasn't Nash, and she wasn't the type to accept as gospel why I continued to torture myself over the matter. She put one of her tiny hands on mine and squeezed.

"Right, she is, which means she should be there to take care of you, and be proud of all the amazing things you do. She should be giddy with excitement about how talented her son is and she should be your biggest fan. What she shouldn't be doing is letting her unhealthy relationship with your dad keep you tied to this town and to her, when everybody, and Jet, I mean *everybody* knows you could be doing so much more on such a bigger scale."

I couldn't argue with her because she was right. Everyone was right, but that didn't change the fact that I was stone-cold terrified of what would happen to the woman if I just washed my hands of the situation, and let my dad finish dismantling her. I didn't know if I could live with myself if I let that happen, and no amount of success or personal achievement was worth that risk. I wasn't even going to mention the offer of the tour with Artifice, because that would just give her more fuel for the fire. If I was here in Denver to keep the old man occupied, there was less of a chance he could totally destroy her.

"It is what it is, for now."

She lifted a pale eyebrow. "But it doesn't have to be. Look at you and Ayd. Things can be one way for a long time and then have to change because there is no other choice."

I just shrugged. "Maybe."

She rolled her eyes at me and climbed to her feet. "I have to go or I'm going to be late. Stop acting like a typical brooding musician and make Ayd talk to you. By the way, she was totally a ten when I saw her this morning, so way to go, killer."

That startled a laugh out of me and shook some of the gloom from my current mood. "I told you one day I would have one."

She laughed and winked at me with her blue eye. "Well, the catch is that you're totally a ten right now, too, and I don't think you've ever been above a five. You're good together, Jet, in any form that happens to be. Don't let her convince you otherwise."

"Yeah. For some reason, I think that might be a lot harder than it sounds."

After Cora left for work, I screwed around for a couple of hours and tried to finish the song I was working on last night when Ayden had ambushed me. It was sad and had a melody to it that made something in the center of my chest hurt. It was missing something I couldn't put my finger on. With my mind spinning about the tour and a certain Southern girl, I couldn't get it right, so I tossed my guitar in the case and went down to the studio. I was supposed to finish up with Black Market Alphas later on tonight, but the mood I was currently in didn't bode well for getting anything accomplished, especially if Ryan showed up flashing his idiotic bravado and unearned arrogance.

I tweaked a couple of the tracks, messed around with some of my own, and sent a text to all the guys in my band that we needed to get together to talk. My dad called me three times and I sent all three directly to voice mail. I debated on calling Ayden and decided that the phone worked both ways. If she wanted to talk, she could get in touch with me. After all, I wasn't the one who left her hanging alone in bed after a night of mind-melting sex.

Before I knew it, the afternoon had blown by and Ryan and the rest of the band were rolling into the studio. It was a shame the lead singer was such a little punk, because the other guys were all cool and I really saw a lot of myself in Jorge. They were getting set up when my phone beeped at me with a text.

I was surprised and admittedly stoked to see that it was Ayden.

Where are you?

At work.

You? Working? ;)

That made me scowl. What did she think I did all day long when I didn't have a show? Of course I worked, how did she think I paid the bills?

When I feel like it. Why, what's up?

I wanted to see if you were hungry. My last class got canceled and I'm starving.

I can't leave. In the middle of a session.

I can come to you.

That was weird. I never let anyone in the studio that I wasn't working with or in a band with. This place was generally my escape from the rest of the world. This is where I came to get away from all the other stuff I normally couldn't deal with. Letting her in seemed like a bigger deal than it probably actually was, and it took me a solid ten minutes to text her back.

All right. But you might hate it. I don't think the guys I'm working with know a single Kenny Chesney song.

Very funny, asshole. What do you want me to bring you?

Whatever. I'm easy.

No Jet, you are anything but that.

I stared at the phone like it would explain to me what she meant. The guys in the band were getting restless, so I told her to grab a couple pizzas and a case of Coors Light so I could feed them as well. I gave her directions to the studio. I couldn't decide between being pleased that she was actively seeking me out or being freaked out about letting her into my inner sanctum. I decided to just hover between the two and focus on work until she got there. Something was going on with the band, half the guys weren't talking and Jorge was a beat behind on three out of four songs. After the sixth time starting the first song over again, I was ready to murder them all.

I slammed my hands down on the mixing board and flipped off the switch that recorded everything in the booth. I cracked my knuckles on both hands and walked into where they were all glaring back and forth at one another, and where Ryan was scowling at me.

"What gives, dude? Today is the last day we have for studio time and we already paid you for it."

I twirled the ring on my middle finger around with my thumb and met him glare for glare. This kid didn't know me well enough to think that I was ever going to be impressed by his youthful overconfidence and mediocre talent.

"What's going on today? You guys suck, and I mean suck. Whatever you're doing is garbage and I'm not messing around with it. Did you forget you're a band and that means you all have to play the same song at the same time? What the fuck gives?"

Ryan puffed his chest up and Jorge threw his drum sticks down. The other two guys frowned at me while Ryan moved to poke me in the center of my chest.

"Watch it. We're paying you, remember?"

I smacked his hand away and narrowed my eyes threateningly at him. "Yeah. You're paying me to put together an album that gets you noticed by a major label and gets you signed, not an album that sounds like a bunch of pots and pans falling out of the kitchen cabinet. My name doesn't get attached to something that isn't listenable. So, what is the goddamn deal?"

Jorge pounded one of the cymbals with the edge of his fist. "Yeah, Ry, why don't you tell him what's going on? Why don't you tell him how you took all the credit for all the songs *I* wrote and all the shows *we* played when that girl from *Shred* interviewed you? Why don't you explain to Jet how this new album is a collaboration between you and him, and the rest of us are just the hired help?" He hit the cymbal again. "You don't need us, right? Why don't you go ahead and finish the album by yourself, because I've had it."

I took a step back as Jorge rounded the massive drum kit. Ryan had turned a lovely shade of purple and was looking frantically between me and where his drummer had stormed off to. I rubbed my chin and made him meet my questioning gaze.

"Can you write songs? Do you know how to put together a melody and a chorus the way Jorge does?"

He frowned and gulped. "No."

"Can you play guitar?"

"No."

"Can you play the drums?"

"I don't see what that has to do with anything."

I rocked back on my heels and crossed my arms over my chest. "Are you a solo artist, Ry? Because if you are, then we need to scrap the tracks we already laid down and start all over."

He balked at me, and the microphone in his hand dropped to the ground. "No. No way. That stuff we recorded the other day was boss."

"Right. It was boss, because Jorge wrote amazing songs and you have an amazing band to back you up. Without that, you're just some little shit jumping around the stage and screaming worthless nonsense. I don't collaborate with worthless nonsense. You better recognize what you can do for them, Ry, not the other way around, because I guarantee if Jorge walks away I can hook him up with another band in a heartbeat. You'll just be a memory for some guy somewhere who saw you play that one time. You need to get over yourself, like yesterday, and stop wasting everyone's time. And if you can't do that, I, for sure, have more important stuff to do than babysit a wannabe rock star."

He stared at me in silence, trying to judge how serious I was. I didn't play around when it came to respecting the rest of your band. I knew that alone I was an all right singer, but that I couldn't do what I did without the rest of the guys, and a talent like Jorge's wasn't to be taken lightly. Ryan and I were in the middle of a stare-down when I heard a low whistle and Jorge called out,

"Who's the babe? On my god, I'm in love. She even has beer and pizza."

I looked over my shoulder and saw Ayden setting the stuff down inside the control room. She had a big silk flower in her dark hair and her glasses perched on her nose. She was wearing a pair of skinny jeans that were tighter than mine, if that was possible, and some kind of flowy white top that hung entirely off one shoulder. Yep, she was a babe all right and now that she was here, inside the inner circle, it wasn't nearly as freaky or as unsettling as I thought it would be. She wiggled her fingers at me in a tiny wave and flopped down in my chair. I lifted my chin at her and turned back to Ryan. On the inside I was wondering why it seemed so right for her to be here.

"Look, my advice to you is, don't screw up a good thing. You guys sound good, but only when you play together. Get

your ego in check and apologize to your band. I'm not putting my name on anything I'm not proud of, and right now it
sounds like garbage. Let's eat some pizza and have a couple
beers and you go make nice. All right?"

He was quiet for a long moment but eventually nodded and begrudgingly walked to where Jorge was standing
in front of the control booth watching Ayden as she messed
around on her phone. I pushed the door open and almost
missed a step when she grinned up at me.

"Hey."

"Hey, back. I missed you this morning."

She winced a little and put her phone down. "I'm sorry
about that, I just had to . . ." She trailed off with a shrug.
"Run."

I bent over her and put my hands on the back of the
chair, so that I was looking down at her, and she had no
other choice but to look up at me. There was something in
those whiskey-tinted eyes, something potent and clear. This
girl was dangerous. I wanted to do things to her, do things
for her that I had never wanted before.

"I have to say, Ayd, I prefer it when you run toward me,
not away from me."

She tilted her head back a little and lifted her hands
so that they were resting on my waist. A mixture of heat
and something more serious coiled in my stomach. I wanted
to imprint everything about her on my brain. I wanted to
remember every look, every touch, and every taste. The
more time I had with her, the more I couldn't shake the feeling that it was like the melting clocks tattooed all over my

forearm; that she was just an illusion, just a dream that I was trying to hold on to before she faded away .

"I wasn't running away, Jet. I'm just not sure what this is all about and what to do with any of it."

"Neither am I, but doesn't it make more sense to try to figure it out together, rather than just muddling through it alone? Whatever it is, it's working fine for right now, so let's leave it alone."

She wrinkled her nose at me, which was too cute with her sexy little glasses on, and I couldn't resist bending down to kiss her. I meant to keep it professional because we had an audience, but she tasted like coffee, secrets, and a place where I really wanted to be. Not to mention, she got her fingers under the edge of my T-shirt and dug them into my sides. I could kiss her all day—forever—but she went to my head quicker than the booze her eyes reminded me of, and I was still a little pissed at her for ditching me this morning. I gave her a little nip with my teeth and pushed back off the chair, which sent her spinning around with a little squeal.

"Seriously, Ayd. We're both smart. Why can't we do this, make sex and something a little more work for us?"

She put her foot down to stop the chair and shrugged a shoulder. "We can. I want to. I'm just trying to be careful about it. When I wasn't very careful about things in the past, it really left a nasty mark."

I reached out a hand, which she grasped as I pulled her to her feet. I tugged her into a hug and tucked her head under my chin. We fit together like that was just how it was supposed to be. She put her hands in the back pockets of my jeans and rested her forehead on my throat.

"If you can tell me how we avoid doing that, Ayd, I'm willing to listen. The only marks I want to leave on you are ones you enjoy being there."

Her soft hair brushed against my neck and she pulled me a little closer. "One day, maybe, but for now let's just try to enjoy what it is, without all the baggage weighing it down."

I felt my eyebrows shoot up, but the guys in the band had made their way into the booth, and we were no longer alone. I ran my hand down her spine and tapped her ass with the flat of my hand. She jumped a little and pushed off me.

"I think the dude is normally supposed to try to sell that arrangement to the chick."

Those amber eyes glimmered with humor, and all I wanted to do was get her naked and put my hands all over her. She was simply something else, and I wasn't sure what to do with her or with the way she wound me up so fast. I didn't have time to keep turning it over, because Jorge forcibly pushed his way between us and started pumping her arm up and down in a way that was comical to watch. I took a few steps back and got a beer, while Ryan tried his best to charm her. She looked at them all with big eyes and sat back down in the chair, while they all chattered at her.

I watched the entire scenario in amusement. She was a very pretty girl and could hold her own. I'd seen her handle drunks with years on these guys and not break a sweat, but maybe because I was watching and we had something as yet unnamed going on, she was watching them carefully and not being her usual laid-back self. They were rapidly firing questions at her; how did she know me, were we a thing, what was her favorite band, had she ever heard of them, what was her favorite song, was she going to stick around and watch them play? She just gaped at them until I guess she had enough, and then came to plant herself solidly next to my side. She put an arm around my waist and regarded them as if they were a pack of wolves and not a bunch of oversexed teenaged musicians.

"Are they always like that?"

"When a hot chick is around, they are. Don't you know most guys start bands, or learn to play an instrument, to get laid?"

She looked up at me and I laughed at the incredulousness shining out of her bright gaze. I handed her the beer and motioned for everyone to get back to work. Now that she was here, all I wanted to do was finish up and get her home, or get her up against the wall, or get her in the back seat of my car. I wasn't picky, but I was impatient. She was like music, something I craved, something that I felt deep in my blood and I wasn't sure what to do with it.

"Why do I think that you didn't need either of those things to get laid when you were their age?"

I looked at her out of the corner of my eye and went back to the mixing board. She followed me and continued to sip on the beer while she hovered over my shoulder. Now that they had such an attractive audience, the boys weren't messing around and they ripped into the track that they had been screwing up royally with renewed vigor and enthusiasm.

"Because I didn't. I learned to play guitar because I wanted to write songs. I joined a band because I had things I wanted to say, and jumping around screaming punk-rock lyrics suited me at the time."

She put her hand on the back of my neck and I shivered a little at the chill, because they were cold from holding on to the beer can.

"And now, you scream and yell heavy-metal songs because you're mad about your dad and your mom all the time, and it suits you." She said it as a statement of fact and it made me shiver again, because she was so dead-on. "I can listen, too, Jet. Maybe you can tell me why you're so angry, and I can help."

I flicked a couple of switches and played with some of the dials to tone down the guitar. "Maybe when you're ready to talk to me about those not-so-smart choices, we can have an all-out sharefest."

My anger had been with me so long, lived in such a dark place inside me, that I didn't know what would happen if I brought it out into the light. I was scared it was going to have the power to cover everything and burn my entire world to ash. Those cold fingers moved from the back of my neck to my shoulder and she gave it a squeeze.

We stood that way for the next three songs. She just watched as I gave the guys instruction and tried to build the best track of each song I could. At one point, she handed the beer back to me and before I realized it, we had the entire album cut and it was almost midnight. The guys were keyed up and wanted to go out. All earlier arguments had been put to rest because they knew, just like I did, that we had just produced a killer album that would no doubt lead them to getting signed.

I wanted to get Ayden alone and ask her to get naked— except for those glasses—so I declined the invite and tried to shoo them out the door. She stayed put and went about cleaning up the mess that five guys, beer, and pizza had made. I was about to shut the door and lock it when Jorge paused, and walked back to where I was standing. He stuck out his hand and shook it like he meant it.

"You really are an amazing musician, Jet. No one else would have been able to do what you just did."

I nodded at the compliment.

"And that girl . . ." He blew out a low whistle. "I would be writing songs about her every chance I got, bro. So whatever you're doing, keep it up, because I totally want to be you when I grow up."

I snorted and flipped him off. When I walked back into the recording room, Ayden went into the studio and was running her finger along one of the necks of my electric guitars I stored there. She was so perfect, so right, that something flipped upside down in my chest and it made it hard for me to breathe for a second. When she turned back around, her eyes were serious and there was something working there.

"Jet, I had no idea you had all of this going on."

"What do you mean?"

She waved a hand around the studio and strummed the guitar, making a shrill sound.

"The studio, the way you were with those guys. I had no clue you were like some kind of rock god. The way you made those boys sound, I mean you know how much I hate that music, but you made it into something so beautiful."

I normally shrugged when people complimented what I could do, but if it made her see something more in me, I wasn't going to brush it off so lightly.

"It's what I love to do."

"It's more than that, isn't it? It's what you were born to do."

"It is." All that whiskey and mystery, all the things that made Ayden so much more than all the rest, swirled around and flashed at me. I still couldn't figure her out but when she grinned at me and hooked her arms around my neck and asked if I was ready to go, the only answer I could give her was "Hell, yeah."

CHAPTER 9

Ayden

I WAS RUNNING LATE, which wasn't like me. But now that I wasn't spending my nights alone and Jet had a thing for waking me up with his hands and mouth in places that made me blush to think about, it was becoming much more common.

I hadn't heard from Asa in two days and while everyone was still on edge from the attempted break-in (which I knew was somehow tied to my brother), I hadn't seen the familiar stranger lurking around anymore. Things were just going along as normal, and I had a sinking feeling that keeping things with Jet on a manageable level was going to be a challenge. The man and the musician in him had layers upon layers that I had never stopped to notice before, and now that I knew that the reality of him so surpassed the fantasy of him, I could feel myself falling into a place I had no intention of going.

Everything he did, he did with an intensity and focus that I had never realized he possessed. He was driven and appar-

ently very much in demand. His phone rang at all hours of
the day and night, and he was always running off to set this
or that show up, or handle this or that crisis for a band.

There was something going on with his own band
that had him keyed up and on edge. He didn't want to talk
about it, but from what I had pieced together, the other guys
wanted him to get on board with some kind of tour, and they
were annoyed that he just wouldn't agree. There were also
the calls that left him moody and surly for hours on end, and
when I asked about those, he would just shrug and change
the subject. Since I wasn't ready to have him pull apart my
past, I figured it was best to just let it go. Only it hurt to see
the way he struggled with whatever was going on. It also
shocked me how much I wanted to be able to help him.

Then there was the fact that he sang to me every night.
I don't know how I was supposed to stop myself from completely falling in love with him, to stop myself from building
dreams of something more with him, when every night I
fell asleep to that amazing voice lulling me with songs about
love and loss. For a guy with a giant tattoo of death on his
chest, and devil horns spiked into his ears, he sure knew a lot
of old country songs and Southern folk songs. Some nights it
was Johnny Cash and Patsy Cline; other nights it was Hank
Williams Sr. and Waylon Jennings. I didn't really like older
country, but there was no denying when Jet sang it to me,
I could see the difference in the quality of the songwriting
compared to what I typically listened to. I also knew that
despite all my best intentions there was quickly becoming
no other place that I wanted to be than in his arms.

It reminded me of being little and thinking that it was so sad that my mom never sang us lullabies when she put us to bed. All good Southern moms sang to their kids. It was just one more thing that I had missed out on, and had found in this new life I had built for myself.

I was trying to remember if I had finished my homework and if I had grabbed my uniform for work, when I came to a grinding halt. At the base of the stairs that led to the Science building stood two familiar figures, and my stomach dropped all the way to my toes. Adam was nodding his head enthusiastically and a familiar blond was using his hands to dramatically gesture, making Adam throw back his head and laugh.

It wasn't good that Asa was here, and it was even worse that he had somehow picked out Adam as someone tied to me. I narrowed my eyes at my brother when he turned around and caught sight of me. He grinned and showed all his teeth, and I immediately knew he was up to something. This was his good-ole-boy act and it was designed to be charming and beguiling, while he robbed his victim blind or left a path of destruction in his wake.

"What are you doing here?"

I tried not to flinch when he wrapped an arm around me, and gave me what was supposed to be a brotherly hug. I knew Asa, and this was his way of warning me to play along or there would be consequences.

"Well, you've been so busy with school, work, and all your friends, I figured I would just come see where my baby sister is spending all her time. I ran into this here fella and he mentioned you guys were pretty close. I told him it was good that you had a gentleman keeping an eye on you, that you deserve only the best."

I glared at him out of the corner of my eye and dug my elbow into his ribs until he let me go. "I told you I was busy. I don't have time to entertain you." I stared at him until he was forced to look away. I didn't want him here and whatever he thought he was doing with Adam was stopping right now. "I'm already late for class. We can touch base later."

I wanted Asa on the first plane back to Kentucky.

Adam touched my arm lightly and gave me his typically friendly grin. "I have some free time. I can show your brother around campus while you're in class, if you want."

Oh hell no, that was the last thing I wanted. Adam was too nice of a guy to be left alone with Asa. My brother was working some kind of angle and I needed to figure out what it was.

"No, that's okay." I said it at the same time Asa chirped, "That'll be great."

We glared at each other out of matching amber eyes. Before, all I had ever wanted was for Asa to protect me, and to take care of me because we were family. I wanted him to see and appreciate the sacrifices made for him. It was only now that I understood that blood didn't make family and that sacrifice didn't matter. I had made bad decision after bad decision time and again for my brother, but now I had my own life and my own path, and he wasn't going to screw it up or drag me back.

Adam must have sensed the tension building between

us, because he cleared his throat and rubbed a hand across the back of his neck. "Well, I'm going to get some coffee. Asa, it was nice to meet you and if you want, the offer of a tour is open, but I'll let you guys figure it out. Ayd, I gotta say it's good to see you, you look good."

I sighed and grabbed my brother's arm as he made a move to follow Adam. "Thanks. It was nice to see you, too."

I held on to Asa until Adam disappeared, then jerked him around so that we were face-to-face. I poked him hard in the center of the chest and was satisfied to see him wince.

"What. The. Fuck."

He rubbed his palm over the place I jabbed and narrowed his eyes at me. "What happened to all those Southern manners you used to have?"

"What are you trying to pull, Asa? I already told you I'm not going there with you anymore. If you think Adam is a pawn, then you are wrong. He's smart and he's broke. College students don't have any money."

He pushed his blond hair away from his face and propped his hip on the stair rail. I saw a couple of younger girls check him out and wanted to scream at them that guys like Asa were poison, and that they should have a natural defense mechanism to warn them away from men like him. He grinned back at them and then turned to me with nothing but cold calculation in his eyes. This was the Asa I knew. This was the brother that I had fought so hard to separate myself from.

"He might be broke, but his family isn't, and that boy is head-over-heels in love with you. When I told him I was your older brother, I think it was all he could do not to ask for your hand in marriage."

I took a step back, like he had physically struck me, and blinked my eyes. "It's not like that between us. We had a casual thing going on but it's over."

"Over for you, not even close for him. He doesn't even care that you're hooking up with the guy in the band. I bet he thinks it's just a phase. After all, what girl can resist a guy in a band, right, Ayd?"

I had to concentrate on my breathing. The fact that he knew about Adam was bad, and the fact that he knew about Jet was worse. I felt my hands curl into tight fists at my sides.

"What is going on, Asa? For real? I'm not playing games with you anymore and if you don't come clean with me, I have no problem letting several very large, very tattooed guys know that you were behind the break-in at my house. I swear it won't end in a way you like."

He narrowed his eyes at me because he hated being threatened, and being threatened by me was just unheard of.

"I told you I was in trouble."

I crossed my arms over my chest and tried not to shiver. "What kind of trouble?"

"I took something that didn't belong to me and now some really bad, really pissed-off people want it back."

Now there was no stopping the shiver. "What did you take?"

Eyes that matched mine flared with genuine fear and I felt my stomach turn into a cement brick.

"Let's just say it wasn't something I can easily replace."

I figured he meant drugs or money and that meant the people were not bad, but really bad. Once again he was in a situation that was going to lead to the jail or the grave.

"How much money?"

He didn't answer for a long time. He looked at something over my head for a solid five minutes before letting his gaze settle back on mine.

"Twenty thousand."

I wanted to throw up. It felt like a punch in the gut. I squeezed my eyes closed and concentrated on breathing in and out slowly.

"Oh my God!"

"I'm in deep, Ayd. They're going to kill me if I don't do something."

"So you're first thought was, of course, to come screw up everything I've worked so hard to build here. It was to come ask me to bail you out like I always do, no matter what that meant for me?"

"We're family, we take care of each other and do what we have to do to survive."

I gritted my teeth. "Yeah, only that always meant I had to take care of you, Asa. I'm done. I'm not sleeping with anyone to keep you from getting your legs broken, because that is the only option. I'm not hanging out with guys that are too old for me, or only interested in using me to get you in the door anymore. I'm not doing lines of coke to numb myself and forget how crappy doing all the things I used to do made me feel. I've got a good thing going on here and I'm not going to let you or your idiotic choices mess it up."

He scowled at me. "You won't help me, but you'll sleep around with any guy who can play the guitar?"

It was as close as my brother, my flesh and blood, had ever come to admitting that he had some kind of idea of the deplorable things I'd taken upon myself to do in order to keep him in one piece. It made me feel worse about it than I normally did, and I had beaten myself up over the truly awful decisions I'd made back then on a regular basis.

I poked him in the chest again and got in his face. "I sleep with *who* I want *when* I want, Asa. You have no right to say anything, after everything I've done for you. I'll tell you one time: leave Jet alone. He isn't a nice guy like Adam. He isn't stupid, and the bumpkin act you have going on isn't going to fool him."

He jumped off the stair and glowered up at me. "Oh yeah, and how do you think all your fancy new friends are going to feel about Good-Time Ayd? Do any of them know what you used to do for fun, how you used to get by? Do any of them know where the real you came from, or do they all just see the polished version and take it at face value? Even if Rocker Boy is cool with it, what about the rest of them? Could he still look at you the same if the rest of them decided you were nothing but trailer trash?"

I sucked in a breath and rocked back on my heels. That was exactly what I was afraid of, but it was a cut that went miles deep coming from him. Half those trips around the block had been because of him because I was forever wanting to save him. Most of the things that I wanted to keep buried now were because of him. To this day I still never had concrete proof that Asa had any idea of the lengths I had gone to to keep him alive and breathing. And if he did know, how he could dare ask me to give him even more. And if he didn't know, the fact that he never asked any questions about it was frankly just as heartbreaking. I loved my brother, and I liked to think somewhere in someplace inside he loved me back, but I just wasn't sure and that's why I could never trust him fully.

I pulled the cloak of indifference that I had been building since the last time I saw Woodward around me and headed up the steps so I could go to class without bothering to engage him further. I was pissed because the class was now almost halfway over.

"It doesn't matter. What I'm doing with Jet is none of your business, and I have no intention of being invested enough to let my past matter or not. Stay away from Adam, and stay away from me. If I can think of a way to help you with the money, I will, but this is it, Asa. I'm not doing this with you or for you. I think it would kill me to have to bury you after everything I've done for you, and I deserve better than that."

"I don't have a whole lot of time for this to happen, Ayd, so even if you can't help I still have to figure something out."

"I guess you should have thought about that before you decided to rip a bunch of criminals off."

He put that smile on again that made my skin crawl. "A leopard can't change its spots, sis. Maybe it would do you some good to remember that."

I watched him walk away and felt like the world was

shifting under my feet. Asa was ruthless—he was a survivor and he didn't care who he hurt or who he stepped on to get what he wanted. I needed to come up with something fast or he was going to systematically dismantle my entire life here in Denver.

I let out a startled yelp when a hand landed on my shoulder. Shaw held up her hands in surrender and laughed at me.

"A little bit jumpy, are we?"

I groaned and shoved my hands through my hair. "Yeah, you could say that."

Her bright green eyes sharpened with concern. "Is everything all right?"

She was my best friend. She loved me and I knew she wouldn't judge me. Only letting her all the way in, letting her have access to all the dirt and vitriol Asa brought up, froze me solid from the inside out.

"Yeah, I guess I'm just on edge still. You know, keeping both eyes open and all that."

"It's probably better to be safe than sorry."

I nodded absently and resigned myself to the fact I was going to miss class and have to figure out a way to get my hands on a whole lot of money really fast.

"What's been going on with you?"

She rolled her eyes and tucked her long hair behind her ears. "Still arguing with Rule about the house. I told him that I would love to move into one with him, if he let me put down half of the down payment. He lost his mind."

I followed her up the stairs and let her talk while I nodded and listened sympathetically. We stopped outside the classroom for my next class and I tugged on the end of her braid to get her to take a breath.

"Shaw, think about this from his perspective for just a second. This is a guy who has a hard time making bonds with anyone, has a hard time committing to anything, and he wants to buy you a home. You offering to pay for half of it makes logical sense to me and you, because you have more money than God, but to him it's taking something he's trying to do for you, for the two of you together, and making it less important. Besides, it's money that comes from your folks, who *hate* him, and he wouldn't want to accept a freaking penny from those people after the way they've treated you. He wants to do this *for* you, Shaw. Why shouldn't he take care of you? You loved him unconditionally for years and years. Can't this be your reward for that?"

She blinked at me with big eyes and then groaned. "Well, crap. Why didn't I see that?"

I laughed. "Because you're trying to prevent yourself from being hurt. That boy would rather chew off his own arm than hurt you again. Just chill out and enjoy loving each other."

She raised a pale brow at me and pushed open the door to the classroom. She already had her phone out and was texting Rule. I really wanted what was best for them. They had had a hard road and deserved a break.

"Where did all this romantic insight suddenly come from? Did Jet get under your skin or what?"

Jet was under more than just my skin. He was doing things to me that were downright scary, and with Asa loom-

ing in the background, I needed to get it all together or risk
it exploding in painful bits and pieces around me. I needed
the control, the firm hand on my life I had maintained since
landing in Denver years ago. I needed to remember that I
was the one in charge of my fate, not Asa and not Jet.

"Jet is a lot different from what I really thought he was.
There's a whole lot there I never really anticipated or fully
appreciated." I wasn't just referring to what was in his pants,
either.

Shaw was smiling at whatever had come back at her on
her phone, but she answered me anyway.

"It's really easy to think that these guys are just one way
because of how they look and how they talk, but once they
let you in it's an entirely different ball game."

I sighed and dug a pencil out of my bag. "I really like
him, Shaw. I mean *like* him. He sings to me at night and it
makes my heart hurt. The way he looks at me, I feel like he's
trying to pull me apart and put me back together in an even
better way."

Her mouth fell open a little. "Wow."

"I know. I'm not ready for any of that with him."

"Why not? If he makes you feel that way, why wouldn't
you just jump in with both feet?"

"Because then I wouldn't be in control of what's happening between us anymore."

She was going to say something back, but had to stop
because the professor started class and we had to pay attention. My life felt like it was suddenly spinning out of control. All I wanted was to build myself a rock-solid road to the

future, a way to never end up back where I was. Now not only was my past staring at me like a loaded gun, but my future was tied up with a guy who didn't care about security and stability, but made me feel like I was the only thing in the world that mattered to him. It was confusing and stressful, and the more time I spent worrying about it, the heavier that brick of cement in my gut got. Jet was a great guy, but the problem was, I wasn't exactly a great girl, and I just didn't know if I was ready for him to know that. I knew for sure I wasn't ready to turn the reins of whatever our relationship was or wasn't over to him.

After class was over, I knew Shaw wanted to rehash what we had been talking about, but I needed to go there like I needed a hole in the head, so I bolted when she was distracted by a classmate asking her about an assignment. I had bigger problems to tackle, like where in the hell I could come up with money for Asa. Realistically, I knew I could ask Shaw for help. She might not have that kind of money just lying around, but she was the only person that I knew who could more than likely come close to getting her hands on it. I had about five grand in savings, but it went quickly between school and rent, and there was no way that would be enough to keep Asa breathing, if he was in as deep as I thought or it was as bad as he was hinting at.

I had two more classes and was scheduled to work a closing shift, but I needed to get ahold of my mom to make sure she was okay. I called her twice but it went to voice mail, and I tried not to panic. It made my skin crawl that Asa could be so reckless and so thoughtless as to how his actions affected everyone around him. I had hoped and prayed that when I left Woodward, I was leaving behind all the awful things my brother dragged around with him.

Shaw sent me a text that let me know, in no uncertain terms, that we were not finished talking, and I started to dread having to work my shift with her. I wasn't sure what to do about Jet, and trying to explain things to her wasn't helping me figure it out. I was running across the parking lot because I was late again and needed to get downtown, when my phone rang. Since my mom was finally calling me back, I ground to a stop and answered her with a breathless, "Hey, Mama."

"Why have you been calling me all day, Ayden? I'm busy."

That was my mother—perpetually stuck at sixteen years old and knocked up. I don't think she had ever emotionally matured beyond that.

"Did you know Asa was coming to Denver?"

"Of course I did. He misses you and wanted to see you."

I had to bite my lip to try not to swear at her. "No, Mama, he owes some people back home a lot of money. He's here so I can help him, as usual."

"Asa is a good boy, Ayd. It's good to help your brother."

It was always the same thing. Every time he went to jail, every time he had thugs pounding on the door, every time he used me or used her, he was always just a good boy in her eyes and that would never change.

"All right, Mama. Just be careful, okay."

"You worry too much, girl. Being at that fancy school

hasn't done nothing but made you like all those folks from here you used to turn your nose up at and run circles around."

I sighed and closed my eyes and tightened my fingers around the phone. "Things change."

She snorted. "No, baby girl, people change. Things just stay the same."

That was the attitude that was going to keep her in a trailer in Woodward the rest of her life. I hung up the phone and was getting ready to climb in the Jeep and head to work when I heard my name. Shaw was running across the parking lot and talking rapidly into her phone. I tossed my stuff in the passenger seat and rounded the hood so I could meet her halfway. We worked the same shift so I assumed that she was having car problems or that something had come up with Rule and she was going to call out. What I wasn't prepared for was for her to grab my arm and gasp, "Jet's in jail!"

At first I thought she was joking. After all, I had left him snuggled up and satisfied this morning on my way to class. I couldn't figure how he had found himself in enough trouble to get arrested between then and now. I laughed a little.

"You have to be kidding."

She shook her head, blond hair flying in all directions. "No. Cora just called me. All three of the guys just left the shop. I guess he called Rowdy to bail him out but they all went. She said she had to threaten Nash with bodily harm to get him to tell her what was going on. She tried to call you, but it went to voice mail."

I looked at the screen of my phone and did indeed have two missed calls from Cora while I had been talking to my mom. I just blinked at it stupidly, while trying to piece together what was happening to my once orderly life.

"Why is he in jail?"

"She couldn't say. The guys all left in the middle of appointments and she was scrambling to reschedule and hold down the fort. Do you want me to take you to the police station? You look a little pale."

I didn't know what I wanted to do. I wanted to run away to a place where Asa was back in Kentucky, to a place where I lusted after Jet in silence and pretended that I could make a relationship with Adam work out. I shook my head and turned back to the Jeep.

"If he wanted me there, he would have called me and not Rowdy. I need to get to work."

"Ayden?" I could hear the question in her tone, but I just held up a hand. I needed some sense of normalcy, some kind of pattern that I was accustomed to, back for just a second.

"Not now, Shaw. I'll talk to him when I get home. I don't know what's going on with him, but if it was bad enough to get him arrested, chances are the boys are a better fit for him right now than I am."

She frowned at me, and for the first time since we had met when we were freshmen, I could actually see her judging me and finding me lacking. "I don't know that I agree with that, Ayd."

I just shook my head at her. "Well, it isn't up to you. I'll see you at work."

I saw her knit her brow in confusion as I pulled out of the parking lot and headed toward the bar. My mind was spinning in a million different directions and I was having a really difficult time putting all my thoughts in their assigned boxes. I was worried about Asa, worried about Jet, and maybe, more important than either of those things, I was worried about myself.

I could feel the control slipping away, feel the walls I had erected to prevent these very things from happening start to crumble, and I was holding it all together by only the skin of my teeth. Who I was and who I wanted to be were being torn into separate parts, and the me that was left was vulnerable and raw. I had no idea how to stitch it all back together again, or even if I wanted to.

CHAPTER 10

Jet

I SHOULD HAVE KNOWN when my mom called me hysterical and crying that it wasn't going to lead to anything good. Normally, she was too beaten down, too cowed to do anything other than be dejected and disheartened. Not today. Today she was sobbing and rambling on and on about how Dad was going to kill her, and while I would have much rather been basking in the afterglow of some very fine morning sex time, I was instead frantically pulling on pants and rushing across town to see what the hell was going on over there.

I brought the car to a screeching halt in front of the house and ran up the stairs like the house was on fire. I didn't bother knocking, just shoved the front door open, and before I could stop to get my thoughts in order or do a thorough survey of what exactly it was that I was dealing with, my dad came barreling out of the kitchen and knocked me back out the door. I landed with a dull thud on the cracked concrete of the sidewalk and saw stars for a second as my head banged hard on the ground. Before I could get my wits about me, or even get my hands under myself to get up, my dad launched himself at me, and his fist connected with the side of my face. I felt the skin on my cheek split wide open and jerked just in time to avoid the blow that would have surely broken my nose. I grabbed at his flailing fists and felt my stomach turn over when I smelled the stale booze and pungent fury coming out of his every pore.

We were about the same size, only I was sober and had been in enough fights in my time to know how to get the upper hand. I shoved him off me and scrambled to my feet, so that I was looking down at him. I poked at my bloody face and glared down at him.

"What the fuck, old man?"

He started to yell something at me, but my mom chose that moment to come running down the stairs. She was a mess. Her shirt was torn and her hair was everywhere, but what made me see red, what made the fire I tried so hard to contain burst forth in an eruption of flame and rage, was the fact that not only did she have a black eye, but also a split lip and tear tracks running down her too pale face. It was clear that, whatever had set my dad off on his drunken rampage, I wasn't his first victim of the day. She was wailing that we had to stop, that we needed to go inside before the neighbors called the police, but I didn't care.

I spit out some of the blood that had trickled from my cheek to the corner of my mouth, and told my dad, in all seriousness, "I'm going to kill you."

He staggered to his feet and glared at me like I was the one at fault.

"Kind of like you killed my dreams? If it wasn't for you and that stupid bitch, I coulda kept on doing what I wanted. Touring the world, seeing great bands. You ruined everything, you selfish little prick. I asked for one thing. Look what you made me do!"

His words made no sense and they didn't matter anyway. All I could see was my mom crying and hear her asking him to stop. There was no stopping it anymore. The flames were raging and I didn't care if they burned him to a charred remnant of himself.

He was still pretty loaded, so when I hit him he went down easily. I heard my mom scream my name from somewhere really far away and felt immense satisfaction that he wasn't nearly as quick as I was. My blow to his nose landed with a gratifying crunch. I don't know how many times I hit him. I don't know who called the cops, or if my mom was crying over me or over him. It wasn't until the handcuffs clicked into place, and the cop who looked like he was the same age as me was shoving me into the backseat of his cruiser, that I realized what I had done.

My dad was lying still as stone on the walkway. His face was covered in blood and a paramedic was strapping an oxygen mask over his mouth and nose. My mom, my poor mom, in all her black-and-blue, tearstained glory, was holding on to his limp hand and telling him everything would be all right. I think something inside of me officially died when she climbed into the back of the ambulance with him to go to the hospital. The young cop gave me a steady look, like he had seen this a hundred times already today and asked, "Want to tell me what's going on?"

I sighed and let my head fall against the back of the seat. It wasn't the first time I had been in the back of a cop car, but I had a sinking feeling it was going to be the most serious reason I'd ever had had for being there.

"He hit her. Normally, he just treats her like shit, and makes her feel bad and worthless, but this time he put his hands on her. I just lost it."

The cop watched me closely. "He do that to your face?" I had forgotten about my cheek and prodded at the inside with my tongue. It still stung but it wasn't dripping blood anymore, so I didn't think it was going to need stitches or anything.

"Yeah. Sucker punched me when I first walked in the door."

My hands were starting to throb, with my knuckles undeniably split open and torn. The reality of what I had done was starting to settle heavily on my shoulders.

The cop nodded and tapped the roof of the car. "They're both saying you started it. The old man wants to press assault charges."

I groaned. I bet he would be willing to drop them the second I agreed to hook him up with Artifice and send him on tour.

"We have to take you down to the station and book you. You have anyone you can call to get you bailed out?"

I nodded and had him call Rowdy. I gave him the Cliffs-

Notes version of events and had no doubt he would bring the cavalry with him, but I had been in enough situations with the law during my misspent youth to know that no matter how quickly he moved, I was still looking at a solid day spent in lockup.

I appreciated that the cop didn't grill me or try to give me a bunch of unwanted advice on the trip to the station. I also appreciated that he didn't ask me over and over if I wanted to know how my dad was doing. I didn't want to know, and I didn't want to know what my mom had to say about it. This was the last straw. I was going to go on the European tour. I was going to look at signing with a label, if that's what the guys wanted. I was going to do it all, everything I held back on because of her. What I wasn't going to do was try to stand sentinel between my mom and that bastard anymore.

They booked me, ran my prints, took my rings and my belt, my wallet and my phone, and put me in a cell with a dude who was clearly in for some kind of drug thing. He was twitchy and kept asking me if I had a smoke, even though there was obviously no smoking when you were locked up. I sat on the hard bench and stared at the ceiling for what felt like hours. As the time passed, more people were ushered in and out of the cell, and I just kept still. I was just trying to blend into the brick walls and make this day go away.

I didn't even want to know how I was supposed to explain any of this to Ayden. We weren't exactly at the "bail your boyfriend out of jail" stage of our relationship. Hell, I didn't even know if we were at the relationship part of the relationship. Something told me this little road bump was going to go over like heavy metal at a funeral. She already couldn't see anything beyond a good time in bed with me, and the last thing I needed to do was prove her right.

It was well after dark when they were finally able to post my bail. I had to show up in court the following week for sentencing, and the same cop who had arrested me walked me to where Rowdy was waiting with a handful of paperwork. He had a serious look on his face and I could tell he wasn't happy. The cop handed me a bag that had all my crap in it and shook my hand.

"For what it's worth, I would have much rather put the cuffs on the old guy. I see it every day. I understand you were just trying to do right by your mom. Too many kids find themselves in that situation, a lot of them are much younger than you."

I just sighed and thanked him for his time.

Rowdy clapped me on the back of the neck and practically dragged me out of the station. I was surprised to see that he was alone, but as we walked to his black SUV he told me, "The cop mentioned you left the Challenger in the Heights with the keys still in it. Nash convinced Rule to go with him to pick it up and drop it off at the house. Didn't know what the old bastard might do to it."

That hadn't even occurred to me, so I muttered a thank-you and looked at him out of the corner of my eye. "Thanks for coming to get me, dude."

He brushed it off. "Whatever."

"Seriously. I'll pay you back."

"Okay, I'm about to punch you on the other side of your face. Knock it off and just tell me what happened."

I jammed my fists into my eye sockets and tried to block it out but all I could see was my mom crying and her black eye. It made me want to beat on the old man all over again.

"It was a total shit show that involved my dad throwing me on the ground, my mom with a black eye, and some pretty serious assault charges leveled at me." I flexed my hands and winced as the scrapes across my raw knuckles pulled and tugged. "I would have killed him. Seriously, Rowdy. I was so goddamn close."

He was quiet for a long minute and I thought maybe I had crossed a line in our friendship, but when he spoke, his voice was steady and there was no censure in it.

"He would have deserved it. No man should ever hit a woman."

I groaned and wanted to pull my hair out. "Now all I can think about is how long it was going on and why she never said anything. She got into the fucking ambulance with him and went to the hospital. She was bleeding and had a black eye and she went with that bastard to the hospital where she works. She didn't say a word when they put cuffs on me and shoved me in the back of the cruiser, not even 'thank you.' I'm over it, dude. Just over it."

"You need to get a lawyer."

"Yeah, I guess I probably should."

"Talk to your mom. Get her to tell them that he hit her first."

I shook my head. "That won't happen. I mean, I guess

I should have seen this coming. It's been getting worse and worse. I refused to set him up with Dario and the boys in Artifice. He wanted to go on tour with them as a roadie. Can you believe that shit? I told him no and he beat the crap out of her and then tried to whip my ass. He's insane."

"What are you going to do?"

That was the question. What *was* I going to do? Since I didn't have an answer, I just kept my mouth shut. I was glad to see the Challenger parked in the driveway. I was also glad to see that Cora's Mini was gone and so was Ayden's Jeep. I wasn't sure what I wanted to say to either of them, and now that I had the time to wash the stench of jail off and try to put my head back on right, I was gladly going to use it. I turned to Rowdy and gave him a lopsided grin that had no humor in it.

"Let the guys know I'm cool. Especially Nash. This isn't the first rodeo with my old man. I doubt it'll be the last."

"We got your back, Jet. Don't sweat it."

I nodded my thanks and jumped out of the SUV. It was closing in on midnight and I felt wrung out and dirty. All I wanted to do was strip down both physically and mentally. I felt like I should have seen this coming from a mile away, and it bothered me that I was still disappointed that it was happening to me. Before I could change my mind, before I could let guilt and anything else get in the way, I sent Dario a text to tell him that the boys and I were in for the tour. I would deal with what that meant for where I stood with Ayden later. Right now, I needed something tangible to focus on and put my energy into, and getting together an amazing set to take overseas was just the ticket. I turned the phone off before I could see what he sent me back, and wandered into the bathroom.

I dropped everything in a messy, bloodstained pile on the floor and turned the water on as hot as it would go. When the steam filled the room, I climbed in and let the scalding burn slide over my head and down over my shoulders. I wanted to wash the entire day away, but that was far-fetched because I still had a dad in the hospital and a looming court date, and no matter how hot the water was, neither of those things was simply going to wash away. I flexed my hands under the water and watched dispassionately as the dried blood swirled with the water down the drain. The slice on my face started to sting and I was going to scrub it, when the glass door to the shower opened and I felt soft hands slide around my waist and rest on my stomach. A feather-light kiss landed on the back of my neck and I felt her lay her cheek on the center of my spine.

She was all soft hands, soft skin, soft breasts, and the sweetest-sounding voice I had ever heard. All the razor-sharp edges and stabbing pain of the day bled away, piece by piece, and started to swirl down the drain with everything else. Some of the awful tension that was coiled inside me started to unwind and I put one of my battered hands over the top of her much smaller ones.

"Bad day?"

Her twang was a little more pronounced than it typically was and I wanted to believe it was because she was worried about me, and that she really did care about me in the same way I was rapidly starting to care for her. I felt her move closer to me, so that her entire front was pressed along my back. I could feel other parts of my body start to tense now, but in an entirely better way. All it took was a touch from this girl and nothing else seemed to matter.

"It wasn't one of the better ones, for sure."

She moved one of her hands up so that it was resting on my heart, which I was pretty sure she could feel pounding at her touch. The other she moved lower and it was almost enough to make me forget about what a crap day it really had been. I wanted to turn around, wanted to put my arms around her, but letting her hold on to me, letting her put me back together was what I needed right now. So I just kept my eyes closed and stretched my hands out to brace myself against the wall. I couldn't see my mom's battered face anymore or feel my dad's face break under my hands. All that mattered was Ayden, and that she could make it right, make me right.

Her fingers trailed a tingling pattern along my cock. I felt each brush, each twist of her hand on my chest. My heart pounded a rhythm that I was sure she could feel, and each time she squeezed me or slicked her hand over the ring through the tip, it thundered and I could feel her smile against the back of my neck. She moved her hand that was on my chest, so that she could run her fingers around the hoop through my nipple, and for a second I thought my knees were going to give out. She normally didn't pay any attention to the hardware I had in places she only got to see when we got naked together. The fact that she was paying extra attention to it right now, that she was just taking care of me so well, I think it was what pushed me over the edge.

She kissed me behind my ear and ran her tongue over the spike that decorated the top. Her clever hands did something with the ring at the tip of my dick that made me breathe out her name, and I knew there was no way I was going to hold out for much longer. I bit my bottom lip and thrust a rhythm into her slick hand. Her palm was soft and pliable, like she knew just what I needed in order to get all the poison out. When she clamped her strong teeth onto the cord of my neck that was straining in effort to prolong the pleasure and to wring out every single second of mindless oblivion she offered, I was done for. She laughed in a soft caress against my shoulder and I felt her rest her cheek on my damp skin. She wrung me out dry, while I panted and she patted the flexed muscles on my flat stomach.

"All better?"

I shook the water out of my face and reached out to turn off the tap. I turned around to look at her. I saw her pretty eyes get big when they landed on the gash in my cheek and I held up my hands backward so she could see the damage to them as well.

"Not even close."

She reached out to touch my face, but I jerked away before she could make contact. I didn't want her to have anything to do with all that ugliness, even if it was just a gesture of comfort and care. I pulled her to my chest so we were pressed together, all wet skin and slick bodies, and wished I could have this moment last forever. She put her arms around me and I almost choked on a sigh of relief. There was a part of me that didn't know where this girl's head was and I really thought seeing the wrecked shape I was in might be enough to make her say, "It was fun, Jet, but I don't have time for this." Instead, she put her hands on my ass and rubbed her soft cheek against the one of mine that was still intact.

"I was supposed to close, but I was worried about you so I harassed Shaw into staying for me. Everyone was freaking out."

I sighed into her hair and pushed open the shower door. I wrapped a towel around her first, which was a shame because there were very few things in life I liked more than a naked Ayden, then hooked one around my own waist. I wasn't sure if she wanted to go to my room or hers, so I followed her out of the bathroom, which had the added bonus of me getting to watch those long, bare legs the entire way. She picked my room, which wasn't a surprise. She liked when I played the guitar and worked on songs, and I think she knew that after the way today had gone, I was no doubt going to need to get something out and on paper before the night was over. I don't know how she got it the way she did, but regardless of where we went with our relationship—or nonrelationship— Ayden Cross was the one person who simply understood me. That alone was enough to make me care for her like I had never cared for anyone else. It would be so easy to fall in love with her, secrets and all.

She let the towel drop and crawled up on the dark red comforter. Those legs, that dark cap of hair and those eyes that just burned with furtive stories and every kind of entice-

ment held me entranced, and all I wanted to do was stare
at her. She watched me steadily for a long minute. I didn't
know what to say to her, so I looked at my torn-up hands
again and frowned as I flexed them open and closed.

"You didn't have to leave work early. I would have made
it until you got home."

One of her sable-colored brows went up and the side
of her mouth kicked up in a sexy grin. She leaned back on
her elbows, which made her breasts do things that any red-
blooded male on the planet would give his left nut to see.

"Stop it, Jet. I was worried about you. I debated all afternoon about coming down to the station, but figured if you
wanted me there you would have called me. I knew the boys
would take care of you in their own way, but I needed to get
to you in order to take care of you in mine. I'm going to ask
you what happened and we're going to talk about it for real,
because I see your hands, Jet. I've had them all over me and
I know that whatever got you to this point is bad. I don't see
any reason for us to have that conversation before we work
out some of that nasty stuff floating around in those eyes,
though, so get that fine ass in gear and get over here."

She tapped the bed next to her and it was enough to star-
tle a laugh out of me. I dropped the towel and let her molten
gaze travel over me. There was appreciation there and something deeper that hit me hard when I grabbed her ankle and
pulled those long legs apart. She hissed out a breath and it
was my turn to raise an eyebrow. She was pretty and polished all over. Everywhere I touched, she was smooth and
silky, and I knew she tasted like cinnamon and sugar. She

looked so right in my bed, I had a hard time remembering what it was like before she became a regular fixture there.

I ran my hands up one of her smooth legs and tickled her knee. She narrowed her eyes at me and I grinned down at her.

"What?"

"Stop playing with me."

She had a flat tummy that curved delicately in between her hip bones. I bent down and kissed her right below her belly button, and then I trailed a wet path to right above her slick folds and stopped and heard her swear at me. She threaded her fingers through my still-wet hair and bent her legs up to my ribs.

"I want to take care of you the way you took care of me." I kissed her again, this time lower, and I heard her gasp and swear at the same time. Her thighs tensed next to my head, and I ran the top of the barbell that was in the center of my tongue over her clit and felt her entire body spasm under the delicate contact. It made me chuckle, which had her pulling at my hair.

"My God, Jet, you're going to destroy my idea of what sex should be like." Good. She didn't need to know what sex was like with anyone but me from now on, and I wanted it to be better with me than it had ever been with anyone before.

I used my tongue on her again, this time deeper and harder and curled it around her, and sucked on her until she bowed underneath me and her skin quivered everywhere we touched. Her nails dug into my scalp and I brushed my bruised and torn knuckles across the velvet peak of her breast until she whispered my name again and started to come apart under my hands and in my mouth. Ayden came like she did everything else, sweet and smooth. I could eat her up all day long for the rest of my life, but she was impatient. Clearly, the taking care of each other portion of the night was over, because she wiggled out from under me and I let her shove me over so that I was on my back. I stacked my hands behind my head and watched with heavy eyes as she leaned over me to fish a condom out of the bedside table.

She was always extra careful when she worked the latex over me. I think the metal down there still kind of intimidated her. I knew she enjoyed it, loved the way it made her feel, but she was always extra gentle when she touched it, like she still wasn't sure exactly what to do with it. There were no words for how badly I wanted her to put her hot little tongue around it, to taste it, feel the metal in her mouth. Not that I could complain; she wasn't shy and I loved what she did to the rest of me. I liked it when she lost control and dug her nails into my back, when she forgot to keep a lid on all that passion and hunger that boiled and frothed between us and used her teeth just a little too hard or pulled my hair a little more roughly than I think she meant to.

She swung a long leg over my waist and rose above me. All I could see was amber glowing down at me. She dug her teeth into her bottom lip when I grabbed her hand and squeezed it hard around the tip of my dick. Both her eyebrows shot up and I saw concern flash across her flushed face. The ring throbbed in the best way possible and I smirked up at her.

"Giddy up, cowgirl."

She flushed a light shade of pink and sank down on me, which made both of us groan. We fit. That was all there was to it, we just fit. She leaned down to kiss me, and the contact of her pointed nipples on my own made both of us hiss out in pleasure. She pressed her forehead against mine and found a rhythm that had me digging my fingers into her hips and swearing under my breath. Every time she lifted up, her swollen flesh pulled and tugged against mine in a way that made me want to explode. We were both pretty sated from all our earlier fooling around, so this slow build up, this tenuous climb toward orgasm had us watching each other intently.

It was far more intimate, far more personal than any sex act I had ever been part of before. I could see it filling her, could feel her inner muscles flutter and drag against me, but it was her eyes—those eyes I wanted to drink in over and over again—that pushed me over the edge. For once I could see her, see that there was something there for me, and I pulled her over into a climax that had both of us sweating and scrambling for air and boundaries as soon as it was over.

She collapsed on top of me, crossed her hands over my heart and propped her chin on them. I moved one hand to her hair and threaded the dark strands between my fingers.

"I beat the shit out of my old man today."

I saw her eyes go to the cut on my face and linger.

"Why?"

I couldn't meet her gaze, so I looked up at the ceiling and

let the events of a lifetime drift through the pleasant after-
math she had woven around me.

"He sucks. He sucks as a parent, he sucks as a husband,
he sucks as a man, and he sucks as a human being in general. He has it in his mind that knocking my mom up somehow derailed the awesome party his life was before we came
along, and has spent years and years blaming both her and
me for it. He wants to drink and party and act like he's eighteen, all while making her feel worthless and awful. I left
home to get away from it and I've always tried to keep him
in some kind of check, but today he was drunk and he hit
her. I lost my goddamn mind when I saw it. He hit me first,
but then I saw her with a black eye, and all I could think
about was killing him. I'm pretty sure I broke his nose and
he had to get hauled off to the hospital, for a second I thought
I might have killed him, but the cops told me I wasn't that
lucky. But, the worst thing . . ."

She didn't say anything, just watched me talk and listened to my heart beating under her hands.

"The worst thing is that she got in the ambulance
and went to the hospital with him, while I got carted off
to jail. She took his side and told the cop I started it, she
blamed me. I just can't do it anymore and that makes me
feel like shit."

She lifted one of her hands and used the edge of her nail
to trace a line around my mouth, which had turned down in
a hard frown.

"The extent to which we can sacrifice our own lives for
our families has to have some kind of end point, Jet. You

can't be angry and hurt forever because she won't let you help her. At some point, you need to recognize that she made her choice, and it clearly isn't you."

Ultimately, that was what hurt the most.

"I have a court date in a couple of days. He pressed assault charges."

"He hit you first. Claim self-defense."

I would, but the fact of the matter was, had the police not shown up when they did, there was a good chance I would be facing a homicide charge instead. I sighed when she pulled my fingers out of her hair and placed a delicate kiss on each of the raw knuckles. I didn't know what it felt like to heal, but I knew enough to know that was what she was trying to do for me. It tempered some of that angry blaze that always hovered so close to the surface in me.

"We can't pick our families or where we come from, Jet. All we can choose is who we want to become in spite of them, and because of them."

I curled my palm around her cheek and ran a thumb over the pronounced bone. To me, she always looked elegant and refined, like she was something expensive to be savored and enjoyed as a reward for really good behavior. I never understood when she hinted that it might all just be a carefully crafted front.

"Why don't you ever talk about where you're from or your family? I don't mean just to me. Cora says you hardly ever say anything about what your life was like before college. Was it that bad?"

I saw the walls go up and the gates close, even though

we were still naked and intimately connected. Her mouth got tight and all the warm fuzzies I had put in her eyes dwindled. I thought she was going to try to pull away from me, so I locked my hand around her neck, under her hair and held her in place. She scowled at me but didn't try to leave. She dropped both her hands and let her head fall, so that her cheek was pressed against the snarling face of the death angel on my chest. She put her hands on my rib cage and answered the wall instead of me.

"*It* wasn't that bad, but *I* was."

"What does that even mean, Ayd?" I soothed my hand up and down the curve of her spine. No matter where I touched this girl, there was no place I felt it more than in my dick.

She huffed out a breath that made my skin pebble.

"It means I wasn't a very good person not too long ago. There were too many boys for too many bad reasons. There were drugs and a general disregard for the law and the only use I had for anyone was what they could do for me. I used whatever—and I do mean whatever—it took to get what I wanted, and I didn't care who it hurt or how it made me look to anyone. I was a mess, and the only real reason I had for being that way was because that's what folks there expected. No one thought I was smart. No one thought I was going to ever get it together enough to leave, and if one teacher hadn't taken an interest in me and forced me to get my act together before it was too late, chances are they would probably have been right."

She was describing a stranger. That person sounded so far removed from this dynamic girl draped all over me that

I couldn't even picture them in the same room, let alone the same body.

"I don't even know what to say to that. I don't know that girl."

Her thumb was skating along my ribs and rubbing at the skin stretched in between each one. It was soothing; she was soothing, and all I wanted was for her to be the balm that put out the fire in me once and for all. I could tell by her tone, tell by how she still couldn't look at me, that forever and me didn't go hand in hand in her mind, no matter how hot we were in bed, or how deeply we affected each other out of it.

"No, but she knows you. She knows you make me feel wild and out of control and that I don't ever want it to stop. She knows that because of you I feel like I'm willing to do whatever it takes to have you, and damn the consequences and whatever gets in my way. Because you get to me like no one ever has and you're more addicting than anything illegal I ever messed with in the past. Mostly, she knows that when I'm with you, all I think about is you and me, and how quickly we can find someplace to get naked, or how long it will be until I can curl up in your arms and let you sing to me. I don't think of the future, or school, or all the other important things I need to work on to have a life for myself. You could own me, Jet, and I don't want that to ever happen."

I curved my hand over her ass and pulled on her thigh so that she was sprawled over me. I needed to get up and take care of business, but I didn't want to move. The arm that had Dalí's clocks on it was wrapped around her shoulder, and once again I couldn't help but think that every minute I spent with this girl was a minute that was going to have to last me a lifetime when she was gone.

"What if it doesn't matter? What if I cared about her as much as I care about this version of you? I don't want to own you, Ayd, I just want to be with you."

She sighed and kissed my breastbone. "I couldn't even care about her, Jet, and I don't think you would be able to help it."

I wanted to tell her none of it mattered. I wanted to tell her how important she was to me. That no one besides Uncle Phil and the guys had ever taken care of me before, and that I didn't know what to do with her worrying about me. I felt like that was huge enough to make me think that I could possibly fall in love with her and want to hold on to her forever.

I wanted to tell her I couldn't see a place in my life or in my bed for anyone but her now, and that she made me feel that every love song I had ever written or sung made no sense until she came into the picture. But I didn't, because I knew she wasn't ready to hear it, and I wasn't sure what it meant to me that I was feeling it.

Just like my melting time, I was going to hold on to her for as long as I could, until the fire got too hot and burned me alive from the inside out, and she would have no choice but to watch it smolder.

CHAPTER 11

Ayden

THURSDAY NIGHT WAS GIRLS' night and had been ever since Shaw, Cora, and I had shared the house. Some nights we just got together with a bottle of wine and watched sappy movies, some nights we got all dolled up and went to a club, and then there were nights like tonight when we all just wanted to forget about whatever it was that had been crawling all over us during the week.

We went out with the sole intent of ending up destroyed and sloppy. I had learned my lesson long ago and no longer took an early class on Friday morning, because nights like this led to terrible morning-afters, and I wasn't stupid.

Shaw had picked a dive bar off Thirteenth Street that was pretty close to where she lived on the Hill. Cora and I took a cab, because it was clear that tonight wasn't going to be pretty and we both knew there was no way either of us was going to be in any shape to drive by the time the party was over. We started with a pitcher of beer, and I blamed the boys. There had been a time when we would have started with wine or margaritas, but after spending so much time with the guys, I think it was just ingrained that we now started with a cold pitcher of Coors Light. One pitcher led to two, and by the time the third one hit the table, Shaw was ready to add shots to the mix. I was a tequila girl, Shaw liked whiskey, and Cora stuck with Jäger. It didn't take long for the conversation to devolve to ridiculous topics and for our laughter to get loud and obnoxious.

Cora's two-toned eyes were huge and Shaw had a hand over her mouth to hold her laughter in. I was just staring at her because in typical Cora fashion she was explaining to us how she never could understand how the three of us could be friends, considering she had up-close and personal knowledge of our boys' junk. I lifted an eyebrow at her.

"All of them?"

She licked her lips and tilted her head to the side. "What do you mean?"

"Have you seen all of them?"

Shaw gasped on a laugh and pushed my shoulder. "Don't ask her that."

"Why not?"

"There has to be some kind of privilege."

I rolled my eyes. "She's a body piercer, not a doctor, and I'm curious."

Cora gave me a naughty grin, and while I had to admit I was super happy she was the one who had put that ring in Jet and not some strange skank, it was still weird to imagine her with her hands anywhere near that part of him.

She ordered us another round and motioned for us to

lean in close. Shaw might have protested on principle, but I knew that gleam in her green gaze and she was just as curious as I was.

"All of them. Well, all of them except the big brother. I've only met him once, and I could tell he was way too uptight and totally not into that kind of thing. Rule has the most hardware, Rowdy has the second most, and Jet and Nash have the same amount. And let me tell you, it is no easy feat to shove a metal needle through the privates of dudes you consider your best friends. I thought Rowdy was going to faint, and Nash took a swing at me."

I had to fan myself a little with a cocktail napkin. Not too long ago, the idea of being with someone who had tattoos all over and jewelry in their privates would have made me laugh. Now I knew how hot it was, knew that no one would ever be able to do what Jet could do. There was no going back to boring and plain, and I saw by the dreamy look on Shaw's face that it was the same for her.

I tossed back the Patrón and lifted the tiny glass in a salute to Cora. "Well, on behalf of the female population of Denver, I salute you and offer you our undying gratitude. Good work, Cora."

That made them laugh, but Shaw nodded her agreement. "Yep, thanks."

"You ladies are very welcome. You know, I had to do something to help those idiots out. It's not like they would ever find good chicks with their personalities alone. They're awful."

Shaw snorted because it was no secret that Rule could be

a real ass when he put his mind to it, but I just shook my head.

"Jet doesn't need it. His personality is fine. He's wonderful."

That had both their heads swiveling in my direction and had I been sober I would have never opened that door for them. Shaw turned her bright eyes in my direction.

"So, what's the deal with all that anyway?"

I wish I knew. "No deal. We're friends, we like to hang out, and I care about him, a lot. We're just being together, nothing more, nothing less."

Only that was a big fat lie. There was entirely more. Jet had been moodier and more withdrawn since his trip to lockup. I knew part of it was his struggle to come to terms with his mom, but something else was going on that had him acting secretive and shady. Every time I walked in the room and he was on the phone, he hung up. He was spending a ton of time at the studio, and it seemed like the band was demanding way more of his time than it had since I met him. From what I could piece together, it sounded like he was planning on going back on the road and I couldn't figure out why he didn't just tell me that. It wasn't like I had any place to weigh in on it, but still, it would be nice to know how long he was planning on being gone. As much as I hated to admit it, the idea of sleeping alone while he was on the road made me feel sick to my stomach.

He also hadn't mentioned a thing about court. He had hired a lawyer and they had pushed the court date back a couple of weeks. I knew he was worried about how the judge's ruling would affect his time, but he didn't seem too concerned about the actual sentencing. I guess he figured he would get a slap on the wrist and some community service, but it concerned me that he never brought it up, or that he didn't once mention his mom and dad in the scenario. I knew he was grappling with some pretty heavy stuff and I wanted to be there for him, but he didn't seem inclined to let me.

"Did he talk to you about why he got arrested?"

I nodded. I knew Rule had the ins and outs of the real reason, but Jet was telling most people he got into a fight, so I didn't feel like it was my place to explain his family dynamics to her.

"He did. It wasn't his fault."

She shook her head and her white-blond hair cascaded around her, drawing the attention of the guys at the table across the bar. They had been casting questioning looks our way the entire night. I normally wasn't above using a well-placed smile to score a free round or two, but now, with a certain rocker in the picture, that just didn't seem right.

"It's never their fault, believe me. I've heard Rule say that over and over again."

Cora rolled her expressive eyes and leaned back in her chair. "That's because those boys scream sex and sin and a whole lot of fun, and no one ever holds them responsible for being a bunch of jackasses most of the time."

"This time the jackassary really wasn't Jet's fault. He was a victim of circumstance."

She turned to look at me and I tried really hard not to squirm.

"I can hear him sing to you at night, you know."

I felt heat flood into my face. I really wanted to change the subject, but I knew that probably wasn't going to be an option. I tried to shrug nonchalantly.

"He has a beautiful voice."

"Yes, he does, but he never used it like that before you started sleeping in his room."

I rested a hand on my throat and refused to meet her gaze. "You know, one of these days you're going to stumble into a guy who's going to knock you sideways, and it's going to be our turn to be all up in your face with the annoying and obvious."

Shaw lifted both her eyebrows and nodded. "Oh boy, I so can't wait for that."

Cora fluttered one of her small hands in the air in front of her. "You won't have to point anything out to me because I'm holding out for perfection."

Shaw and I shared a look and then both of us gaped at her. Shaw was the one who sputtered, "You have to be kidding me."

Cora shook her head. "No, I'm not."

"There is no such thing as perfect, Cora. Look at Adam. Good-looking, sweet as could be, amazing future all lined up in front of him, not to mention we had tons in common and I actually really enjoyed his company. None of that matters, because he didn't do a goddamn thing for me, and all Jet has to do is look at me, grin a little tiny bit, and I'm ready to jump him and combust on impact."

Shaw nodded vigorously. "My version of perfect tried to

beat me within an inch of my life and rape me. There is no such thing, girl. You're only going to be disappointed."

She waved us off and reached for her beer. "Jimmy broke my heart, smashed it into a hundred million little pieces. I never knew anything could hurt that bad until I found him with that girl. I'm never going through that again. I'm holding out for the guy who is perfect—no issues, no drama, and no history of emotional unavailability or instability. There has to be someone out there who just fits the bill."

She pointed a finger at me. "And Adam wore sweater vests, so clearly he wasn't right for you." She aimed the same finger at Shaw. "And you were in love with Rule forever, so even if everyone else thought crazy-pants was perfect, you always knew deep down inside that Rule was really the only one for you."

That made both of us lapse into silence, so I just sighed. "Cora, we love you, and yes, you are annoyingly right most of the time, but I just think in this case you are setting the standard too high."

She muttered something I didn't hear and tried to lighten the conversation by pointing out, "It's not like most guys are going to pass muster with the Terrible Trio anyway. They're a hundred times worse than a dad with a shotgun."

We all burst into raucous laughter that had Shaw wiping tears out of her eyes. "Aww. The big bad tattoo artists just love their little pixie."

Cora scowled and threw a damp cocktail napkin at her, which had Shaw in turn flick her straw wrapper at her. Since we were morphing into kindergartners, I decided it was time to take a trip to the restroom. We had opted for the dive bar, so I had on my cowboy boots and a denim skirt with a tight black T-shirt that had the Jack Daniel's logo on it on. It was cute, but low-key, and I was glad I wasn't trying to navigate between tables and chairs in heels, considering I was wobbly at best.

The bathroom was gross, so I took care of business as fast as I could and scrubbed my hands like I was getting ready for surgery. I was slicking on a layer of lip gloss and trying to ascertain just how drunk I was by touching the tip of my nose with my index finger, when the door to the small room rattled. I jumped away from the mirror, and hollered that I would be out in a minute, but that didn't deter whoever was trying to get in. Had I been sober, I probably would have been way more freaked out. As it was, when the shabby knob finally gave up the fight and the figure crowded into the room with me, it was all I could do to muster up some startled surprise.

I most definitely hadn't been expecting the lurking stranger that I had seen around my neighborhood, the man who I was sure had tried to manhandle Cora, to appear in this gross bathroom and be instantly up in my face. He grabbed my shoulders and shoved me against the sink. Now that only a fraction of space separated us, I no longer had a hard time placing him.

"Silas."

I said it like people said the word *cancer*, which is really what he was. Silas Anderson was all the bad things to all the bad people, and if he was who my brother was running from, then whatever Asa had told me was only half the story. The reason I hadn't recognized him earlier was that life clearly had not been kind to him since I left Woodward. He was a year older than Asa but looked like he was fifty. His skin was gross and taunt, his eyes wild and sunken, and his once decent hair hung stringy and oily around an ugly face. It was hard to believe that at one point, this guy had been considered a catch. It was equally hard to believe that at one point, I hadn't considered sleeping with him to be all that bad of a chore, if it kept him off my brother's back. Now, the idea made my stomach lurch and my head spin.

"Where's the book, Ayd? I know Asa is here. I knew that pussy couldn't resist running to you to fix his shit, like always. I need that book back now."

I tried to shake him off, but the space was too small and he was fueled by desperation and panic.

"I don't know what you're talking about." My teeth clicked together hard when he started to shake me.

"I don't know what your idiot brother told you, but this isn't small-time stuff he stumbled into. If he doesn't give the book back, these people won't just kill him, they'll take out their anger on your ma and then they'll come after you."

I got a hand on his chest and shoved him back enough so that I could wiggle toward the door.

"What are you talking about? Asa told me he owes someone twenty grand for something he took."

Silas barked a laugh that made my skin crawl. "No way. That moron jacked the little black book from one of the local MCs. It has the totals due and money owed from anyone and everyone over most of the fucking south. I don't know what he thought he was going to do with it, but now he has everyone and their goddamn mother on his ass to get it back. You know he'll sell you out faster than a greased pig to get out of this mess, Ayd. Just tell me where it is."

"Did you try to break into my house?"

He looked around the room and his eyes were buggy and wild. "Little bitch almost Tasered me in the nuts."

"You're lucky she didn't shoot you. She's from Brooklyn, and she doesn't mess around."

"Stop avoiding the question. I know he's here. I followed you around for days waiting for him to ask you to make it all better. Just like he always did."

I tried not to convulse in disgust when his eyes raked over me from head to toe.

"I don't do that for him anymore, any of it. This is his mess to clean up." I made sure my point was clear. "I don't know where he is and I don't know anything about a book."

Silas swore and I jumped when his meaty fist smashed into the dingy mirror over the sink, shattering it into a shower of glass bits.

"This isn't a game, Ayd. This is a bunch of pissed-off bikers who run drugs and guns, and they have no problem putting your entire family in the ground in the backwoods if it suits them. Asa screwed the pooch and I'm just trying to minimize the damage."

"By following me? By scaring the crap out of my roommate and trying to break into my house? This isn't Woodward. None of that is going to fly here."

I pulled the door open and glared at him over my shoulder. "I'll talk to Asa. If I can get him to hand that book over, you better make sure nothing happens to my mama. But chances are he already did something stupid with it and he lied about needing the twenty grand so he could disappear. This is Asa, you know what he's capable of."

Silas's gummy eyes skirted over me from the top of my head to the worn toes of my boots. "So do you, Ayd, and if you think for one hot second that piece of shit would be above selling your fine ass to an MC, if it meant keeping his own skin safe, than you're dead wrong and that fancy college didn't teach you shit."

I walked out the door shaking from the inside out. I had tried so hard to keep the past from interfering with my new life, tried so hard to forget about the things I'd done and the way I had lived, but it seemed like fate was bound and determined to keep right on cramming it down my throat. At that moment, I could say in all honesty that I hated my brother, hated everything he represented, and yet I was still going to have to try to figure out a way to keep him breathing. It grated that I couldn't just let him hang from the noose of his own stupidity and greed.

When I got back to the table, I wasn't at all surprised to see that we had visitors. Shaw was sitting on Rule's lap while he finished her beer, and Jet had taken up post in the seat I had recently vacated. They were all laughing at something Cora was saying, and I felt my heart sink. This was the family I had always wanted. These were the people who I could count on, who would love me through the good and the bad and not ask a thing of me in return, and all I had done was fool them into thinking I was worth more than I actually ever was.

Jet's dark gaze found mine and I tried to force a smile. There were so many questions shining out of those dark depths. I wished so badly that I could just answer a single one of them. I stopped at his side and smiled for real when his hand curled around my hip.

"What's going on?"

"We were hanging out at Rule's when Shaw called in an SOS. I figured since I was close by I could just scoop you two knuckleheads up and take you home, so you didn't have to wait for a cab."

It was sweet; he was sweet, and so ridiculously hot. Man, oh man, was he hot. His black hair was standing all over the place like it tended to do and he had on a tight, black long-sleeved T-shirt with a pentagram and cow skull on it. I'm sure it was some band logo that I had never heard of, but it looked good on him, almost as good as those painted-on black jeans he liked to wear, which were tucked into the top of his unlaced combat boots. I liked everything about him, from the silver rings on every finger to the devil spikes at the top of each ear. He looked like a rock star and I knew firsthand that those skills extended way beyond the stage. I licked my lips and felt his fingers press even harder into the soft skin on my hip.

"Well, that was awfully nice of you."

I didn't want to think about Asa, or Silas, or my mom. All I wanted to do was get somewhere alone with him and let him make me forget everything. I could fall asleep with him singing in my ear, and pretend that everything would be all right.

Rule laughed and lifted one of his dark eyebrows. The barbells made him looked wicked and sinister, and I had no trouble seeing why Shaw had been his for the taking for so long.

"You don't have to thank us. It's totally to our benefit that you're all liquored up and ready to get down to business. I told Jet on the way over, girls' night out is one of my favorite nights of the week. Shaw always comes back ready to play."

She gasped in outrage and smacked him on the forearm. The guys shared a laugh and I couldn't help but grin when she turned hot pink under the scrutiny. Playing with Jet, drunk or sober, sounded like a whole lot more fun than hanging out in the bar, so I tried to catch his eye and indicate anytime he was ready, so was I. Cora ordered one more round of shots and by the time we finished them it was way past time to go. She was draped over Jet and me, and he had to fold her small frame into the back of the Challenger. He gave us both a level look and warned that if we puked in his baby, we were cleaning it up, wasted or not. Cora found that hilarious and laughed and laughed, until I heard her gasping for air.

Jet let out a low whistle, and honked the horn when we drove past Rule's massive truck. I saw Rule flip him the bird, but it in no way deterred him from whatever he was doing to Shaw. He had her pressed up against the driver's door with her arms around his neck and her legs around his waist.

I tried not to wince when the music came blasting out of the speakers. It was so loud and so violent sounding, and I hated that it was what he related to. He turned it down with a shrug.

"Wolves in the Throne Room."

"What kind of name is that for a band?"

He shot me a look out of the corner of his eye. "An awesome one."

I snorted and settled back into the seat. We were never going to see eye to eye on musical preferences, just like I was never going to ask him to go line dancing. Plus, if he ever tried to drag me into a mosh pit, I was going to strangle him. It was a good thing we connected on so many other levels.

Cora was rambling something in the back and had flipped herself over, so that she was lying on her stomach with her face smashed into the leather seat. I jumped a little when one of Jet's hands landed on my thigh, right where the hem of my short skirt had ridden up.

"You looked stressed out when you came back to the table. Is everything okay?"

It was on the tip of my tongue to tell him all of it—Asa, Silas, and the whole ugly, sordid mess—but instead I put my hand over his and moved it higher on my leg.

"The bathroom was dirty, and I was surprised to see you. You've been really busy the last couple of days. I thought you would still be at your studio."

His thumb brushed back and forth across soft skin and climbed even higher until I had to remind myself to breathe and that we weren't alone.

"Yeah, I'm just working on getting things together."

I was drunk, but not drunk enough not to know he was being purposefully vague. "Getting things together for what?"

He sighed and went from stroking to squeezing. I shivered a little and shifted in my seat, which gave him even better access to flesh that was rapidly getting wet and ready.

"You really want to get into this now?"

I blinked at him and narrowed my eyes in irritation. "Well, I was starting to wonder if you were going to say anything at all, or just ask me for a ride to the airport one day."

His thumb hit the edge of my panties and for a second I forgot that I was working on getting pissed at him, because I saw stars.

"I'm going on tour for a couple of months."

I sucked in a breath through my teeth when I felt him maneuver the lacy material out of his way. I wanted to peek back at Cora to make sure she was still out of it, but I was scared to move, afraid I would give away all the naughty things he was doing to me.

"Why is that so hush-hush? Don't you go on tour all the time?"

He sighed again and I almost punched him, because he removed those questing fingers entirely. I snapped to attention when I saw that we were parked in front of the house. I was twisting around to help Cora out of the car, when she literally barreled over the back of the seat and scrambled across me to get out the door.

"I have to pee right now!"

She bolted for the front door so fast no one would have ever known she was close to comatose a second ago. I laughed and was going to follow her into the house, but Jet reached across me and pulled the door back closed. He turned the car off so that the radio went silent, and it was just me and him in the quiet cocoon of the front seat of his car.

"I'm going to Europe. We're going with Artifice, so it's kind of a big deal. I've never been gone for that long of a stretch before, or gone that far, because I was always so worried about what would happen to my mom. Now I have other reasons for being all torn up over it."

"Because you're worried that he might hit her again?"

"Come on, Ayd, you know that isn't what I'm talking about."

His dark eyes were even darker in the silence around us.

"Every day, I'm waiting for you to tell me it was fun, but you have better shit to do. I don't even want to tell you what goes through my head when I think about telling you that I'm going to be on the road for three months."

I bit down hard on my bottom lip. I braced one hand on his shoulder, and used that and the steering wheel to lever myself over him, so that I was straddling him in the driver's seat. I put my hands on either side of his face and leaned down to kiss him. I didn't want him to worry about me, about where my head would be, while he was gone. I wanted him to go on tour and do what he loved for once, just for himself, with none of his baggage. I slicked my tongue across his, played with the barbell in the center of it and let my teeth nip and bite at his bottom lip. I kissed him like he always kissed me, like he was the last guy on earth I would ever put my mouth on.

I ran my hands down his shoulders and looked him straight in the eye. "Are you going to sing angry anti–love songs to anyone else while you're gone?"

He coughed out a laugh and moved his hands so that they were on my ass, where my skirt had risen up to an indecent level.

"No."

"Are you going to find someone else to sing sappy old country songs to before bed?"

He stiffened because I had managed to get my hands between our bodies where we were pressed together so tightly and to snag the buckle on his belt. I wasn't so sure about having enough room to maneuver with those tight-ass pants of his, but I was more than willing to give it the old college try.

"No, Ayd. I only have ever wanted to do that for you."

He fell, hot and heavy into my hands and he must have been ready to move the show on the road, because I heard the sound of ripping fabric and felt the chilly night air hit bare skin where my lacy underwear no longer covered my backside.

"Then stop worrying about everyone but yourself. I'll be here when you get back and maybe by then I'll be ready to have this conversation you're clearly itching to have. Moment by moment, remember?"

He groaned when I leaned down to kiss him again. I was tired of talking, tired of thinking. I just wanted to get him inside me and I didn't care that we were outside in his car, when there were two perfectly good beds less than a hundred yards away. I had a much harder time ignoring Bad Ayden when he was all hot and bothered and throbbing so deliciously between my legs. The run-in with Silas and everything building with Asa had her close to prying off the lid of the box I'd so ruthlessly shoved her in.

"We need to have some kind of conversation before then, Ayden, and you know it."

He was right where I wanted him, the tip and that cold ring all against the wet and needy parts of me. I was ready to slide down, to engulf him and disappear in the sensation only he could provide, when his long fingers suddenly dug painfully into the globe of each ass cheek. I lifted my head to look down at him, needy and frustrated that he was being difficult. The sexual buzz he offered was way more intoxicating than an entire bottle of Patrón, and he was about to get hollered at if he didn't give me what I wanted like he did yesterday.

"Jet, seriously, this can wait until later."

I tried to wiggle free, tried to sink down and seat myself on him, but he had too tight a hold on me and I was stuck between his hard hands and the steering wheel.

"We can't do this here, Ayd. I don't have anything on me."

Well, that sucked. I was ready, beyond ready, and I could feel that he was, too. I kissed him again and Bad Ayden out of the box, I was just so tired of trying to keep it closed.

"Don't care."

And I didn't, at least I didn't right then. Tomorrow, I

undoubtedly would. Hell, in five minutes I would probably be in a full-blown panic, but right then, I just wanted him. It had nothing to do with the tequila swirling around in my blood. It was enough that he cared, that he was worried enough about me to put the brakes on when I could feel how hard he was, and feel that he was as close to the precipice as I was.

He was still trying to hold me off him, but it was futile. I was too buzzed and he was too hard, and there was just something a little crazy and a whole lot sexy about hooking up in the front seat of his car. There was no way we could hold out for much longer.

When I felt that cold press of metal, unfettered for once without the covering of latex, I nearly passed out. My eyes fluttered and I thought I heard him swear, or maybe he told me he loved me. Either way, it was lost in the sensations that were burning up my spine and making me pant against his throat. His hands were rough enough that I was going to have bruises, and I was so glad I'd had to foresight to put on a skirt that I wanted to give myself a high five, until he pushed me up and hauled me back down, and I couldn't even remember what day it was anymore.

I said his name over and over again because it was the only thing that made any sense to me at the moment, and I heard him growl something dirty and incoherent. I was going to lose it, going to shatter all over the place and take him with me, when he suddenly shifted under me and I felt him pull out. I was too far gone, too close to the finish line for it to matter. I shivered and quaked, broke apart all over him and heard him groan and whisper my name. When I was able to pry my eyes back open and catch my breath, all I could do was look at him with huge eyes. He kissed me on the cheek and moved around to get us back in some semblance of order. He was still hard, still pressing against me like a steel rod, and I didn't miss that he looked like he had swallowed something sour.

I grabbed his jaw with one unsteady hand and forced him to look at me. His muscles clenched and unclenched, and those dark eyes with their unholy halo did a better job of stripping me bare than anything he had ever used on me before.

"Why did you do that?" My voice was husky and sounded totally sexed-up even to my own ears.

He put his hands on my waist, and shifted me off him just enough so that I wasn't smashing that impressive erection between the two of us anymore. He let his head flop back against the seat and narrowed his eyes at me.

"I'm not going to let you use me to make bad decisions that give you an excuse to walk away from me, Ayd. When you go, it's going to have to be for a real reason, and not just because you can lose control with me when we hook up and it scares the holy hell out of you."

I didn't know what to say to that, because even through the lovely buzz I still had working, I knew he was right. In the harsh light of day, unprotected sex in the front seat of a cool car was exactly the kind of thing that would send me running from him as fast as I could. That was exactly the kind of thing I liked to think I had left well behind me. I was looking for a way to get some space between him and the new me, and the best way to do that was to let the old me finally have her wicked way with him.

I let him collect me in a hug that had the best parts of us lined back up. I didn't know what I was going to do with him in the long run. I had a sinking feeling that I was going to end up breaking his heart and mine right along with it. Right now, all I wanted to do was take care of him as well as he always took care of me.

"Take me inside, Jet." I didn't have to ask him twice.

CHAPTER 12

Jet

I KNEW SOMETHING WAS off before I even opened my eyes the next morning. Normally, there were endless legs tangled with mine and a cloud of feather-soft black hair all in my face and spread across my chest. Not this morning. She was curled on her side, facing away from me. Her hands were folded under her cheek and she had makeup smudged under her still-closed eyes.

It almost looked like at some point in the night she had been crying.

Granted she was bound to be hungover after the tankard of tequila she had drunk, and I hadn't been very gentle with her last night. But there was something else, something working that I couldn't see, but sure as hell could feel. That was the only way I had been able to stop in the car last night. It felt like there was someone standing physically between us that I couldn't reach around to get to her. It almost killed me; it had made my dick swear an unpleasant and ugly revenge on me, but I had known on some soul-deep level that all she needed was an excuse like that, a simple slip for a reason to walk away.

I was going to wake her up, kiss her bare shoulder and maybe some more interesting parts that the scarlet comforter covered, when my phone went off in an angry blast and the wailing strains of Mastodon filled the room. I scrambled to answer it before it woke Ayden, but it was too late. She moaned and grabbed her head, like that would help. By the time I answered, she had pulled the covers all the way over her face and was swearing at me in a way that would make all my boys proud.

I chuckled a little and tapped the round curve of her ass under the heavy blanket. It wasn't like Von to call before noon, but the entire band was running at full speed to get our act together for the tour.

"What up?"

There was a lot of noise in the background, the clash of angry voices, and the wail of sirens combined with my guitar player's panicked voice. A cold chill raced down my spine.

"Dude, you have to get down to the studio. Now."

I was already on my feet and searching the floor for a pair of pants.

"What's going on?"

I didn't see Ayden poke her head out of the covers, but I could feel her bright eyes watching me as I scrambled into a T-shirt and my boots.

"Someone broke in. Everything is gone."

I blinked because that didn't make any sense. "What do you mean?" I probably sounded like an idiot but my head was spinning in a million different directions. All I could think was, if my old man was involved, no court on earth was going to stop me from killing him for real this time.

Ayden swung her long legs off the bed and I distractedly watched as she got back into her clothes from the night before. Only this time, she put on my long-sleeved shirt with the cow skull on it. I shouldn't have been able to process that she looked superhot, but it was her, so I totally did.

"Everything. The instruments, the recording equipment, all of it. It's like someone backed up a truck and cleaned the place out. I called the cops, and the rest of the guys in the band, but you need to get down here since you're the owner and everything is in your name."

I shoved my free hand through my hair and grabbed my keys. Ayden snatched them out of my hand and shook her head. She mouthed "I'll drive" at me and pushed me out the door. Luckily, Cora was still down for the count, because I didn't have the time or the inclination to explain why we were running out of the house like my bed was on fire.

"Tell the cops the entire building is alarmed, and there are also security cameras, if that helps."

I saw Ayden cut me a look out of the corner of her eye that I couldn't read, but I was too busy tallying up the total loss of equipment in my head. The instruments alone were close to twenty grand, but the recording equipment and all the high-end gear that went along with it easily tripled that number. I didn't even want to start thinking about trying to replace everything in a pinch we would need in order to go on tour. The idea made my blood boil and red streaks flash before my eyes. If it was my dad, there was nothing in the world that was going to stop me from burning his entire world to the ground and dance on the bare, bloody bones of our relationship.

I heard Von repeat the information I had just given him and heard someone close by in the background swear long and loud.

"The cops want to know if everything was insured."

I snorted and tugged at my hair in frustration. "Of course it is. Even metal heads need insurance."

That startled a laugh out of him and I sighed because I was suddenly exhausted.

"It doesn't matter, though. We're going to need to replace all of our stuff, at least to make the tour."

"We can use backup equipment if we have to."

"No. We committed to the tour, committed to be a solid opening act in order to make Artifice a worldwide name, I'm not going to let Dario down. We'll just get new shit."

"Can we afford it?"

"Probably not, but it is what it is. I'll see you in a minute."

I looked over at Ayden and noticed that she was worrying her bottom lip something fierce. She must have seen me studying her, because she looked back at me and forced a smile that I didn't buy for a second. She was back to being all smoke and shadow, and the Ayden I was getting to know, the one I was pretty sure I was falling in love with, was gone, and in her place was this girl who was looking at me like we were merely strangers.

"You don't have to stick around. Just drop me off and I'll have one of the guys give me a ride when I'm done with the cops."

She didn't say anything, but I noticed her hands tighten on the steering wheel and I would have given anything to know what was going on inside that overly complicated mind of hers.

"I bet you a million dollars my dad is behind it. He's pissed that we have to go to court, that I just didn't give in and give him what he wanted. This is probably his way of getting back at me and for once it's pretty damn effective."

"You have security cameras?" The question sounded strained.

"Yeah. That equipment is expensive and the instruments are top of the line, plus I sometimes have other bands' gear stored there so I always try to keep it safe. Why?"

She wouldn't look at me but her mouth was pulled in a frown that looked like it hurt. I almost wanted to forget the cops and make her drive us somewhere quiet and secluded so I could force her to talk to me, but that wasn't realistic. She shrugged and continued to worry her lip.

"Just asking. I didn't realize how much it was all worth."

I blew out a long breath and shoved the heels of my hands into my eye sockets.

"It's not just some hobby, some band that I jam with on the weekends. It's my job, my livelihood, Ayd. Of course I took steps to protect it."

We lapsed into a tense silence. I didn't know what to say to her, and I was too wrapped up in all the nasty stuff swirling under my skin that I didn't want to lash out and make whatever was going on worse. When we pulled up in front of the studio, the building was lined with cop cars, and all the guys in the band were standing out front looking both pissed and frustrated. I put my hand on the handle of the door and flinched when her soft hand landed on my arm before I could climb out of the Jeep. Those topaz-colored eyes were as hard as the precious stones they resembled, and I knew before she said anything that whatever waited for me in that studio was going to be nowhere near as devastating as whatever she was going to say next.

"I'm so sorry, Jet. Whatever this is or isn't, I can't do it. This . . . It just isn't working for me anymore. It doesn't feel like a moment-to-moment thing anymore and I can't handle that."

I could have made it easy on her, just let it go. After all, we weren't in a relationship, but I was feeling raw and split open and she had some fucking badass timing to pull this now. I narrowed my eyes at her and shook her hand off.

"Yeah right, Ayd. You should be sorry for the simple fact that I can get you off and a douche bag in a sweater vest can't."

I saw her grimace, and she whispered my name like I had hit her. I held up a hand and shoved the door open.

"Just don't. Don't tell me whatever reason you managed to cook up after last night, because whatever it is, we both know the real reason, the real problem is that you won't even entertain the idea of letting me in. That's just fucked up because I could have fallen in love with you. Hell, I probably already did. I have shit to take care of, so I guess I'll see you around."

She didn't say my name again, and I didn't look back, but I sure as hell took massive amounts of pleasure in slamming the door shut behind me hard enough to make the entire machine rock on its chassis. Von and Catcher walked over to me, and I refused to look over my shoulder when she pulled out of the parking lot. There was a hole in my chest that Ayden had left behind. Her rejection creating a wide-open place for all that fire and burning emotion I tried so hard to control to escape from. The irony was that the only person who had ever offered any relief from the heat, and any escape from the blaze, was the one who had ripped it open and released it all. Ripped it open and left it gaping, for all that awful venom to flow into the world.

We spent hours trying to put a list together of all the lost gear for the police. They pulled the security footage and I told them not to be surprised if the image of the thief was my dad. I told them I wanted whatever charge they could come up with pressed against him. The rest of the band was stressed out and were getting on my already frayed nerves, so I shooed them off with a promise to take care of everything while I waited for the insurance adjuster.

It sucked having time to turn things over and over in my head. I had known the deal with Ayden wasn't a permanent thing, but I still felt like she had pulled my heart out of my chest and handed it back to me after deciding she had no use for it. Moment to moment my ass, it was more than that, always had been, and I never should have let her distract me

from having that conversation in the car the night before.
I wasn't sure why her switch had flipped so suddenly; all I
knew was that it hurt and I felt like she had pulled further
away from me than she'd ever been.

It wasn't fair to either of us. There had been so much
tension, so much attraction, that I should have known all
along that just sex was never going to work out between us.
But something told me that if all those months ago, I had just
taken her up on her offer, I wouldn't be in this mess now. If
I had gotten her when those defenses were down, there was
a chance I could have gotten under the wall before she built
it back up. Now it was too late, and I was just going to have
to focus on figuring out the current mess and act like yet
another woman I cared so much about hadn't picked something else in life besides me.

By the time the adjuster finally showed up, I had worked
myself up into a state of vibrating rage. I was pretty sure
the guy was terrified to walk into the empty building with
me, but considering it was his job, he didn't have a choice.
All that was left of my gleaming and shining equipment was
a tangle of useless black cords and the swivel chair I sat on
in the booth. The pictures of the band and the posters used
to decorate the walls hung haphazardly and a lone Coors
Light can was on its side, leaking onto the floor. The studio
was empty and hollow and looked like a dump, and totally
reflected how I was feeling inside.

After emailing a bunch of pictures I had of the instruments and the recording equipment on my phone to the
adjuster, who couldn't get away from the murderous vibes I

was throwing off fast enough, I slowly paced back and forth in the stark and empty space while rubbing my temples. All I could see was the barren landscape, and all I could feel was the place inside that was hot and smoldering in a dangerous way.

Before I knew what happened, something at the core of me broke loose. It was like when I had witnessed my mom with the black eye, only this time it was my future that was broken and battered. It was the one thing I had ever loved that had unconditionally loved me back, and it had fallen at the hands of some unknown abuser as well. I let out a scream that bounced off the walls, and picked up the only furniture left in the place and hurled it through the glass that surrounded the recording area. A million shards cascaded all over the floor and tinkled against my ears. I pulled all the remaining pictures off the walls, tore the posters down, and reopened all the wounds on each and every knuckle until blood dripped off the tip of each finger. I kicked the Coors Light can across the floor, spilling stale beer in every direction and I tore all the cords and plugs out of the wall and threw them into a pile on the floor. I made a mess. By the time I was done I was panting and sweating, and the fury that was scorching inside me had subsided to a manageable level. I wanted to hit something, to tear someone apart, so I put my hands on my knees and bent over to catch my breath before the heat burned my vision black.

I don't know how long I was like that, but when a low whistle echoed through the now-barren space, it startled me enough that I jerked and whirled around ready to fight. Rowdy had his hands in the pockets of his jeans and those ocean-colored eyes were sympathetic as they roamed the devastation, made worse by my current state of freak-out.

"What are you doing here?"

I didn't mean to sound surly and ungrateful, but it was the crap day to end all crap days and I didn't have one ounce of play nice anywhere in me at the moment.

"Ayden called me. She gave me the rundown. She thought you might need a friend, or someone to box with. I'm here to fill either roll."

I swore at him and finally just collapsed on the floor. Some of the broken glass from the booth poked into the denim covering my legs but I couldn't muster up the energy to care.

"She also tell you that she bailed on me? Left me hanging because it is what it is and she doesn't want it to be anything anymore?"

He was looking around, taking everything in, and I could tell by the set of his mouth that he knew how bad it was, how hard it was going to be to pull everything together before the tour.

"No, but she sounded like shit, so I figured something must have happened."

I snorted and closed my eyes for a second.

"I told her I was going on tour, told her I could love her, and I stopped her from having seriously awesome, bare-back sex in the front seat of the Challenger. Then she effectively dumped me, right after I got the call that all my worldly possessions had been stolen. Today can suck it."

"She give you a reason why?"

"She didn't have to. It's not like we were dating or in a relationship or anything solid like that."

"That doesn't sound like Ayden."

My heart squeezed so hard in my chest I actually had to rub the area with the palm of my hand to relieve the pressure.

"Well, I'm the one sitting here feeling like I got kicked in the nuts and then run over by a truck, and I'm pretty sure it was a whiskey-eyed brunette who did it. So, yeah, that sounds just like Ayden."

He shook his head and not a single blond hair moved out of that fifties style he liked to slick it up into.

"I just think it's probably more complicated than that. She sounded as torn up as you look, and any idiot that gets within a few feet of you two can feel that there is something powerful there. Hell, I saw that the very first time you laid eyes on her at the Goal Line and I was trashed."

"Sex." I blew out a breath. "We have awesome chemistry and really hot sex, that's all it is, all she ever wanted it to be."

"I just don't think that's the entire story."

"Well, that's the one she's telling, and now I've got all this to figure out, and court, and my fucked-up family. I don't have time to try to do revisions or rewrites."

He toed the crumpled can that had faced my wrath earlier.

"Do you think your dad had something to do with this?"

"Who else could it be? He's too arrogant to ever ask about what I'm doing, so I doubt he knew about the security setup."

"Maybe if you have him on tape you can use that to get him to drop the assault charges."

"If I have him on camera, I'm putting his dumb ass in jail

for as long as I can. I'm not scared of community service or anger management classes, but if I can get him locked up for at least as long as I'm on the road, then I'll know he won't be able to put his hands on Mom while I'm gone."

"Good point." He put his hands on his hips and took one final look around the destruction.

"Do you want to stay here and sulk some more, or do you want to go find some dark bar to sit in and get wasted?"

What I really wanted to do was go get my guitar and find someplace quiet and alone where I could write the saddest songs ever, about a girl who simply didn't want what I had to give her. That sounded more dangerous than drowning myself in Jameson, so I took the beefy hand he offered and let him pull me to my feet.

"Bar it is."

TWO THINGS BECAME APPARENT as soon as I pried my eyes open the next morning.

The first was that I didn't have any pants on, and the second was that trying to drink an entire bottle of whiskey in order to forget a girl with whiskey-colored eyes was a terrible idea. I groaned and tried to turn my head, only to have pain and a starburst of bad ideas explode in every direction. Luckily, I could feel the leather material of the couch sticking to my bare legs, so I didn't have to shove out an exploratory hand to make sure I was alone. I was all for drowning my sorrows, but going home with someone else just for spite didn't seem right or fair to the other party. I was grateful that while he hadn't seemed to care that I wanted to punish my liver, Rowdy had seemed to keep my hurt feelings out of my pants, wherever those might be at the moment.

It took me a solid five minutes to roll over and another ten to work up the courage to open my eyes. When I did, all I could do was groan and swear that I was never going to drink like that again. As usual, it was a vow I ended up breaking as fast as I could.

I heard Rowdy moving around the kitchen and I heard the tinkle of female laughter, so I made the Herculean effort to sit up and try to find my pants. I was in no state to be nice to whoever he had brought home from the bar with him, and I most assuredly was in no shape to do that in just my boxer-briefs. A groan escaped me and a herd of hippos started to river-dance behind my eyes when I swung my legs over the edge of the couch. I heard him and his friend walking toward me, but there was nothing on earth that was going to make me move any faster.

I gratefully took the mug of coffee Rowdy handed me over the back of the couch, and tried not to grimace as I tossed back the handful of painkillers he dropped in my hand. I tried to avoid the curious gaze of the blonde walking to the door. She was good-looking, at least I thought she was from what I could see through the haze of my hangover, and I vaguely remembered her and a friend joining us at some point in the night. She gave me a smile that I didn't have the faculties to return and looked over at Rowdy, who had propped a hip on the back of the couch and was outright laughing at my sorry state.

"Too bad he was such a bummer. Heather would have loved to get her hands all over that."

Considering I was mostly naked, I just closed my eyes and fell back against the couch cushions and prayed for the morning-after gods to swallow me up. I heard Rowdy chuckle and the front door open and close. None of us were strangers to the one-night stand, and this one had made less of a scene than some of them were prone to. It sucked that I was the one feeling like I had been caught doing the walk of shame, and I hadn't even slept with her.

"What the hell happened last night?"

Rowdy moved off the back of the couch and plopped his big frame in the recliner across the room. His eyes were serious and he didn't look amused, so I wondered if maybe he had had to work a little harder to get the blonde to come home with him, considering what a train wreck I had been.

"You never told me you were in love with Ayden."

I blinked in surprise, which made my head throb. I would have frowned but something told me that was going to kill me, so I just tilted my head a little to the side and watched him cautiously.

"What are you talking about? I told you I was all jacked up over her."

He shook his head and pointed a finger at my face. "Jacked up is not the same thing as being in _love_. Why in the hell did you just let her walk away yesterday?"

"I still don't know what you're talking about." That was a lie, but I didn't know where he was getting his information from, so I wasn't ready to admit defeat just yet.

"Jet." He sighed so deeply I could practically feel his exasperation through the floorboards. "You drank your weight in whiskey last night. For most dudes, that would mean you spent the night puking in the john or passed out in a yard somewhere. You, my friend, spent the night telling anyone who would listen about a girl with whiskey-colored eyes who just broke your heart. When that wasn't enough, you told a very nice, very pretty girl who happened to think it was sweet and romantic that you were acting like a love-sick fool, that you were never having sex again because you weren't a stud for hire, and that if it took a sweater vest to make her love you, then you would just argyle it up.

"Said hottie was still willing to come home with you, and, in fact, had her hand almost down the front of your pants, when you called her Ayden, not once, not twice, but three freaking times. Then she just thought you were sad. You were a mess, still are, and I don't get why, if you feel that way about a girl who obviously has some pretty intense feelings for you as well, you're just letting her slip away."

I was in no mood for this kind of heart-to-heart. In fact, I was in no mood to think about Ayden or anything that had happened yesterday at all, but Rowdy wasn't going anywhere and it wasn't like I was in a hurry to go back to the house and face either her or Cora.

"She's always running away. She tells me over and over again that I really don't know her and she made it pretty clear, even as far back as last winter, that all she wanted was a quick hook-up. I don't have it in me to be someone's mistake. Look what that did to my mom.

"I'm going to go on this tour. I'm going to write an entire album of songs about how shitty it feels to get your heart two-stepped on by a chick with mile-long legs and cowboy boots, and then maybe when I get drunk enough, I'm going to take a hot Spanish girl to bed and let her whisper all kinds of things I don't understand in my ear."

We stared at each other for a long time and I grunted when he tossed me my pants from the other side of the room, and they hit me in the center of my chest.

"I think you're an idiot for believing that any of those things are going to help. I think you should just tell her how you feel. I think you should demand to know exactly why she can't handle more than that right now. Your mom accepts the blame for your dad's unhappiness, and she feeds into it, letting him act like the lunatic he is. Ayden is just convinced she needs something different, and if you could show her she was wrong, I think it would save the both of you a lot of unnecessary heartache. Besides, you don't speak Spanish."

It took way more concentration than it should have to get the first leg into the tight denim.

"That doesn't matter. I'm in a band. That language translates across all barriers."

He shook his head at me and pushed up out of the recliner.

"What are you going to do about her until you leave? You do recall you live across the hall from her, right?"

I froze, because I hadn't thought of that. If she brought someone home, some guy with a blazer and an attaché case, some guy with perfectly coifed hair and nerd glasses, some guy that was the opposite of me, there was a good chance the rage exploding out of me would burn the house to the ground, and all the relationships that lived inside with it. Even if she didn't bring anyone home, there was still bound to be an awful awkwardness between us that was enough to make me shiver. Throw in Cora's big mouth and tendency to pick at any open wound for her own amusement, and the next few weeks would be a nightmare.

I knew Rowdy would let me crash on the couch for as long as I wanted, but I had no desire to watch his parade of his morning-after castoffs. Normally, I would have just posted up at the studio, but seeing it all broken and stripped down was too much for me to take right now. Nash and Rule didn't have any room, and while I could couch surf from place to place with the guys in the band, I needed a solid home base to operate from until the replacement stuff for the tour was locked down. That meant I was just going to have to suck it up and face my gorgeous tormentor head-on, like a grown-up.

"I guess I'll just deal with it."

"You're going to have to keep it in your pants. Cora won't let you drag groupies home regardless of the fact that it was Ayd who called it quits. She'll claim she's just protecting her."

I swore. "I'm not in the market for a horde of groupies right now."

It was true. Anonymous sex with nameless and faceless girls had served its purpose in my life, but now I could see how hollow and shallow it was. Being on the receiving end of being used for a sexual outlet, and nothing more, gave me

an entirely new appreciation for all the chicks I had mercilessly skated out on the morning after. It was the reason I
had initially turned Ayden down for so long ago. Even then,
I knew one night with her had the ability to ruin me.

"Jet, I'm going to tell you this because I really think the
two of you have something that could be forever. When you
find someone, someone who gets you, who understand you,
it's worth fighting for. The last thing you want to do is be five
years down the road and look back and wonder what could
have happened. Trust me, that kind of regret, that kind of
what-if, can gnaw on your soul until there is nothing left."

I looked at him like I had never really seen him before.
Rowdy was the fun one. He was the one who was always
quick to suggest a bar or the after-party. He was the one
who came equipped with a joke and easy smile. In all the
years we had been friends, all the times we had drunkenly
spilled our deepest and darkest secrets, he had never hinted
at something like that in his past.

"Are you speaking from experience?"

He just stared back at me and shrugged. Clearly it wasn't
a subject he wanted to delve into deeper, which was probably a good thing, considering I still smelled like the inside
of a whiskey bottle and my head pounded like a drum solo
from a Slayer song.

"Look, dude, I get that your mom and dad gave you a
messed-up idea of what a solid relationship looks like, and I
know none of us are going to get gold stars in the monog-
amy and happy-ever-after department. But I think you can
see meant-to-be when it's staring you in the face."

I knew that what he was saying to me had validity threaded through it, but I just couldn't reconcile trying to be who Ayden figured she needed in order to be happy, with the guy I really was and planned on being forever. I just didn't think there was any way for us to be together when she wouldn't let me all the way in, and I couldn't get the fire inside me all the way out. Not that together was an option for either of us anymore.

CHAPTER 13

Ayden

ONE MORNING YOU JUST wake up and realize the way things have always been doesn't mean that's the way they have to always be. I was so used to being called a whore, a slut, white trash, and all the things that just went along with the life I was living, that it didn't even occur to me until it was almost too late that leaving the place where I was that girl would mean leaving all of that behind. From the minute I crossed the state line out of Kentucky, the Ayden that was lost and so accustomed to being used and using was gone. Normally, I don't miss anything about her, but lately that hasn't been the case."

I was squeezing the cup of coffee between my hands and staring into the dark liquid like it held all the answers to every question the universe had ever asked. I could feel Shaw's bright gaze picking me apart and dissecting me, but so far she had kept her mouth shut and just let me talk. We were in the corner of a coffee shop down by the school, and I could tell by the stiff way she was sitting that she wasn't exactly happy with me. I had called her in a panic yesterday and she had agreed to the outrageous favor I'd asked, with the one condition that I come clean about every sordid detail of why I was currently in the horrendous situation I was in.

"I never knew my dad and, frankly, I don't think my mama really knew him either. We lived in a crappy trailer on the poorest side of town that really only has a poor side, and it wasn't uncommon for her to bring strange men home, or for all of us to go without food or lights for long stretches of time. Now, looking back I understand that she did what she had to do to keep a roof over our heads, which could very well be why my brother, Asa, turned out the way he did. People aren't people to him, they're just a means to an end, and for a long time, I was his favorite pawn to get those ends to meet."

I could feel shame burn in the back of my throat, but those tears had long since fallen, and if I was going to cry now, it was going to be for the absolute look of betrayal, of disappointment that had crossed Jet's face, without my even having to say a word.

"I was young and stupid, and at first I thought it was so cool that all my brother's older friends wanted to hang out with me, and wanted to hook up with me. I thought I was popular and that I was living beyond the stereotype of trailer trash. Eventually, it became clear that Asa was using me, and he used my well-earned reputation of party girl—the girl who never said no to anyone or anything—in order to have access to the kids with money, the kids with drugs, the kids with whatever it was he wanted to get his hands on at the time. It's amazing where a short skirt and a bad reputation will get you, and Asa exploited it for all he was worth. Had I been smarter, maybe more aware of myself and what was going on, I could have saved myself a lot of regret and painful memories."

I finally risked a look at Shaw and some of the bitter edge had faded from her green gaze, but her mouth was still pressed in a tight line that didn't look at all forgiving.

"I started messing around with drugs to make it more tolerable, to make it seem less like I was exactly what everyone was saying I was. Half the time I was doing what I was doing to keep Asa out of trouble or because I thought it would help a situation he had created, which made me feel awful time and time again. To this day I never asked if he knew what it cost me to help him in any way I could. He's never said because I don't think either of us could look the other in the eye if the truth was out there."

Shaw's mouth went flat with concern, but she waited silently for me to continue. I wasn't sure the concern was for the old me or the new me, but either way I just needed her to understand why I was making the decisions the way I was.

"I had a science teacher in high school, Mr. Kelly, who was keeping an eye on me. I always managed to get pretty good grades, even though I missed more classes than I ever attended. I guess he saw the wasted potential, the girl trapped by circumstance, and I think he had dealt with Asa a few years earlier, so he knew what my brother was capable of. He threatened to call the Kentucky Cabinet for Health and Family Services and get the state involved if my mama didn't get her act together, and I guess it was enough to get her motivated to have Asa back off. Mr. Kelly forced me to fill out scholarship application after scholarship application, and hounded me until I practically got a perfect sixteen-hundred on the SAT. I guess I knew it was my one shot to get out of Woodward and if I didn't do it, I was going to end up strung out and paying rent on my back, just like my mama."

I shifted uncomfortably in the seat and shot a look around to make sure no one was listening in on our conversation. I was embarrassed to have all my dirty laundry out there. Not that I didn't trust Shaw; it was just a wound that had never healed completely, and having someone else look at it made it open and bleed all over again.

"I got a partial scholarship to DU. Not enough to cover everything, but room and board were included and Mr. Kelly was so desperate for me to get away from Woodward and Asa's influence that he pulled money out of his retirement account to make up the difference. Once I qualified for student loans, I paid him back as soon as I could. I got the Jeep at a junkyard and some of the guys who took auto shop fixed it up for some weed I stole from Asa. I hit the road and never looked back. When we moved into that dorm together, and I saw you all proper and elegant, I told myself that was what I was going to be from now on. No one was going to make me do anything I didn't want to do, no one was going to question my worth or my value as a woman, no one was ever going to doubt that I was intelligent and driven. I was going to be all the things no one had ever given my mama a chance to be, and I wasn't ever going back to Woodward. Asa was effectively dead to me. I had to get out from under the cloud of what I had let myself become."

I blew out a breath and saw Shaw raise an eyebrow at me. This is where the favor I asked for came in.

"Only Asa isn't dead or in jail. He's here in Denver and he brought all the crap from Woodward here with him. There's a guy named Silas in town who does really awful things for really terrible people back home. He's the one who tried to break into the house when Cora was home. Apparently, Asa took something—some important book—from a biker gang and they want it back, bad. Silas will do whatever it takes to get the gang's book, and I know Asa well enough to know he'll do whatever he has to in order to keep it, if he thinks he can make money off of it. Asa has always counted on me to fix all his problems and I have no doubt my mom sent him out here for me to take care of him."

Shaw clicked her fingernails on the table and tilted her head to one side.

"All right, Ayd. That sucks, really sucks, and I'm glad you finally told me all of it. I could kill the people who've hurt you. But I just don't understand what any of this terrible story has to do with you breaking up with Jet, when you are clearly head over heels for him? When he would never treat you badly."

I cringed, because there wasn't anything in this world that was ever going to erase the look on his face when I dropped him off at the studio. The light that circled the outside of those midnight eyes had dimmed to the point of being black.

"We weren't together, so I didn't really break up with him." That was as much as I could minimize the damage even if it was a blatant lie. I hadn't just walked away from him and whatever it was we were building together, I had done what I do best—run.

I was startled because even though Shaw was tiny, when she wanted to, she had enough attitude to seem much bigger. I wasn't expecting her to push away from the table and I wasn't expecting her to glare down at me like I had just kicked her puppy across the room.

"We agreed on the truth, Ayd. If you can't do that, then I'm not sitting here listening to this anymore. I'm already pretty pissed that you think any of that stuff in your past would have mattered to me. You know for a fact Rule was a manwhore, probably more of a slut than anyone really knows, and I loved him anyway. I would like to think that after our friendship took root, you would have known that I would have looked past anything to see all the wonderful things that make you, you."

She was going to leave. She was actually walking away from me in a huff when I reached out a hand and clamped onto her arm. My brain was having a hard time getting around the fact she was angry about Jet, about how I had treated him, and not the fact I was asking to borrow twenty grand and the fact my past was so ugly and that I had kept it from her for so long.

"Shaw." I was trying to find the words but she was on a roll.

"No, Ayd, you listen to me. I saw you with him the

other night. Hell, I've seen the way you've watched him for over a year. No, he isn't a guy who's going to work in a cubicle and push paper around for a set salary. He is the guy who will turn you inside out, and make you forget about all those stupid boundaries you've set for yourself because you're scared. Jet isn't going to care about your past; he has one of his own that isn't pretty. But, like a coward, instead of talking to him about it, you ran away from him when he needed you. You dropped him when he's getting ready to go on tour for three months, and practically dared him to stick his dick in every European groupie who looks his way, just to get you off his mind."

I pulled her back into the seat across from me, and waited until the curious stares her outburst had garnered died down. My heart already felt like a heavy stone in the center of my chest. When Jet hadn't come home last night, every worst-case scenario I could come up with played through my head on an endless loop for hours. For the first time in forever, I cried myself to sleep while I was still wearing his shirt and wishing he were there to make it better.

"Look, I had to break things off. You don't know my brother, but robbing Jet's studio, taking everything that's important to him, is right up Asa's alley. I refuse to let someone I care about be my brother's victim, because of me. Jet deserves to go on this tour, to have something just for him, finally. I did what I did to protect him."

She sighed heavily and squeezed my hand. Some of the heat had faded out of her jade gaze.

"I think Jet is a big boy. I think if you were honest with

him, he would not only be able to protect himself, but you as well."

I shook my head vehemently. No.

"Asa is trouble and he just needs to go away."

"So what? You think if he burglarized the studio, you can offer him the money and get the stuff back? I don't understand."

"I want the money to see if I can get the book back and get Silas out of town, and off my back. Asa is all about protecting Asa. If I tell him the studio had cameras, there's a good chance he'll take the money and run."

"What if it was Jet's dad? Rule and Nash were talking about it last night. They seem to think Jet's dad is the most likely culprit. Apparently, there is a really ugly story there that neither one of them was inclined to share with me."

It was my turn to sigh.

"I can't take that risk. If it wasn't Asa this time, it will be Asa next time. All this has made it pretty clear that no one is safe from him and the kind of havoc he can wreak. The closer you are to me the worse the destruction tends to be. I'm not willing to put Jet in that line of fire."

We stared at each other for a long moment. I could see the wheels turning in her head, and could see her trying to put all the puzzle pieces together. I knew no matter what, she would come through for me. Shaw loved me, and since I had been with her when her world went upside down and sideways, I knew there was no way she would hang me out to dry when mine was hanging so precariously. Gulping down the fear, I bit down on my bottom lip and told her the truth that I had been shoving back for so long.

"Look, I don't know about love, or being meant for someone, but I'm infatuated with him. He makes me smile just by being in the same room. When he touches me, I forget to breathe and when he sings to me, oh my Lord, when he sings to me there are no words to describe what that does to me. He has his own struggles, and his own bright and hot place that's hard to get around because of the heat it generates, but that never stops him from trying to get to me. I've never felt about anyone the way I feel about him. I hate that he ever thought I was so pure, so breakable, but now I feel like I'm shattered into a million pieces of remorse and regret, because he knows just how fallible I really am. I might be in love with him, but I can't be, because I'm not willing to be the one who destroys him."

I could feel pressure and moisture build in my eyes, so I dug my nails into my palms to hold it back.

"I haven't cared about his plans for the future, or compared what a life with him would look like instead of with a guy like Adam, ever since he kissed me in the bathroom on Valentine's Day at the Fillmore. He's just . . ." I trailed off and had to close my eyes to keep the emotion from spilling out. "Everything. He is just everything I want."

Shaw swore softly under her breath. "Then don't do this, Ayd. You're making a terrible mistake. I don't just think he's everything you want; I think he's everything you need."

This conversation had shades of familiarity. We had gone rounds when she was trying to figure out what to do with

Rule, so I knew she was coming from a place of honestly wanting what was best for me and wanting to see me happy. But she just didn't understand what I was dealing with; no one that hadn't had to deal with Asa could. That on top of the struggle Jet had on his hands with his messed up-parents I don't know why I thought I could ever play with that kind of fire and not end up seriously burned. We were two people forever marked by those around us, and it hurt to know it was enough to keep us apart.

"Look, Shaw, I really need your help. Things with Jet are what they are, but things with Asa are going to keep snow-balling until Silas doesn't have a choice but to come after me or— God forbid—Cora. Let me handle it and maybe, just maybe, when Jet gets back from tour, we can figure something out."

Granted, that idea made me want to throw up, but I was nothing if not realistic. "I understand that Asa is a piece of shit and doesn't deserve me going to the trouble to help him. I hate him most of the time, hate the way he made me feel about myself when I was younger, but my mama did anything, and I do mean anything, that was in her power to keep us together and keep us in a warm, dry place. I don't owe her much, but I do owe her trying to save Asa from himself this one last time."

Shaw grabbed my hand and pressed her palm hard against it so that I understood what she was going to say to me was serious and close to her heart.

"You don't have to sacrifice Jet for Asa, when it's clear one could love you forever and the other just wants to use you for whatever it is you can do for him. You know, I'm speaking from experience."

I did know, but I also knew that if Silas got his hands on Asa and handed him over to whomever he had stolen the book from, it was going to end badly. I really didn't care what happened to Asa, but if I could spare my mom from having to suffer the heartbreak and indignity of burying her son in a pauper's grave, I was going to do it. And the truth was I couldn't just watch him die. The added bonus was I got to keep Asa away from everyone I cared about, Jet first and foremost .

"And if anything happens to you, if so much as an eyelash gets damaged while you are messing around trying to clean up your brother's mess, I won't hesitate to call the police. You better let him know that I will tell Rule all about this, so he better beware of a whole lot of pissed off coming from the guys when they hear the entire story. He cares about you and he doesn't take kindly to people he cares about being manipulated and maneuvered unfairly by family."

I rubbed my hand across my forehead and tried to get all the stampeding thoughts in line. It was nice to know I had an entire army of tattooed and decidedly dangerous dudes to take up for me, but it was also frustrating that nobody understood I just needed to handle Asa in my own way. If he was responsible for the theft at Jet's studio, I was going to destroy him myself.

Shaw dug around in her purse and pulled out an envelope and slapped it down on the table between us. I looked at it like it was a live snake, ready to bite me. I couldn't believe she was just going to hand over that amount of money, that she wasn't going to make me sign an agreement in blood guaranteeing I would pay her back. Her eyes were locked on mine and I hated the sympathy that was shimmering there.

"I took a cash advance from one of my credit cards. Dad's been so wrapped up in the divorce and trying to cover his ass that he won't notice it for a while."

I gulped and had to swallow back the sudden rise of bile in my throat. It all felt so dirty and wrong.

"I'll pay you back."

She waved a hand, like twenty grand was only twenty dollars. "Eventually. If you want to pay me back sooner, get your head out of your ass and fix things with Jet. Tell him why you're doing what you're doing; he deserves to know before he leaves."

That made me suck in a breath and grit my back teeth together. She got to her feet and leaned over the small table to kiss me on the cheek.

"I love you Ayd. I really hope you get this all fixed before it isn't just broken, but ruined."

I watched her walk out of the coffee shop and felt the world tilt on its axis. I had to blink rapidly to avoid the darkness that was starting to swirl around the outside of my vision. Everything, and I do mean everything, I had worked for, the person I had tried so hard to become, was mocking me. She was looking at me from that trailer in Woodward and reminding me that no matter how much distance I put between me and her, I was always going to be Ayden Cross, white trash, and perpetual fixer of all wrongs done by the Cross kids. I took the money off the table, added it to the five grand I had pulled out of my own account, and waited for the menacing figure who had been seated across the coffee shop the entire time I sat there with Shaw to make his way over to me. I wouldn't put it past Silas to take the money and then demand to know where Asa was, so I had to put together a plan that kept everyone safe.

Silas looked even worse out of the dim light of the bar bathroom and I hated the way he ran appraising eyes over me.

"Where's your bother?"

I wrapped my hands back around the coffee cup and met his stare head-on.

"I don't know, but I'm going to find him and get the book back."

He didn't say anything for a long moment and I saw his gaze flicker to the bag on the floor where I had stashed the money.

"You think you can work this so he gets outta Dodge, scot-free?"

I shook my head a little.

"I'll get the book for you, but Asa is off-limits. He gets to go to Canada, Mexico, wherever the hell he ends up, and you leave me and my mama alone."

"The people he stole from aren't the kind of people that work that way. Retaliation in blood, Ayd. You're smart enough to know that. Hell, you were always too smart for the shit Asa dragged you into. None of us could ever figure out what you were doing there, not that we didn't appreciate it while you were. Probably the only chance most of us were ever gonna get to have a piece as hot as you."

It made me want to hurl, but I just rolled my eyes. I knew how to get guys like Silas to give me what I wanted. I could flirt, could make suggestive come-ons, could take him to bed and make him forget his own name, but the part of me that refused to let that Ayden back just gave him a bored look and tapped short fingernails on the table.

"If you want the book, that's the deal."

"How do you even know Asa still has it, or that he'll give it to you?"

I didn't, but my brother wasn't the only skilled liar in the family.

"He will, otherwise I'm handing him over to you to do with what you will. I didn't ask for him to show up and get his sticky fingers all in my perfectly nice life here. If Asa doesn't want to play ball with me, he can take his chances with you and the bikers."

He narrowed flinty eyes at me. "I'm going to need some kind of insurance."

I didn't even act like I was surprised by that. I bent down and dug out the five grand. I shoved it at him, careful to make sure no part of him touched me.

"This is the last favor I'm doing for Asa. If he wants to steal and tangle with people who would kill him just as soon as they would look at him, I'm done. I'll get the book, Silas, but if you follow me, if you harass my roommate or my mama anymore, I'm telling you that there are plenty of people here in this town that are willing to make sure you never make it back to Kentucky."

He watched me without blinking. I think he was weighing how serious I was, and considering the fact that I felt like I was leaking poison and pain all over the place, he must have seen whatever it was he was looking for.

"I need the book by tonight."

I narrowed my eyes.

"I'll call you when I have it."

"Time is running out for all of us, Ayd."

I scooped up my bag and pushed away from the table.

"It's a good thing I've always been fast then." I made him write a contact number down on a napkin before leaving the coffee shop.

When I got to the Jeep, the first thing I did was call home. I asked my mom a hundred and one times if she had anyway for me to contact Asa, but she stonewalled me at every turn. I tried to let her know just how bad things were, that she might be in danger, but as usual she just blew me off and told me that moving to the city had made me paranoid.

I called the strange Kentucky number on my phone over and over again. I even texted it a couple of times, but there was no response. I was going to freak out, and have a hissy fit because I couldn't start to fix things if I couldn't get my hands on Asa in the first place. I was about to bang my head on the steering wheel and scream in frustration, when a lightbulb went off. I called Adam with shaking hands, and felt even worse when I heard the genuine pleasure in his voice when he answered.

"Hey, Ayd. I didn't think I would be hearing from you anymore. Is everything okay?"

I closed my eyes and rested my forehead on the steering

wheel. I felt so cold, and not from the chilly Denver weather, just cold and frozen from how everything in my once perfectly normal life was going.

"No, no, nothing is okay." I didn't mean to blurt that out, but I couldn't control myself.

"Uh, is there anything I can do for you? Are you all right?"

This guy was just inherently nice, just a good guy all around and it made me feel even worse that I just couldn't return his affection. It also made it pretty clear that whatever I had with Jet was just so much bigger, so much more consuming than anything I was ever going to have with anyone else, and I had just walked away from it. My heart folded in on itself and made me gasp in acute pain.

"I just need to know if you've heard from my brother. He's a pretty friendly guy and I figured since he was in town, he might have made good on his threat to get in touch with you if he was bored."

There was silence on the other end of the phone and I had to restrain myself from tossing it against the windshield.

"Is that all? You sound pretty bad, Ayd."

"Things with Jet didn't exactly work out, and I'm having a hard time with it right now."

He cleared his throat and it rasped across my skin like a bunch of tiny razors.

"I have to say I'm kind of surprised to hear that. As much as I wanted things to work out between us, I think it was always pretty clear that there was someone else you would rather be with. I just figured out it was him on Valentine's Day, but I feel like I should have seen it sooner."

"Unfortunately, things don't always go the way we plan. But seriously, I really need to find Asa and he didn't tell me where he was staying. I can't get him on the phone."

Adam was quiet again and I found myself holding my breath. Finally, he sighed so heavily that I could feel it hit me through the phone line.

"I met him at a hotel across the highway a few days ago for a drink. He's staying at the one over by the stadium. I like your brother, Ayden. He seems like a really nice guy and he says he's just worried about you being out here all alone, without any family to watch out for you."

Oh, Asa was the nicest guy in the world all right, when he wanted something from you, and the only thing he was worried about was how I was going to help him out of his latest jam.

"Did he ask you for money?"

If Adam had already played the role Asa had scoped him out for, I was going to be screwed. There was no way he was going to stick around and barter with me if he already had cash in hand.

Adam sighed again and this time it annoyed me. Granted I would probably always feel bad for wasting his time for so long, but I had life-and-death matters at hand, and I needed him to be on board with things, and the sooner the better.

"No. He did ask how much you were working and a bunch a questions about what your days looked like. Like I said, I think he's just concerned about you. He made it sound like you don't make too much of an effort to stay in touch with your family back home."

I could hear the disapproval in his tone, but I didn't let it bother me. Adam had never even gotten close to the heart of me, so it was all right that he thought I was just a bad sister and a bad daughter. Things were beginning to be clear to me now. All the parts of me that I had hated, and had buried so far down, were the parts that were responsible for me being all the great things I was today. If wonderful people like Shaw and Cora and a guy like Jet could care about me, then both parts of me deserved a break, finally.

"Okay, thanks, Adam. You take care."

"Hey, Ayd." All I wanted to do was hang up and go find Asa, but I couldn't do that to him, not when he had never done anything but care about me. "When you're ready, when things with the rocker don't seem as painful, maybe give me a call."

My hand clenched reflexively on the phone. The idea of going back to Adam, that he still wanted me, should have made me giddy. He was the picture-perfect mate for my dream future, but the thought of being with anyone who didn't have black-velvet eyes and a voice that made me quiver and shake, made my skin crawl. Jet was going to be it for me, and I was just going to have to learn to live with the fact that I had let him go.

"Thanks, Adam, but I don't think I'm going to be ready for any kind of relationship anytime soon."

"Well, even if you need a friend, I'm here."

I ended the call and tossed the phone onto the passenger seat. I felt turned inside out but things were bright and clear, and the direction I had to go was sharp and defined. For the first time since I came to Denver, I felt like I wasn't living a lie.

I drove across town to the other side of the interstate, where all the hotels and motels next to Sports Authority field were located. The entire way, I kept an eye on the rearview mirror to make sure Silas wasn't following me. The hotels here weren't as nice as the places downtown, but they were right up Asa's alley. I found the hotel Adam had mentioned and went inside. I knew no one would just give me my brother's room number, but luckily I had watched him enough to know that if there was a pretty girl behind the counter, she would undoubtedly have fallen victim to his charms by now.

There was a redhead who looked a couple years younger than me who fit the bill perfectly. She looked fresh-faced and sweet, the perfect victim for all of Asa's machinations. I plastered a pleasant smile on my face and waited until she was alone at the desk. I crossed my arms on the counter and tried to look as innocent and unthreatening as possible. I made sure my accent was on in full force so that there would be no mistaking that Asa and I were related.

"Hey there. I'm supposed to be meeting my brother here. I just got into town and I forgot what room he's staying in. Do ya think ya can help me out?"

I saw her look at me in surprise. The eyes were enough that anyone would know Asa and I were brother and sister, but the different hair color could be misleading. She bit her lip and looked from side to side.

"What's your brother's name?"

I smiled even bigger.

"Asa Cross. He's a handsome devil, and I just know he

would be so grateful if you helped me out. Denver is a lot bigger than the city we come from, and I've been feeling a little overwhelmed so any help would sure be appreciated."

I made sure to layer on the yokel as thick as I could and batted my eyelashes at her. I should feel guilty for being another person who was manipulating her to get what she wanted, but my end game was more important than her feelings.

She fiddled with her hair and continued to look around, like she was afraid of getting caught doing something wrong.

"Um, I'm not allowed to give out room numbers, but I can call up and let him know you're here, and you can ask him what room he's in."

I didn't trust Asa as far as I could throw him, but I figured he was going to want to hear what I had to say, so I nodded in agreement and kept an eye on the lobby for any sign of trouble. The girl made the call and it only took a moment for her to smile at me and blush at whatever my brother was telling her on the other end of the phone. She giggled, which made my skin crawl, and scribbled something on a piece of paper.

"He said he's been expecting you and he's so glad you finally made it." She put a hand over her chest and leaned a little over the counter, making me rear back to avoid having her right in my face. "He is so cute, and nice. My name is Heather. Feel free to let him know I was super excited to help you out."

I gritted my teeth and forced my smile to stay friendly and not turn nasty.

"Well, thank you, Heather, I'll be sure to pass that along. You were just a doll."

I snatched the paper with the room number on it and almost ran to the elevator. I knew where he was, now I just had to get him to let me in. The ride to the floor he was on felt like it took forever and somewhere along the way, a woman with a crying toddler got on, and kept apologizing for the kid. I wanted to tell her that I understood, because on the inside I was just as upset, crying just as loud as her baby, but I just smiled and shrugged at her to let her know it was just part of life.

When I found Asa's room I stood in front of the door for a second trying to decide the best course of action, if he decided not to let me in, but it turned out I was worrying for nothing. Just as I was raising my fist to pound on the door, it opened and I found myself being yanked inside by my wrist. I stumbled a little, which made Asa laugh, and I wanted to slug him on principle alone.

He had on sweatpants and looked rumpled and well rested, not at all like he had a herd of angry bikers all over his ass, demanding retribution.

"What's going on, sis? Took you long enough to find me."

I shoved him away from me, and stalked into the room so I could flop down on the edge of the unmade bed.

"Silas is here."

I saw his eyes open wide and he began to pace back and forth in front of me.

"He's been here waiting for you to show up. He told me about the book, about the biker gang. What were you thinking, you idiot?"

Eyes that looked just like my own flared with heat as he glared at me.

"I was thinking that book has every marker, every debt owed, in every county in the south. Do you have any idea how much power that is? Do you know what I can do with that information? It's more than a get-out-of-jail-free card; it's a move-out-of-the-trailer-park-and-play-with-the-big-boys card. It was one of the smartest things I've ever done. I can take care of Mama with it, I can make sure none of us ever has to work for anything ever again with it. You could come home and we could be a family again with it."

I wondered if he actually cared about Mom at all, or if he was just using that as an excuse, and I had no idea he thought I was ever returning to Woodward. Asa was a pretty man with pretty words, and that was what had always made him so dangerous.

"It also has people very willing to kill you, and to hurt Mama and me to get it back. This is a nightmare, Asa, and you know it. You came here for me to fix it, so that's what I'm going to do, but first you're going to tell me if you had anything to do with Jet's studio getting robbed. If you did, I'm handing you over to Silas and walking away."

He balked and narrowed his eyes at me.

"The rock-and-roll guy? I didn't even know he had a studio. I was focused on the nerd with the rich family. That guy is so in love with you, I thought it would be a sure thing. The guy in the band seemed a little harder to get at."

I sighed and leaned back on my elbows. I didn't know if I believed him or not.

"He has security cameras, so if you're lying, I'm going

to find out and it's going to be your ass, because those guys make Silas look like a Cub Scout."

"I swear, Ayd, I didn't do anything to the studio. Even if you had something serious going with that guy, he doesn't come across as the type who would be easy to work. You know I pick my marks smarter than that."

We sized each other up, him looking for some sign of whatever it was I was working on and me, for some sign he was lying about Jet. I dug around in my bag and pulled out the envelope stuffed with the money from Shaw. I tapped it on my thigh and saw his eyes track the movement.

"I want you out of town. I want you as far away from me and from Mama as you can get. I got the money you asked for to make that happen." I lifted an eyebrow. "Give me the book to give to Silas."

His eyes darted from the money to my face and back to the money. I could practically see the wheels turning in his head and the drool collecting at the corner of his mouth.

"Where did you get the money from?"

"None of your business." I growled at him, actually growled like an animal, because I was pretty sure I was going to go for his throat at any minute.

"Take the money, Asa. Give me the book. That's the only way to fix this."

"The book is worth way more than twenty grand, Ayd."

I clenched the wrinkled bedding in my fingers and told myself to calm down. If I got all worked up, Asa would use it to his advantage and I needed to be the one in control.

"Your life is worth more than twenty grand, as well. I

know it would kill Mom if I had to go home and identify your body, Asa. Take the goddamn money and get the fuck out of my life, once and for all. This offer has a time limit. Once I walk out that door, you are on your own come hell or high water and I will do what I have to do to protect myself and Mama and you from yourself, just like always."

"What does that mean?"

He sounded bored, like he didn't believe I would go through with any threat I made. Maybe old Ayden wouldn't have, but I was a kickass hybrid of old and new, who had no time to mess around with my brother's games, not when I was broken-hearted and feeling so raw.

I got up and held the money out to him.

"It means take the money or I'm calling Silas on my way out the door. Like I said, he's been following me all around town, and he might even be out in the parking lot now. If you don't work with me, Asa, I honestly don't care what happens to you from this point on. I don't have it in me to save you, to do anything and everything for you the way I once did."

He must have seen the seriousness in my face, and the fact that I had nothing left to lose, because he snatched the envelope from me and peeked inside. I saw his eyes get big at the sight of all that green, but he made no move to get me the book.

I crossed my arms and tapped the toe of my cowboy boot on the floor. I think he was waiting to see what I was going to do, so I just stared him down until he swore. He took his sweet time going to his suitcase and digging out the little leather-bound book that was about the size of my palm.

Why criminals didn't just digitize all their illegal doings and password protect that shit was beyond me. I caught it in one hand when he threw it at me, and tucked it in the back pocket of my jeans. It felt like it weighed as much as my heavy heart at the moment.

I put my bag over my shoulder and made my way to the door.

"I'm serious, Asa. This is the last time I'm doing anything for you or because of you. I like my life here, I like the person I am here, and I'm willing to do whatever it takes to keep it. Even if you are blood and family."

He crossed his arms over his bare chest and his radiant eyes glinted at me.

"You've changed, lil sister. You're a lot tougher than you used to be."

I looked back over my shoulder. "Damn straight, and you would be smart not to forget it."

"I know you won't believe me, Ayd, but the things I did, the things I never told you not to do, even though it was obvious it was killing you inside, I was just trying to get us by. I always loved you more than anything. You've always been the only one who ever had my back."

I turned to look at him and had to fight back tears. "When did you ever have my back?"

He looked confused for a second, but Asa was good and could look anyway he wanted to. It sucked that I couldn't trust whatever was shining out of those eyes that were so like my own.

"What are you talking about, Ayd?" For a split second it

looked like he was going to move toward me, to try to hug me or comfort me, but it was way too little and far too late for any of that to exist between us now.

Maybe he really didn't know, maybe he didn't want to know, either way it was too late and all those things and him were in the past. It wasn't a conversation I felt like I wanted or needed to have with him. When I closed the door on him without answering, I was closing the door on more than just my brother. I was closing the door on a past that had held me hostage for too long. I wasn't sure Asa even knew what love looked like, but I knew that now I did. I had been living a life that was driven by things that seemed like a good idea but had proven to be superficial and were really just armor to insulate myself. Moving forward, it was going to be all about the balance between what I wanted and what I needed. It sucked that Jet Keller was the only thing that fit both those criteria, when I was pretty sure he was never going to want to have anything to do with me again.

CHAPTER 14

Jet

THE LAST WEEK HAD been torturous. I was emotionally exhausted and running on fumes and a flurry of avoidance. Between scurrying all over hell and back to replace the stuff we would need for the tour at the end of next week, and trying desperately to avoid any kind of run-in with Ayden, I was scattered all over the place and barely holding it together.

So far I had managed to spend most of my time with the band, practicing and working our asses off, to the point that I was just crashing overnight at the studio on a blow-up mattress, or dragging myself home long after Ayden returned from her shift at the bar. I was writing songs that made my head hurt and my heart ache, and I think the guys in the band were sick of ballads about broken hearts.

I didn't know what to say to her, and didn't know how to look at her without having it rip me into shreds and burn me up more than I thought was possible. I didn't want to be constantly mad at her or let her know that the chasm she'd rebuilt between us was killing me, so I thought that distance was my best bet for holding on to my sanity. On occasion, our paths would cross in the morning on the way to the bathroom, or at the kitchen table for breakfast, and I had to admit she looked about as broken as I felt. None of that made me feel any better, and the fact that Cora wouldn't leave it alone just made it easier to avoid the house as much as I could.

At the moment, I was sitting in court, and even though I had been waiting for this moment, I felt like an igniter on a stick of dynamite. My lawyer kept telling me to stop twitching and fidgeting, but I was anxious, because my dad was sitting on the opposite side of the room, with his bruises healing and looking madder than a sack of wet cats. My mom was sitting behind him, her gaze nervously moving back and forth between the two of us. Her black eye was artfully covered with makeup and I could tell she was trying really hard not to cry. I was also uncomfortable as all get-out in a pair of pinstriped pants and a white, button-down oxford cloth shirt that made me feel like a big, fat phony. Court clothes sucked, but I could tell by the way the judge was eyeballing my hair and the spikes in my ears, that dressing up had been to my benefit.

My dad's lawyer opened up by going on and on about how assault was a serious charge, and how I had put my dad in the hospital. He said I had brought trauma and damage to the family. He brought up the fact that I had been in trouble before, and generally tried to make me out to be some kind of wild hooligan who was out of control.

My lawyer countered that my dad had instigated the

fight, and that I had only been acting to protect my mom. It went back and forth like that for a while, with my dad huffing and puffing the entire time. I tried to sit still, tried not to glare daggers across the courtroom. The judge interjected that he had seen cases like this far too often in his court, and even though my old man wanted me in jail, I got just what I had predicted—a million hours of community service, probation for a year, and fines out the ass. They also made me responsible for my dad's medical bills and ordered an immediate protection order that said I couldn't go within a hundred yards of him or the house for ninety days.

I readily agreed to all of it and had the added benefit of watching my dad go purple when I asked about postponing the community service and making sure the terms of my probation didn't prohibit me from leaving the country for the tour. I heard my mom gasp when the case was ruled closed, but the same cop who had put me in the back of his car came around the table and slapped a heavy folder down in front of my dad. I wanted to get up and do a victory jig. It had taken every favor my lawyer had hanging in the legal world in order for it to go down like this for me and I was beyond stoked that the same cop was the one who had the honor of arresting the old bastard.

"Do you know what these pictures show, Mr. Keller?"

My dad's lawyer was freaking out, calling out all kinds of crap that no one was paying attention to, and my mom was holding her hands up to her mouth when the clear, bright images of my dad trashing and emptying out the studio spilled onto the table in an array of visible guilt.

My dad went from purple to some other color I had never seen before, and stood up in his chair so violently that it fell backward, making the officers of the court tense.

"That's not me!" He pointed a finger at me. "You little shit! You set me up!"

I leaned back in my chair and tried hard not to smile.

"I had security to prevent something like this from happening. It's not my fault you got caught, and you bet your ass I'm pressing every goddamn charge he can think of."

I tilted my head at the cop who was putting my dad in the cuffs.

"You've messed with me for the last time, old man. This is it, and I hope you rot."

"I'm your father, Jet!"

I just shook my head and got to my feet.

"No, you've never been that."

I couldn't look at my mom or at the judge, who was watching the entire debacle with sad, knowing eyes. I didn't even want to think about all the families in worse shape than ours who had come before his bench. I shook my lawyer's hand, and agreed to sign all the stuff he needed to get together for my community service and legal fees. I asked him to check with the cop about getting the stuff my dad had stolen back, but he didn't sound hopeful that that was an option.

I was walking out of the courthouse and pulling my leather jacket on over my stupid button-down shirt, when I heard my name called. I didn't want to stop, didn't want to talk to her, considering I was still bleeding from her picking that asshole over me the last time. There was something encoded on my DNA that made me turn around and wait for her to catch up to me, though. Out here in the bright light of day, I could see every line, every mark on her face that indicated a life lived in misery and suffering. She looked so awful and so far away. There wasn't even a shadow of the woman that I wanted to call "Mom" in there anymore.

"Jet, wait just a minute, please."

I swore under my breath and wished that I smoked so I had something to do with my hands. I shoved them into the pockets of my jacket and tried to keep my expression blank.

"I don't think we have anything left to say, Ma."

She fidgeted with the strap on her purse and refused to meet my gaze head-on.

"He's your father, Jet. You can't send him to jail."

I sighed. I knew it was coming, but it still felt like a blow.

"Yes, I can. He stole from me, and he dismantled my livelihood because I wouldn't cave in to his demands. Not only *can* I send him, but it's where he belongs. I'm going to Europe for three months, Mom. I'm not going to be just a phone call away the next time he tries to use you as a punching bag. I'm not going to even be on this continent the next time he spends all your mortgage money on booze and hookers. So maybe locking him up will finally make you see you're better off without him."

She involuntarily touched her still-yellowish bruised eye.

"He only did that the one time and he wouldn't have been so riled up if you just would have helped him, like you always help me."

I laughed, and it was so broken, I felt it lash across both of us.

"Are you seriously trying to blame him smacking you around on me? Nice try, Ma, but that isn't going to fly with me anymore. I'm finished trying to force something better on you, trying to pull you into the light. If you want to live in the dark, it's your choice, Ma, and you have no one left to blame but yourself."

I was going to walk away, but her hand on my elbow stopped me. Her bottom lip was quivering and I would like to say it broke my heart, but I knew her concern wasn't for me or for herself, but for that selfish bastard sitting in a cell for trying to kill my dreams.

"If you go and he's in jail, I'll be all alone, Jet. I can't be alone." The last word was said on a whisper that I barely heard.

"You know what, Ma? Alone is better than one second spent with that asshole. I've spent my entire life trying to make you see that I would take care of you, that I would never leave you alone. That all changed when you let them shove me in the back of police car for trying to protect you. It's time you start protecting yourself."

I shook her hand off, which was surprisingly easier to do than I thought it would be. I couldn't look at her anymore, couldn't let her shadow pull me under with it, so I took a step away from her and said, "I'll call you when I get back. Maybe the time alone will do you some good and we can talk. If not, I'm done with this. If the old man thinks he's going to fuck with me, fuck with my band and my music, he better get a wake-up call. I tolerated it for years, because I was so worried about you and what he would do, but now I'm only worried about me. Bye, Ma."

I walked away with the sinking feeling I was walking away from her for good. I pulled my phone out of my pocket and called the Marked, the tattoo shop where Cora and all the boys worked. Since the shop had caller ID, Cora was less than professional when she answered the phone.

"Hey."

"Hey, is Rowdy around?"

"Did you just get out of court?"

Man, that little pixie was like a pit bull when she had something in her teeth.

"Yeah."

"How did it go?"

"Fine. Seriously, Cora, I want to talk to Rowdy if he isn't busy."

"You know all of them are going to be hounding him to know what happened as soon as he gets off the phone with you anyway, so you might as well just tell me, so I can tell them. It saves everyone time."

I sighed and relented.

"I got a ton of community service, a million fines, and a restraining order. The old man got the cuffs and a ticket to lockup. I'm sure my mom is going to try to bail him out, but the cop assured me the theft was enough to keep him there a for a good long while, and that the bail isn't going to be cheap. I'd like to say he was gonna be there for the whole time I'm gone, but I don't know that it's very realistic. I'm fine, Cora, really."

She muttered something under her breath and I heard her call Rowdy's name across the shop.

"I'll consider you fine when you stop playing hide-and-seek with Ayden and just talk to her."

I snorted. "That ship has sailed, girly."

I think she was going to snap something back, but I heard the sounds of a scuffle and Rowdy's gruff voice came on the line.

"Yo."

"And it's team Jet for the win."

"No doubt, dude. What's up?"

"What does your schedule look like today?"

"Hold on a sec and I'll check it out, that is if I can get the Tasmanian Devil to move her fine ass outta my way."

I heard Cora shriek in outrage, and more scuffling sounds, only this time male laughter rang loud in the background.

"My last appointment is at four and it should be quick. Some girl who just wants a little fleur-de-lis on her foot."

"Wanna start something for me?"

"What did you have in mind? Something big or something little?"

"Big."

"We won't have time for that before you leave."

"I know. I just want you to draw it and get the outline done."

"Talk to me."

I had been thinking about it since the studio got trashed, since Ayden had pulled out my heart and tossed it away. I wanted something that captured the way music exploded out of me, the way the fire flowed in and out of me with the words when I was onstage.

"I want an old-school microphone broken, like split open, with a bunch of fire spilling out of it. It needs to look shattered and rough, not old-school or traditional."

I could hear him scratching stuff down on paper as I talked.

"The fire needs to be hot and out of control and I don't care how big you make it. My whole back is open, so you have whatever space you need."

He whistled between his teeth.

"All right. I'll get something sketched up and text it to you. If you like it, stop by around five."

"Don't worry about the text, just draw it and let's go. Come on, dude, you know me; this tattoo is all about me and my music. I know you got it."

"You can be totally insane, you know that, right?"

It was funny because for the first time in a long time, I was feeling like I had things figured out and insanity played no part in it.

"Don't they say all great art comes from suffering or madness?"

He laughed. "I think you have both of those covered. I'll see you later."

I had avoided going to the house during the day, on the off chance I would run into Ayden, but I didn't want to be in court clothes anymore, so I decided to risk it. I swore out loud when I saw her Jeep was still parked in the driveway. I locked my jaw and decided I was grown-up enough to handle a run-in with her, even if looking at her made all my exposed parts hurt.

I pulled the front door open and stopped dead in my tracks. Clearly she had just gotten back from a run, because she was in those stretchy black pants that made her legs look like something out of a wet dream, and a sports bra and nothing else. That was entirely too much skin, and too much Ayden for me to deal with in my current state of mind, so I was just going to slide past her, and totally pretend like I didn't even see her in all her too-hot-for-my-own-good glory. Apparently she had other ideas, because she put down her water bottle and leaned back against the sofa to stare at me.

"How was court?"

It was on the tip of my tongue to ask how she knew where I had been, but then I remembered the fancy duds and the fact that Cora had the biggest mouth ever. I shrugged out of my leather jacket and tossed it next to her, and counted backward from ten until I felt like I could talk to her. I wanted to interact with her without spilling and choking on all the bitterness I struggled with every day.

"It went fine."

I saw her look away. Clearly she was as uncomfortable as I was.

"That's good. I'm happy for you."

I let out a bitter laugh and shoved angry hands through my hair.

"Yeah, it's every kid's dream to send his dad to jail because he ripped them off and tried to screw them out of a chance-of-a-lifetime opportunity." The sarcasm was like a blade that sliced through the discomfort between us.

She cleared her throat and pushed up off the couch, crossing her arms over breasts that I would dream about until I died.

"You deserve to be happy, Jet. You deserve to take care of yourself for once."

"Yeah, I guess." I would much rather have her take care of me, much rather take care of her, but since that wasn't an option anymore, I guess taking care of myself was the only choice left.

I was going to head to my room, so I started unbuttoning my shirt. Those eyes of hers were sharp and followed my every move. Her phone rang from the kitchen table and I moved to toss it to her. Everything inside me went cold and still when I saw the name on the caller ID. Sweater Vest. Goddamn Sweater Vest was calling her and I was going to incinerate the whole planet with a single thought. Without a word I handed the device to her and went to storm past her. I stopped when her hand fell on my shoulder. Those gilded eyes glowed at me with an emotion I couldn't identify, but I was so tired of this girl twisting me up and letting me go. I couldn't just spin out of control anymore. Being dizzy was only fun for a second.

"It isn't what you think, Jet. None of this is what you think it is."

Her voice quivered a little and I wanted to care, wanted to kiss her and take her to bed. I wanted to sing to her, wanted to beg her to come on tour with me, wanted to put a ring on her finger and ask her to be mine forever. Unfortunately, all I could do was shrug her off and narrow my eyes at her.

"I try not to think about it at all, Ayd."

I heard her gasp but I just kept moving to my room. I didn't want to hear anything she had to say to the idiot in argyle, so I slammed the bedroom door and pulled the clothes that were suffocating me off, all the while wishing I could pull the emotion she had me tangled in off as easily.

I turned on Venom as loud as it would go, to dissuade her if she tried to follow me and talk. The music was so loud it made even my head hurt, but it distracted me long enough that I got a few last-minute things done for the tour, and set in place a few details I had hanging with the recording for Black Market Alphas.

Really, helping start-up bands, getting new bands out into the world for other people to hear, made me happier than anything else at the moment. There was just so much good music out there that no one ever got a chance to hear, because they never made it big, never made it to the radio or on one of the big tours. It was a shame, and any part that I could play in changing that gave me more pride than anything that I produced for myself did.

When I left to head to the tattoo shop, there was no sign of Ayden and I didn't know if that made me feel better or worse. I chose not to think about it too hard and headed downtown. I hated to leave the car parked on Colfax, so I went farther down where Nash and Rule lived in a converted Victorian and parked there. It took me a few minutes to walk back up to the shop, and even though I was a few minutes late, Rowdy was still working on a girl who barely looked sixteen.

Cora rolled her eyes and told me that the girl had been late and she was proving to have a low pain tolerance, so that my boy was struggling with it. I told her I would wait, but Rule came walking out of the back frowning at his phone and asked me if I had a minute. I wasn't really in the mood to have him bust my balls, but the shop wasn't that big, so I didn't really have a choice. I nodded a greeting at Nash, who watched us walk out the front door with a frown. He was working on something intricate on a guy's calf, though, so he didn't say anything or make any move other than the frown.

Rule muttered something at the screen of the phone and tucked it into the pocket of his hoodie.

"Rome is headed home for good in a few months."

I wasn't expecting that, so I wasn't sure what to say. Rule's older brother was cool, and a total badass, take-no-shit kind of guy, and I liked him a lot. I knew there was some tension there with the family, and the fact that Rule's twin brother—who was no longer living—had managed to take a pretty big secret to the grave with him.

"That's cool."

"It would be, if he would stop being an asshole. I want him to take over the lease on the Victorian when he gets back, so he doesn't have to worry about trying to figure out where he's going. I know he won't go home right now. He's still not talking to the folks."

I rubbed my hand across the back of my neck and won-

dered why he wanted to talk about this away from everyone else.

"If he moves into the Victorian, where are you and Shaw
going to go?"

"I'm going to buy her a house."

I balked a little because I had known Rule for a long
time, and while the idea of him settling down with one girl
had been a shock, the idea of him making a permanent home
with one was downright unthinkable.

"Wow, dude, that's a huge step."

He shrugged a shoulder and leaned back against the
glass window that was the front of the shop.

"It doesn't feel like one. She's it for me."

I lifted an eyebrow and copied his pose against the chilly
glass.

"You thinking marriage and babies there, Archer?"
It baffled me. He was the original lone wolf, and his track
record with women was legendary and almost scary in its
length. But once he had decided that he was going to commit to Shaw, he had done it with the same intensity that he
applied to everything else in his life.

"Honestly, man, it's whatever she wants. She wants a
ring, I'll by her one the size of her head. She wants a kid,
I'll take her to bed every night until she has one, and I won't
complain about it at all. If she wants to keep things the way
they are now, until the end of time, then I'm cool with that,
too. All that matters is that it's her and me at the end of the
day. That's what I wanted to talk to you about."

His eyes were serious and pinned me to the glass. It was

hard to look away from that winter storm when he turned its full force on you.

"When the right one comes along, Jet, you figure it out. You move mountains, you change your life and you do whatever it takes to keep them with you. I would be half the man I am without Shaw. She makes me better, she makes me happy, and I can see that Ayden does that for you, too."

I was going to interrupt, going to tell him that I wasn't the one who had walked away, that I had dealt with her secrets and her evasion, and still fallen in love with her anyway, but he held up a hand and stopped me.

"I know things with her are convoluted. I know she isn't making it easy to love her, but that's when it's most important that you do it anyway. Trust me, I've been in her shoes. Shaw explained a little of what Ayd's dealing with, and it isn't pretty, and it sure as shit isn't easy, but I know you could handle it if you just pushed through."

I frowned and tried not to let his words rattle around in my head. I appreciated where he was coming from, appreciated that he really did think that love was something that could just prevail. It was beautiful coming from a guy like him, but he wasn't the one trying to battle the walls Ayden had up, and he wasn't the one there when that damn phone rang this afternoon. I sighed and looked at him out of the corner of my eye. I wasn't going to lie about how I felt about her, but I also wasn't going to pretend like I had hope for things working out beyond the way they had.

"Thanks, Rule. Seriously, I understand where you're coming from and I wish, I truly wish I could have with

Ayden the same kind of thing you have going on with Shaw. It just isn't like that. I know what happens when you try to force something on someone, just look at my folks."

We stared at each other for a long minute, his pale blue eyes glittering like chips of diamonds as he turned my words over in his head. Finally, he sighed and pushed off the glass.

"I just know that if you think the person is worth it, that the end game is worth it, then you shouldn't give up."

I followed his lead and pushed myself off the window. A group of girls walked by and checked us out, but neither one of us returned the attention or the flirty smiles sent our way. I wanted to kick something.

"I guess happiness is all relative now."

We went back inside the shop and Rowdy was walking the girl he had been working on to the desk. Cora was giving her the stink eye and being particularly snarky as she cashed her out. Rowdy and I exchanged a fist bump, and he jerked his head toward the back room where they all had drawing stations and a little break room.

"Come back and check out what I threw together. If you don't like it, I have enough time to change it up."

Rule clapped me on the shoulder.

"He's been working on it all day. It's fucking amazing."

I lifted an eyebrow and followed Rowdy to the rear of the shop.

"Thanks for pulling it together so quick."

"It isn't often I have a client who gives me free rein to just do what I want, so I had a good time with it."

The stencil was massive. It would cover one entire side

of my back, from the top of my ass to the base of my shoulder blade. The fire was the main focus, with twisting, twining flames that licked over an old-fashioned microphone that was split open in the center and looked similar to a screaming mouth with more swirls of flame spitting out of it. It was nasty, it was mean, it was bright, and it was full of life. It looked exactly like what I felt when I was onstage, and the colors he envisioned, the flow he found for it, was more like a watercolor painting than the typical hard lines of a tattoo. I stared at it in awe for a long minute, until Rowdy cleared his throat, and I noticed that he looked a little nervous.

"Is it kind of what you were after?"

I laughed, really laughed. Laughed so hard I felt water build in my eyes.

"Dude, if I didn't think you would punch me in the face, I would kiss you. It's perfect. It's exactly what I wanted."

"It's big. All we're going to be able to get done tonight is the outline, and you're looking at a solid four to five hours for that alone. You need to decide what side you want it on."

"The side opposite the angel of death." I figured that would look more balanced than having them on the same side, even though the death angel took up most of my chest.

"Cool, give me a few to set up and get the transfer ready. Nash said when he was done with the guy he's working on, he'll run out and grab pizza. Rule said he was gonna get a case of beer and come back. You have to wait until you're done getting inked to drink though, otherwise you'll push the ink out. We're all just gonna hang out here."

I readily agreed and kicked back while he went to take

care of business. My family was as settled as it was ever going to be, my music was in the prime of its success, and I had the coolest group of friends ever. It was a shame that none of that seemed to do any good at filling the place in me that was still gaping wide open because of a whiskey-eyed brunette. Nothing made the fact that she was still talking to Sweater Vest easier to swallow, and none of it made the fact that we just couldn't figure out how to be together suck any less.

Letting Rowdy hammer on me for a few hours with a bunch of needles seemed like a good way to get the endorphins and adrenaline flowing, and a good way to let some of that scorching, blistering emotion Ayden stirred up bleed out.

CHAPTER 15

Ayden

SACRIFICING SO THE PERSON you loved would be better off should have made me feel altruistic and at peace. Unfortunately, in my case it was making me miserable and uncomfortable. Walking away from Jet before Asa could get his grubby paws into him, or before all the nasty things I thought I had a handle on could come between us was so much harder than I thought it would be. I didn't know what was worse, the awkward encounters I had with Jet when I ran into him in the house, or the nights he didn't come home at all.

My head would spin around like a crazy person, trying not to wonder who he was with or what he was doing. I had always wanted him on a purely chemical and sexual level, but now that I knew him, now that I understood all the things going on behind those dark eyes of his, I wanted him for everything else as well. It broke my heart into a million pieces every time he looked at me like I was a pane of glass, and that he had no interest whatsoever seeing what was on the other side. It killed me when he just gazed right through me. The reality was, if he looked close enough, he would see all those shattered pieces of my heart in places they didn't belong. They were in my throat, in my hands, and lost somewhere in the pit of my stomach.

He was leaving today. When I left for my run earlier, he had been getting his stuff together by the front door and talking on the phone to whoever was coming to pick him up. Part of me was glad that the tension that rolled between us would ease now that he was going to be thousands of miles away, but a bigger part of me, a louder part of me, was screaming that once he was out of the door with that guitar, it was over for good between us. I knew he deserved to know the real reasons why, but I just couldn't seem to find the right words to tell him.

I hadn't heard from Asa or Silas in more than a week. I hoped my brother had taken my advice and found a deserted island to hole up on, but knowing him, I had my doubts. I wasn't stupid enough to meet Silas alone, so I had given that little book that had turned my life so upside down to Lou, and had Silas come to the Goal Line to get it. Lou was cool about it and didn't ask a million questions. Plus, he had the benefit of looking like he could pull Silas's arms off and beat him with them with very little effort, so I felt safer having him take care of the hand-off.

I tried to call my mom and explain the whole situation to her, but she was as disinterested as always, and wanted to talk instead about some guy she met at a bar. Apparently, he wanted her to go on the road with him in his big rig and she was all excited about it. As usual, I tried to be the voice of reason, telling her she didn't know the guy, and that if they got into a fight or she decided she didn't like him, that he could end up leaving her stranded wherever he liked. She didn't want to hear any of it. She didn't even say thank you or seem at all grateful that I had come up with a way to keep Asa breathing, at least for now. All of it reminded me why I had been so desperate to get out of Woodward in the first place, and why I wanted my life to look so different now.

Adam had taken to calling once or twice a day, now that he knew Jet and I were no longer involved in whatever it was we had been trying to do. I could tell he was honestly concerned about how I was doing, but I had had to tell him more than once that I just wasn't interested in dating or starting anything with someone else. The fact of the matter was that no one was ever going to be safe in a relationship with me, secure financial future and corporate career or not. The things in my past, the people in my life, were always going to be a threat and there was just no way that I ever wanted to risk subjecting someone I cared about to that. It wasn't fair.

When I got back to the house, I stopped to catch my breath and I stumbled a little, because Jet was coming out the front door and headed down the steps. He stopped short when he saw me and looked down at the toes of his combat boots. The look in his eyes broke my heart, and all I wanted to do was wrap him in a hug and tell him everything would be okay. I knew that wasn't really true, so I just propped a hip on the wrought-iron railing and looked up at him.

"Are you okay?"

He didn't even look up at me, but I saw his shoulders tense

and his nails dig into his palms. I didn't know if I was in love
with this man, but I thought I was, and I knew for absolute
certain that all I wanted for him was that he never feel the
way he was obviously feeling right now again. If I had to
stand between Jet and whatever was making him sizzle and
pop with anger the way he was at the moment, I would do
it, even if that meant I kept myself away from him as well.
He deserved some measure of peace, some respite from the
demons that constantly hounded him, and even if it meant
not being part of his life, I was determined to see that he got it.

"I'm fine."

He lifted his head to look at me and those eyes were so
dark and so angry that I felt them singe across my skin. I
understood better than he could ever imagine about being
hurt by someone who you loved, and I wanted to tell him,
wanted to explain the entire ugly mess to him. But then he
would just want to fix it and there was no fixing Asa, and no
going back in time and fixing the girl I used to be. There was
just moving forward and getting the things we had worked
for, and building a better life from here on out, and hopefully being better people along the way.

"Well, have fun on tour. I'm sure you're going to be
amazing."

It was stilted and awkward, as all conversation between
us was anymore. We used to be able to talk to each other,
just look at each other and know what the other was thinking. Now we were just two people hurting for different reasons, trying to pretend like it didn't rip us apart to breathe
the same air.

I wasn't expecting him to move but suddenly he was in my face with a rattle of the chains that hung from his wallet to his belt, and a clinking of the rings on his fingers. He grabbed the metal rail on either side of me. Those blazing eyes were millimeters from my own, and I could see the way his anger pulled down the corners of a mouth that had loved me in so many different ways. I knew Jet had a lot of rage inside him, knew that he struggled to keep a lid on the volcano of emotion that roiled inside him, but I never expected to see it unleashed on me. It burned and popped across all my exposed skin and all I could do was stand there and take it, while he glared at me and growled,

"Does it even matter?"

I wasn't scared of him, wasn't scared of that anger. What terrified me was being another person who had ultimately let him down, who had picked someone awful and abusive over him. That wasn't my intention, but it was what I had done nonetheless.

"Of course it matters. What was between us always mattered; you matter. We both knew going in that it was never supposed to be long-term, just a good time remember? We aren't good for each other, Jet."

The words tasted like dirt on my tongue. I wanted him forever, wanted him to sing me to sleep every night, wanted to watch him onstage and know he was coming home with me. I wanted all of it, and none of it was the future I had ever planned for myself, but more than that, I wanted him to be happy. I wanted him to have something that no one could tarnish or soil; not his dad, not his mom, not me, and sure as hell not my jackass of a brother. He was great and more talented than one person should ever be, and I knew he deserved greatness. I refused to stand in the way of that.

He bent down, leaning in even closer, so that our noses were practically touching. I was shivering from head to toe, because it had been far too long since I had pressed up against the long, hard lines of that lean body. I was always going to want him, always going to be tempted by him, and it took every ounce of self-control I had not to grab him and slam my mouth over his, not to beg him to come back to me, not to demand that he keep it in his pants while he was on the road. But I didn't have the right to do any of those things, so I just watched him carefully and tried not to quiver.

"Why can't you just say I'm not good for you, that I'm not what you want? It doesn't have anything to do with me or what I think or want, Ayd. I could see forever with you, and could promise you every day that it'll just be me and you."

That made my heart seize. I wanted to grab his face, wanted to kiss that mouth that looked like it tasted sour and bad. I just wanted to make it better, but there was no way I could. I sighed and shook my head a little bit.

"I want what's best for both of us. I know you don't understand that, and I can see that you don't really believe it, either, but it's true. I know I'm not what's best for you, Jet. I have things going on and so do you, really. I don't think the universe or that girl from my past was ever going to give us a fair shot."

I wasn't ever going to be what was best for anyone, but that was neither here nor there.

He was looking at me like I was killing him slowly, over and over again. He pushed off the railing in a violent move that made me flinch a little. He scowled at me and shoved his hands through his messy hair. He took a few steps down the stairs, so that I was standing above him. When he looked up at me, the pain in his eyes tore away whatever was left that I was hiding behind. None of it mattered anymore and the truth was just too strong to ignore.

I loved him, loved him like I had never loved anyone or anything ever, and I realized that was why I could let him go. I could see how much it hurt him, imagined that I looked just as bad, but knowing I was doing it for the right reasons, because I did love him, made me believe we would both be okay in the end. Letting him go for his own good, to protect him from all the things that he could suffer from if he loved me back, was worth it.

"That's funny, Ayden, because when I'm with you, I feel better. I behave better, I sound better, and some of the nasty shit that eats me up inside doesn't seem so bad. No one has ever done that for me before, so if you aren't what's best for me, I can't imagine what you think would be."

I bit my lip and caved. I hopped down to the next step and grabbed his frowning face in both hands. His rough cheeks abraded my palms and he was warm, as if all that stuff he was feeling on the inside was trying to find its way out through his skin.

"You don't need anyone to make you better, Jet. You're already the best."

I meant to just brush my mouth across his, to just touch

lips to lips, to try to soothe some of those broken edges we seemed to keep stabbing each other with. As usual, when it was me and him, it went from sedate and light to a full-blown inferno in half a second. My hands wrapped in his hair, his hands locked on my waist, and it went from a good-bye peck to the kind of kiss people share when they know there is a very good chance they will never see each other again.

His lips were hard and his tongue was insistent against my own, and there was a level of desperation in both of us that made the kiss twist into something more dangerous than I could handle now that I realized how deeply I cared for him. Everything about Jet was passionate—his mouth, his hands, and the way he held me like I was going to escape and run away at any minute. He kissed me like he loved me and it broke me even further. I had no doubt had we been inside, and not standing in front of the house when the van with the rest of the guys in the band pulled up, that they would have interrupted something a lot more intimate than us kissing.

Someone honked the horn and Jet pulled away. He left a little bite to remember him by and now, instead of being angry, those oh-so-pretty eyes with that gold halo just looked sad.

"Bye, Ayd."

I had to hold back tears. I put his shaking fingers to my mouth, like maybe I could hold him there, keep him with me forever, and whispered back, "Bye, Jet."

He hauled all his equipment to the van and I stood fro-

zen to the spot. Right before he closed the door, he looked
at me and forced a lopsided grin. I lost it. Before the van
was gone from the front of the house, I bolted to my room
and threw myself across the bed. I cried because I couldn't
help but feel like he was telling me good-bye forever, and
I cried because there was no way I could have him. I cried
because my mom was never going to grow up, and I was never
going to get my childhood back. I cried because, as awful
and manipulative as Asa was, I still loved the rat bastard.
But mostly, I cried for me. I had spent so much time trying
to deny who I was, and working toward a future that was
secure, that I wasted Lord only knew how long avoiding
and denying the one person who wanted to actually promise me a forever. It was a mess.

I didn't hear Cora come in, but I felt my bed sink down
when she sat on the edge of it. Her fingers were cool when
she pushed my hair off my face.

"That was brutal."

I sniffed and tried to wipe the moisture away with the
pillow case, but my eyes kept on leaking.

"How much of it did you see?"

"Enough to watch two of my best friends' hearts break.
Come on, Ayd. Why are you doing this? Clearly you guys
belong together."

The tears came harder and harder and my heart squeezed
so hard I thought I was going to stop breathing for a minute.

"It's for the best." I wasn't sure how many times I had to
say it before I actually started to believe it myself.

She didn't say anything else, which for Cora was like an

act of God himself, but she did stay and continue to stroke my head until I was all cried out.

THE FIRST WEEK HE was gone was the worst. I threw myself into school and picked up every extra shift I could at the bar, and not only because I had to pay Shaw back an exorbitant amount of money. I had to stay busy or I felt like I would crack into pieces.

My friends asked how I was doing every day, and every day I lied and said I was fine. I even gritted my teeth and listened to Cora when she gave me updates on how the tour was going. Apparently, Enmity was even more popular than the band that was headlining, which wasn't surprising at all. Jet was a rock god and now all of Europe knew it, too. I wondered if, when he got back, he was finally going to sign with a big label and shoot to real stardom. He deserved to be recognized for how wonderful he was.

I ran more than I had ever run in my life. It was the only thing that wore me out enough so that I could fall asleep at night, and even then I still woke up and rolled over to reach for an empty side of the bed. When that happened, I tossed and turned and then finally gave up, and eventually just got out of my bed and went across the hall to sleep in Jet's empty bed, because it still smelled like him and made my heart hurt less.

I thought I was doing a good job keeping it all together, but sometimes I would see Shaw watching me like she was afraid I was going to shatter or do something crazy, like beat

Loren to death with her own stupidity. There were times Cora would say something and then just look at me, and I realized I was supposed to laugh or chime in with my two cents, but nothing really seemed funny to me anymore. It sucked. I felt like I was empty and hollow, and that hurt way worse than having anyone know what my life used to look like did.

Week two was a little better. I stopped listening for the sad strains of a guitar and I managed to stay in my own bed for most of the week. The only rough spot was when I overheard Cora talking to him on the phone, and I wanted to chase her down and steal it from her to ask how he was doing, ask if he had found some crappy European version of me to help heal his broken heart. That night, not only did I sleep in his room, but in his shirt as well. It was pathetic.

I had about a thousand unsent text messages on my phone that I battled day in and day out not to send to him. I wanted to tell him that I missed him, that I loved him, and that no one would ever be to me what he was. Instead, I listened to sad country songs (new ones, not old ones) and told myself over and over again that it was all for the best.

By the time week three rolled around, I was faking being okay like a pro. Shaw wasn't giving me the eye anymore, and Cora was talking about Jet like it didn't cut me open every time she said his name. I had even agreed to have a couple strictly platonic coffee dates with Adam, just to reinforce to him that I wasn't interested, and that while I thought he was a super guy, my heart just simply belonged to someone else. He took it with a grain of salt, but continued to call, and as long as I had everyone watching for cracks in my facade of indifference, I decided it didn't hurt to keep him around.

I was getting used to the absent feeling I was carrying around, getting used to the idea that this is what my life was going to look like now, because there was no replacing someone like Jet. There was no getting around that he was what my future was supposed to be when my past decided it wasn't done toying with me yet.

I was getting ready for work, standing in the bathroom subconsciously looking for all the junk Jet used to leave lying around, when that same odd number from Kentucky that had been calling for weeks popped back up on my phone. I was going to ignore it, but then I figured it was just Asa, and since I hadn't heard from him in more than a month, I decided it would be best to answer and let him check in, or ask for money, which was more likely. I propped the phone between my ear and shoulder while I fussed with my hair, and answered.

"Hello?"

It wasn't Asa. It wasn't Silas. It wasn't my mom. It wasn't anyone who I would have ever expected to hear from again.

"Hello, Ayden."

I blinked for a second and stared in shock at my own reflection in the bathroom mirror.

"Mr. Kelly?" There was no mistaking that kind voice with the familiar Southern drawl. It was the voice that had broken me free from Woodward. It was the voice that had convinced me I was better than all the things I was doing wrong.

"I'm sure this is a surprise, but I had to call to tell you about Asa."

I could see my own bewilderment reflected back at me.

"Asa?" I was sure I sounded as confused as I felt, but I was having a hard time putting two and two together.

There was a sigh on the other end of the phone.

"You know I always believed in karma. I thought that by helping you, getting you out of that trailer park and out from under your brother's thumb, my universe would be in alignment, and for a while it was."

"Have you been calling me the last month or so?"

"I have. I knew they were going to send Silas after Asa, so I wanted to check in on you. I figured as long as you answered, you were okay."

I leaned against the sink because my knees were suddenly weak.

"What's going on with my brother, Mr. Kelly?"

There was another sigh, and this one I could almost feel the heaviness of. I owed this man my life, but I had a sudden, sneaking suspicion he was about to move to the category of "no good things come out of Woodward."

"Asa didn't give you the entire book when you paid him off. There were a couple of pages missing from it and the motorcycle club isn't happy."

That was just like Asa. Leaving good enough alone was never his style and greed was just too powerful a motive.

"Asa is long gone, Mr. Kelly. I gave him enough money to sit on a beach and sip margaritas for as long as he wants. I can't get those pages back."

"Oh, I know that, Ayden, and you don't have to worry about the missing pages. The club already retrieved them, and that's why I'm calling."

My stomach rolled and I felt the blackness start to swirl. "Is my brother dead?"

There was a lot of silence on the other end of the phone and I thought I was going to pass out.

"No, but you might want to come home, because I honestly don't know how much time he has left. He's in bad shape. He's at the hospital in Louisville."

I gagged a little and sank to the floor. The cold tile on the back of my legs brought a little clarity to my rapidly spinning mind.

"How are you involved in all of this?" One thing was clear to me now, this man had never helped me out of the pure goodness of his heart.

"I wish I wasn't. I wish I could have just watched you drive away and never thought of you again, but that isn't the case when you live in a small town like this."

"Mr. Kelly, please just get to the point."

"My name is in that book, has been for years."

I coughed a laugh out that sounded more like a wounded animal dying.

"So you saved me, just to sacrifice me when it was convenient for you?"

"Your brother courts trouble, Ayden. Blame him, not me. When I decided to help you I had to get the money from somewhere and there was no way a teacher has those kinds of funds lying around. I gamble, I have for years, and some-

times my luck is better than others. I was on a hot streak
when I helped you out and now . . ." There was a long drawn-
out pause and I could almost feel him struggling with the
words to use to minimize the damage this call was creating
in the fabric of my reality. "Now all that luck is gone and it
was get Asa and the book or end up in a morgue. I'm so sorry
you had to be involved Ayden."

"Why on earth would Asa go back to Woodward, knowing what was waiting for him there?"

I was so lost, so confused, but one thing was obvious, this
was just one more person who had used me as a means to
an end. One more person who couldn't see past what they
thought I should be. As it turned out, being the only person that knew where to find me, the only person back home
with a clue as to how my life was progressing out in the
mountains, had proven too good a bargaining chip for him
not to use.

"Because I called him and passed on the message that if
he didn't come back, the club was going after you."

I hissed out a breath through my teeth. "You would have
sent them here?"

"It's a lot of money, Ayden. One day, maybe you'll understand. I'm the one who called the ambulance when they were
done with your brother, so maybe instead of judging me,
you should thank me. After all, the life you're living now, no
matter how you came by it, is because of me. I knew I was
absolutely doing the right thing when I saved you from this
town. I knew you had greatness in you and I wasn't wrong.
You have become a remarkable young woman with so much

potential. It does a guilty part of me good to know I had a hand in that."

"Asa came back because of me?"

That didn't make any sense. My brother was selfish, he was arrogant, and really, the only person he cared about was himself. The idea that he would have sacrificed himself for my safety was just crazy.

"He did. He knew whatever the club did to him wouldn't compare to what they would have done to you, if they got their hands on you. For what it's worth, your brother got less than he deserved, and if he pulls through, maybe he'll have learned a lesson. I really am sorry it had to go this way, Ayden. You deserve better."

The phone went dead on the other end of the line. I let mine rattle from my numb hand onto the floor. I put my forehead against my knees and concentrated on not passing out. It was all a lot to take in. My brother, Mr. Kelly, the way things were with Jet, all of it came tumbling down around me, like a house of cards. Thoughts of things I should have done differently started slamming into my head, left and right. The decisions I had made, bad and good, began chasing each other in a circle so fast that I was dizzy and sick at the same time.

I heard the bathroom door open and looked up at Cora with startled eyes. I must have been quite a sight, because she freaked out a little when she called my name.

"What in the hell is going on? I thought you fell in the shower or something."

I just gazed up at her, this little punk-rock pixie who I

loved, and realized that Mr. Kelly was dead wrong. The life I had now had nothing to do with anyone but me. These people loved me for me and would love me in spite of me. They loved whatever me I gave them, no questions asked. Bad choices and a life lived unwisely before I got to this point weren't worth suffering an eternity for, and trying to save Jet from me was stupid. He was the only person I had ever cared about who wanted me just for me, and not for what I could do for him. If I had let him, he would have loved every part of me, and made sure that both of us were safe from the things that the past kept trying to drag us back into.

I blinked up at Cora right before she was going to smack me to get my attention.

"I have to go home." My voice cracked. I think all of the things that made me who I was were starting to leak out, but I wasn't afraid of anyone seeing it anymore. I wasn't afraid of seeing it in the mirror every day anymore.

"Home? Home, like Kentucky? Why?"

"My brother is in the hospital. It doesn't sound good."

She got on her knees in front of me and put her tiny hands over mine, where they were resting on my knees.

"Oh no, do you need me to go with you? Do you want me to call Shaw? I didn't even know you had a brother."

I just shook my head and let it flop back until it banged against the cabinet door.

"No. My mom took off with some trucker named Earl or Daryl or something. Not like she would come back anyway. Mother of the Year she is not. It's just me and Asa, and normally really it's just me, but he got hurt trying to do something right for the first time in his sorry life. Now I have to go back home and hope he pulls through, so I can kick his ass and thank him, in that order."

She had a look of shock on her pretty face.

"I think that's the most you've ever said to me about your past, ever."

I closed my eyes and blew out a breath.

"That's because it's not a pretty tale and I spend a lot of time pretending it never happened. Only now, it's right in my face and it caused me to push the only guy I've ever loved away. I thought Jet wasn't right because he made all the old parts of me want to break free and take control of this wonderful life I have here. I think I've been punishing myself for things I've done in the past. Jet would have been a reward, and I refused to take it, because I didn't think I deserved him."

She moved so that she was sitting cross-legged on the floor in front of me. I couldn't look away from those odd-colored eyes. The blue on one side was intense and sad, and the brown was dark and filled with sympathy.

"Ayd, I don't know who you think comes from some kind of *Leave It to Beaver* background. Rule barely talks to his folks, Shaw's mom is the Wicked Witch of the West, and Nash hates his mom's husband so much he moved out when he was just a little boy. Rowdy doesn't even know who his folks are, my mom took off before I could walk and left me with a dad who conveniently forgot I was a girl every chance he got, and we all know how bad Jet's dad treats his mom. None of us is shooting sunshine out of our asses, girl, so I don't know why you think you should suffer alone."

I wrapped my arms around her neck, and let her hug me back. It was so nice just to appreciate my friend, to know that she was simply there for me. Everything else that was facing me back home didn't seem nearly as daunting.

"Thanks, Cora."

"You're a great person, Ayden, and you deserve the best."

I pushed my hands through my hair and let her pull me up off the floor.

"I had it. I let it go."

"He didn't go far. Just call him."

"Maybe after I figure out what's going on with my brother, I can tackle that issue. Asa really might not make it." I was surprised that the thought choked me up.

"Let me come with you, or call Shaw. You know she'll drop everything and probably even charter a private jet or something."

I shook my head and headed toward my room.

"No. I need to do this alone."

"But Ayd, if something really bad happens, you shouldn't have to deal with it alone."

"If something really bad happens, I promise I'll call in the troops, okay?"

She just watched me for a second, then squeezed my arm. "Promise?"

I hugged her again. "I promise."

"All right, well, while you pack I'll call and make you a reservation, and get you going, okay?"

"I adore you, Cora."

"Well, I am adorable, so that is totally understandable."

She scampered toward the phone, and I started throwing together everything I could think of into an overnight bag. I called work and told them I was going to miss a few days and called Shaw to give her a quick update. That took longer than anticipated, because she demanded to come with me and it wasn't until Rule wrestled the phone away from her and told me that he would sit on her until I landed, that I managed to get out the door. Cora took me to the airport, since I was lucky to get a flight out right away, and it only took a few hours until I landed in Louisville.

Being back in Kentucky was like a smack in the face. Everyone moved a little slower and talked a little sweeter, and by the time I was in the rental car on the way to the hospital, I was starting to feel like I'd never left. It was a quick drive into the heart of Louisville, because Woodward was too small to handle Asa in the condition he was in. All the while, all I could think was that Asa had to at least make it until I got there. It didn't matter what kind of self-ish prick my brother tended to be, no one deserved to die alone and scared. I called ahead and found out he was still in the trauma unit and that he was unconscious. It made my skin pebble up when I heard the sadness in the nurse's voice. Clearly he wasn't in good shape, and I hated that he was that way because of me.

I didn't even have to ask where he was when I got there. The admitting nurse was obviously waiting to see if anyone was going to come for the pretty broken boy. Even on the brink of death Asa still had that effect on women. They led me back to a tiny little room and I almost fell over when I finally laid eyes on my big brother.

My larger-than-life brother looked like a broken marionette. There were tubes and wires coming out of him everywhere. I couldn't see his face because of the gauze wrapped around him. He had a ventilator in his mouth and I could see the unnatural rise and fall of his chest, indicating he wasn't breathing on his own. Both arms were in heavy casts and his leg had something that looked like a medieval torture device on it. Bad shape didn't even begin to cover it. He didn't look human or alive.

I gulped and walked to the bedside. I put a hand over the plaster on one of his hands. A doctor came in with a chart and looked slightly startled to see me.

"Are you family? We've tried to get ahold of his mother but she said she was in Illinois and wouldn't be back for a few weeks."

I cleared my throat.

"I'm his sister."

The doctor looked at me over the top of his glasses. "You might want to impress upon your mother that the situation is very serious. She might want to get here in case his condition deteriorates further. His brain was bleeding. We put him in a medically induced coma to help with the swelling and to see if we could get it to stop. It's very touch-and-go."

I wrapped my hands around the rails of the hospital bed.

"I'll stay with him. She won't come back."

"It doesn't look good. Even if he wakes up, there is no

guarantee he'll be the way he was before. Frankly, it's a miracle he survived this long. I've never seen a beating like this. He must have made some very bad people pretty angry."

I closed my eyes.

"He has a particular talent for that."

"The police are doing a comprehensive investigation. Hopefully, they'll come up with something."

They wouldn't. Woodward was a small town and things didn't work that way out here. This was just good old-fashioned justice, an eye for an eye, and Asa would be lucky if he survived it. I bent down and kissed him on his thickly bandaged head. I still had all my stuff in the car. There was no way in hell I was going back to that trailer, and it looked like I was going to be here awhile, so I needed to find a hotel close to the hospital.

"I didn't think we had anything in common anymore, Asa, but it looks like protecting the people we love, even if it nearly kills us, is a Cross trait. We really gotta be smarter than that, big brother."

CHAPTER 16

Jet

THERE WAS A NAKED blonde in the bed, across from where I was sitting at the little dinette in the hotel room. It was a sad testament to the state of affairs that I was far more interested in the bottle of whiskey in front of me than I was in her. She hardly spoke any English and had come along with one of the guys in Artifice after the set, but for whatever reason she had been all over me all night, even though I wasn't remotely interested. Maybe it was the language barrier. I didn't understand German, and all she seemed to understand was that the more booze I tossed back, the more appealing she became, so there had been an endless supply since coming back to my room.

She was good-looking, tall with a great rack, and had miles of blond hair and pretty, big blue peepers. The problem was, she had all of those things and was in my bed where there should have been an amber-eyed brunette. Part of me was dying to climb in beside her and let the whiskey and a soft girl eliminate the ghost of Ayden for just a minute.

Unfortunately, a bigger part of me knew that was only a temporary fix, a fix that would make me feel like shit in the morning, and make the guys in the band worry about me more than they already were.

Being on this tour was wearing on me and I don't think I was hiding it well. The girls, the parties, the booze, and the drugs—it was all a lot to process while I was trying to deal with a broken heart, and no matter what my own guys threw at me or what Dario and his boys tried to tempt me with, it held no appeal. I missed Colorado. I missed the boys at the shop, I missed Cora, and despite everything, I was worried about my mom. There was no hiding the hole in the center of my very being where Ayden should be and it went without saying I missed her most of all.

However, the real reason, the real issue that was keeping me from climbing all over the naked blonde and letting her teach me the German word for Jet, was Ayden. I couldn't stop thinking about her, and couldn't stop seeing all the things I was feeling reflected back at me in her honey-tinted eyes. I felt so alone without her, and I didn't for a second think she was going to be waiting around for me when I got back, not even after that kiss good-bye.

So far, the best thing about Europe was the opportunity to see a bunch of really great bands. In every country we stopped in, in every bar we pulled up to, there were underground bands playing. Amazing groups made up of kids often years younger than me, and it made me happy every time we got to hear them play. It reminded me just how much I loved listening to other bands play, loved discovering new talent and getting them exposure, far more than I liked being the one adored and fawned over while onstage. Sure I loved to play, loved to write songs and perform, but I absolutely didn't want to do this for a living.

Being on tour, no matter where in the world it was, got to be a drag after a while. I wanted my own bed, preferably with a pretty Southern girl already in it, and I wanted a night not spent in a bar, fending off groupies and metal heads. I wasn't cut out to be a rock star, but I was a perfect fit to make others into one. When I got home, I was going to rebuild the studio and look into starting up my own record label. The idea had me excited in a way the naked blonde could only dream of doing. Luckily for me, the rest of the guys in the band seemed as burned-out as I was.

Von missed his girlfriend and his kid, and spent more time on Skype than he did in the bar. Catcher spent most of his time with the guys in Artifice, but really was just happy to be along for the ride, and Boone we all watched every day, to see if he was struggling at all with his long stretch of sobriety. Being on the road was hard, and for this long and this far from home, we all worried he might slip. I don't think anyone was thinking about signing with the label and I was glad. The band was solid and I would have hated for us to break up because we wanted different things. That thought just hit a little too close to home right now for me.

Dario insisted we were the better band, that we could go places and do things Artifice had only come close to, and while I took it as a compliment, they were things I just didn't want. The only thing I wanted, the only thing that mattered, didn't think we were right for each other and that's where I seemed to be stuck.

I lumbered to my feet, drunk but not drunk enough, and eyeballed the girl. I needed to get her under me or out the door, and my tired brain wasn't sure which option it was going to go with, when my phone trilled the very screamy Jucifer from my back pocket. The time changes across the ocean still weirded me out and the fact that Shaw was the one calling me made my blood go cold. It didn't even register to me that the girl in the bed was swearing at me in a foreign language, or that she hurled the remote at my head as I went into the bathroom to take the call. She was going to be a pain to get rid of, but I didn't deserve anything less for some seriously piss-poor judgment.

"Hey, Shaw is everything all right? Is Rule okay?"

Worst-case scenarios were running through my head at a rapid pace and I couldn't slow them down. Angry German was rumbling though the closed door along with hammering fists. If I had been just a shade more intoxicated, this entire situation would have been so ridiculously hilarious there was a chance I would have killed myself laughing over it.

"Hey, sorry to interrupt you, but I needed to call you even though Rule threatened to hide my phone if I did."

"What's up?" She sounded nervous, which made me nervous and mad that Colorado was an entire ocean away. Something really heavy hit the door, and I absently wondered if the girl had bothered to put on clothes before throwing her tantrum. It struck me as funny that no matter where

I was in the world, a pissed-off groupie was still just a pissed-off groupie.

"It's Ayden."

And just like that the world stopped. There was no angry blonde in the next room. There was no band. There was no anything but Ayden, and the fact she was too far away. I stopped breathing long enough that the room got a little hazy and it took Shaw snapping my name to get me back in focus.

"What's up with Ayden?"

I tried to sound casual, but knew I failed miserably when Shaw just swore softly.

"Look, there is a bunch of stuff she needs to tell you, that you need to make her tell you. I understand why she pushed you away and you just have to believe me that she really did it because she thought she was protecting you, but right now, she's alone and she needs you. She wouldn't let me go with her and she refused to let Cora go with her, but she needs someone, and honestly that someone is you."

"Shaw, you realize I'm in Hamburg right now and I'm supposed to be in Berlin tomorrow afternoon, right?"

She sighed and what sounded like her head thunking against something hard came across the line.

"I know. But she needs you."

"I think she made it pretty clear I'm the last thing she needs in her life, Shaw." Something on the other side of the door shattered and I cringed. It looked like the cost of my room just went up exponentially.

"Her brother is in the hospital, Jet. He got beaten within

an inch of his life and no one knows if he's going to make it. Ayden's mom is a flake, Ayden's sitting in a hospital in Louisville all by herself, waiting to see if her only sibling is going to die. Come on, I know you don't fully understand why she pushed you away and left you hanging but the reality is she just wanted to keep you at arm's length so that you didn't get hurt. She was trying to protect you."

"From what?"

"Another situation that was ugly and full of really awful things. She's in love with you."

I ground my teeth together and absently kicked at the bathroom door.

"I didn't even know she had a brother. If she loved me, don't you think that would have come up before now? Shaw, I know you're just trying to help, but I think you're grasping at straws."

Now she swore loudly, and I heard all kinds of Rule in her attitude when she snapped back at me.

"Stop being such a stupid guy! You don't need to give her anything, all you need to do is show up. She just needs you to show up, Jet. It's not that hard." I didn't get a chance to respond before she went on. "I know you're hurting, but so is she, and the only thing that will make either of you stop is for one of you to realize that you just need to be together. Plain and simple. If you can't see that, then you didn't deserve her in the first place. I'll talk to you later, Jet."

She hung up on me, leaving me stunned and reeling in a bathroom, a million miles from home. My instinct was to throw everything in a bag and run off to the rescue, only the last time I had tried that, I had ended up in jail. I was so tired of trying to save people, women in particular, who ultimately didn't want me to be their hero at all. The idea of Ayden suffering alone, the idea of her trying to handle something like that by herself, turned me inside out, but she didn't want me. If she didn't want me, there was nothing I could do for her that her girlfriends or Sweater Vest couldn't do. Besides, I had a naked and very angry German girl I had to wrangle, and that was at least a tangible problem I could fix.

WE WERE ON THE train to Berlin the next day and I felt awful. I hadn't slept at all the night before and getting rid of the St. Pauli girl on steroids had proven more difficult than I anticipated. I couldn't get my mind off Shaw's phone call, and being cooped up on the train with a bunch of hungover metal dudes and loud German families was enough to make me want to pull every last hair out of my head and run screaming for the hills. Von was sitting across from me, alternately napping and messing around on his phone, seemingly oblivious to the noise around us and I envied him the peace he seemed to just naturally have.

"You all right, man? You've looked ready to bail out the window all day."

I shifted restlessly in the seat.

"I'm straight."

"Really? I call bullshit. You haven't been straight since things went south with you and Ayden. Your body might be

here, but your head has been back in Denver since we picked
you up."

"I'm cool. Just takes time to get over someone like her, is
all. I keep thinking maybe I should call her."

"Dude, who do you think you're talking to? I've know
you since you were a punk-ass little kid. Girls were just girls,
until Ayden. She's different, we all saw it. Fuck, you sang oldies on Valentine's Day, Jet. Do you think we're all stupid? We
knew who you were singing to."

"She just got to me, is all."

"Good. She's smart, she's a knockout, she has enough
attitude to put up with all your moods, and I bet she isn't
scared of all the Keller family skeletons. Goddamn Jet, you
write better music than anyone else in the world, you're a
better front man than pretty much anyone else who has ever
stepped on a stage, and you're an all-around really fucking
good dude. You should have someone like Ayden in your life.
Stop thinking you need to do some kind of crazy penance
because your dad is a douche rocket and your mom refuses
to see it."

"Whoa, where did all that come from?"

"Coming on this tour was a great opportunity. We all
needed to do it to see where we stood with the band. It isn't
what I want and it's easy to see it's not what you want, either.
I love playing music and doing a festival here or there and
playing at Cerberus is just fine for me, but it's fine for me
because I go home to Blain and the baby. They're what I
want, they're where I want to be, and I see that in you now.
Before, it was fear. You were scared for your mom, scared of

what would happen if you just let go and did you, but now it's different. You want to be where that girl is, even if she told you that it was over."

I lifted an eyebrow at him.

"Last year, if we had been on this tour you would have had a different girl in your room every night. You would be drinking your weight in whiskey and acting as crazy as the guys in Artifice have been. Face it. You've changed."

I rested my forehead on the window and watched mindlessly as the German countryside sped by.

"The only other person that has ever made me feel that bad is my mom."

"We all have things we're trying to handle and deal with. You have an outlet for all your crazy—you can get onstage and scream it out. Maybe your girl doesn't have one of those things."

I closed my eyes and let all the things of late float around in my mind. He had a valid point. I'd always thought of the anger that lived inside me as fire—heat and flame—and things that could burn down the world I live in. Well, if I was fire, Ayden was water. She was constantly shifting and moving, reflecting things back and changing form at will. She was cool, and she ebbed and flowed with whatever life handed her. We shouldn't work together, but we did, and when you put us together everything got hot and steamy, which really was all I could ask for in someone who I wanted to keep with me forever.

"How am I supposed to fix this when we have a show tonight and one tomorrow night? How am I supposed to do anything when I'm here and she's there? What am I supposed to do if she doesn't even want me there, and Shaw was wrong and just reading more into it than there really ever was?"

"Stop being a pussy and just do it. If Blain needed me, you bet your happy ass I would leave you jokers hanging."

"Asshole."

He laughed a little and stretched his legs out in front of him.

"You aren't going to be able to get anything done today anyway, so you play the show tonight, figure your shit out tomorrow, and let me and the boys handle the next couple of shows until you get back. I can cover most of the vocals, and what I can't do, Catcher can. We won't be half as good without you, but who cares?"

I closed my eyes and turned it all over in my mind. I didn't want to let the guys down; we were a team and this was a big deal, but I also knew I wasn't going to do anyone any good when everything that made me so good onstage was wrapped up and focused on something else. Even if she ended up telling me to get lost for good, at least I tried. I dug out my phone and called Cora.

"Hey."

"Hey, what's going on?" She sounded sleepy and again I remembered the time change.

"I need to know where in Louisville Ayden is."

"What?" The sleepiness was gone out of her voice now.

"Shaw called me and told me about Ayden's brother. I'm going to her."

"Oh, thank God."

"Come on, Cora, help me out here."

"I talked to her yesterday. They had to rush him in for some kind of emergency surgery. She sounds terrified and so sad. Shaw and I were about to draw straws to see who was going to ignore her and fly to Kentucky anyway. Her brother is at Baptist Hospital East or something like that. It's right downtown. She needs someone, Jet. Don't screw this up."

I thought it was ironic, considering Ayden was the one who had left me hanging, that everyone was suddenly so concerned that I was going to mess everything with her up.

"I'm trying to fix it, which is pretty weird considering I don't think I'm really the one that broke it."

She snorted at me and I popped my knuckles and twirled the ring around my thumb absently.

"I have to play the show in Berlin tonight and I'll work on getting to the States tomorrow, but it's still going to be a while before I can get to Kentucky. You guys probably need to keep an eye on her until I can get to her if it's as bad as Shaw said."

"We have been. We love her, too, you know?"

I snorted. "I do know."

"Are you going to tell her you're coming?"

I was debating that myself. I wanted to shoot her a message, something to let her know she was on my mind, that she wasn't alone no matter what happened. I knew if she ignored it, or told me not to bother her right now, there was a good chance I would scrap the entire idea and just keep on going forward with the band and the tour.

"No. I think it'll be better just to show up. That way, if

she doesn't want me there she can just tell me, and it doesn't have to be some long, drawn-out thing."

"Jet, even if she tells you she doesn't want you there, she's lying. It's your job to know that and stay anyway."

Women were entirely too complicated.

"Thanks, Cora. I'll shoot you a message later to let you know how everything works out."

"It'll work out the way it's supposed to. I have faith in you guys."

I grunted and hung up the phone. I flipped it around in my fingers for a few minutes, and stared at the blank screen until I finally gave in and typed a message to Ayden. We hadn't spoken since that kiss in the yard before I left, and I could still feel every part of her inside me.

I've been thinking about you. I miss you.

There was no response back for a solid half hour, but she was in a different time zone and I didn't know if she was stay-ing at the hospital or not, so I tried really hard not to think about it too much. Instead, I scrounged up a pen and a piece of paper and worked out the chorus of a new song that had been tugging at me since we left. I was so lost in thought that when my phone dinged with a message, I almost ignored it until I remembered that I had sent a text to her.

I miss you, too.

Simple and to the point. It was all I really needed to hear.

CHAPTER 17

Ayden

I WAS SO EXHAUSTED I could barely see straight. I had spent the last three nights sleeping in the most uncomfortable chair in the world in Asa's room and I was sick to death of arguing with my mom on the phone.

Asa had a seizure my first night back in Kentucky and had been rushed in for major surgery. The doctors had to drill a hole in his head in order to reduce the swelling and give the pooling blood a place to escape. Asa's heart had stopped beating twice, and they told me lucky didn't even come close to covering it with how close my brother had come to dying. He still wasn't awake, and it was really touch-and-go, but I had to take a shower and if my mom called to tell me she just simply couldn't make it home one more time, I was going to murder everyone. I couldn't believe she was acting like this was just another scrape that Asa had gotten himself into. Not when I told her that the hospital staff had declared him dead, not just once but twice, while he was on the operating table. If he died and she made me bury my brother alone, it was the last time she was ever going to hear from me.

The hotel wasn't exactly five-star accommodations, but it was within walking distance of the hospital and they had plenty of open rooms, so it would do until I knew one way or the other what I was dealing with. I sent a quick message to the girls to let them know what had happened and then spent ten minutes assuring both of them I was fine, and that neither one of them needed to get on a plane. They were the best, but I needed to handle what was to come on my own. I promised to call if I needed them and then stared at the message Jet had sent the day before.

I had been sitting in the waiting room during Asa's surgery when it came through, and it had taken me a half hour to stop silently crying long enough to write him back. Just knowing I was on his mind had been enough to get me through the endless hours of waiting, and when they had come out and told me about Asa's heart stopping, it was the simple *I miss you* that had enabled me to keep it together.

I toyed with the idea of sending him a quick little message to let him know I was thinking about him as well, but I was too tired to think straight and no words seemed right to convey everything I wanted to say to him. I wanted to tell him that I needed him, that this was the scariest thing I had ever had to do on my own, that I was done pushing him away for his own good, that if he could love all the parts of me, they were his for the taking. I just didn't want to shovel all that at him while he was concentrating on the tour. He had obligations to things bigger than me, and I could be patient. I would

talk to him when he got back and hope that somewhere along
the way he hadn't found a replacement for me

I rubbed my gritty eyes and trudged up the concrete
steps that led to the floor my room was supposed to be on.
I had only been in the room for five minutes to drop off my
bag and brush my teeth. There were families on either side
of me who had been cheery in passing, but now I hoped they
were out for the day, so that it was quiet and I could just
crash for an hour or so until I had to head back to the hospital. I blinked a couple of times when I got to the landing
because it looked like a long, lean figure was sitting against
the closed door. I shook my head for a second to make sure
my sleepy brain wasn't playing tricks on me, because there
was only one person on the planet I could think of who
would be wearing skintight purple jeans in the middle of
redneck country, and he was supposed to be a million miles
away being a rock star.

"Jet?"

The word whispered out as more a breath than an actual
sound, but he must have heard me, because his head turned
and he finally saw me. He pressed back against the closed
door he was propped up against and levered up to his feet.
He had on dark sunglasses and a tight black T-shirt that had
some kind of flaming skull and pentagram band logo on it.
His dark hair looked like he had slept on it for days, but his
mouth kicked up in a half grin and suddenly he was all I
could see. There was no rundown hotel, there were no kids
screaming in the pool down below, there was no brother
barely hanging on to life—there was just Jet, and he was all

I wanted in the world. I wasn't aware of the fact that I was moving toward him, that I was running. I wasn't aware that I was crying, yet again, and wasn't aware that he caught me when I slammed into him hard enough to drive him back a step or two. All I could feel was his arms wrap around me and his lips touching the top of my head, while I collapsed against him. I tried to climb him like a jungle gym, so that I could get my legs around him as well.

"What are you doing here?" I wasn't sure the words made any sense through the hysteria I was dripping all over him.

He put a hand under my ass to hoist me up higher and ran his other hand over my seriously unbrushed hair.

"It's where I'm supposed to be. Good thing the teenager in the room next to yours took a fancy to those long-ass legs, or I would still be wandering around the parking lot. I was going to come to the hospital if you didn't show up in another hour, but I figured here was a better bet, just in case things with your brother were really bad and you didn't want me there."

I buried my nose in the crook of his neck and just breathed him in and out. He felt so solid and real. I swore to myself I was never going to let him go again. He tasted salty from the Kentucky humidity and from my tears running down the side of his neck and into the collar of his shirt.

"I want you here."

"Want to give me the key to your room so we can stop giving the nice family from Michigan a show?"

"It's in my back pocket."

I felt him digging around in the pocket of my cut-off jean shorts and his chest move up and down as he chuckled a little against me.

"I gotta tell ya, Ayd. I'm a fan of the South if this is what you're gonna be wearing while you're here."

I had on cut-off jean shorts and my cowboy boots with a tank top, which was pretty much the uniform while I was home, and not really appropriate for Colorado, since the weather there never wanted to make up its mind. I felt him get the door open and move us inside. He kept his hold on me and sat down on the edge of the bed. I wanted to tell him it was probably gross and he should pull the comforter off, but more than that I just wanted him to keep holding on to me and make everything feel better.

"I'm so happy to see you."

He rubbed the back of my neck and I closed my eyes and just let him soothe me.

"You could have called me at any time, Ayd. I would have been on the first plane out."

"I don't know what I'm doing, Jet. I don't even know how I got this far alone." I exhaled against his neck and felt him shiver. "I need to tell you some stuff and I need you to promise me that it's not going to make you go anywhere when I'm done."

I felt him tense a little under me but his hands stayed steady and his voice was calm when he replied, "I'm not going anywhere, Ayd. I just flew all the way across the fucking globe to be here. You don't scare me, this doesn't scare me."

"That makes one of us."

I pulled back so that we were looking at each other and wiped my cheeks with the back of my hand. He reached up and tucked some loose strands of my hair behind my ears and the gesture was so sweet, so caring it almost made me start bawling all over again. I took a deep breath and let it all unravel.

I told him about my mom. I told him about the trailer. I told him about the boys. I told him about the drugs. I told him about the sex. I told him about Mr. Kelly and school, and finally I told him about Asa. I laid it all out as bare and naked as I could. I pulled back the curtain to show him all the secrets that were hiding there. He never blinked, just kept watching me, kept those dark eyes on mine the entire time, and those halos around the outsides got several degrees brighter and sharper the more I talked.

I told him about being entranced by him the first time I saw him onstage. I told him about how bad I wanted him that first night he turned me down for being too good of a girl, and how that played with my head for months after, because I was no one's idea of good. I told him all I wanted was to protect him, and that the idea of Asa being behind the studio robbery had sent me running into a blind panic, and that was why I had to make him go. I was trying to get it all out, explain all the decisions, either right or wrong, that had led me here. I was going to tell him that I missed him so bad, that I loved him, and that I never wanted him to go, but I didn't get that far, because he just stopped me by putting his mouth over mine.

It was an effective way to stem the flow of words, and

it also had the added bonus of making me lose my train of thought and settle more fully into his lap. He ran his hands up the outside of my bare arms and his rings trailed little paths of cool metal all along the skin.

"Ayden," his tone was serious and his dark eyes were intent. "You never had to do any of this alone. I would have been there for you,"

I let my forehead fall forward to rest against his. This man, who was all metal and tattoos that bled out anger and frustration, really had the softest and kindest heart I had ever encountered in my life. Now that I knew how easy it was to snap in half, I told myself it was going to be my job to take care of it from here on out.

"I know you would have, but you're here now when I need you the most, and that's all that really matters to me. If you still want my forever, it's yours, Jet. No one else has ever come close and you're the only one I have ever wanted to offer it to."

He lifted a dark eyebrow and grinned at me.

"You in love with me, Ayd?"

I closed my eyes and kissed him like he had just kissed me. We just made so much sense together even if we made no sense at all.

"I'm in love with us, Jet."

That made him laugh out loud and wrap me in an even tighter hug.

"That's even better. For what it's worth, I shouldn't have let hurt feelings and my own fears stand in the way of us being together. I knew you were a runner from the get-go, and I shouldn't have been such a jackass and given up the chase so easily. Now that I know what you were trying to sort through all on your own, it makes me feel like even more of a pansy. Just a fair warning, if your bro pulls out of this mess, there is a good chance I might put him right back in that hospital bed."

I sighed against his mouth and moved to climb off him. It did my heart happy when his hand clenched just a little to hold me close, before he finally let me go.

"You might have to get in line for that. Asa is Asa. He's always going to be the way he is, but he's also always going to be my big brother and he did the right thing by me when he ultimately had to. Come on, you know it's nearly impossible to turn your back on family."

He leaned back on his elbows on the bed and watched me with hooded eyes as I moved around the room.

"I finally let my mom go."

I looked at him over my shoulder and sucked in a breath. If I wasn't exhausted beyond measure, if my mind wasn't still on Asa and his precarious condition, I would have jumped on him and not let him up for hours. I wondered if it was always going to be like that between us, or if the allure of all that tattooed skin and those dark eyes and devil spikes in his ears was going to wear thin.

"You didn't let her go, you just finally gave her some room to find her own way. There is only so much you can do there."

"I'm not letting you go, Ayden, and I'm not going to give you any kind of room, so you better be prepared to deal with all of that for a long time. You promised forever and I plan on holding you to it."

The hesitancy in his voice tore at my heart. I hated that I had put it there, hated that I had added to his insecurity. I knew all about wanting a steady and secure foundation for the future. I just never knew it was going to come in the form of a good-looking boy in too-tight pants holding a guitar and singing to me in a beautiful voice.

"Old me, new me and everything that's in between or yet to come, all of it is yours, Jet."

He pushed off the bed and stalked toward me, until we were toe-to-toe and I had to tilt my head back to look him in the eye.

"We can wait until your brother is all better to talk about this stuff. I have a couple days before I have to head back, and you look dead on your feet. I'm here to take care of you, not the other way around."

I grabbed one of his hands that was hanging loosely at his side. It took a little bit of work to pry the fat silver ring off his finger, but when I had it free, I held it up between the two of us and looked him dead in the eye. He was watching me cautiously but didn't ask me what I was doing.

"Do you love me, Jet? Despite it all, do you love me?"

"Ayden, I'm here. Of course I love you. I loved you before, I love you after, and I'll love you for everything in-between."

Had we not been in a grungy hotel room in Kentucky, there was a good chance that I would have gotten down on one knee to make the moment more dramatic, to prove to him just how serious I was about not running away anymore. But a girl had to have standards. I grabbed his left hand and put a kiss in the center of his palm.

"Jet Keller, I love you, and there is no future for me without you in it. I'm never going to bed with a man who isn't you again. I don't care if you're a rock star or a car salesman, I just want there to be a 'you and me' forever. Will you marry me?"

I held his ring out in front of him and waited for him to answer me. His mouth opened and closed like a fish, and his eyes looked like they were going to bug out of his head. The entire thing would have been comical, if I hadn't felt like I was going to swallow my tongue or pass out at any second.

"Are you serious right now?" I was surprised that his voice cracked a little. I had seen Jet in a lot of ways, but speechless and choked up wasn't one of them.

"It doesn't have to be today. It doesn't have to be tomorrow. Hell, it doesn't have to be this year or five years from now. I want you to understand I'm here, I'm not going anywhere, and I'm never going to pick anyone over you, Jet, never again not even myself. This is it. You are it."

"Shouldn't I be giving one of those to you and singing you ballads?"

If he didn't just answer me, I was going to kick him in the nuts.

"Jet, you already picked me. This is me doing the same thing now. Can you stop being difficult and just answer the damn question?"

He took the ring from me and put it back on his finger where it normally lived.

"Yes, Ayden Cross, I will gladly marry you. Supersmart chemistry major or barefoot country girl, it doesn't matter to me, either. I just want me and you."

I jumped into his arms and let him swing me around. This time when he kissed me it was full of promises and all kinds of good things to come.

"Now, as much as I want to put you in bed right now for a different reason, you really do look like you're about to keel over, and I don't even want to tell you how long I was on an airplane over the last few days. Let's grab a few winks and get you back to your brother. You can share the good news with him."

I nodded against his chest and let him lead me to the bed. I threw the ugly comforter on the floor and was glad to see the sheets were clean and at least visibly free of stains. I toed off my cowboy boots and flopped down, face-first, and groaned as my head hit the flat pillow. As happy as I was to see him, as glad as I was that things between us were straight and there were no more secrets to hide, there was no way I could keep my eyes open any longer. I had to take a nap and get back to Asa. Jet climbed in beside me and pulled me on top of him so that I was using him as a pillow. I put my cheek on his heart, resting it on top of the death angel tattooed there, and closed my eyes. He stroked a hand from the top of my head to the base of my spine.

"Are we really gonna get married?"

I laughed a little. "Sure. Why not?"

"What if I want to do it sooner rather than later?"

I tapped the ball on his nipple ring through the fabric of his shirt with the tip of my fingernail.

"Whenever you want, Jet. I told you I'm not going anywhere."

"I feel like I need to put a big-ass rock on your finger before I get back on that plane."

I sighed and wrapped my hands around his waist.

"You can do whatever you want as long as I get a nap first."

He snorted and said something I didn't hear, because I couldn't fight the pull of sleep anymore. With him here, I finally had a sense that everything had a chance of working out fine.

I slept like a log for two hours. The alarm on my phone went off after only one hour, but apparently I had been so out of it that Jet had turned it off and let me sleep for another full hour. When I woke up, I was rushing around, trying to take a quick shower and change into clean clothes, while he texted everyone back in Denver to update them on what was going on. He didn't look any more rested than I felt, but he never complained, and when I told him I was probably going to have to stay overnight at the hospital again, he just shrugged and told me he would hang out until they made him leave.

When we walked into the intensive care unit, I noticed the way the nurses looked at us—well, looked at Jet, and not just because we were in the South and his style stood out. There was something about his wild hair and general swagger that just drew attention, primarily female attention, but

I was okay with it. He was hot, he wore pants that were tight enough to leave little to the imagination, and he had eyes that were enough to break your heart between each blink. He was just something special and he was mine, so I was going to enjoy it. He put his arm around my shoulders and tucked me into his side when we walked into the room.

Asa didn't look any better. He was still all bandaged up and he was still unconscious, but his chest was rising and falling in a steady rhythm so he wasn't dead and at this point I was considering that a win. Jet sat in the chair that had been my home for the last few days and I reached over the side of the bed to pat the cast that encased Asa's hand.

"Hey, big brother, I brought someone to meet you. You should wake up and say hi."

I was a little choked up. It was hard to see him like this, and it was awful to think he might not wake up and that if he did, he wouldn't be the same ornery son of a bitch he had always been.

Jet pulled me down on his lap and we sat like that for a long time. We talked about the tour and how he was tired of being on the road, but that seeing Europe was amazing. He told me about how he was considering starting a record label, which sounded like the perfect career for him, and how that meant he was going to have to do more traveling between Colorado, L.A., New York, and Austin. He sounded excited, and that meant I was excited for him. I told him about growing up in Woodward and how Asa was the best liar, the slickest con artist that had ever lived. I told him that he was nearly impossible to not love, but somehow when it mattered, he came through and acted like a big brother should. I told him about Silas and how he was the one who tried to break into the house. At that point, I thought he was going to stage a full-blown lynching party, and I offered to go scrounge up some coffee and snacks to calm him down.

When I walked past the nurses' station, the two young nurses had their heads bent together and were talking about Jet's very memorable backside. They both gave me a startled look and all I could do was shrug and agree. "I know. Believe me, I know."

The line at the little café took a lot longer than I thought, and I wasn't really hungry for anything, but I didn't know when Jet had eaten last, so I grabbed a whole bunch of different stuff hoping something would tide him over. When I got back to the room, the door was open a crack so I could slip in, but I stopped because Jet was on his feet next to the bed talking to Asa's prone form. I didn't mean to eavesdrop, but he sounded intense and I didn't want to interrupt.

"I'm going to marry your sister."

The idea that I was going to be with Jet forever still gave me the shivers.

"That means I'm going to protect her. That means I'm going to keep her safe and make sure nothing ever hurts her again. I'm going to give her everything she ever wanted and anything she ever needs. When you wake up"—he paused and I could almost feel how hard he was trying to impress upon Asa what he was saying even though he was unconscious—"if you try to be anything to her but an awesome brother, a supportive, loving part of our family, I swear on everything you believe in, that what those bikers did to you will look like a picnic when I'm done with you. I love her and I will not let anyone use her, or manipulate her again. I hope nearly dying gives you the wake-up call you so clearly needed, because you have an amazing sister who loves you and is willing to put up with a lot of shit. We can have this chat again when you can respond, but I thought it was best to just get it out of the way now."

I wasn't sure if I wanted to laugh or cry at that, so instead I just cleared my throat so he knew I was coming, and made my way the rest of the way into the room. I handed him the coffee and the snacks and put my hand on his lower back and kissed him on the cheek.

"The nurses outside think you have a nice butt, even if it is encased in some girly-ass purple pants."

He lifted and eyebrow.

"I like my pants."

"Me, too. I like what's in them even more."

He groaned and opened one of the sandwiches I handed him.

"Don't go there, Ayd. It's been a while."

I looked at him over my shoulder and stroked one of Asa's finger with mine. It was about the only visible skin on his body that didn't have a tube coming out of it or gauze wrapped around it.

"There was no pretty French girl or sexy Spanish chick to keep you company?" I didn't really want the answer to that question, but I figured I should ask. It wouldn't change things, but I felt like I needed to know.

"No. What about you? Sweater Vest was blowing up your phone when I left."

I shook my head in the negative.

"Adam is a really nice guy, but he isn't you. That was the problem with him all along."

I felt him run his hand up the back of my bare thigh and I had to suppress the shivers that trailed in their wake.

"When do you have to leave?"

"I have four days and then I need to hook back up with the guys in Amsterdam. If you need me to stay, I will."

I looked back at him and gave him a sad, lopsided smile. "No. I don't know what his condition is going to look like over the next few days. If I need to, I'll call the girls."

"You should let them come anyway. They're both worried sick over you."

I sighed and went over to prop myself up in the arm of the chair. He put a hand on my knee and I covered it with my own.

"It was just me and Asa growing up. Mama was always off doing her own thing. Granted, he wasn't always the best caretaker. Frankly, he was a piece of crap most of the time and he used me in ways I don't really want to think about right now, but we're family no matter how dysfunctional it is. I kind of feel like it should be that way now. If he takes a turn for the worse, it needs to be me and him, ya know?"

"I'm sorry you have to deal with this, Ayd, and I'm sorry for whatever you felt you had to do in the past."

"Me, too."

We fell into a kind of pattern the next two days. I didn't

want Jet to have to be at the hospital the entire time, so I sent him back to the hotel to sleep when visiting hours were over, and I stayed with Asa. I would go back in the morning for a shower and we would grab breakfast and then spend the bulk of the day keeping vigil over my brother. There was no change in his condition, which everyone tried to convince me was a good thing, but I wasn't sure I bought it. He was still unconscious, still needed a ventilator to breathe, and there was no miraculous recovery showing on any of the scans of his brain.

Jet was a champ. He took it all in stride and never once complained or griped that he had come all this way to sleep alone in a sketchy hotel and drink awful hospital coffee by the gallons. If I hadn't already loved him, this would have sealed the deal. He was just rock solid, and the only entertainment we had during the day was watching the nurses, all of them from the sixty-year-old ladies to the younger techs, try to get his attention. He was quickly becoming the star of the intensive care unit. At one point, he decided to sing me every old Southern folk song he could think of—"Little Birdie," "I Am a Man of Constant Sorrow," "Amazing Grace"—it was like a private little concert, and by the time he was done, every single female who worked in the intensive care unit was as in love with him as I was.

It was the day before he had to leave and we were both tired and starting to think things with Asa were at a standstill. I could tell Jet felt bad that he had to go, that he was worried about me, and the idea of leaving me alone made him nervous. I had to promise to call if Asa turned a corner either way, and he insisted that if I was going to be there for another week, I should bring in reinforcements. It was bittersweet. He was so wonderful for putting his life on hold for me, and made it so clear that he was in this for the long haul, that I wished he was going back on tour knowing I would be fine. I wished that Asa would wake up and things would just go back to normal. Since none of that looked like it was going to happen, I just tried to reassure him that everything would be fine either way, and that I would still be here when the tour was over.

I was talking to Asa in a low voice, telling him all about the crew back in D-town, about Rule and Shaw and their crazy love story. I told him all about Cora and how wild she was, how fun and unpredictable she was. I told him about Nash and Rowdy, and explained that my guy had the best friends that anyone could ask for, but mostly I told him all about Jet. I told him about how talented he was, how kind he was, how I had loved him from the first minute I saw him onstage. I told him all about the rocky road I had traveled to finally reach him, and how I never really thought someone like Jet was going to be my end game. I talked and talked and somewhere in the middle of my telling him how happy I really was and how great my life was, even if he had stumbled in and messed it all up, his fingers started to twitch.

At first I thought I was just imagining things. I thought it was just wishful thinking, but then they did it again and I looked up, and eyes that matched my own were looking back at me.

I freaked out and had every nurse on the floor rushing in

to poke and prod at him. I was systematically shoved out of the way while people moved around him and took his vitals and nudged at all his tubes and wires. They were droopy and unfocused, but those whiskey-colored eyes stayed locked on mine and I knew, just knew, that he was going to be okay. When Jet showed up, I was an incoherent mess. All I could really explain was that Asa had opened his eyes and that his fingers had moved, and that all the medical staff seemed optimistic, which was a good sign. It was such a good sign, in fact, that the staff insisted I finally go to the hotel for the night since this was a huge hurdle cleared. I initially didn't want to go, in case he woke up again and was aware, but it was Jet's last night and he was going to be gone for a solid two months. Sexy text messages and phone sex only went so far.

Jet got me into the rental car and when he left the hospital parking lot, I didn't even notice when he went the opposite direction of the hotel. I was lost in thought, and so elated that Asa had at least opened his eyes, that I paid zero attention until he pulled up in front of the Brown Hotel. He was taking us to the nicest, most elegant and expensive hotel in town. My shorts and boots, and his combat boots and Lacuna Coil T-shirt were not appropriate wear for this old and expensive place, but he didn't seem to care.

"What are we doing here?"

"It's my last night in town. It's the only night I get to spend with you for the next two months, so I'm doing it in style."

I didn't argue and he clearly already had a reservation.

We checked in with the guy behind the counter sneering at us the entire time. That seemed to amuse Jet to no end, so I just kept my mouth shut and let him haul our stuff up to the fancy room. I had to admit the idea of sleeping in a real bed with sheets that I knew for a fact were clean turned me on almost as much as the idea of getting him naked on top of them.

"Oh, Jet, this is just . . ."

Where I hadn't wanted to get down on one knee on dirty carpet, he didn't have the same problem here. I gasped a little when I turned around and found him on his knees in front of me. I put a hand to my mouth when he handed me a ring that was as unique as he was. It was platinum and in the center was a sparkling topaz, surrounded by a bunch of tiny canary yellow diamonds. I had never seen anything like it and had no idea where he had found something like that here.

"I told you I wanted to put a big-ass rock on your finger before I left."

I took the ring with shaking fingers. "It's so pretty. Where on earth did you find it?"

"Rowdy. I told him to find me something that matched your eyes and send me a bunch of pictures, then overnight the sucker. My boy has good taste and you have beautiful eyes."

"He does. I love it. I love you."

"I just wanted you to know that you weren't alone when I left. This makes it feel more real to me."

I put the ring on and just looked at him. He was perfect,

tattoos, piercings, messy hair, and too tight jeans, all those things that made him Jet were wonderful and unique. With him I could always just be *me* whatever form that happened to be, and that was a gift no one but him had ever been able to give me. It would keep me tied to him forever. I had his ring, I had his love, and I had him, and there was only one way I could think of to thank him and show him my appreciation and the fact that I would be a happy girl to just *be* with him forever. He didn't know what to do when I tackled him to the ground and started kissing him all over on the plush carpet of the fancy hotel room. Well, he didn't know what to do for a second, but this was Jet after all, and he caught on real quickly; we were bound to set the place on fire in no time.

CHAPTER 18

Jet

I WAS GOING TO marry Ayden. However, first I was going to try to not lose control while she systematically stripped me of my T-shirt and pants. Granted, we both probably had a lot of pent-up sexual frustration to work out, but I think there was something about putting that ring on her finger that made her slightly more zealous in her pursuit of getting me all kinds of naked and under her.

Not that I was complaining. I couldn't have asked for a better outcome to my journey back to her. All I wanted was for her to know she wasn't alone, that I cared about her, and wanted to work on us being together. Now I had her forever and there was no more doubt, no more nagging fear that she was going to run from me the first chance she got. We were just two people who were meant to be together and that was all there was to it.

I wanted to spend the night with her in a fancy place, show her that even though it was rushed and we were prob-ably too new and too young to really talk about forever, that

I meant it, that this was serious and meant everything to me. I also wanted her to have something nice to hold on to if things with her brother nosedived. Only she had turned the tables on me, like she was fond of doing, and now I was on the floor with her on top of me. It was a pretty great place to be, but it defeated the purpose of what I was trying to do for her. I was getting ready to tell her that, to roll her over and pick her up and carry her to that massive king-sized bed that took up the majority of the room, but before I could form a coherent thought, she did what I had been dying for her to do all along, put that sassy mouth around my dick, piercing and all. I guess she wasn't scared or hesitant about it anymore.

I let out a string of swear words that were totally out of place in an establishment this old and regal, but that somehow made what she was doing with her lips and her tongue that much better. I don't think I had ever been this hard, this in tune with what was happening to my body, and I wanted to alternately high five whoever had taught her how to give head and murder them in cold blood. My girl clearly knew what she was doing, and if I didn't put some brakes on the situation soon, our night together, which was supposed to be memorable and romantic, was going to be over before it even started. I had every intention of telling her that, only her clever little tongue did something with the hoop at the head of my cock at the same time her fingers found their way to the ones in my nipples, and my poor brain short-circuited and all I could do was lie there and let her have her way with me.

I mumbled her name and I was pretty sure I told her I loved her and that I would do whatever she wanted me to do for the rest of my life, and that made her laugh. With her mouth where it was, that just made the situation harder to handle, so I gave up trying. I threaded my fingers through her soft hair and just let her do her thing. Every time she ran the tip of her tongue around the ball on the ring of my piercing I thought the top of my head was going to come off, both of them. Her hands traced over the angel of death on my chest and wound around the unfinished piece on my back, all the while working me over and taking me to a place I had never been before. I was about to explode, so I used my hold on her head to pull her off me with a slick *pop*. Those eyes of hers turned me inside out, and I swore that I could get drunk just looking into them when she was looking back at me the way she was now.

She licked her bottom lip, which was puffy now, and I wanted to bite it. She lifted a dark eyebrow and crawled over me so that she was sitting on my stomach all damp heat and ready to go.

"You did tell me to enjoy it."

I could tell she was pleased with herself by the saucy gleam in her golden eyes and the smirk on her face. Not to be outdone, I slid my hands up under the edge of her tank top and along her ribs. Her eyes got wide and she offered little resistance when I pulled the fabric over the top of her head and tossed it to the side. Her bra was pretty and lacy, but it was in my way, so it joined the steadily growing pile of clothes on the floor next to us. Having the opportunity to get this woman naked anytime I wanted was most definitely on the top of the list of perks of being with her for the rest of eternity. Miles of tanned legs, sweetly curved waist, high, round breasts topped with pretty pink nipples, luminous eyes and silky black hair, all of it was mine, and she was my dream come true.

"My turn." I got to my feet and took her with me. It was a little tricky getting those shorts off over her cowboy boots. She gave me a look when I tossed her on the center of the massive bed and moved to climb over her. I bent down to kiss the point of each of her prominent hip bones and shivered when she ran her hand through my hair.

"I still have my boots on."

"Yep." I loved those black cowboy boots. Loved them on her. Loved that they kept her tied to her roots and still fit the new Ayden that she was when we were together. I was totally taking the image of her wearing nothing but those boots with me back on the road. That alone would be enough to tide me over until I got back to her.

I kissed her on her belly, and dipped my tongue in the sexy little indent of her belly button, which made her shiver against me. The heels of her boots dug into my ass and it made me smile before I bent down and kissed her even lower. She gasped my name in a way I hoped I could make her do when we were old and her hands got tighter and more insistent in my hair. I ran my tongue all along her damp cleft and flicked her hidden little clit with the tip of my tongue. She arched up hard and squeezed me with her legs. Now it was my turn to chuckle against the most sensitive part of her. I loved the things we did to each other. She was just right for me and I wanted to make sure she knew it.

I licked and kissed and got her all worked up, so that when I finally moved my tongue in and out of her like I was planning on doing over and over again with my very eager dick in a few seconds, she didn't have too far to go and broke apart under me, saying my name and writhing against me in all the best ways. I pulled back and kissed one of the creamy thighs that had gone limp next to my head, and worked my way back up her prone body. She put her hands around my neck and grinned up at me with sated and glowing eyes.

"Yee-haw . . ." It was barely a breath of sound.

That made me laugh. I brushed a thumb over the arch of her dark eyebrow and kissed each corner of her mouth.

"You're the best, too. You know that, right?"

She wiggled a little, so that all the necessary parts were better aligned, and every time the leather of her boots moved against me, I swore it made my dick twitch in anticipation.

"I think we're both actually pretty screwed up, but together we just work and we make each other better."

She hooked one of her arms around my side and across my back, and dug the edge of her heels in my ass to get me to move. I was going to tell her to let me get a condom, but this time I was the one that was impatient and not willing to slow down. I slid all the way in, hard, hot, and bare and we both groaned aloud at the searing contact. I swore and her eyes fluttered closed as I began to move. I bent down to kiss her and it was a kiss that sealed our fate together. There would never be anyone else for me, and I knew the same held true for her. We were just two sides of the same coin, and when she nipped at the ball in the center of my tongue, all semblance of romance and building a moment were gone. I just wanted to get in her as far and as deep as I could.

I pulled her hips up hard enough that she was probably going to have the imprint of my fingers in her skin in the morning. I pounded into her until we were both out of control and I felt her start to spasm around me. I felt the prick of her nails in my shoulders and greedy grasp of her body on mine, and it took me over the edge as well. I sank my teeth into the tendon of her neck when she threw her head to the side, and then softened the bite with a little kiss. I collapsed on top of her, careful to keep as much of my weight off her as I could. When the rings in my nipples brushed against her still puckered ones, it made both of us inhale a little.

"Ayd, you're going to kill me, and as much as I like all this skin-on-skin contact, if we aren't careful we're going to end up dealing with something neither one of us is really ready for."

The idea of putting a kid in her didn't terrify me nearly as badly as I thought it would have, considering my own less-than-stellar example of fatherhood, but the timing wasn't right. I was honest enough to admit that. I'd just gotten her, so I wasn't ready to share her yet.

She danced her fingers down my spine and turned her head so that we were looking at each other. Those eyes of hers were liquid and smooth and clearer than I had ever seen them.

"I went on the pill after the hit-and-miss in the car."

I felt an eyebrow shoot up. "You dumped me the next

day." If she had planned on going back to Adam after that, there was a good chance my head was going to implode.

Her fingers went back up the other way.

"I didn't dump you. I was just confused and I think I knew deep down it was always going to be you. You make me burn, Jet. You always have. Better safe than sorry."

I wrapped her in my arms and rolled us over so that she was sprawled on top of me.

"You know, that's what I always felt like. Like I was on fire on the inside, I was so angry with my dad, so frustrated with my mom and just kind of burning through life doing whatever, whoever I wanted, and I think I was probably eventually just going to burn out. When I met you, it tempered it a little bit. I didn't need the stage to get it all out. You would just look at me, or say something in that Southern drawl, and I felt like I could keep a lid on it. If we burn together, and have a fire that's all our own, I guess that isn't a bad thing."

She was using the pad of her finger to trace the face of the angel that sat over my heart.

"You need it. The fire is your passion, it's your creative drive. You feel strongly about things, and care deeply about the people you love. I can handle the fire in you, Jet. It's just part of you."

That's why I loved her. It was just like Rule had said, I would move mountains for her, just so that in the end, it was only me and her.

"As much as I would love to keep you in this bed all day, I'm sure you want to check in on Asa."

She nodded under my chin and wiggled off me. She pulled on my T-shirt and scrambled around to find her phone. I pulled my jeans back on and scrounged up the menu for room service. I figured the least I could do after going at her so hard for the last hour was feed her. I ordered a bunch of stuff that probably was going to cost as much as my plane ticket back overseas, and hung up when she scooted up behind me and wrapped her arms around my shoulders.

"He's in and out. They aren't going to pull the ventilator yet because he's so unstable and they can't really tell how he was affected by the brain trauma yet. They said he's responsive, which is a good sign, so I'll take it."

"I ordered some food. We can chow and head over there if you want."

Her hair was silky against my cheek as she shook her head in the negative.

"No. You have to leave in the morning and this is important, too."

"I'll be back in no time. I don't want you to worry about him."

"I'm still working on forgiving him for being an awful person most of the time. I hope this is some kind of divine intervention, but there's a good chance Asa will still be Asa. When you leave, you're taking my heart with you, Jet, and that is never going to change."

I leaned farther back so I could kiss her, and it was just getting good, when there was a knock on the door. I ordered her to get those legs covered up and went to let the guy in with the food. I gave him a pretty hefty tip because he didn't even so much as flutter an eyelash in her direction, but when I mentioned it to her she laughed so hard that tears actually leaked out of the corners of her eyes. She told me that the dude's eyes had been glued to me since I hadn't bothered to fasten my jeans.

I just rolled my eyes and we set up on the bed to feast. She told me a little bit more about growing up in the trailer, about how small towns worked, and, oddly, it reminded me of how my mom ended up under the thumb of my old man. It made me even more proud, more impressed by her that she had fought back, and found her way out to a place of awesomeness. She was just damn impressive all the way around.

We spent the rest of the day in bed, and by the time the sun went done, we were both exhausted and raw in the best way possible. I fell asleep with her curled into my side, and the thought that she was going to be there from here on out put something in me at ease that had never been still and quiet before.

The next morning I woke up with her hands and mouth doing things to me that were designed to make leaving her here damn near impossible. When she was done, I was convinced I had done my best to ruin her for anyone else who might try to press up on her while I was away. We were both breathless and running late when we climbed into the rental car to go to the airport. I had to fly to New York and sit around for two hours before flying to Amsterdam, and the idea of being away from her for two months flat-out pissed me off. I was still worried about her brother, but I had obligations I needed to fulfill and this was just going to be part of our relationship.

The ride in the car was quiet so I found myself humming "Whiskey River" by Willie Nelson. She cast a sideways look at me and tapped her fingers on the steering wheel.

"How do you know every old country song on the planet, but can't sing me Tim McGraw to save your life?"

I rolled my eyes a little and settled back in the passenger seat.

"My mom. She loved country. She used to sing it to me when I was little. She actually has a pretty good voice."

"And your dad was a rocker?"

The irony was suddenly right in my face. "Yeah, but he was also a sadistic bastard, so history will not be repeating itself with you and me."

She reached out and put her hand on my knee. "I know that. Plus, I hate to admit it, but the house was almost too quiet without all of that racket you call music blaring from your room."

That made me snicker and before I knew it, we were pulling into the passenger drop-off area and we had to say good-bye. She came around to my side of the car and leaned against the door. I put my hands in the back pockets of her shorts and pulled her so we were flush. She put her hands around my neck and I kissed the tip of her nose.

"I'll be thinking about you all the time."

"Don't. Just go have fun and be a rock star. You being here was everything I needed."

"Call me if you need me."

"I'll always need you. I'll just call you because."

"Fair enough." I pressed my mouth to hers with enough intensity to let her know she would be missed. When I pulled back there was moisture in her eyes and I was ready to rip up my plane ticket on the spot until she gave me a half smile.

"I really do love you."

"Good thing I'm going to marry you, then." I winked at her as she smacked me on the arm.

We said another good-bye and this time she kissed me. Saying good-bye sucked, but it was bearable because unlike the last time I had left her behind, this time I knew she would be there when I got back. She had on my ring, and she gave me her heart and her trust. I was her future and she was my entirety. Damn, I might be in the first metal band that sang love songs after all.

Jet

A Few Months Later, The Fourth of July

I CAN'T BELIEVE YOU have a yard with grass, sprinklers, and a barbeque. That is some serious adultlike shit." I handed Rule a cold beer good-naturedly even though he glared at me.

"I'm not the one rocking a wedding ring."

I absently looked down at the wide titanium ring on my left hand. The same topaz that sat on Ayden's finger rested on mine. I had told her we could wait until she was done with school, that I could wait until I had the new business up and running, to actually get hitched, but after being gone and apart for two months that wasn't something either of us wanted or had the patience to wait for. As soon as I got back to the States, I packed her up and hauled her to Vegas for a long weekend. It had turned from a simple ceremony between the two of us into an epic party weekend, when all of our friends had decided to crash the event. I knew she wanted something more formal, more traditional, but every time I brought up doing a reception or some kind of ceremony here for everyone, she would roll her eyes at me and tell me that she had to pay Shaw back and that Asa's hospital bills weren't going anywhere. I was going to let her get away with that excuse for a little while, and then I was just going to plan one for her anyway.

"I didn't say it was a bad thing. The house is awesome and this yard is badass. I just never pictured you manning a grill and being all domesticated."

Those pale eyes of his were still as sharp as ice shards and he still mixed it up with his hair; today it was his natural dark brown and a startling lime green that was spiked up in a hundred directions. Now, though, there was just something inherently more settled about him. I wondered if Ayden did that for me, wondered if it was so obvious to other people that with her, I had found my place and had been able to put out most of the bonfire that used to burn me alive.

He tilted his head to where the girls were sitting on the deck that jutted out from the back of the house. Shaw was cracking up at some story Ayden's brother was telling and Ayden was leaning back watching me talk to Rule. I lifted an eyebrow at her and she just shrugged. Asa could charm the pants off a nun, but ever since he had gotten mobile again he had been on his best behavior. His recovery had been long and tenuous. He had had not one but two major setbacks, and Ayden had just decided to repeat the semester at DU until he was out of the hospital because she had missed so much school taking care of him and being in Kentucky. As soon as she was able, she had packed him up and brought him to

Denver with her, so not only did I have Cora's big mouth to contend with, but also Asa's slicker-than-slick charm.

Asa and I weren't exactly friends. I didn't trust him as far as I could throw him, but he seemed to be operating on the up and up. I think he had a healthy fear of what I would do to him if he messed with Ayden in the slightest, and his brush with death had seemed to give him some brief bit of clarity. As much as it bugged me because I now knew exactly how complicated their dynamic was, I could see he really did love her. I know Ayden was hoping for a total transformation, but the guy was just too smooth, too good at reading people and playing games, for me to believe that was going to be the case. I really felt like he wanted to go straight for his sister, so for that alone I was willing to give him a chance. Since I was on the road at least once or twice a week with the new label, I liked having him at the house with the girls, even if he still had a cast on one arm and a walking boot on his foot.

"He's almost as pretty as she is, isn't he?"

Rule's question snapped me out of my reverie and I gave Ayden a wink before turning back to him.

"He's a pain in the ass."

Rule snorted and turned over the burgers he was watching.

"Shaw likes him, which surprises me after everything he put Ayden through, and Cora thinks he's a riot."

"That's because they're chicks and that dude has more game in his pinkie finger than we have combined. It's unreal."

Rule squinted his eyes a little, in the direction where the rest of the group was sitting in a circle lounging on lawn chairs on the grassy lawn. Rowdy and Nash were messing around with a whole pile of fireworks that looked illegal as hell. I assumed they probably came from across the state border in Wyoming. Cora was sitting next to Rule's older brother Rome and neither one of them looked too happy with the situation or the company.

"I know all about siblings being a pain in the ass."

I had only seen Rome a few times since he had gotten back from Afghanistan. I knew through the grapevine—the grapevine being Rowdy—that he and Rule weren't exactly feeling the brotherly love. I guess Rome was still pissed at his folks about something to do with their other brother and it was pretty obvious whatever had happened involved Shaw, because the older Archer brother was barely civil to her and this was her house. I knew Rome and Rule were tight, so whatever was going on was going to have to be addressed, but I guess Rome was wound pretty tight and had been pretty unpredictable since his return. Nash had mentioned a couple times, since they were roommates now, that he had never seen the big guy drink the way he did now. I knew the guys were worried about him, but Rome was the oldest and by default the leader, so I think they were having a hard time addressing any of it with him.

Rule's pale eyes flicked back to me. "How are things with the rest of the family?"

I shrugged and watched as Ayden got up and started down the steps of the deck. I wondered if my heart was always going to turn over when it realized she was coming to me, always to me. I could watch her move all day on those killer legs and I elbowed Rule in the ribs when I caught him checking them out as well. He just lifted an eyebrow like it was an involuntary response.

"The same I guess. Mom hasn't forgiven me for not inviting them to the wedding in Vegas, even though I told her she could come as long as she left that bastard at home. She just doesn't get it. Ayd's even tried to talk to her, tried to explain that as long as she stays with him that she won't be part of our family. God forbid we have kids, because the old man is coming nowhere near them. Sometimes, it looks like the sun is shining through the clouds, only for it to disappear again. I have more important things to worry about and focus on, so that's what I do."

When Ayden reached my side, I hauled her in close with an arm around her neck and planted a kiss on her temple. Her arm went around my waist and she leaned against me lightly. Rowdy was almost done with the piece that took up my entire ribs on the backside and she was used to having to be gentle with the tender skin and new ink.

"What are you two over here gossiping about like a bunch of girls?"

Rule narrowed his eyes at her and I chuckled. "Family drama."

She made a face and snagged the beer I was holding out of my hand.

"Yuck. Hey, are you going to be in town all week? I was thinking about taking a summer interim class to catch up on some of the stuff I had to miss last semester, but if you're going to be around, I don't want to do it."

It was a tough balancing act with both our schedules. I was gone more than I had thought I would be, because starting the label meant finding bands, and finding bands meant I had to go places where bands played. With her being in school, that meant she couldn't come with me. Which sucked for both of us, but we were learning to adjust.

The first band I actually signed and agreed to work with was the new band Jorge had formed after finally getting tired of Ryan's crap with Black Market Alphas. The band was amazing, even better than Enmity was, in my opinion, and I really thought I could make Jorge into the star I always thought he was. I loved it and had clearly found my calling, even though I still played with the guys in town and wrote songs when I found the time. My favorite time to sing was when I sang Ayden to sleep at night. I still refused to learn any of that new country junk she liked, but luckily the old stuff still rattled around in my brain and she never complained about it.

I was going to tell her to take the class regardless, because it was important to her and we had the rest of forever to spend time together, but I never got the chance. Across the yard, Cora screeched, and the next thing we knew Rome was soaking wet as she dumped her beer over his dark head, a feat that would have been impossible if the guy had been standing, because she was itty bitty and Rome was a giant. Nash scooped her up before she could lunge at the glaring soldier and Rowdy stepped between all of them. Shaw bolted to her feet and came running down from the deck as Rule stomped off in the direction of the fray. Asa could only watch from the deck since his gimpy limbs kept him pretty immobile, and Ayden and I just watched the entire thing in silence.

"You're an asshole!" Cora's voice was sharp and loud as Nash hauled her over in our direction. She was pointing a finger at Rome and her heated anger was almost alive in its intensity. Nash kept right on walking past us and I heard Rule holler at his brother.

"What in the hell was that all about?"

Shaw looked anxious at Rule's side when Rome climbed to his feet. The guy easily topped six and a half feet and looked like he could bench press a semi-truck without breaking a sweat. He also looked good and pissed off on top of being soggy and irritated that his brother was getting in his face. I glanced down at my wife (hell, yeah, I called her that any chance I got) and gave her a questioning look.

"What do you make of that?"

She lifted a shoulder and rested her hand on my stomach under the edge of my shirt. Her pinkie finger snuck below the waistband and it made me suck in a breath. She still went to my head faster than a shot of Jameson and nothing would ever be better than that as far as I was concerned.

"Who knows? Cora has a big mouth and isn't afraid to give anyone her opinion, even if they don't want it, and Rome doesn't strike me as the kind of guy to just sit back and let her steamroll him. He's kind of intense."

She moved her finger a little lower and I narrowed my eyes at her. She just gave me an impish grin and batted those bright eyes at me.

Things in the yard escalated when Rule reached out and shoved his brother in his massive chest. Shaw screamed something I didn't hear, and Rowdy yanked her out of the way as the older Archer brother returned the favor by putting Rule on his ass. Some really angry and heated words were exchanged and the next thing we knew, Rome was storming past us and slamming the back gate to the fence on his way out. The roar of the Harley he had arrived on rattled the tension in the air and everyone just kind of looked at one another in silence. I sighed and reached out to put my hands in Ayden's back pockets.

"It's never boring with this crew, is it?"

She stood on the toes of her boots—these were red and my new favorites—and kissed me on the underside of my jaw.

"We're a family, and when you're a family, there's going to be issues. They'll get it figured out. Shaw will make them. Let's go watch the fireworks."

"It isn't even dark out yet."

She wiggled around until she was plastered to my front and wrapped her arms around my neck. This girl was just the best part of my day, every day, and I would never take that for granted.

"Those aren't the fireworks I was talking about."

She made me laugh. She made me happy. She was my family and my future, and while it might have taken both of us letting go of what we thought we wanted and needed to be happy in order to see that all we needed was each other, it was so clear to both of us now.

"You already lit the fuse, Ayd. You better be ready to deal with the boom that follows."

She licked her bottom lip and gave me the look that told me she would never be afraid of the fire and the heat I threw her way. She just stood in the center of it and let the embers fall all around her. Every time she walked away unscathed, and I had a little less of it inside me burning things up. We were going to leave without even saying good-bye to anyone, when Cora's head popped over the edge of the deck. She still looked mad but there was something else moving around in her two-toned gaze.

"See . . . like I always said, you two are just perfect. That's what I want." She sounded so sad and wistful that it concerned me.

"I keep telling you that your expectations are too high." Ayden nodded.

"Love isn't perfect. It's hard work and sometimes it's more effort to be in love than it is to just run away. If you keep looking for perfect, the real thing is going to pass right by you."

She waved a hand and walked over to sit down next to Asa, who was watching the entire show in silence. I could swear I could see wheels turning in his head.

"I'll know it when I see it."

I didn't have a response to that because even though Cora was a good judge of character, when it came to her personal life, she was kind of like a lion tamer, always fending everyone off with a whip and a chair no matter how fierce or tame the predator was.

I looked down at Ayden and I could tell she was more than likely thinking the same thing.

"You ready to go?"

"Yep."

And that's how it was. We walked the same way, no more running, no more fear, no more secrets. Just me and her, in sync and together, even though we came from two separate sides of the spectrum. I was her perfect future and she my perfect love and that was how every good love song should end.

So it ends . . . at least for now

Jet's Playlist

You might need earplugs for this one if you don't like metal
Slayer: *"Love to Hate"*
Danzig: *"Twist of Cain"*
Neurosis: *"Black"*
Metallica: *"Master of Puppets"*
Dystopia: *"Backstabber"*
Morbid Angel: *"Rapture"*
Mastodon: *"Black Tongue"*
Wolves in the Throne Room: *"Astral Blood"*
Jucifer: *"Contempt"*
Lacuna Coil: *"Heaven's a Lie"*
Memphis May Fire: *"The Sinner," "Vices," "Prove Me Right"*
(they get the most because this is how I think Enmity sounds
and how Jet would sing)
Venom: *"Black Metal"*

Jet's Playlist for Ayden

Crosby, Stills, Nash & Young: *"Love the One You're With"*
George Jones: *"Tennessee Whiskey"*
Waylon Jennings: *"Good Hearted Woman"*
Merle Haggard: *"Today I Started Loving You Again"*
Willie Nelson: *"Always on My Mind," "Whiskey River"*
Conway Twitty: *"Hello Darlin' "*
Johnny Cash: *"I Walk the Line"*
Hank Williams: *"So Lonesome I Could Cry"*
Patsy Cline: *"Crazy"*
Tanya Tucker: *"Would You Lay With Me"*

Ayden's Playlist

(Courtesy of my favorite person in the whole world: My mom!)

Zac Brown Band: *"Colder Weather"*

Kenny Chesney: *"You and Tequila"*

Eli Young Band: *"Even If It Breaks Your Heart"*

Brad Paisley & Alison Krauss: *"Whiskey Lullaby"*

Carrie Underwood: *"Blown Away"*

Lady Antebellum: *"American Honey"*

The Band Perry: *"If I Die Young"*

Kid Rock & Sheryl Crow: *"Picture"*

Blake Shelton: *"Drink on It"*

Hunter Hayes: *"Wanted"*

About Me

First off, I'm a chick. I wouldn't think I needed that in the "about me" but after some of the emails I've received I figured it was good to let folks know Jay is short for Jennifer.

I'm a native Coloradoan, and if you live here you know why that is a source of pride. I love all the things Colorado has to offer and that is why I choose to set my books in this familiar setting. I try to write about things I know and am familiar with, which is why my stories feature plenty of rock and roll and body modification.

I've been in the bar industry since I was in college and I spend more than forty hours a week watching the interactions between men and women in a unique way. I think my nine-to-five job offers me valuable insights into how relationships start and evolve in a social setting. I love it.

I like to write New Adult novels because I remember being in my early twenties and thinking I had it all figured, out only to be proven wrong time and time again. When I look back, those were the years that defined who I am today, and good or bad, those decisions ultimately set me on my current path, and that's what I like to explore in my writing.

Wanna talk at me? Feel free to touch base with me at any of the following locations. I do like to hear from readers. Feedback has been an important part of this entire process for me:

Jaycrownover.blogspot.com

@jaycrownover on Twitter

facebook.com/jay.crownover on Facebook,

or like my fan page,

Author Jay Crownover

Jaycrownover@gmail.com

Can't get enough of the
Marked Men?

Good news, there's much more to come . . .
Up next
Rome

On sale January 2014 from William Morrow

Cora Lewis is a whole lot of fun, and she knows how to keep her tattooed bad boy friends in line. But all that flash and sass hide the fact that she's never gotten over the way her first love broke her heart. Now she has a plan to make sure that never happens again: She's only going to fall in love with someone perfect.

Rome Archer is as far from perfect as a man can be. He's stubborn and rigid, he's bossy and has come back from his final tour of duty fundamentally broken. Rome's used to filling a role: big brother, doting son, super soldier; and now none of those fit anymore. Now he's just a man trying to figure out what to do with the rest of his life while keeping the demons of war and loss at bay. He would have been glad to suffer it alone, until Cora comes sweeping into his life and becomes the only color on his bleak horizon.

Perfect isn't in the cards for these two, but imperfect might just last forever . . .

Turn the page for an exclusive sneak peek

Rome

I couldn't believe that crazy little sprite had the nerve to dump beer on my head. First of all she barely came up to my shoulder, and second of all she looked like a walking, talking piece of candy. Everything about her was so colorful it almost hurt to look at her.

I should be furious at her, but she was right, I was an asshole. There was no reason to talk shit to Nash, no reason to get into it with Rule, I was just looking for a target to vent my frustrations at and those were the people closest to me. Maybe it was easier to unleash my aggravation at them, because I knew instinctively they would forgive me. I needed to find a place to have a drink and try and get my head together. A place that was dark and quiet and where no one expected me to be anything, or act a certain way. I was tired of not meeting expectations. I was not an idle man by nature. I was used to action, used to being in charge and taking the lead and the only things I had managed to be on top of since coming back to Denver was pissing everyone I encountered off and drinking my considerable body weight in vodka. I was on a downhill slide that was bound to have an ugly-as-hell impact at the bottom, and I knew it but seemed powerless to stop it. Today was the proof of that.

I pulled into the first bar that looked like it could handle the mood I was in. Independence Day my left nut. I had had about enough of the revelry and good cheer to last me a lifetime. I just wanted to bury my head in the sand and go back to a point in time that felt comfortable and familiar. I hated feeling like a visitor in my own life, and no matter what I told myself when I woke up in the morning each day, I couldn't shake feeling like everything I had come back to after my contract with the Army was up was a life that belonged to someone else. My family didn't feel right. The new dynamic in my relationship with Rule didn't feel right. Trying to get used to Shaw being taken care of by my wayward and reckless little brother didn't feel right. Crashing with Nash while I tried to get my shit straight didn't feel right. Not having a job lined up or any clear direction of how to support myself doing something other than fighting a war quite possibly felt the most wrong out of it all.

The bar was dark and not a place for those out for a fun Fourth of July cocktail. In the back, around several well-used pool tables, was a bunch of guys in biker gear sporting colors and looking like they meant business. Toward the front were several older men who looked like they never even got off the barstool to go home and shower. Neil Young was blasting on the house speakers, even though no one seemed like the type to sing along. This was not a place for the hip and trendy urbanites who flocked to Capitol Hill when the weather finally warmed up. I took a spot on an empty seat at the bar top and waited for the guy manning the bar to wander down to me.

He was almost my size, which was rare, only he had a solid thirty years on me. He had a beard that looked like it could be the home to a whole family of squirrels, eyes the color of charcoal, and the grim countenance that could only be found in men who had seen the worst the world had to offer and came out on the other side of it. I wasn't surprised at all to see a Marine tattoo inked on his bulky forearm when he propped himself up across from me and put a battered coaster down in front of me. I saw him size me up, but I was used to it. I was a big guy, and other big guys liked to figure out if I was going to be the kind of trouble they could handle or not.

"Boy, you already smell like a brewery. You sure you need to have another one?"

I frowned until I remembered the little blond pouring her beer over my head. She could have found a better way to make her point, though, as I remembered the soggy state of my T-shirt. I didn't know what to make of Cora Lewis. She was around a lot. We never really talked much. She was too loud and tended toward the dramatic, hence the Coors Light shower I had just received. Being around her made my head hurt and I didn't like the way her mismatched eyes seemed to try and pick me part.

I took my sunglasses off the top of my head and hooked them in the collar of my T-shirt.

"I picked a fight with the wrong pixie and she poured her drink on my head. I'm straight."

The guy gave me a once over and must have deemed me okay because without asking a tankard of beer was set in front of me along with a shot of something amber and strong. Typically I was a vodka drinker, but when the burly brute poured himself one and wandered back over to where I was seated I didn't dare complain.

He lifted a bushy eyebrow at me and touched the rim of his shot glass to my own.

"You Army?"

I nodded and shot back the liquor. It burned hot all the way down. If I wasn't mistaken, it was Wild Turkey.

"I was. Just got out."

"How long did you serve for?"

I rubbed a hand over my still-short hair. After wearing it cropped close to my head for so long I really didn't know what else to do with it.

"Went in at eighteen and I turn twenty-eight at the end of this year. I was in for almost a decade."

"What did you do?"

It wasn't a question I normally answered, because frankly the answer was long and anyone who hadn't served just wouldn't get it.

"I was a field operations leader."

The bear of a man across from me let out a low whistle. "Spec ops?"

I grunted a response and picked up the beer.

"I bet they were sad to see you go."

The thing was, I think I was sadder to see them go. I wasn't cleared for active duty anymore. My shoulder had taken a beating when we rolled over an IED on my last deployment and there was all kinds of shit rattling around in my head constantly taking me out of the game. Sure, I could have taken a desk job, stepped down and trained the generation coming up after me. But I wasn't the best teacher, and being tied to a desk was the same thing as retirement to me anyway. So I got out and now I had no fucking clue what I was going to do with the rest of my life.

"What about you?" I motioned to the tattoo on his arm. "How long did you put in?"

"Too long son. Way too long. What brings you in here today? You aren't one of my regulars."

I cast a look around the bar and shrugged. For now this place was a perfect fit for my mood.

"Just out having a drink to celebrate America like a good patriot."

"Just like the rest of us."

"Yep." I had to fight the urge to chug the beer down and order him to keep them coming.

"I'm Brite and this is my bar. I ended up with it when I got out and started spending more time in the bar than I did at home. I've been through three wives and one triple bypass, but the bar stays true."

I lifted the eyebrow that had the scar above it and felt the corner of my mouth kick up in a grin.

"Brite?" The guy looked like Paul Bunyan or a Hells Angel, the name didn't really fit.

A smile found its way through that massive beard and pearly white teeth were the only bright spot in the dim bar.

"Brighton Walker, Brite for short." He extended a hand that I shook on reflex.

"Rome Archer."

He dropped his head in a little nod and moved down the bar to help another customer.

"That's a good name for a warrior."

I closed my eyes briefly and tried to remember what it was like to feel like a warrior. It seemed like it was a million miles away from this barstool. The music switched to AC/DC and I decided this was my new favorite place to hang out.

I was on my Harley, so I knew I should probably cool it with the booze. A DUI would just be the icing on the crap cake I was currently being served on a daily basis, but as the beer mixed with the potent bourbon from earlier, none of that seemed to really matter anymore.

At some point I did another shot with Brite and the barstool next to me was abandoned by the grizzled old man that had been complaining about his wife and his girlfriend for the last hour and quickly occupied by a redhead with too much makeup on and too little clothes. Had I been three less beers in I would've seen her for the trouble she was worth. As it was, Brite told her to scram, which she promptly ignored. She was cute, in that "I'm-a-good-time-take-me-home" kind of way, and I couldn't remember the last time I had randomly picked anyone up from a bar. When I was overseas there had been a female intelligence officer that was down to be friends with benefits whenever we were in the same place at the same time, but it had been months since I had seen her. Maybe a quick, sleazy hookup was just what I needed to break through the black cloud that had been hovering over me since my return.

"What's your name, Sugar?"

Her voice was squeaky and hurt my head but I was loaded enough to ignore it.

"Rome."

I saw her heavily made-up eyes dart back to someplace over my shoulder and that should have been my first clue that this wasn't going to end up all fun and games.

"That's a different name. I'm Abbie. Now that we're friends, why don't we get out of here and get better acquainted?" She ran a painted fingernail over the curve of my bicep and for some reason the blood red color of it made other images of things that color start to flash behind my already hazy vision.

I started to pull away, to get those hands that were making bad things happen in my foggy brain to let me go, when a heavy hand fell on my shoulder from behind. I was a trained soldier, but more than that I was a man who had a brother born and bred into trouble. I knew what trouble looked like from a million miles away. I knew what trouble felt like, what it moved like, how it sounded and yet I had kept right on drinking and ignored all the signs as it built up around me. Out of the corner of my eye I saw Brite frown at whoever was standing behind me, and even in my stupor of bourbon and beer I knew this wasn't going to be good.

Sighing under my breath, I shook off the talons that had me seeing blood spilling out of a young soldier's throat onto the desert sand and turned around so that I was leaning back on the bar with my elbows. It shouldn't have surprised me to see that almost the entire back pool room of bikers was now gathered around me and the bar area. The guy with his paw on my shoulder was a scrawny little fella, and I felt my boozy brain register that he wasn't wearing the club's colors, which meant he was either a hang-around or a prospect and I was the lucky bastard he had picked to try and prove his worth with. Sometimes it sucked being a big-ass dude.

"Can I help you?"

The redhead was long gone and Brite was making his way around the end of the long bar. The old guys stayed posted up and ignored the brewing hurricane like only lifelong drunks were capable of doing.

"You trying to start something with my girl, GI Joe?"

It was boring and so predictable that I had to roll my eyes. I had been in enough shithole places in the world to know that a bar brawl was a bar brawl, but throw in a wannabe biker and it could get really foul.

"No. I was trying to get drunk and she interrupted me."

I don't think they were expecting that, because a couple snickers tittered throughout the group. Scrawny puffed up his chest and reached out a finger to poke me in mine. Normally I could just walk away from this kind of thing. I was typically a level-headed kind of guy. I didn't fight unless it was in defense of something I really and truly believed in, or in defense of someone I loved, but today was the wrong day to goad a reaction out of me.

I swatted the guy's hand away and did a quick survey of the room. I didn't see any visible hardware, but bikers were known for stashing knifes in hard-to-see places, and Brite seemed like a cool enough guy. I didn't want to trash his place if I could help it.

"Look, dude, you don't want to do this and I *really* don't want to do this. We both know you sent the chick over here to try and start shit, so just leave it at that. I'll bounce, and you and your buddies can go back to smoking up and shooting pool and nobody has to bleed or look stupid. Okay?"

In hindsight, trying to drunkenly reason with a bunch of bikers probably was bound to have a low success rate. Before one blink and the next I had a bottle broken over my head and found myself in a serious chokehold. Scrawny guy looked like he wanted to kill me and the rest of the crew was just hanging back waiting to see what he could do. I didn't really want to hurt the guy, but the bottle over the head had taken a nice chunk of skin off with it and a river of red was steadily flowing into my eyes. Just like with the red nail polish on the tramp's fingers, the sight of my blood took me to another place and time, and it wasn't me struggling with a stupid, show-off biker, it was me battling for life, for freedom, for the security of my family and friends at home, and just like that the poor kid had no idea what hit him.

I already had a distinct size advantage on the guy, throw in the fact I was a soldier battle-hardened and trained by the country's best, and it got nasty and bloody fast. It didn't matter that the numbers were so obviously skewed in the biker's favor, I was getting out of the bar in one piece no matter what I had to do to make that happen.

Barstools were broken. Glasses went flying. Heads banged against the floor. I think at one point I heard someone crying and somehow when it was all over I was hunched over with my hands on my knees and blood now dripping not only from my lacerated head, but also my hands and a nasty knife slice across my ribs. The bikers had scattered for the most part, and I wasn't surprised to see Brite holding a baseball bat and glaring at me.

"What the hell was that?"

I would have laughed, but I think the knife cut in my side was worse than I originally thought.

"A really shitty 'thanks for you service'?" My humor was not appreciated, as the older man swore at me and pulled me painfully into a standing position.

"Doesn't look like that little punk is gonna get patched in anytime soon."

I got a critical once-over and was met with a sigh.

"You need a doctor."

It wasn't a question.

I tried to wipe the blood off my face with the back of my hand, but just ended up smearing it all across my face while my side steadily leaked onto the floor.

"I rode in. Don't think I can handle the bike right now."

He shook his head at me and put two fingers in his mouth and let out an earsplitting whistle.

"Everybody drink up and get out. Consider this last call."

A few diehards grumbled, but it only took five minutes and Brite was hauling me out the back door after locking the front and shoving me into the battered cab of an old Chevy pickup truck.

I rested my head back against the seat and gave the older man a rueful grin.

"I'll pay for any damage to the bar. I'm sorry about that."

He snorted in response and gave me a narrow-eyed look. "Try not to bleed out before we get to the emergency room, son."

Like I had a choice.

"The Sons of Sorrow hang out in the bar all the time. The old-timers are a good group of guys. A bunch of them are ex-military and get what my bar is all about, so I don't usually gripe about them coming in. It's all the younger kids trying to make a name who stir shit up. It wasn't the first time blood has been spilled on that floor and I doubt it'll be the last. You come see me when you sober up and get all sewed back together and we'll talk about what you can do to repay me for the damages. Gotta tell you, you're one hell of a fighter, son."

I would have shrugged, but the slice on my ribs was starting to burn and I was having a hard time ignoring the sticky, warm blood oozing between my fingers. I just grunted in acknowledgement.

"I'm really not. I hate fighting. I did it for a living for too many years, but the only way to come out alive is to be better at it than the other guy."

I closed my eyes and silently prayed we didn't hit any more red lights. My vision was starting to blur around the edges.

His voice was gruff as we pulled into the parking lot of the emergency room. "That's a damn shame, son."

I didn't have a response, because he was right. It was a shame.

I didn't get admitted right away. I guess a knife wound and a split-open scalp took a backseat to fingers blown off by fireworks on the Fourth. I didn't want to keep Bright waiting, so I called Nash and left a garbled message that I was going to need a ride at some point in the night. I knew I should have called Rule or Shaw, but I just wasn't up to dealing with that headache right then and I knew Nash would come with no questions asked even if I had been a royal ass earlier in the day.

"I gotta leave my bike at your bar tonight. I would appreciate it if you kept an eye on it for me in case Scrawny is a sore loser."

Brite nodded and again I saw that flash of white buried in that massive beard. "Well, I would say it was nice to meet you, Rome Archer, but of all the things I've been in this life, a liar has never been one of them."

We shook hands and I promised that I would touch base with him when I was in a more functioning order.

I had to wait longer than I was comfortable with to see someone, and by the time they took me to the sterile little room and pulled the curtain around the bed, I was pretty sure I was staying conscious just by the sheer force of my will alone. I was peeling my ruined T-shirt off over my head when the curtain moved back and a really pretty nurse holding a chart came in. She had her head bent over whatever she was reading and it gave me to opportunity to check her out. She had long auburn hair twisted in a braid away from a truly lovely face. She looked a couple of years younger than me, and I couldn't help but appreciate that she was rocking some kickass curves under those boring scrubs all medical professionals seemed to wear.

"Hey."

She looked up at the sound of my voice and blinked wide, dove-gray eyes at me. I don't know if it was the sight of my naked chest or the fact that I was now covered head to waist in blood that had her looking apprehensive.

"Hello, Mr. Archer. It looks like you had a rough night."

"I've had better, that's for sure."

She snapped on some latex gloves and came over to stand beside me.

"Let's have a look at what kind of trouble you got yourself into, shall we?"

She poked and prodded at my head and I tried not to stare at her boobs. She really was a pretty girl and it made the sting of her jabbing at my newest battle wounds hurt just a little less.

"What's your name?" I didn't really need to know it, I probably would never see her again after I got stitched up, but her eyes were just so soft and pretty I couldn't help but ask.

She gave me a friendly smile and looked like she was about to oblige me when the flimsy curtain was yanked back and Nash came barreling through. His cornflower-blue eyes were on fire with a mixture of anger and concern. The flames tattooed on the side of his head were standing out as the vein under them throbbed in irritation.

"Do you have any idea the kind of hell I'm going to get from Rule when he finds out about this? Goddamn it, Rome, what the fuck is wrong with you lately?"

I was going to respond when his attention switched from me to the lovely nurse who was staring at him with her mouth hanging slightly open. I was used to Nash's dramatic look and larger-than-life presence. He and Rule had always drawn a lot of attention, so it never fazed me, but the pretty little nurse suddenly looked like she was seeing a ghost, and it looked like Nash was trying to place where he might have seen her before as well.

"I just need to get stitched up and then you can yell at me on the way home."

The nurse cleared her throat and tossed her now blood-stained gloves in the trash. "You're probably looking at staples for the laceration in your head. It's pretty nasty and deeper than it looks. The slice on the side is pretty clean, so you might get away with just a topical liquid suture on it. The doc will be in shortly."

Her entire demeanor changed with Nash in the room. I could tell he noticed something was off with her as well. He scrunched up his nose and stared at her until she was uncomfortable enough to look up at him.

"Do we know each other?"

She shook her head so hard that she dislodged the pen she had tucked behind her ear.

"No. No, I don't think we do."

He scratched his chin and narrowed his eyes at her. "Are you sure? You look really familiar to me."

She shrugged and fiddled with the stethoscope that dangled around her neck. She was hot and if I was so inclined I could see working up some really nice nurse fantasies where she was the main attraction.

"I get that a lot. I must just have one of those faces. I have to run. No rest for the wicked." She gave me a little grin and disappeared around the corner, leaving both of us staring after her, me in pure male appreciation, Nash in puzzlement.

"I swear I know that chick from somewhere."

"She one of your one-hit wonders?"

"No. Maybe Rule's pre-Shaw?"

I snorted and contemplated the ceiling while my head and side continued to burn. "She seems too smart to fall into that category."

"Maybe. It's going to drive me nuts until I figure it out. What the hell happened to you tonight? Picking a fight with Rule wasn't enough, you had to take on a whole biker bar?"

"'Merica!" I gave a bitter laugh at my lame joke.

He scowled at me and took a seat on the doctor's wheelie chair, dwarfing the thing.

"Seriously, Rome. You need to knock this shit off."

I didn't have to answer, because the doctor chose that moment to come in. He was a guy in his fifties who clearly was at the end of a long shift, because he was no-nonsense as all get-out and wasted no time in fixing me right up. When he was done he gave me a serious look and told me I might want to lay off the booze, considering my blood test came back potent enough to start fires, and all I could do was silently agree.

He scribbled a prescription for painkillers that I hoped I wouldn't need to fill since I was already struggling with my reliance on another dangerous substance, and told me the nurse would be back in a few minutes to discharge me. I was stoked I would get one more chance to get my flirt going but as soon as she stuck her head back in it was clear she was all business and wanted nothing more than to see us go.

"Take care of yourself, Mr. Archer, and thank you for your service to our country."

She spun around to leave when Nash suddenly hopped to his feet and snapped his fingers. It made the nurse wince and made me frown.

"I knew I knew you! We went to high school together, didn't we? Aren't you Saint Ford?"

We could have heard a pin drop, she went so still and got so quiet. She stared at him like he had just crawled out of the sewer.

"I am. I'm surprised you recognized me; most people don't."

He tilted his head to the side and gave her a considering look. "Why did you say we didn't know each other, then?"

She cleared her throat and fiddled with the end of her braid. She was clearly very uncomfortable with the conversation.

"Because high school was a million years ago and about a hundred pounds ago. It's not a time that comes with the fondest memories; in fact, I prefer to pretend it never even happened. I'm sure that's not something a guy like you can understand. Have a nice night, try to avoid any more knife-wielding bikers if you can, Mr. Archer."

She swept out in a haughty cloud leaving both of us dumbfounded and gaping at each other.

"Whoa. Were you a dick to her in school or something? That was a whole lot of hostility for something that happened so long ago."

He shrugged and helped me get up onto my feet. I wobbled a bit from the mixture of alcohol and blood loss, so he didn't let go until I was steady.

"Probably. Rule, Jet, and I were a bunch of punks. Remy was the nice one."

"What do you mean *were*? You probably teased her for being fat or something."

He had the good grace to look ashamed. "That is entirely possible. I wasn't exactly in a great place when I was in high school either. There was too much stuff going on with my mom and that idiot she married for me to really give a crap about anything or anyone else. Man, that blows. She's a total babe now."

I didn't even consider putting my blood-soaked shirt back on as I hobbled out of the emergency room.

"She sure is."

We got to his fully restored '73 Dodge Charger and I slumped down in the seat. It wasn't the worst Independence Day I could remember having, but it sure wasn't one of the best either. All I wanted to do was crawl into bed and forget about everything, not that that seemed to be working out for me so great as of late.

"Listen, dude, I'm sorry about today. I'll touch base with Rule and make things right. I'm just a little off balance right now."

The massive motor rattled so loud it made my teeth hurt.

"We all get that. You just aren't giving anyone a chance to try and help set you straight."

"I'll chill out." I wasn't sure how I was going to go about that exactly, but I knew I needed to get on it. "You can tell the rabid pixie to back off."

He laughed. "No can do, my friend. Cora is like a pit bull. When she sinks her teeth into something or someone, she doesn't let go. You might want to try and apologize. She just wants to look out for all of us, and she does a good job of it."

I closed my eyes and let my head drop back on the seat.

"I remember when that was my job."

Heavy silence filled the car and I didn't think he was going to say anything else about it, but after a minute he muttered, "You went off to save the entire world, Rome, we just did the best we could while you were gone."

Just like being a big guy often had its disadvantages, wanting to be a hero to everyone and anyone often had the same dangerous pitfalls. I got used to everyone needing me, to their relying on me, and now that I wasn't needed anymore I simply just didn't know what to do with myself. That honestly terrified me more than any war zone or bar brawl with armed bikers ever could.

On Sale January 2014!
From William Morrow